not my ROMEO

OTHER TITLES BY ILSA MADDEN-MILLS

Very Bad Things

Very Wicked Beginnings

Very Wicked Things

Very Twisted Things

Dirty English

Filthy English

Spider

Fake Fiancée

I Dare You

I Bet You

I Hate You

Boyfriend Bargain

The Last Guy (w/Tia Louise)

The Right Stud (w/Tia Louise)

not my ROMEO

ILSA MADDEN-MILLS

This is a work of fiction. Names, characters, organizations, places, events, and incidents are either products of the author's imagination or are used fictitiously.

Published by Montlake, Seattle
www.apub.com

Amazon, the Amazon logo, and Montlake are trademarks of Amazon.com, Inc., or its affiliates.

ISBN-13: 9781542021883
ISBN-10: 154202188X

Cover design by Hang Le

Cover Photography by Daniel Jaems

Printed in the United States of America

not my ROMEO

Chapter 1

Elena

If I smoked, I'd have one in my mouth right now. Maybe two.

But I don't, so I settle for chewing on my thumbnail as I whip my little Ford Escape into Milano's jam-packed parking lot. Glancing around, I take in the stone-and-cedar exterior, the flickering gaslights by the door. It's a five-star restaurant, one of the best in Nashville, with a monthlong reservation wait, yet my date managed to get us one on short notice. Points for that.

A long sigh leaves my chest.

Who, *tell me who*, agrees to a blind date on Valentine's Day?

Me, apparently.

"I'm breaking the seal!" I announce to no one.

That's right. Tonight, I'm meeting Greg Zimmerman, the local weatherman for the NBC affiliate here in the Music City. Supposedly he's tall, dark, handsome, a little nerdy, and fresh from a breakup. Perfect for me. Right?

So why am I so anxious?

For a brief moment I contemplate a pretend headache. Dang it. I can't do that. For one, I promised my roommate, Topher, I'd follow through; two, I have nothing better to do; and three, I'm starving.

And this is *just* a quick dinner, no matter what Topher says. I recall him in the library today. He'd been wearing his Grateful Dead T-shirt and skinny jeans, bouncing up and down in the romance section as he mimicked riding a horse. *Straddle him like a thoroughbred, Elena. Take those reins, dig your spurs in, and ride him until you can't walk the next day. Pound him so hard he can't even say "Cloudy with a chance of snow" the next day.*

I blow at a piece of hair that's fallen out of my chignon, then tuck it neatly behind my ear. No horsing around tonight. I'm here for a nice meal. Italian *is* my favorite, and I'm already picturing a nice bowl of pasta and garlic bread.

Just say hi, be nice, eat, then get out.

Besides. What can go wrong from meeting someone new?

I pull down the rearview mirror and check my appearance. Pale as paper. After scrambling around my bag, I pull out my cherry red and roll it over my full lips, then blot them with a tissue. I sigh, studying my features as I adjust my pearl necklace and matching earrings. The truth is there's nothing spectacular about me. My nose is a hair too sharp, and I'm annoyingly short: five feet, three inches and a quarter in bare feet. That quarter is very important. Floating somewhere in between a true petite and the "standard" size, I'm stuck with clothes either too long or too short. If I want something that fits well, I make it myself.

Another glance in the mirror. Another sigh.

I hope Greg isn't disappointed.

I get out of the car and approach the beautifully stained oaken double doors, where a doorman dressed in a black suit gives me a smile and opens the door. "Welcome to Milano's," he murmurs, and I swallow down my qualms as I step into the foyer and squint around the dark interior.

Dang.

Dread inches up my spine.

Why did I insist on not seeing a photo of Greg before the date?

Mostly I just wanted to be . . . surprised. When your existence is as boring and mundane as mine, it's the little things that spice it up. Instead of my normal coffee, let's try the peppermint latte. *Mind blowing.* Instead of wearing my hair in a bun, let's make it a messy topknot. *Amazing.* Instead of seeing a picture of your blind date, go anyway, and look for the guy wearing a blue shirt. Sounded exciting at the time, but I'm cursing myself as I check out the interior. There's no one waiting for me in the foyer. I did text him to let him know I was caught in traffic, yet I got no response back. Perhaps he's already seated and waiting for me.

The hostess whisks a lovey-dovey couple to their seats in the back of the restaurant, leaving me alone and fidgety. I brush down my black pencil skirt. Maybe I should have changed into something flirtier? I do have a closetful of slinky dresses Nana left me—

Nope.

This is the real me, and if he doesn't like what he sees, then, well, he can suck it.

I am who I am.

After five more minutes have passed and the hostess still hasn't come back, my nerves have ramped up, and I've broken out in a small sweat, the nape of my neck damp. Where did she go? Is she on a break?

I take a seat on a long bench, whip out my phone, and send him another text.

I'm here in the foyer, I send.

No reply comes back.

Annoyed and running on hunger fumes, I decide I can find him myself. Feigning confidence I don't have, I waltz out of the foyer and make a quick perimeter of the restaurant. A few minutes later I feel like a stalker as I peer at the patrons, so I move to stand in the shadowy alcove next to the restrooms, scanning for men alone on Valentine's Day.

Topher should have chosen a different night for us to meet, considering I have a horrible history with Valentine's Day. At my high school Sweetheart Dance, my date, Bobby Carter, drank so much spiked punch that he barfed all over my white dress. My college boyfriend's idea of a romantic night was ordering in sushi—his favorite—then playing video games with his friends online. I can't recall one decent Valentine's Day in all of my twenty-six years.

Bam. My eyes land on a tall dark-haired man wearing a blue button-down, the sleeves rolled up to his forearms. He's in the far corner, sitting apart, almost tucked away. His table has several empty ones around it, and I find it curious that he's managed to get privacy on such a busy night. A waiter sets down his food, and my lips tighten.

He's eating without me?

I spy his phone next to him on the table. The nerve! Why hasn't he responded to me?

He's taller than I expected, judging just from how he sits in his plush leather armchair—

Wait a minute. He *does* look vaguely familiar, like a face you've caught briefly but can't put a name to. Mama and Aunt Clara always have the TV on at the beauty shop, so it's possible I have actually seen him on the news.

I pull my white cat-eye glasses out of my purse and slide them on for a better look. My heart flip-flops as butterflies take flight in my stomach. Oh heck no. That can't be him. He's . . . he's . . . freaking gorgeous, and I don't mean regular handsome but like a movie star: dark hair swept off his face, the strands wavy and unruly with copper highlights, soft and silky brushing against his cheeks, and too long for a newscaster, in my opinion—but what do I know? I don't own a television.

He lifts his arm to shove his hair back, and my eyes pop at the tightly roped muscles of his forearm and biceps straining through the fabric, the impossibly broad shoulders that taper to a chest.

Well, would you look at that.

And this has to be him, right?

I'm in the right restaurant. He's alone. He's wearing a blue shirt. He has dark hair. Odds point to yes. Usually the most simple explanation is exactly what it appears. Therefore, he must be my date.

The man in question turns to look out the window, tapping his fingers on the table impatiently, and I take in his profile. Long straight nose, full dark arching eyebrows, and a sharp, bladed jawline. Sensuous lips, the lower one decadently full. Almost wicked. He's the kind of hot that draws your eyes over and over just to make sure it's not a mirage. I knew guys like him at NYU—sexy, athletic gym types who played a sport. And those types never gave me a second look. I'd watch them work out while I fumbled my way around one of those god-awful butterfly machines, while beautiful, tall, svelte girls who weren't sweating fawned over them, bringing them towels, water bottles, and sexy promises.

He isn't beefy, though, like those brawny guys with thick necks and flushed faces. His muscles are taut and powerful, nothing too overstated, yet tight and no doubt firm—

Elena. Enough with the body. It's to your taste. Move on.

He takes a sip of an amber liquid, long tanned fingers grasping the fragile container as his eyes rove across the room. They prowl around the restaurant, as if he's assessing every person in sight, and I feel the sizzle of him even from twenty feet away. Prickles of awareness skate down my spine. Greg has massive raw animal magnetism coming from him in waves. *I'm the alpha,* his body language yells. *Come and challenge me.* I watch as a few ladies eye him—even some of the guys are turned and checking him out. Some are whispering. Interesting. I guess he has quite the following on the news.

His gaze drifts right over me without stopping.

Not surprised.

I duck back into the shadows.

Dang it. My hands clench. I wanted nice and nerdy, not this . . . sexy beast!

And judging by the scowl on his face, he's grumpy. *Life's too short to be dour, Mister.* And what is he annoyed about? I am here!

And he did see a picture of me. Topher said so.

Yeah, maybe he doesn't really want to meet you.

Maybe he's hoping you won't show up.

I tap my foot. I should leave. Really.

I have a ton of things to do at home. Some sewing, snuggling up with Romeo—

The smells of Milano's waft around me, spicy and tantalizing, and my stomach lets out an angry howl. I move from one foot to the next. Every place to eat between here and Daisy is going to be packed. I could always hit a drive-through on the way back home—but how pathetic is a Big Mac and fries on Valentine's Day? Plus, I'll have my entire nosy family to answer to tomorrow. They've built up this blind date so much: *Oooooh, Elena has a date with a weatherman. Ask him if that's a barometer in his pocket or if he's just glad to see you.* That nugget came from Aunt Clara. If I chicken out now, there'll be hell to pay, because no matter the brave face I put on, everyone knows I haven't been myself in months.

I give myself a mental pep talk.

Grow some balls, Elena.

You can't keep living life on the sidelines.

Sometimes you have to go out and take what you want.
So what if he's hot enough to suck the dew off a rose.
So what if he's got a dangerous look on his face.
You are hungry. Do it for the pasta.
He is your date. Go get 'em, girl.

I gather my resolve, point my little black pumps in his direction, and start marching.

Chapter 2

Jack

"Um, you're him, right?" A nervous laugh. "*The* guy?"

I glance up from my glass of scotch and take in the petite auburn-haired woman standing in front of me as I try my best to enjoy my meal—damn hard to do these days with my face all over the media. Every eye in the place is either glaring at me or pointedly turning their noses up.

She's wearing a shirt buttoned all the way to her neck, a black pencil skirt, and low-heeled shoes. I move my eyes up to the intruder's face, taking in the uptight hairstyle and big white glasses.

Dammit. Another reporter. My hands tighten in my lap, and I dart my eyes around for the server. A deep exhalation leaves my chest when I don't see him. I lean back in my leather chair and glare at her. Part of me is nervous; the rest of me is pissed.

"Yeah, I'm the guy." *What the hell do you want?* my face says.

Dark lashes flutter against a creamy complexion as she seems to gather herself, a determined grimace on her delicate face. She swallows, and before I can protest, she's taking the seat across from me.

I blink.

She exhales. "*Thank God.* It was the blue button-down that gave it away—and the fact that you're alone." Her eyes roam over my chest, lingering for a moment on my shoulders. "I'm just glad I found you. Forgive me for being late. I did a photo shoot for Romeo—he has quite the following on Instagram—and then the downtown Nashville traffic is just insane."

Forgive her for being late?

And photo shoot with Romeo? The name's familiar. New player in the league?

"Hmm." I hide my confusion by taking another sip of scotch, keeping my gaze on her, distrustful. Lawrence, my PR guy, mentioned a female sports blogger who was sympathetic to my most recent falling-out with fans and who might be willing to write a favorable story.

But he knows I detest reporters.

And why didn't he let me know?

Dammit, he's always doing shit without telling me.

I consider calling him to confirm who she is, but . . .

"So you're the blogger?" I ask.

Her eyes widen, her face paling. "I *have* a blog."

"Hmm."

She stares at me for several moments and shakes her head. "Gah, I'm going to skin Topher alive for telling you that. Of course, he thinks I should tell everyone. Only he doesn't understand how small towns work, especially Daisy. Once they know your deepest secrets, it's literally all they think of when they see you on the street. And the whispers . . . goodness."

I watch her with lowered lids, assessing. I don't know anyone named Topher. And why would she hide her blog? Maybe it isn't the sports blogger. I'm used to women coming up to me, mostly jersey chasers. In the past, especially in college and my early years of professional football, I ran with it, choosing the most beautiful and taking them up on their offers: keys to hotel rooms, phone numbers pressed in my hands, girls who tagged along to our VIP parties—but this girl doesn't fit that category. No tight dress. Minimal makeup. Studious looking.

She continues. "True story: my aunt Clara sneaks her boyfriend in through her back door to keep people in town from seeing him. He parks his car behind the church and walks to her house—and she's forty. I wish she'd just tell everyone she's in love with the mailman." She arches an elegant eyebrow. "Scotty is ten years younger than her and quite the catch."

"I see." Black Pumps talks a lot. And not about football.

She gives me a half smile. "You must know how that is, wanting to stay out of the limelight and keep your personal business quiet."

Indeed. Even enjoying a nice glass of whiskey in public makes me paranoid. I picture everything I do as a headline. *Jack Hawke drinking! Does this mean another DUI for the Nashville quarterback?* That DUI happened five years ago, my second year in the NFL, yet no one forgets. I partied a lot in those early years. I thought fame and money made me invincible. Stupid.

"Yes. I like my privacy very much." I take a bite of my pasta, chewing and swallowing, eyes on her, taking in the stiffness of her shoulders, the way she's breathing in long, slow breaths, as if she doesn't really want to be here.

Shit. Perhaps she isn't sympathetic at all.

Perhaps it's all a ruse to get a story from me.

Several seconds go by as neither of us speaks, and she squirms a little in her chair, her eyes following me. It's rude to keep eating, but no reporter or blogger or random person is going to keep me from—

She chews on her plump red lips, as if she's angry. Full and overly lush, they're a deep crimson. A little sinful.

Behind big white glasses, her eyes hold mine for several moments. A vivid aquamarine color, outlined in black and heavily lashed, they spear me with sudden ferocity. "You know, I think it's rude you started dinner without me—even after I texted you and said I'd be late."

"Didn't see your text, and I was starving. Sorry." I shrug nonchalantly, not sounding sorry at all.

The server scurries over to our table, straightening his black suit.

"Sir." He darts his eyes at . . . whoever she is . . . and then comes back to me. "I'm so sorry she got past. You know it's the busiest night of the year. Please forgive me. Would you like me to call security?"

Black Pumps goes from all nerves to annoyance. She glares at the waiter with laser focus, her face indignant. "I'm sitting right here. And I'm supposed to be here. It was *arranged*. This is a *date*."

My eyes flare. Surely she means *work* date?

She straightens her spine and sends a longing look at my pasta. "And I'd like whatever he's having with extra bread." She waves her hand at my bowl of half-finished bolognese. "And a glass of red. No. Make that a gin and tonic with a double shot of Hendrick's with a cucumber. In fact, if you could just keep those drinks coming, that would be fantastic. Thank you." Her voice has just a tiny bit of that southern accent that makes everything she says sweet yet layered with a tenacity that almost makes my lips twitch. She reminds me of a little poodle my mom had once, ready to pounce at any moment if there's an injustice.

The waiter blinks at her, then glances back at me, a pleading expression on his face. "Sir, again, my deepest apologies—"

I wave him off, making an impulsive decision, brushing away the reminder that those ideas tend to get me in trouble. "No worries. Let's feed the lady, yes?"

He bows deeply and darts away, and I turn my eyes back to the girl.

I study her features carefully, cataloging them more, instead of the cursory glance a few minutes ago. She's not beautiful in a magazine way, but there's *something* captivating about her. Could be the stuffy, conservative clothes that hint at soft curves underneath. Maybe it's the lips. Most definitely the lips. And whether it's unintentional or not, she's using them to her advantage, one minute pursing them, the next chewing on the bottom one.

As one of the best quarterbacks in the league, one of my special skill sets is reading facial expressions and tics that telegraph a play on the field. And I can't help but notice that she looks at me as if I'm no one special, no glint of excitement in her eyes, no fluttering lashes, no awe at the weight the name Jack Hawke carries. Fascinating.

"Is that . . . are those tiny flying pigs on your shirt?" I ask as I narrow my gaze, taking in the white shirt buttoned up to a black velvet Peter Pan collar.

"Yes. The fabric is from a designer in New York. I ordered it a month ago and went crazy. I even made Romeo a pillow."

"Is that the new wide receiver for the Saints? Drafted last year?"

She cocks her head. "Hardly. He's my little potbellied pig. A teacup. He's a rescue and the sweetest. Okay, maybe not the sweetest, but I couldn't resist taking him in when someone dumped him off at the Cut 'N' Curl across from my house. He was near death's door. Just last month, someone left a box of kittens on my front porch with a note addressed to me; can you believe it? It's like they *know* I'll take care of them. I found homes for all of them except for one of the males. You interested? He's black and gray, adorable, and litter trained; I swear."

I huff out a laugh. This girl is—

If Romeo is a miniature pig and not a football player—what the hell is going on?

"I'll pass on the cat."

"Every man needs a cat. Might make you softer."

"Do I need to be softer?"

"Wouldn't hurt. Might take more than one cat to do the trick, though. You seem . . ." She waves her hands around. "Tense."

She has no idea.

"I see."

"Are you a dog person, then?" she asks.

"I don't have time for pets."

She grimaces. "Well, if you change your mind, I recommend the cat. Nothing against dogs, but they will love just about anyone. Cats are pickier, and the men who have them can appreciate moodiness and definitely handle personality issues—which might be key in a relationship. Also cats are hilarious. Do you have any idea how many cat videos there are on the internet? Over a billion! Isn't that crazy?"

Is *she* crazy? Who the hell is she?

Yet I'm hanging on her every word, slowly warming up, feeling . . . interested.

"You mentioned fabric. You made your shirt yourself?"

She pushes her glasses up. "Stores don't market to my tastes or to my figure. In fact, the majority of clothing in stores is designed by people who have no idea what a woman like *me* wants. But then if you know about my blog . . ." Her face flames red. "Then you know my specialty is lingerie."

Lingerie? The plot thickens.

I tap my fingers on the table, some of that earlier interest waning. Is she looking for an endorsement from me? I briefly dated a girl who wanted me to promote her makeup. People, whether they initially intend to or not, somehow always circle around to using me in some way.

I can see it now.

NFL superstar Jack Hawke likes blah-blah lingerie for his girlfriends.

The waiter sets down her drink, and she gulps it down completely, then plops it down on the table as a long sigh comes from her. "God. I've needed this since the moment I walked in and tried to find you."

Surprisingly, sympathy rises up and eclipses any misgivings. "Bad day?"

She huffs out a laugh. "Bad year. I moved back to Daisy two years ago from New York, and it's been one insane day after another. My family, my job, my small town."

I set my fork down. "It's been a shitty week for me as well."

She nods. "Let's try this again, shall we? Tell me about you. What's it like being a weatherman on TV?"

I'm in the process of taking a sip of my drink when the question comes, and it gets caught in my throat, and I sputter, then cough, grabbing my white napkin to cover my mouth.

"Are you okay?" Her eyes are huge, luminous, the color of the sea.

"Fine," I say in a strangled voice.

She thinks I'm a . . . *weatherman.*

What. The. Hell.

I shake my head, processing what she said . . . about sending the text . . . her comment about my blue shirt . . . her indignation with the maître d' . . . and it all clicks into place.

A date. Obviously a blind date.

But girls have tried all kinds of tricks to get in my bed. Once, on the road, I walked into my hotel room and found a naked girl in my closet. Took hotel security to remove her as she screamed "I love you, Jack!" the entire time.

"You've *seen* me doing the weather?"

She grimaces. "Actually, no. The news is worrisome; plus I rarely watch TV."

I rub my neck. "And you agreed to this date without seeing my face? That's rather . . . bold."

She gives me her first real smile. "It's my version of living dangerously."

"You a football fan?"

"Men pushing each other around in tight pants, fighting over a ball? Please. Very caveman. I prefer books and podcasts. You?"

I take in the blank look on her face. *Well, damn.*

About ten seconds go by as we stare at each other.

I feel a brush of excitement rising inside me, gently at first, then all at once, flooding my senses. No. Freaking. Clue. She doesn't know me! I want to hug her. Maybe take that cat. Kidding.

I laugh for the first time in a week. It's as if I'm in a parallel universe where I get a do-over. Shit. It's a clean slate, sparkling white.

But . . .

Jack. You can't not *reveal who you are . . .*

If she thinks I'm her date, I should come clean right now and tell her the truth. Save her the embarrassment of dragging this out further.

But . . .

What do I have to go home to but an empty apartment and my face on ESPN?

Plus, she's hot in an understated way, everything all buttoned up and just waiting to be unleashed—

My gaze brushes over that tight-fitting shirt, taking in those full curves straining against her blouse.

And I'm a tit man.

Tell her. I open my mouth, and she speaks.

"What's your favorite part of doing the weather? Is it the snowstorm, when you know the city is hanging on every single word, when they run out and buy bread and milk?" She takes a huge bite of pasta the waiter has set down, using a fork and a spoon to twist the pasta, giving me a couple of seconds to think of a reply.

"Hmm, I like clouds. And rain. It's . . . wet."

She gives me a swift look and pats her mouth delicately with her napkin, capturing my attention with the ultrafine bones of her wrists, the elegant way she moves. Once, a long time ago, when I was just a poor kid from Ohio, I might have wanted to draw those hands, the delicateness of them. She looks as if she might break in my arms—

"Wow, you like *clouds*?"

"Yeah, those puffy cumulus ones." I have no clue. "They're . . . white."

"I see." Her brow wrinkles. "It's me, isn't it? I'm talking too much, and I was late and rude to the waiter, and you are so not into this—"

"Elena? What are you doing here?" The words come from a stocky, well-dressed, brown-haired man who's stopped at our table. He moves his gaze to me, and I see instant recognition in his face, the way his mouth gapes. Yep, there it is. He knows me.

I glance at *Elena*—thank you, Jesus, for the name—and she's gone white, her hands twisting the pearls around her neck. I frown, my gaze darting from her to him, wondering what the connection is.

"I'm on a *date*, Preston. Isn't it obvious?"

He sputters, his eyes widening as he looks from her to me. "Tonight? I assumed you'd be . . . home."

Elena stiffens. "I'm not pining away."

Preston smooths down his tie, lips tightening. "Of course. It's just if I had known you'd be here, I never would have come here with Giselle." He nudges his head toward the middle of the restaurant without taking his eyes off Elena. "We just arrived, and we're sitting over there. I was on my way to the bar to grab another drink and happened to see you—"

Her eyes flash like lightning, and I think I see pain in those depths. "Well, forget you saw me. Go back to Giselle."

He pushes his hands inside his slacks. "I never meant to hurt—"

"But you did." She points to her pasta. "Also, I'm trying to eat here, and you know how much I *enjoy* my food. Remember?"

He opens his mouth to speak.

"Piss off," I say, rougher than I intended.

He isn't budging, his eyes squarely on my . . . date. They sweep over her, from head to toe, his face settling into disapproval. "I can't believe you'd be interested in *him*," he says under his breath.

My body tenses up, shoulders tightening.

He takes a step closer to her. "Everyone wants you to move on, but this guy is *not*—"

I stand, my six-four frame towering over his, and you can tell he's forgotten how tall I am, bigger than I seem on TV. My fists curl, everything from this week building up and threatening to erupt. Usually I'm in tight control of my temper, knowing that every little thing I do is scrutinized, but I'll be damned before I let him talk to her as if she's a child.

"Go back to your table now, or I'll have you removed," I murmur softly. "This is *my* restaurant."

He holds his hands up, as if to ward me off. "See. Trouble, Elena."

She shrugs. "Maybe trouble is just what I need, Preston. A little adventure."

He darts a glare at me, then scurries off across the restaurant before taking a seat with a blonde lady.

I settle back in my chair and meet her shiny gaze.

Nah, please don't cry. Females weeping always make me think of my mother. I saw her cry more than she ever smiled. And it makes me want to fix things . . .

"Are you okay?"

She nods, seeming to gather herself as she clears her throat and stares down at the table. "Thank you for running him off. I had no idea he'd be here."

"No problem," I say gruffly.

"You own this place?"

I shrug. "Just diversifying. I don't want to be a chef or anything. It looked good on paper, and I bought it."

"Why did he say you were trouble?" She slides butter on a piece of bread, eyes down.

I pause. "When you're famous, people either love you or hate you."

The waiter takes my plate and sets down another gin and tonic for her.

"Your ex, right?" I finally say. "And let me guess . . . you aren't over him?"

"Long story." She sighs, still not looking at me, and it's driving me a little crazy, this need to have her eyes on me. People always stare at me. Why doesn't she?

I picture her in my penthouse, her auburn hair down, her body spread out on my bed—

Damn.

Where did that come from?

You don't know *her, Jack.*

You just met her.

Ease up.

Chapter 3

Elena

Well.

Well.

Well.

I keep sneaking little glances at my drop-dead-gorgeous blind date. Who knew weathermen were this hot? And that classically handsome face? He's a Greek god on steroids. No wonder the TV loves him. He's the most beautiful man I've ever seen. Also, a bit of a badass. Giddiness races over me at how he handled Preston, towering over him, barely restrained anger held at bay. I don't think two males have ever gotten into a disagreement over *me*. Especially when I'm wolfing down food like it's my last meal.

I clear my throat. "Topher mentioned you'd broken up with someone. Have you tried those dating sites like Tinder? I haven't been brave enough."

He frowns. "Those sites make me wary. Don't do Tinder unless you're looking for sex, Elena. Even then, it's dangerous."

I've been blushing all night, but now my cheeks flush with heat even more, and I put a hand up to my cheeks. Yep. Hot. "Well, um, yeah . . . maybe that wouldn't be so bad. 'Be good and you'll be lonely.'"

He arches a brow. "Mark Twain?"

Interest fires through me. "You read classics?"

"Try not to look so surprised." His eyes lower, grazing over my face, lingering on my lips. "What kind of books do you enjoy, Elena?"

I pause. Not a good idea to mention all the steamy romance I consume, so I stick with the basics. "I'm a librarian. I read everything."

"Shut up. An honest-to-God librarian." He shakes his head. "Should have guessed it."

But didn't Topher tell him?

"Why are you smiling?" I ask instead.

He leans in over the table, and I get a whiff of his scent: male mixed with leather and fine scotch. "Because you fit every guy's fantasy of a librarian: intelligent, studious, big glasses, tight pencil skirt." He flashes a white smile.

Oh.

Oh!

My leg jiggles under the table, and I push my glasses up on my nose. They've been sliding down constantly, and I know it's because the room seems warmer now, the tension in the air thicker.

"Guess I should have stuck a pencil in my hair tonight and carried a book in my hands to complete the look."

"Hmm. Next time, maybe."

My heart pounds at the way he's looking at me, as if I'm a fine piece of Belgian chocolate. I look around the room. What universe is this where a guy like him has fantasies about girls like me? My nerves kick in even more.

Deflect, redirect. "Right. So what happened between you and your ex?"

His lips compress, his features hardening. "My ex left me for a professional hockey player, then wrote a tell-all book about me, right down to our sex life. She also said I was an abusive alcoholic."

Crap. "Is it true?"

"No!"

"Why'd she do it?"

"People do crazy things for money, even people who say they care about you."

He wears a distant, faraway look on his face. I understand gossip and the havoc it can cause. Preston and Giselle have kept everything that transpired between us quiet, but the entire town knows he dated me first. I've caught everyone's pity-filled glances, and there's no telling the stories they've concocted in their heads. *Poor girl. Preston dumped her for her prettier, younger sister.* Not quite the truth, but I shove those memories down.

"Want me to kick her ass? I can throat punch with the best of them."

He laughs. "Nah."

I take him in, letting my gaze linger on his powerful forearms, the light-brown hair there, the length of his fingers, the careful way he's slowly rubbing his index finger over the top of his whiskey glass—his lingering glances. My buzz has definitely kicked in, because I say, "I'm just guessing here, but I bet the sexy bits were complimentary." I take a sip of my drink. "You know, just trying to find the positive. What did she say, exactly?"

His finger stops, and those tawny-colored eyes spear mine. I blink. They're not brown, not yellow, but somewhere in the middle, golden and piercing and intense, the color of a warm sunrise even in the dim lighting. A small grin starts slowly, easing up the chiseled lines of his face until it's a full-blown smile. "Oh, Elena. She'll never get over me."

A tingle dances up my spine.

It's such an arrogant comment, but dang it, curiosity wins out.

"Why's that?" My heart thuds in my chest. We've gone from Mark Twain to a sex discussion, and I'm on the edge of my seat.

"Are you really asking how I am in bed?"

"Guess I can read the book myself. What's it called?" I pull out my phone. "Everything's on Amazon, right?"

It's a challenge I've thrown down—and he picks it up.

"Please don't."

"Then tell me, and save me the money and time."

He stares at me for a full ten seconds, lids lowering. His chest rises.

I swallow. I've gone too far. I shouldn't press him. About sex! What is wrong with me? I blame it on seeing Preston and Giselle.

"Elena," he says softly, as if tasting my name on his lips, dragging out the three syllables. His voice is low and husky, like an exotic silk, deep and rich with colors of gold and navy, gliding through my hands. "Let's just say I know how to satisfy a woman, to have her crave me every moment we're apart."

I volunteer as tribute.

What?

No.

I suck in a deep breath.

Seriously, did they turn off the air in here?

Why am I sweating in February? I glance at my drink. I should really stop drinking.

"Nothing to say?" he asks softly.

I get it now. Greg is way ahead of me in the sexy-times department. I bet he's banging chicks left and right. Weather groupies. After all, he's practically a celebrity in Nashville—with a book about him! And here I am. Wasting away my prime years with a vibrator.

"That sounds lovely." I keep my face composed, hoping it's not bloodred. Heck, Preston wore a full set of pajamas to bed. A full set! Including socks. Those stinky, smelly black socks.

"Lovely?" He smiles. "That's one way to describe it."

I change the topic. "Preston is dating my sister. Do you see her over there?" My back is to them, but I nudge my head toward the middle of the restaurant. "She's the tall pretty one. They met at our Fourth of July family barbecue last year when she moved back to Nashville."

"Shit."

"Double shit." I gulp down the rest of my drink. The waiter dashes over with a new one.

"My ex wanted me to put a ring on it. Couldn't do it, so she got back at me with the book." He pauses. "She wasn't the one."

I snort. "The mythical *one*. I've come to believe there is no special person."

He nods eagerly. "I'm with you. I'm not into relationships. All they bring is pain."

I lean in over the table until we're closer. "Preston couldn't even find my c-l-i-t. It's like . . . he didn't try hard enough with me, and I guess something inside me, woman's intuition, knew something was missing, but I ignored that voice in my head." I wince as soon as I realize what I've revealed.

What am I doing? I'm being too flirtatious. I spelled *clit*! I sigh, backpedaling. "I'm sorry. I keep rambling. This whole Valentine's Day blind date was a mistake—"

"Not a mistake, Elena."

Chapter 4

Jack

I can't believe I brought up Sophia and her tell-all about me. She may have been beautiful and said she loved me, but in the end, her true colors came out. I swallow, glancing down at my scotch. I've only had one, for Christ's sake, yet I'm saying way too much. For some reason the thought of Elena reading about me being a bad-tempered jock with a penchant for drinking and hitting women is unsettling. It isn't the image I want to leave her with at all.

She's so . . .

I bite back a smile. She's *almost* shy, yet not, speaking with a directness I appreciate.

Feeling a gaze on me, and not a friendly one, I look over her shoulder and frown at Preston, who's sending me furtive side-eyes in between cooing at his date.

I try to imagine what it must be like for her to live in a small town and see them constantly.

Pure hell.

I know how reporters and fans look at me. Party boy. Rude. Super Bowl loser.

She leans in over the table, and her scent wafts around me, sweet and fresh, like honey mixed with spring flowers.

How long has it been since you got to meet someone who isn't judging you on your past?

Fuck that.

How long since you got laid?

"What's it like to be on TV?" She's wrapped up in her pasta, her movements graceful, yet she's consuming every bite. She gets another piece of bread.

Anxiousness tugs at me. I don't like lying to her. "All eyes are waiting for me to make a mistake, and after the week I've had, my career might just be over." It's the truth.

Her hand that's resting on the table reaches out and touches mine briefly before pulling back. "I'm sorry. That sounds terrible."

When she moved, the candlelight accentuated the sheer quality of her shirt, and I freeze at the color underneath, something pink and sexy. Heat, hot and searing, flashes straight to my dick.

I'm caught up in wondering how she'd feel underneath me, those legs tight around my waist, her full breasts against my bare chest, those little heels digging into my back—

Just stop, Jack.

I grow silent, frowning, my head going back to the long line of faceless women who've drifted in and out of my life. Elena isn't my type. She's nursing a broken heart, and she's . . . nice. But damn, this knot of worry and tension in my chest is killing me.

My fingers tap the table; I watch her as she eats the last piece of bread. I'm wired, my eyes moving from her to the people in the restaurant as I finish my drink, wondering when someone's going to come over and ask for an autograph or tell me I'm an asshole, and shit, I don't want her to know what people really think of me . . .

She studies me. "You're quiet."

"Yes."

"Why?"

I frown. I don't know how to explain what a tough week it's been without revealing who I am.

Which I should! Right now.

"I'm normally quiet."

"I'm not. I talk way too much."

"I see."

Tell her, Jack. Tell her you aren't her date.

She grabs her drink off the table and chugs it down. With a sigh, she folds her napkin in elegant movements and then stands, a look of accomplishment on her face, as if she's just completed a hard project.

I straighten in my chair.

She's leaving?

After digging around in her purse, she pulls out a wad of twenties and places them on the table.

"What are you doing?" I ask.

She grimaces. "Heading home. Thank you for a lovely meal. This should cover my part. It was . . . great to meet you. Maybe I'll even decide to watch the news." She fidgets, her heels already pointing in the direction of the door.

"Wait, Elena." I don't have a clue what I'm going to say when I stand. She's so small next to me, her frame about five-five in heels. My eyes go from the top of her head to her feet; that black skirt clings to her delectable hourglass figure, full and curvy and lush—one I didn't notice before. Damn.

"Don't go," I murmur.

Abort, abort, my common sense yells, but I shove it down. I don't know how the rest of my life is going to play out, and part of me . . . wants to just push it all away and forget about it—with her.

"Come on. This has been terrible." She exhales. "I was late. You didn't text me back. My ex showed up. It feels . . . off."

"I admit, my social skills suck." I pick up her money and stuff it back in her hands, our fingers brushing. "Why don't we both get out of here and go somewhere else?"

Here I go, being impulsive.

"Where?" An uncertain expression crosses her face.

I could say another bar, maybe for a nightcap or dessert, but there'll be people who know me; there's only a handful of places where I feel comfortable, and this is one of them. Since Sophia's book came out a year ago, I don't get out much anymore. I've battened down the hatches and retreated inside myself, trying to protect my reputation as much as I can.

"My place. It's not far from here."

I take a step forward and tuck her hand through the crook of my arm. "Besides, your ex is here, and don't you want to walk out of here with me by your side?"

"He really didn't like you at all." She stares at the floor, then back at me. "But I don't go home with men I don't know."

"Elena . . ." My voice trails off.

"Yes?"

"What if I told you that c-l-i-t-s are my specialty."

She laughs, color flaming on her cheeks, her head dipping. "I never should have told you that."

"Every word we use has meaning and purpose—and you said it. Why do you think that is?"

She bites her lip, and there we are, standing face to face, staring at each other for a little too long, and people are staring and probably snapping pics with their phones.

"It's Valentine's Day. What else do you have planned tonight? Crying into your ice cream over your ex?"

"Maybe."

"I'm better than ice cream."

"Obviously you haven't had Ben & Jerry's Rocky Road."

"Obviously you haven't met me before." I reach out and briefly touch her plump bottom lip, grazing my thumb across her silky skin, my cock swelling inside my slacks.

Her eyes close, and her throat moves as she swallows, her mouth slightly parted. "Um . . . I don't know."

"Elena, are you going to make me beg for it?" My eyes are hot, this need for her rising and growing every moment we stand here looking at each other.

Please say yes.

Chapter 5

Elena

I look around the room, a penthouse on the top floor inside the Breton Hotel, a posh place near the restaurant. I glance over at Greg, who's at the minibar, making us drinks. I don't need another drink, obviously, because I've had enough already, and I'm buzzing, and *What the hell am I doing*?

I was ready to cut the date off early because he grew quiet on me, and I knew I was rambling too much about exotic pigs, stray cats, and Preston. Jeez. I need a dating class.

But was it ever worth it to walk out of Milano's on his arm, with Preston and Giselle gaping at me. Greg tossed his arm around my shoulders and pulled me close to him as we waltzed past them. Then he phoned a town car he said he had on call and whisked us over to the hotel.

The ride over was quiet. He kept darting me little glances, his eyes on my face, but when I'd look back, he'd drop his eyes and stare straight ahead. He looked as if he wanted to say something, and I chalked it up to him being as nervous as I was.

We walked inside the lobby, and he whispered for me to ignore anyone I might see. There wasn't anyone around, except for the security guard who stood sentinel outside the double doors of the penthouse the elevator took us to on the twentieth floor.

His back is to me, and my gaze eats up those impossibly broad shoulders, the way his mahogany-colored hair has highlights, as if he spends a lot of time outdoors. He's wearing expensive gray slacks that have to be tailor made, the fabric clinging to his powerful thighs, tapering down to a narrow leg opening.

He slides around the bar, adding tonic to my gin, the movement lithe and precise, like a tiger in the jungle. Greg may walk and talk like a man, but he's pure animal underneath.

I lick my lips, one side of me ready to bolt, but the other side has had a slow flame burning inside my body since the moment he stood up to Preston, using that low husky voice of his—

He turns, and I start.

He walks—no, stalks—toward me.

You don't even know him and . . .

I need this, I counter. Plus, he's Topher Approved. I've been sitting on my butt at home for months, and I need something, just *something*, to knock me out of this funk and get me on with my life.

You are only confined by the rules you set for yourself. Live your life, Nana says in my head. She told me that when I dropped the bomb on my family that I wasn't going to medical school. She wanted me to be true to myself. I think she would have approved of the weatherman.

He hands me my drink and takes a sip of his, his eyes at half mast, a hint of wildness there. I suck down my G and T, holding his gaze. I want to be wild. I want to be wild with *him*.

No you don't, the rational side of me counters.

"Is this where you live?" I set my glass down on the table. *Dumb question, Elena.*

He pauses for a moment. "I own an apartment nearby, but the penthouse is close to work."

A restaurant and two residences? Greg is wealthy.

"I see."

I eye the king-size bed in a bedroom I can see down the hall, the opulent white down comforter, the millions of fluffy pillows. I've been with two men in my life. One was Tad, my college sweetheart, who moved to Silicon Valley after graduation. He didn't ask me to move with him—he needed to get a foothold on his new job and find a place to live—and I didn't press him. We parted ways with promises of keeping in touch and flying out to see each other, but for some reason, neither of us ever did. We had a benign, comfortable relationship, and after a few months of him being gone, I found that I hardly thought of him at all. About a year ago, I looked him up online and saw that he'd recently gotten married. Then came Preston, and look how that turned out. Men keep leaving me, and I wonder if it's something missing in me.

"You look nervous, Elena. Don't be."

Right. That's like telling my pet pig to not eat cucumbers.

"If you'd rather me call you a car to take you home, I will. I just thought you and I . . . we seem to . . . have . . ." His voice trails off, as if he's not quite sure what to say.

"No, I want to be here."

"Good." We look at each other for several moments, and I fidget, moving from one foot to the next.

He comes closer, setting his glass down on the end table where mine is. "May I take down your hair?" His voice is hesitant, and it comforts me to think that he really is nervous.

"Okay."

He tugs at the upswept hair I carefully arranged before work this morning.

He sighs when it's down, running his hands through the long strands as they fall to the middle of my back. My hair is my treasure, long and thick and lustrous, a coppery color with gold highlights. Topher is always telling me to wear it down, that it's my best attribute, but it's easier up or pulled back with a headband.

"Beautiful. I didn't realize it was so long," he murmurs.

His hand massages my scalp in a way that makes me step closer to him, my body loose and melting under the intensity of his golden eyes.

"I need you to sign some papers. Are you okay with that?"

Papers?

I blink.

His thumb tugs at my bottom lip, brushing against it softly like he did at Milano's. "It's just basic stuff about confidentiality, an NDA form. Because of who I am and what my ex did, I don't take any chances. Cool?"

"You aren't *that* big of a deal."

He stills and takes a step back from me, and I immediately want him back.

"Elena, there's something I should tell you . . ." He rubs at his face. "Shit."

He's wavering.

I exhale. Preston's taking Giselle home, and even though he'll be in his full set of pajamas and smelly socks, I'll be the one alone tonight.

"Are you married?" I ask.

"No!"

"Girlfriend?"

"No."

"Serial killer?"

"No, but would I admit that if I was?" He smirks.

"Do you have an STD?"

He scoffs. "Hell no. I just got my physical. Plus, I never have unprotected sex."

Then why does he look so conflicted? Maybe it's me. I'm not his usual.

"Then we're good. This is what it is, right? Just sex between two lonely people."

He releases a sigh and gives me a lingering glance. "You should never be lonely, Elena."

My entire body softens at the sincerity—and heat—in his voice. I like his growly tone. Masculine and nothing like Preston's. He takes my glasses off, and I stare at his lips. They're insanely lush, full, and totally bitable, a deep indentation on the bottom. No man should have such a wicked mouth.

"Which is why we're going to do this," I murmur.

He seems to come to a decision and guides me to a huge modern kitchen, where he pulls a few pieces of paper out of a drawer and lays them down on the white marble countertop.

I do my best to focus on the papers, but it's difficult when he moves behind me, his body pressed against mine as he lifts my hair to the side and brushes his lips lightly over the sensitive skin on the back of my neck.

Fire licks at me, rising higher and higher, from the brief contact. We haven't even kissed for real yet, and I'm already incinerating from the outside in.

With a shuddering inhale, I give the papers a cursory look. A nondisclosure agreement. Gross. I'm a trustworthy person. I'd never share my dalliances with anyone. Good grief, I have my own secrets to keep! Hello, sexy lingerie.

His hands are undoing the clasp on my pearls, the soft graze of his hands against my skin making my legs weak.

"Hurry up, Elena."

The soft words shoot straight to my core, heat pooling as I shiver. I grab the pen and scribble in a name and address.

I turn to face him, chewing on my lip. "All done."

He wears that wild look in his eyes again when I face him, his chest rising rapidly as he takes me in from head to toe. I don't know what he sees except that my hair spills around my shoulders, and I'm pretty sure my nipples stand at attention.

I put my hand on his chest. "First, tell me three things about you."

His fingers unbutton the top button of my shirt. "Let me see. My middle name is Eugene, and coupled with the fact that I didn't hit my growth spurt until sixteen, it got me beat up a lot in middle school." He undoes the second button. "Secondly, I'm absolutely terrified of water. You'll never see me swimming or on a beach vacation."

He's so athletic looking. "Why?" I breathe as he goes for the next pearl button.

He puts his face in my neck, inhaling. His lips brush at my ear. "Not telling you. Fuck, you smell good. What kind of perfume is that?"

I let out a ragged breath. Something Topher gave me. "I can't recall, and third?"

He fingers the last button on my shirt, not quite undoing it. "You really need to know?"

I nod, my body tingling when his hand pulls at my hair, the hold making me arch my neck up. It's a little commanding and sharp, that motion, but it only sends sizzles of electricity down my spine.

"I like my sex hard and dirty. Does that scare you?"

"As long as you don't pull out the handcuffs." I must be drunk because I might not mind those one little bit.

He kisses my collarbone. Barely. "And you didn't ask for a fourth, but the truth is I may have to jack off in the bathroom before I fuck you, Elena."

A long breath comes out of me. "Greg . . ."

He winces and drops his hands. "Don't call me Greg."

"Okay, Eugene."

He huffs out a laugh. "Tell me about you."

"My middle name is Michelle."

He gives me a long look, his eyes darkening as I undo the last button on my shirt, picking up where he left off. I'm doing this. And the freedom of it, knowing that this man wants *me*, makes me bold.

"Tell me more," he murmurs, eyes low, watching me like a wolf might watch its prey.

"I love books—the smell of them, the weight of them in my hands. Before I was a librarian, I used to edit romance books in New York."

He holds my gaze, his mouth deliciously close to mine. "Nice. What else?"

"When I'm nervous, I spell words." I blush.

"I make you nervous. Filing that away. What else?" he growls.

"I've never had an orgasm with a man."

His eyes go to half mast. "Sweet Elena, I'm gonna take care of that first thing."

A long exhalation leaves my chest, part exhilaration, part excitement that licks over me at the way he's looking at me, as if he's going to devour me bit by bit. That feeling of confidence roars. With a skilled motion, he slides my blouse off, and it falls to the floor.

He swallows, his throat bobbing as his eyes burn over every inch of me. He takes a step back, his eyes hot flames.

I might be a librarian, but my lingerie screams *sex kitten*.

I unzip my skirt and step out of it, kicking it to the side. It lands near the kitchen table.

And I know exactly what he sees—a three-piece pink sequin set, a bra and panties with garters featuring handmade Italian lace on the straps.

His chest rises. "Fuck me."

Oh, I will.

I cup my full C cups, sliding my hands over the material, showing him how the sequins change from pink to silver. "There are little unicorns on my breasts when you move the fabric." I drift my fingers over the waistband of the panties, feeling brave, oh so brave, by what I see on his face. I touch the top of my mound. "And here, when I move the sequins"—I slide the fabric resting on my small bundle of nerves—"is a little heart." It's funny how easy this is with him when I was never able to model for Preston any of my designs. He took one look at the mannequins and dress forms in my sewing room and left the room, chagrined, his face livid. He yelled at me and said I was going to ruin my entire family with my *proclivities*. I should have seen then that we weren't the same. That he wasn't the *one*.

Because the *one* is supposed to get you, accept you.

But the man in front of me is not looking at me with distaste at all. He rubs at the scruff on his jawline, a flush on his cheekbones. "Elena, you are not what I expected. Or maybe you are. I don't know." He shakes his head. "Can't really think straight right now."

I dance my fingers down to my thighs, to the scraps of lace there, unsnapping the clasp and letting the garter fall.

"More," he pushes out, palming his slacks.

I unclasp the tiny triangle bra, twirl it for a moment before letting it fall from my fingers and drift to the kitchen tile.

He bites his lip, eyes skating over me before coming back to my face.

I shimmy, and my panties fall to the floor.

Who am I right now? Who is this crazy girl? I don't know, but I like it.

"Elena." He says my name with a groan and drops to his knees right there in the kitchen. His hands encircle my waist as he presses an openmouthed kiss to my hip bone, sucking and nipping at my skin as he works his way down to my apex. A finger brushes my nipple, skating from one to the other as his tongue paints me with ownership, with scalding heat and dark promises. My body ripples with desire, clenching, nerves quivering as I shudder and arch into him.

All coherent thought vanishes.

A delicious frenzy spirals inside me, wet and slick, passion wrapped in the feel of his lips and tongue. Every groan he makes, every touch of his hands, every lick is amplified, expanding into an unrestrained ache until I'm lost in this reckless universe that is me and him. He flicks his tongue and moves his fingers in a wicked way inside me, and a star explodes in a bright light somewhere overhead, drenching me with the fallout, glowing sparks and embers bursting around me. Throwing back my head, I cry out, gasping as my entire body undulates, surging and swelling, my skin reveling in this beautiful release.

Moments pass as I grapple with the aftereffects. The room spins as he sweeps me into his arms, then carries me away from the kitchen and down the hall to his bedroom. We don't speak, or maybe he does, but I'm not tracking, limp and loose in his warm embrace. The wolf has caught me, and I couldn't be happier.

I may not recognize this daring part of myself, but he is what I want right now. This moment. This bliss. This one night.

I'll worry about tomorrow later.

Chapter 6

Jack

Hours later, I snap awake and stand straight up from the bed, fists raised, heart hammering like a freight train. *Fuck.* The nightmare again. Slowly I rub at my left shoulder, where my scar is, easing the ache there. I sigh and sit back on the bed with my head in my hands. Deep inhale, long exhale. I close my eyes, hoping to banish the dream from my thoughts, but it doesn't work . . .

Harvey tosses me against the wall, his hand tight against my throat. He hovers over me, cigarette breath in my face. I'm not a match for him at thirteen, and I flail around, my lanky arms reaching up to pull his meaty paws off me. His road-map eyes glare down at me, and I see darkness there, emptiness that alcohol or Mama can't fix. He reeks of dissatisfaction, discontent, a grenade that's itching to be pulled.

My mouth opens, gasping for air. Black spots dance in front of my face.

"Get off him!" Mama yells from behind, but he doesn't even turn around. He gives me an oily grin and presses harder. My nails scrabble at the old paneling, grasping.

"He smarted off to me, Eugenia. Need to teach this boy some lessons. Might do him some good. Little pussy. Always getting on my nerves."

I look over his shoulder at Mama as my lids shut. This is it. And maybe I always knew it would come to this, Harvey getting sick of me being around and under his feet, another mouth to feed. Mama can't quit him. Even after busted lips and cracked ribs on her body. Belt whippings he did to my back.

Dimly I'm aware of Mama running into the bedroom and dashing back. "Let him go, or I'm going to shoot you, Harvey."

He lets his arms fall, and I sink to the shag carpet, sucking in air, but all I focus on is Mama—and those two trembling hands that clasp the gun.

Shoot him, shoot him, *I scream in my head.*

He advances toward her, creeping in, the stillness of it frightening me more than any of the fast jabs he takes at me.

"Mama," I croak, and in that instant when she looks at me, he pushes her down to the floor, takes the gun from her hands, and fires two bullets at her. He points it back at me—

Stop.

I scrub my face, then grab my phone and check the time. Five o'clock in the morning. Too close to my workout time to go back to bed. Besides, there'll be no more sleep for me. Once that dream hits, it digs its claws in deep, rocking me, taking me back to the hell I grew up with. Twenty-eight years old, and that shit still sticks to me, like dirty gum you can't get off your shoe.

A soft snoring sound reaches my ears, and I start and jerk back off the bed, nearly stumbling as I blink down at the girl in my bed and study the lump she makes under the white quilt, her body curled up in a ball. Her hair, a mix of red and gold, is splayed out on the pillow, her soft pink lips parted as she breathes. I trace over the soft curve of her cheek, the elegant arch of her auburn eyebrows. Part of me is tempted to crawl right back in with her, to wake her up the way she deserves, but my head isn't there. Once that nightmare hits, I crave time alone.

Plus, today is going to be hard enough anyway. I may as well face it.

Being as quiet as possible, I head to the bathroom and look at myself in the mirror. Dark shadows are under my bleary eyes, and I've lost a few pounds since the Super Bowl, when I should be bulking up and prepping for summer camp.

Even though I'm headed to the gym, I get in the shower and let the hot water slide over me, trying to shake the last vestiges of that dream out of my head. My back stings, and I glance in the mirror from the see-through glass of the shower. Long scratches are across the yellow-and-black tiger tattoo that takes up most of my back, and a small laugh comes from me. She quieted all the shit in my head last night, a bandage to the turmoil. I recall the way she stood in front of me, all curves and fire, the sound she made deep in her throat as she came under my tongue that first time, her hands deep in my hair, showing me what she wanted—

My cock is hard again.

I ignore it.

Once she finds out who I really am, she'll probably be just like everyone else . . .

Whatever.

There's no reason to make something into more . . .

Once out of the shower, I ease back into the darkened room, and moving as quietly as possible, I toss on my workout gear and shoes. On the way toward the door, I stop by the kitchen and grab her NDA, sticking the papers inside my duffel without looking.

It's the flash of sparkly pink that makes me stop. Lying near the kitchen island are the little panties she wore last night. Memories of her flood my head. Impulsively, I bend over and snatch them up and tuck them in my joggers. I grab a pad of Post-its from the desk; then I scrawl a note for her and leave it on her pillow. I owe her the truth.

I exit the penthouse, and Quinn stands at the elevator, big and muscular, all of twenty-one. He's one of Lucy's former foster kids, and I hired him a few months back to be on call whenever I need him. It makes me antsy that someone else might figure out where I periodically spend time. My apartment is a block away, but that building came with top-notch security—the hotel, not so much. I called him last night and told him I was headed to the penthouse, and he came over. He's got zilch experience in security, but he's tough looking, and when Lucy asks for something, I move heaven and earth to make it happen.

"Morning, sir. The stadium?"

I nod. "Yeah, and you don't have to call me *sir*, Quinn." We have the same conversation every time he addresses me.

"I'll call a car for you now, sir. Or I can drive you?"

I wave him off. "I'm going to drive."

He looks disappointed, and I figure he's bored just standing here all night—although he still looks fresh. He probably napped in the big leather chair near the elevator. My head nudges toward the closed door of the penthouse. "Will you make sure the cleaning lady skips today? Call down, and let them know."

His face splits in a grin. "Nice evening?"

I frown. "We don't discuss my private life. Whoever comes in and out of that room is my business." I pause. Yet . . . "Tell her I'm sorry, will you?"

He gives me an odd look, then straightens and gives me a nod. "Of course, sir."

"*Quinn.* Call me Jack, please. The same lady raised us. We're practically family."

Not really. He came along long after I left Lucy's house and went to college, but damn, sometimes I wish I had a *real* brother.

He nods. "Sorry, it's just I'm thankful for the job, sir—Jack. Not many people want to hire someone who's been in jail."

Lucy told me all about his drunken skirmish with another college kid, who happened to be the son of a senator. That kid ended up in the hospital with a broken arm and broken ribs. Quinn got six months, a tough sentence for a kid just starting his life, and from what I've seen of him, he's polite and good at what he does, and he definitely looks the part with that brawn. And I'm a big believer in going with my gut, and my gut says Quinn's a good kid.

"Hey. Forget that. It's how you live your life now that matters."

He exhales. "It was self-defense, sir—Jack. He brought it on himself, and I took it and took it until I snapped. The media blew it out of proportion."

"No need to explain it to me. I've snapped a few times myself." I recall a skirmish I got sucked into on the field just this last season, after a helmet grab that took me down hard and hurt my shoulder. And even though I didn't start that fight, you better believe people think I did.

I slap him on the back. "Never look back, Quinn. Let people talk." That's my motto.

He gives me another hopeful glance. "You think you'll need me tonight? I don't have any plans. I can be here or wherever you need."

I don't really need him tonight. But I can tell Quinn wants to be busy. "Devon's got a birthday party at the Razor. You can hang out if you want the hours."

He grins. "Yes, sir."

An hour later, I've gotten fifteen miles in on the treadmill when Aiden waltzes into the gym, his face fucking perky for the early hour. Looks like someone else is working on his game. Most of the team is on vacation right now, chilling out in some faraway place, enjoying their families or significant others during the off-season. Not me. Here I am, working my ass off to keep my number one spot.

And Aiden . . . yeah, he's a real go-getter too.

Twenty-three and a superstar draft from Alabama, he's been breathing down my neck since he got on the roster, just waiting for me to screw up so he can step right into my shoes.

He doesn't speak as he walks past me, but those eyes are all over me. A little smile curls his lips as he leans on the treadmill next to me.

I click off the machine and tug out my earbuds. "Like what you see? Need some pointers on how to run?"

A lot of this game is in the head, and nobody's as good at that as me. Sure, my private life might be piling up around me, but I know when a young buck is aiming for my heart. Football is *all* I have, and I'll do anything to protect my game.

"Ease up there, old man. I'm just here to work out."

Uh-huh. He's been here every morning like clockwork, staying as late as I do.

"You need some help with your passing game? You hesitate half a second on a blitz. You better fix that before you even dream of taking my spot."

He frowns.

I grin.

"I do not hesitate."

"Yep. You do." I shrug and grab a towel and wipe the sweat from my face, knowing he's playing back that last horrible game we had.

He rolls his shoulders before picking up a barbell, doing reps for his arms. "I just want what's best for this team—"

"And you think that's you?"

He sets down his weight and pushes back brown hair, flashing me a cocky grin.

"Yeah, man. Think about it. You've been here for seven years, and I don't see a Super Bowl ring on that finger. You messed up that game good, Hawke. Five interceptions. *Five.* You choked last month in front of millions, and this town remembers. And now . . ." He laughs as he sets the barbell back on the shelf, grazing his hands over the selection, idly picking up a heavier one. His eyes meet mine in the mirror. "Dude. You're practically handing me the starting position. You *hit* a little kid in your big-ass Escalade last week. They might have forgiven you the loss of that trophy, but a young fan . . ." He lifts a shoulder nonchalantly.

Anger ratchets up. "I didn't see you out there trying to score when they put you in that game. You couldn't move the ball one inch. You. Hesitate." I continue, "You might be bright and shiny now, but you don't have the grit, Alabama."

He bristles.

The double doors of the gym open.

I turn as head coach John Connor walks in, his gaze beady. "Everything all right?" He moves his eyes between us.

I cross my arms. "Aiden and I were just jawing."

"Yeah," Aiden adds. "Jack was saying how great I am."

I bend down to grab my water bottle on the bench; my lips tighten as a fissure of pain races down my left shoulder, tingling all the way to my arm. Gritting my teeth, I force my shoulders to relax. No way do I want Aiden to get a whiff of weakness. Or anyone. I shake it off, rolling my shoulders, relaxing as it fades.

Coach frowns as he takes in my running joggers and sweaty face. "The press conference is in two hours. You know what you're going to say?"

The press conference.

A tight feeling grows in my chest. *Do I know what I'm going to say?* No.

I pray I can speak at all.

I give him a tight nod and stalk out of the gym. Lawrence meets me out in the hall, his Armani suit gray and as sharp as his face. He straightens up from the wall he was leaning against. "First things first, you look like shit."

"Thanks." I rake a hand through my hair. "Late night."

"Also, there's a pic of you online in Milano's with a woman, drinking. What part of keeping your head down until this blows over did you not understand, Hawke?"

"It was a date. And it was one drink with dinner."

His mouth gapes. "A date?"

I scrub my face. "Wasn't planned."

He nods, eyeing me carefully. "There's a video of you getting in some guy's face too—"

"I did *not* get in his face. God damn it, Lawrence. I have a life. Why does everything I do have to be picked apart?" I push off past him, and he follows, his legs considerably shorter than mine, so he scurries to keep up.

"Because you're you, and the media hates you."

"They love the lies."

"But it makes for a good story."

I walk into the locker room and yank open my locker, eyeing the clothing I have there, everything from street clothes to a couple of suits.

Lawrence looms over my shoulder, rifling through the rack and pulling out a yellow polo with the Tiger emblem and a pair of designer jeans. "You need to dress casually for the reporters, nothing flashy. I know you like your pressed shirts and slacks, but look relatable. Be nice. Try a smile. Soften that growly voice."

My shoulders tighten as I take in a deep breath. "I am relatable. I grew up poor as shit. I won the Heisman my junior year in college. Why doesn't anyone remember that, huh?" I send him a side-eye. "And we both know I can't stand those reporters in my face. I can't do it, Lawrence. I don't know why I'm even going to this thing."

"Because Coach is making you."

I turn to face him and see the sympathy on his face. He knows the panic I feel whenever a crowd is hounding me. I wasn't this way in high school, or maybe I was and just didn't recognize the symptoms because I never really had to put myself out in public. In college, I recognized it right away as soon as I came off the field after a big game and a reporter stuck a microphone in my face. I brushed past them and kept on going. Sometimes I'd be okay if my helmet was on. A few times, my teammate

Devon would stand next to me, and I'd let him do the majority of the talking. Lord knows he can't shut up anyway. Later, after I was drafted and came to Nashville, everyone expected me to be friendly with the media, give interviews to the local guys whenever they wanted, be the MC at galas. Never in a million years.

And my reputation as an arrogant, unemotional asshole was born.

"The press conference isn't a bad idea. You've barely spoken at one in years, and trust me; they'll be salivating in that room."

"Not helping, Lawrence."

"Too much has been said about you in the past—including Sophia's lies—and you've never defended yourself. You lost the Super Bowl. You ran over a kid—accidentally. It's time to buckle down and think about putting yourself out there. Look, you hired me to fix your image issues. You have this anxiety thing when it comes to reporters in your face, but just *try* this time. Stare at the ground if you have to. Just get the words out about what happened. It wasn't your fault, Jack, but when you won't even tell people, they form their own opinions."

I stand there, mulling. I don't even know the root of the fear. It's just *there*.

He exhales. "People like a villain, Hawke, and you make a great one. There are rumors of trading you."

"Rumors from whom?"

"I don't have specifics."

I close my eyes.

There are always rumors, especially after a big loss, but if they do trade me . . . it's a death sentence. It says, *Jack has problems, and Nashville doesn't want him.* Plus, this damn shoulder. I rub it for a moment, then grab the hangers he's holding and head to the showers.

He keeps pace behind me, his headset from his phone in his ears as he talks to someone. Probably my agent.

I flip on the water and give him a look. "Are you gonna talk to me the whole time I shower?"

His lips press together. "If I have to. We need to run through a few responses to questions I'm anticipating. We're going to spin it and blame the kid. He never should have been outside the stadium in a restricted zone anyway. It wasn't your fault you didn't see him—"

"Lawrence, he's a *kid.* I can't blame him. Get out of here, okay? Let me think." I pause. "Also, find out what you can about a girl named Elena."

He crosses his arms. "Not your secretary."

"Personal assistants. That's what they call them these days. But you are my PR guy."

He rolls his eyes. "A girl, huh?"

I grab my gym bag and pull out the NDA, scanning it. "Yeah. The one from last night." My stomach drops. "Dammit!"

"What?" He looks over my shoulder.

I groan, dread filling my stomach as I scan the papers. "She didn't sign the NDA with her real name."

He shrugs. "Juliet Capulet? Has a nice ring to it. Maybe Elena is her middle name?"

"Hardly." My lips tighten.

"Is there an address?"

I grimace. "Home address: Verona, Italy."

"Is she Italian?"

I huff out a laugh. "Dude. *Romeo and Juliet.* How the hell did you ever pass freshman lit?"

He shrugs. "Your dick is going to get you in trouble."

I slam the papers back in my bag. "Just find out who she is, okay? I left her this morning with my digits, but she may not be in the best mood when she wakes up. She thinks I'm the local weatherman, Greg something—"

Lawrence sputters. "You lied to her? That alone is enough to make the NDA invalid. What if she runs straight to the media?"

I wince. I wasn't thinking straight last night . . .

"Just find her, and we'll do a new one, true?"

He throws his hands in the air. "Unbelievable. You actually want me to hunt down some random you screwed—"

My finger spears him. "Not a random. Don't talk like that, Lawrence. She is a person."

And I liked her.

His eyebrows hit the roof. "I should just quit this job now."

"You threaten to quit once a month, and no one believes you. 'Cause you like me too much, and I pay you well." I slap him on the arm. "I need you. I have two good friends in this town, you and Devon. Do you have any clue how lucky we are to be together?"

Lawrence, Devon, and I all attended Ohio State and played football and won a national championship our senior year. I was drafted to Nashville—first round, first pick—and Lawrence's family lives here. Football wasn't a lifetime career for him, so I hired him as PR, not even realizing how bad I'd come to need him in the next few years. And Devon—he was traded to Nashville from Jacksonville a couple of years ago, our best wide receiver and my go-to guy on the field.

Lawrence scowls. "I don't know how to find a girl."

"Liar. You're like a pro, man, all stealth and spy-like. You're a laser with sharp focus. You're a ninja who scales tall buildings. Hell, you're—"

"Fine. I'm awesome. I have skills." He studies his carefully manicured nails. "But this is different. Maybe this girl doesn't want to be found. Does she live nearby?"

I stop, recalling our conversation. "Daisy. Small town. I've never heard of it, but then I don't leave the city much."

He paces around the locker room. "Daisy, Daisy, why is that so familiar . . ."

"Lawrence, I need her signature. I'm paranoid as hell."

He nods, whipping out his phone and taking notes. "Elena something who lives in a town named after a flower—a weed, really, if you think about it." He gives me an assessing look. "I hope she's worth all this trouble."

My body heats, my cock twitching at that memory of her big eyes, the way her back arched when she was on top of me last night, her long hair brushing the tops of my legs—

"Hawke, are you listening? I barely have anything to go on here."

I put my back to him to hide the tent in my workout pants. "She's a librarian. Can't be too many of those in Daisy."

A long sigh comes from him. "All right, you get showered while I make some calls."

Chapter 7

Elena

My mouth has a million cotton balls inside it. I groan, my hand pressing against my temples as a slow painful thudding starts in my head. Hello, Armageddon of headaches. I wince and curse. That's what I get for slamming back gin and tonics. I'm never drinking again.

I move around and plop my hand over my eyes to block out the light that's coming in from a huge window. At least the sheets under my skin are silky and plush. Hmm, I must have changed them. My hand pats the bed. Where's Romeo—

Dang. I am so not in my own bed.

Everything from last night floods my memories.

I'm sore in the most delicious places, and it makes me smile. Greg. Greg. Greg. He's . . . fuck . . . yeah, he gets the f-word, because that man knows how to make a woman happy, and he definitely knows where my c-l-i-t is.

I glance at the clock on the nightstand. Seven o'clock in the morning, and I turn over, fully expecting to see Mr. Weatherman right there, but the huge bed is empty, just a small indentation where his head must have been. There's a note there. I squint at it, but it's no use, and I have to hold it close to my face to get a good look.

My name is Jack. I'm sorry about the mistaken identity thing. 861-555-5144.

I have to read it three times. It's so . . . to the point. Where's the part about what a great time we had?

And mistaken identity? Is this a joke?

I lie back on the bed, thinking, playing back our meeting at Milano's. I thought he *said* he was Greg.

I asked him if he was *the guy*, and he said *yeah*.

Uneasiness causes me to sit up and flick on the lamp. I focus more on the night before, as much as I can with my head hammering. I didn't know what Greg looked like, and when I saw the guy in the blue shirt, I thought he was Greg. I pause, chewing on my lips. I approached him and sat down and started talking.

Disbelief makes my heart race. No! Is it possible I sat down with the wrong guy, and he . . . he didn't say one word? And all that talk about the weather—and *rain is wet*!

Mortification feeds anger.

What kind of person pretends to be someone else's date?

Who exactly did I have sex with?

I snatch a white sheet from the bed, and I drape it around myself and stand up. One hasty look in the mirror on the wall tells me I look . . . well, like I've had a drunken one-night stand; my hair is everywhere—one side sticking straight up, the other flat as a pancake. Dried drool is on my chin, and my eyes have smudged mascara underneath them. I look deranged. That explains it. No wonder he snuck out.

I scrub at my face while I dart to the kitchen to gather up my clothes. My skirt, shirt, bra, and garters are still on the tile—no panties.

A few minutes later after scouring the kitchen, then dashing to the den and turning over every chair and even crawling under the desk and the minibar, I still can't find the pink underwear. *Jack, or whatever your name is, those panties cost more than my skirt and blouse put together when you count the material and the hours it took to hand stitch the tiny sequins onto the silk.*

I need those for an important fashion meeting I may or may not go to!

Did he take them?

No way. Why would he?

So I restart, being slower this time as I walk through the entire penthouse. I even check under the bed and crawl the perimeter of the kitchen floor near the baseboards. Nada.

There's only one explanation, I think as I stand up and clutch the note he left. My fists curl.

Jack is a liar *and* a thief. *Major douchebag.*

I'm already envisioning the note I'm going to leave him, and I'm muttering loudly as I kick one of the chairs, only it just hurts my foot, and I call out, tears springing to my eyes.

There's a soft knock at the door, and I hobble over to it, peeking through the peephole to see a tall young man, concern on his face. He's wearing a black turtleneck and black pants. Very James Bond.

I whip the door open. "Who the hell is Jack?" are the first words out of my mouth, using *teacher voice*, short and direct, the one I reserve for the kids who come in the library, especially the high school variety. A group of them were just there last week, looking up research for their term projects, and I caught a pair of them kissing in the stacks, like the Daisy Public Library was their own personal make-out spot.

He blanches, his eyes taking in the makeshift toga-style outfit I have going on. I should have gotten dressed right away, but I was too worried about my underwear.

"Ma'am. Good morning. I, uh . . . are you okay? I heard a commotion in here and wanted to check."

His gaze lands on the pink bra in my hands, and a slow blush starts up his cheeks.

I tuck it behind me. “I’m fine. No need to check on me.”

He swallows and stares at a point over my shoulder. “Sorry to bother you. It’s just once a reporter broke in here and went through his things. One time, a girl got in. Stole all his clothes.”

“Good for her!”

He blinks. “Ma’am. I just wanted to check on you. Jack gave me this job out of the goodness of his heart, and I don’t want to mess up.” He pauses. “He said to tell you he’s sorry.”

“He’s sorry? Oh my God! The nerve of him to send you to apologize.”

Young James Bond fidgets. “Most girls Jack dates are happy—”

My anger races up. “You aren’t helping the situation here.”

He dips his head, lowering his eyes. “I’m sorry, ma’am. I shouldn’t have said that about other girls. Hasn’t been one here in a very long time.”

Jeez. I need a better look at this guy so I can read his face. I hobble over to my purse and pull out my glasses and slide them on, turning back to check out the young man. All at once, I’m relieved. He looks antsy and uncomfortable.

He clears his throat, keeping those arms crossed in front of him like a soldier.

“You’re security for Jack?”

He gives me a tight nod. “Yes, ma’am.”

“Please stop calling me that. You can’t be much younger than me.”

“Yes, ma’am—sorry. Southern boy. Can’t help it. May I run out and grab you something? Or call you in breakfast downstairs? The staff here is phenomenal.” He keeps those eyes off me, and I feel at ease.

My stomach rumbles, growling, and I sigh. This is *not* the time to be hungry. “I’m sorry; I missed your name?”

He sticks his hand out. “Quinn. I’m here for whatever you need.”

I give him a firm handshake. “And Jack? Where did he run off to?”

He gives me an odd look, as if I should know. "Uh, he's at the stadium. Big press conference today and all."

"I see." My mind churns, recalling his powerful body, those tightly roped muscles. Stadium means either hockey or football in Nashville, and since Jack said his girlfriend dumped him for a hockey player . . .

"I guess football keeps early hours."

He gives me a big smile. "He's the hardest-working quarterback in the league. A real legend. Brought Nashville four AFC championships since he was drafted. He finished the regular season with four thousand one hundred and four yards passing, five hundred and fifty-one yards rushing, and thirty-one touchdowns. I know we haven't won a Super Bowl yet, but that isn't all on him. This next season is the *one*. I can feel it." He blushes.

"Uh-huh." Sounds Greek to me. "Go on. I love football stats. What else has Jack done?"

He gives me an odd look, but you can tell he wants to talk about Jack. "Well, people are still sore about our loss to Pittsburgh this year, but it takes a team to win. We need better guys on defense. He just gets a bad rap because of his past."

"I know. His past. Man, it follows him everywhere. Such a shame." I look expectantly at Quinn, who's nodding along with me.

"Right! So what if he got a DUI once and was benched. That was years ago. I mean, come on; at twenty-two he got a twenty-four-million signing bonus, fifteen more million than the quarterback that played before him. He made some mistakes. That kind of money can mess with a kid who never had a pot to piss in." He grimaces, as if he's said too much.

Indeed.

"I see. When was the Super Bowl?"

He starts. "Last month, ma'am. You didn't watch?"

"Missed it."

He gives me a disappointed look, as if I've failed horribly. "That's a shame."

I keep the dawning realization of who Jack is off my face. A jock. A freaking athlete! A famous one who makes millions!

It's so ridiculous that it must be on my face, because Quinn frowns. "You okay, Miss?"

"Call me Elena, please. I insist," I say absently, trying to come up with how to glean more info from Quinn.

"So back to Jack. How did he seem when he left this morning?"

Quinn hesitates. "A little tired, maybe. He's got a lot on his mind. You know what he's dealing with. The media hates him and for no good reason. He's one of the kindest people I know. He took care of that kid that got hurt and even paid all his medical expenses, although he'd never tell anyone."

Kind? He lied to me and took my underpants!

Kid? What kid?

I straighten my shoulders. I'm not leaving this place until I figure out exactly who Jack is and why he . . . why he . . . I bite my lip . . . he made me feel so . . . beautiful.

Whatever. He deceived me, and that trumps everything.

My stomach rumbles. "When's he coming back?"

"Not sure he will. He usually stays at his other place. You can hang out here as long as you like."

Oh, I see. *This is the fuck palace.* I do my best to hide my simmering emotions.

"Well, Quinn, does Jack keep his fridge stocked?" I'm already marching into the space, flinging open the French-style stainless steel fridge.

He tags along behind me. "I keep it up for him. If you're okay, I'll just go."

My eyes glaze over when I see eggs, green peppers, and a drawer full of premium cheese.

"Oh, Quinn," I sigh. "There's gouda here. And dang . . . fresh spinach." I squeal. It feels like centuries since dinner. Plus, I've practically run a marathon since then. "You hungry?"

He gives me an unsure glance, his head turning to look back at the door. "Um, yeah. Gouda. There's some gruyère as well."

"You know how to shop, Quinn. You can stock my fridge anytime."

He just stares at me, and I see a hint of anxiety. He's a little afraid of me. Good.

I open three cabinets before I find the mixing bowls and give him a smile over my shoulder. And I know how crazy I must look, hair and bedsheet, but desperate times call for desperate measures.

"I best be going . . ." He trails off, watching me crack eggs against the granite countertop and then drip them into the bowl.

Teacher voice is back. "Have a seat, Quinn. No one's going to charge the front door this early in the morning. Now, come beat these eggs, and chop some spinach while I go make myself presentable, and when I get back, I'm going to whip us up an omelet, and you're going to freaking love it."

And you're going to tell me all *about Jack.*

"Uhhh . . ."

I push the bowl at him and smile. "Aren't you hungry?"

He nods grudgingly. "Kinda. I usually just call up the restaurant downstairs, and they deliver food to me."

I smile. "Big strapping guys like you need a home-cooked meal. Me too. Look, we already have something in common. We're gonna be besties. Be right back."

After grabbing my purse and clothes, I dash into the marble-tiled master bathroom, taking in the opulent wall-to-wall white stone. I catch my reflection in the mirror again and groan. *Rode hard* comes to mind. *By a lying football player.* Not that I have anything against athletes, but me? I'm not the sexy-jock-type girl. I'm drawn to the intellectual types: lawyers, teachers, computer programmers—weathermen.

After washing my face and combing out my hair and putting it up in a messy knot, I dress hurriedly, minus the panties. I'm almost out the door when I turn back around. After fumbling through my purse, I pull out my cherry red and write on his mirror: *Jack. I want my underwear back!*

Chapter 8

Elena

A few hours later, after a not-as-informative-as-I-would-have-wished breakfast with Quinn, I'm driving the twenty minutes back to Daisy on Interstate 40, my hands tight on the wheel. All Quinn wanted to discuss was Jack's football career and nada about him personally. I did like him, though, and it's not his fault Jack lied to me.

I'm feeling ashamed of my one-night stand, and I'm sure every car I fly past on the interstate can see the huge scarlet *A* on my face. Weak, I was weak. Throw in the gin and tonic, and all my inhibitions disappeared.

Okay, okay, also it might have been his kissing too.

And the fact that he's hotter than a blazing fire.

My phone buzzes again with a text, and I figure it's Topher checking on me, but I don't text and drive or even talk on the phone while I'm behind the wheel. Plus, I sent him one earlier from the penthouse. I'm alive and on my way home. My cell goes off again, then again, and I dart my eyes over to the passenger seat where my phone is. *Sexy Lawyer* is the sender, and my jaw tightens.

Why haven't I removed Preston from my contacts yet?

Cursing under my breath, I find an exit and pull off to the side at a gas station. I totally should ignore him, but Preston did see me leave with Jack, and I'm curious about what he has to say. I snap the phone up and read a series of texts from him; the first ones were sent earlier, but I missed them.

I came by your house this morning and you weren't there.

Did you spend the night with him?

Elena. Are you crazy? He's not a good person.

And then the latest one: Call me.

Call him? I sputter, that familiar hurt and anger rising up at the months I invested in him, in how I thought he understood me—until he didn't. We met when he showed up at the library, decked out in a suit and tie, an engaging smile on his handsome face. Fresh out of law school to work at his uncle's firm, he stayed for an hour talking to me, his warm-brown eyes the hottest thing I'd seen in Daisy since moving back. He left with two Stephen King audiobooks and my phone number, and we quickly became a thing in town. While the sex wasn't off the charts, I just figured it would develop as our intimacy did.

Why does it matter?

My sister swept into town, and that was the end of that.

I change his name to *Two-Timing Lawyer* and get back on the road.

Taylor Swift is blaring "You Need to Calm Down" as I whip into the paved driveway that leads to my two-and-a-half-story white house on East Main. Over a hundred years old, the five-thousand-square-foot Victorian-style house was left to me by Nana when she passed away. It needs constant updates and renovations—obviously including a garage to hide my car from nosy people—but it drips in southern charm, the white wood pristine and crisp, a gingerbread-house-style turret on the right side. A small iron historical placard reading **Belle of Daisy, established 1925** sits near an azalea bush. It has been owned by three generations of my family. Stately pillars dot the broad front porch, and magnolia trees line either side of the yard. The house itself is bookended by two regal weeping willow trees. A gray-and-blue stone sidewalk leads to the porch, and I take it all in, letting the comfort of my home ease that tight feeling in my chest. On days when I feel like this small town is going to drive me bananas, coming home makes it worthwhile.

Topher opens the front door and takes the steps two at a time to reach me. Wearing white skinny jeans, an REM shirt, and ragged black Converse, he's holding a wriggling pink Romeo, currently decked out in a red sweater I knit.

He stops in front of me. "Where have you been?" Without waiting for a reply, he continues, glaring down at Romeo. "Hog from Hell chewed up the toes on a vintage pair of Chucks I have. Lime green! High-tops! Do you know how much those are worth?"

I roll my eyes. My age, with a mop of long wavy white-blond hair and a slender build, he looks like he belongs in California on the beach with a surfboard in his hand. But he's just a good old southern boy, a little misunderstood and a whole lot of wonderful. We met at the Daisy Community Center theater program when I first moved back to Daisy. He was Peter, and I was Wendy in *Neverland*. He moved in soon after, when his lease ran out on his small rental. Lord knows I have enough room: six bedrooms, four baths, and acres of beautiful rolling hills behind the house.

"Didn't you get those at the Goodwill, Topher? And are they really worth money?"

He smirks. "Doesn't matter where or how much I paid. Lime is my color, baby girl. I look good in it. Hog from Hell needs obedience school."

Romeo grunts and sends a glare up at him, but Topher doesn't try to hand him over.

"Nice sweater you put him in," I say.

He shrugs. "It's chilly."

"Uh-huh."

No matter what he says, he likes the tiny pink pig—a little.

"Fine. Forget the stupid shoes." He kisses me on both cheeks, a look of concern on his normally amused countenance. "Greg texted me this morning and said he had the flu and was so out of it he didn't get back to you last night when you said you were going to be late. He's sad he missed you, begs forgiveness, and plans to call you, blah-blah-blah." He pouts. "I'm sad because I just knew you two little nerds were perfect for each other."

"Flu, huh?" He better have been sick as a dog.

"He wants to reschedule."

"Not after last night. It's just bad timing. I'm not ready to meet anyone right now."

His summer-blue eyes rove over my disheveled shirt and skirt. A slow grin takes over his face as he lets Romeo down to follow us and hooks his arm through mine as we walk down the sidewalk. "So you didn't go out with Greg. Which begs the question: Where have you been *all night*? Please tell me you weren't crying somewhere over Preston."

My lips compress, shoving down that hurt and grabbing onto anger instead. "To quote Aunt Clara: 'Preston is a turd in a punch bowl.' But I did see him last night at Milano's with Giselle. Apparently, that's the go-to place for Valentine's Day. I had another date."

He holds his index finger and thumb up within an inch of each other. "Well, I was this close to calling your mama when you didn't come home."

I freeze. "Traitor. I will stab you in your sleep if you even hint—"

"Sweet baby Jesus, I'm joking. She terrifies me." He grins. "So *who* was your date with?"

I feel a slow blush building as I pick up Romeo and give his ear a little scratch. He buries his face in my arms, a long shuffling sigh coming from him. "No one important."

"Did you pick someone up at the bar?"

Pretty much.

I dart a look over at the Cut 'N' Curl across the street, Mama and Aunt Clara's beauty shop, the place in Daisy to get your hair done and hear the latest gossip. The parking lot is packed, a typical Saturday. They opened at ten this morning and no doubt saw that my car wasn't here. I could say I was out for errands if they ask, but Aunt Clara lives right next door and doesn't miss a beat.

"No one's popped by. They're clueless," Topher says, a gleam in his eyes. "But if you don't tell me what's going on, I might just have to go in for a trim and let it drop that a certain librarian didn't come home."

I smack him on the arm playfully and walk inside the house, but inside I'm not as perky as I let on.

He reads me like a book. "Stop that right now, Elena. You do you. So what if you had a fling with some guy you picked up—"

"Who said I had a fling?"

"Your hair is crazy, and your clothes are rumpled, and your lips have a deliciously swollen look to them."

"What a vivid imagination you have."

"I know what a good night of sex looks like." He grins, white teeth flashing on his tanned face. It might be the middle of February, but he's a sun worshipper and hits the tanning beds in the winter.

I set down my purse on the sofa and plop down in a faded-blue armchair, lace doilies Nana made draping the back. I still haven't gotten around to updating the furniture in the house, mostly because I don't have the money for it—and part of me likes the old furnishings because they hold memories.

"Who was it? Was it one of those Tinder guys—"

"No," I murmur. "Um, Jack Hawke."

He does a slow blink. "*The* Jack Hawke? Quarterback for the Tigers? Hot as hell with guns big enough to crush a grown man? That Jack Hawke?"

"Yeah?"

Glee grows on his face as he lights up the room with his smile.

"Stop grinning," I groan, rubbing at the headache that's decided to pop back up. I let Romeo down, and he runs in circles before darting off to his small tent set up in the den. I hear him rooting around before he gets comfy. "It was terrible."

"The sex? Ah, dammit, I've had daydreams about that man, the way he—"

"Stop!" I hold my hand up. "I just want to forget it ever happened."

"Well, then how did it happen?" He takes a seat on the old velour sofa across from me and crosses his legs. "I'm picturing it now—you at the bar looking all sad that Greg didn't show, and in waltzes this hot jock who takes one look at your dainty black pumps and does a double take."

If only that had been how it happened, then maybe I wouldn't feel so bad.

"Not exactly."

"Stop tormenting me. I want every detail."

I shake my head. "I walked up and sat down at his table."

He leans forward. "You picked him up? Oh shiiiiitttt. This is going to be so good. Spill, Elle, spill."

"You are annoying."

"Am not."

"Are."

"Fine, maybe I'm a teensy bit annoying, but I did take care of Hog—"

"Romeo."

"Whatever. Just tell me. Please. Ever since Matt and I split, you know I'm living through everyone else's love life."

I let out a sigh. He's over Matt, but I see what he's doing. He's worried about me. I guess he has been since Preston and Giselle.

"Fine. I sat down at Jack's table because I thought he was *Greg*. He had a blue shirt on, and he was alone and broody, and you know I don't follow football. Daisy is so small we never even had a football team growing up. Plus, no TV . . ." My hands cover my face for a moment of embarrassment. "It's ridiculous! You'd think I would have at least recognized his face from . . . somewhere . . . like a bar TV, and he did seem a bit familiar, but I just assumed it was just Greg—that I'd caught him on TV before."

He laughs. "You fucked the baddest, sexiest jock in Nashville. Do you have any clue how women have chased him his entire life? I hear he even needs security." He grabs his diary from the coffee table. "I'm writing this down. It's going in that great American novel I'm going to write—"

"Not a good idea," I mutter, recalling the NDA. I stand up and pace as he eyes me, frowning.

"Do you plan on seeing him again?"

"One-time thing."

He looks crestfallen, slumping back against the cushions. "Was it good, at least? Is his lower body proportional to the rest of him?"

My face flames as my entire body clenches, recalling the orgasms I had. Oh boy. He *did* deliver on that front. The first one in the kitchen with him on his knees; the second time on the floor in the master bedroom, him behind me; the third time, we finally made it to the bed—

I suck in a breath.

"Your face is redder than a stop sign." Topher chuckles.

"Here's the kicker: Jack didn't tell me who he really was, and he left before I woke up."

He winces, closing his notebook. "Ouch. That is not diary worthy at all. Asshole."

I exhale, thinking again about how I assumed he was Greg. "He mentioned my blog, and I assumed he meant where I post my designs, but I wonder if he thought I was another blogger . . ." I frown. "Why wouldn't he just tell me he wasn't my date? Why keep it a secret?"

He shrugs and waggles his eyebrows. "You wore your naughty things?"

"Unicorn set."

He lets out a low whistle. "Nice."

"And he kept the panties."

"Not nice. We need to get those back." Topher knows how important my work is, how much I love creating fanciful pieces, things *I* want to wear. Not those ill-fitting, basic, run-of-the-mill scraps of lace sold in stores. I yearn for unique clothing, something eye catching and sexy yet quirky. Made for full-figured women with moxie.

Topher's frown turns into a scowl, deepening. His feet shift around as he stands, walking over to me. "Elle, honey, I have other news, and I want to tell you before you find out some other way."

I groan. "Please tell me it's nothing to do with Mama or Aunt Clara." They are constantly popping over. I've even taken to locking my sewing room.

He shakes his head, his pretty hair swishing around his shoulders.

"Okay, tell me."

"I ran over to the Cut 'N' Curl to get a Sun Drop a few minutes ago. You know they have those from the distributor, when we can't even buy them at the Piggly Wiggly. Giselle was there . . ." His voice trails off, and my stomach drops.

"She saw me with Jack."

He watches my face. "She didn't say a word about you and Jack . . ."

"But?"

He grimaces and takes a big breath, his eyes soft and careful. "She was showing everyone her ring. Flaunting it around, waving it in people's faces. I'm so sorry."

A huge chunk of lead lands on my heart, and I wrestle to throw it off, to eviscerate it from my chest and make it go away. I feel winded. "Ring, huh?"

He sits on the arm of the chair. "Preston proposed last night. Had the ring hidden in the cheesecake. So stereotypical. What a snooze fest."

I clasp my hands together. Part of me knew this was coming. It was apparent in the Sunday lunches where I've been forced to sit across from them. Giselle can't keep her eyes off him. She's completely enamored with him.

I recall how she waltzed into my Fourth of July party and met him for the first time. She'd been living in Memphis, and somehow the two of them had never crossed paths in the six months I dated him. Tall, leggy, and blonde, she's three years younger than me—and beautiful with her heart-shaped face and baby-blue eyes.

I recall that sinking feeling when I introduced him to her, the way his eyes flared when he took her hand in an energetic handshake.

I barely notice as Topher dashes to the kitchen and returns with a splash of bourbon in a glass. "I think this calls for the expensive stuff."

I take a small sip. "Nana's twenty-year Pappy. So much for never drinking again."

"She'd want you to have it. Lady was a rebel. Like you."

I slump down in the chair, feeling incredibly tired and not like a rebel at all.

"I've said it once, and I'll say it again. Preston wasn't right for you. He's a pompous jerk with a stick up his ass. I mean, what man doesn't see you and all the sweet things you do for . . . for . . . even an ugly pig!"

Romeo sticks his head out of the tent and glares at Topher, and his eyes clearly say *I know what you said about me.*

"He's smart, you know." When someone dumped him in the parking lot of the beauty shop a year ago, he was near death, wrinkled pale skin that clung to his bones, so weak and thin, barely breathing. I cried the entire way to the vet's office, begging the heavens to let the little thing live, promising to take care of him forever.

Topher picks up Romeo and gives him a reassuring pet. "Fine, he's a little bit cute. And even though he has hooves—freaking hooves, okay—I let him get in my thousand-thread-count sheets last night when he was running around looking for you."

"Did you give him a bath too?"

"Of course. Hog from Hell likes to make a mess, water everywhere. He also chewed up a rubber duck."

I smile at that, but I'm not feeling it.

"But seriously, Elena, Preston doesn't see the woman underneath, all this amazing talent you have."

"Stop." I smile wanly.

He gives me a tight hug. "Come on; go put on some comfy clothes, and we'll pile up in my bed upstairs and read. Later, though, I'm taking you out. You should consider a nap, old lady."

"I'm only six months older than you, and no, please, I do not want to go anywhere. I just want to hermit-crab and stay home." Plus, I could get some sewing done, especially if I want to really commit and meet with the lingerie company.

He winces. "You can't. It's Michael's birthday. Remember?"

Ugh. I totally forgot. Michael is one of Topher's friends from Nashville who periodically hangs out with us. He's straight, but he and Topher go back to high school days.

He gives me a careful look, and I know he's still gauging my reaction to the engagement, but I paste on a brave face.

I sigh. Maybe I should go out, forget everything, dance myself silly. "I'm never good at nightclub outfits."

He presses his hand against his chest. "It will be my pleasure to pick out your clothes."

I study his face, seeing the merriment he's barely hiding. "Uh-huh. I know that look on your face. Is this shindig one of your themed parties?"

He nods. "I confirmed with Michael yesterday. It's *Grease*, baby. I'm John Travolta, and you're Olivia Newton-John." He claps, clearly excited.

I wail. "No, please no. I just want to wear regular clothes."

"Elena Michelle. We are going to party in style because I took care of your wretched pet. You owe me."

"Don't you double-name me. You are not Mama."

But he's already waltzing up the polished cherry staircase in the hall. "Look at me, I'm Sandra Dee, lousy with virginity—"

"You are incorrigible!" I call to his back, but he's still singing. "And now that song is in my head!"

He pauses at the top of the staircase. "Also, later, I demand to hear all details about Jack Hawke and his sexual prowess. You went a little light on the details."

"Never gonna see him again, so it doesn't even matter."

"Evil woman." He disappears in his room, and I swoop up Romeo, who's darted back out of his tent, and plant a big kiss on his face. Everything from last night and the news about the engagement settle like rain clouds on my shoulders. I heave out a sigh. "Romeo, what am I going to do?"

He looks up at me and grimaces.

"I slept with a famous football player," I tell him. "He *stole* my panties. Plus, Preston and Giselle are getting married, and I guess . . ." I swallow. "I need to be happy for them. What do you think?" I glance down at him.

You've got some serious problems, lady, his eyes say.

Chapter 9

Jack

"The vultures are circling," Lawrence murmurs next to me as we push through the throng of cameras and reporters inside the press conference room, a place with a long table at the front, a row of microphones at each seat. The crowd parts as we walk in, and I keep my gaze straight ahead. I gave myself a good rousing pep talk in the locker room, and I'm feeling like, okay, maybe, *just maybe,* I can do this.

I take a seat in the middle, and Coach sits on one side of me, Lawrence on the other.

Devon rushes in the room and jogs to the front, giving me a fist bump. "Fear no more. The favorite is here." He waves at an attractive reporter close to him. "Hey. Good to see you. Call me sometime."

She blushes. Yeah, he's probably tapped that.

"Devon," I murmur. "You didn't have to come. But great late entrance. Everyone's looking." I feign confidence I don't have. Something I've been doing my whole life.

"My plan, of course." He waggles his brows and tosses out a wide grin as he rubs his hand across his dark purple-tipped spiked hair. "Plus I look good on camera."

He sits at the end, slouching down in his seat, and proceeds to give the room a lazy look, winking at anyone who meets his gaze.

Lawrence leans over, and I hear him hiss, "Stop that shit, or you'll be paying me to fix your image next."

"Nashville loves me, Lawrence," he replies, his tone amused. "Get over it. I can do no wrong."

"Give them time," Lawrence mutters. "Fans are fickle."

Coach takes the podium and gazes out at the mass of reporters and cameras. "Thank you for coming today. I'm sure you're all anxious to hear from the team." He shoots me a look.

A muscle in my jaw pops.

"First off, let me answer the first question I know you want to know. Jack Hawke's toxicology is back, and there's no evidence of alcohol or drugs in his system when the accident occurred. There are no plans or even a reason to suspend him from the team. The truth is we're all behind Jack. We support him. He's still the leader on the Tigers football team." A long pause. "Now if you'd like to ask questions, Jack is ready to answer them. As I'm sure you're aware, Jack hasn't answered reporters' personal questions in years, but he's agreed to speak today."

My heart pounds so hard it feels as if everyone in the room can hear it.

Then Aiden waltzes in the back of the room and leans against the wall, his eyes taking in the throng. He turns to talk to the Adidas rep who dropped me this week. I grimace. That's right. Jack Hawke is no longer the face of Adidas. Not surprised they let me go; I've been waiting on this since Sophia's book came out. I guess this week was the icing on the cake.

The door opens again, and my eyes flare. Timmy Caine, the kid I ran over, arrives in a wheelchair with his arm in a cast; his mom is right behind him. They ease inside and stand on the other side of Aiden.

He shouldn't be in this mess. He's just a boy.

I forget that as reporters surge toward me at the table, cameras flashing.

"Jack, have you been charged with assault in the accident?"

"Jack, are you aware the boy you ran over is only ten years old?"

Clearly, they haven't noticed he's here yet.

"Jack, over here. Are you aware that fans have started a petition to remove you from the team—"

"Jack, is it true Sophia Blaine is writing an article about you for *Cosmo*? She claims you forced her to have an abortion while you were dating."

No. I didn't. I swallow, my throat dry. I feel dizzy.

"Jack, why don't you give interviews?"

All the voices are talking at once, rising over each other as the crowd stares at me, and I'm hot all over. I clench my hands under the table, praying to God no one notices that I want to hurl. I dig deep to keep my face composed. *Cool. Be cool. Keep your voice low. Remain calm.*

A young guy in jeans and an ESPN badge pushes ahead of the rest, and I recognize him as John, a talk show host, one of the big guns. "Jack, can you tell us exactly what happened?"

I nod, but my voice refuses to come. Inhaling four breaths, I practice my calming exercises—deep inhale, long exhale.

"Yo, catch this!" It's Devon from the end of the table. He's standing, holding a football I didn't see him come in with.

Working on autopilot, I stand, and it's instinct when I catch the ball.

"You can't shut up when you've got that ball. Always telling us what to do." He grins, and I paste one on my face too. I can't deny the way the ball feels in my hands, leather tight in my grip. Comfort. *Home.*

His eyes glint with understanding, and he takes his seat, back to his slouch.

So here I am, standing in front of my critics—and the kid I hit—holding what I treasure.

You have *to talk to them.*

You have *to be relatable.*

The room is hot, and my face feels red as I turn toward the reporters.

Everyone in the place is staring, waiting, some frowning and scribbling as they write on pads, probably jotting down what an idiot I am. They don't see the awkwardness underneath, the fear of having people I don't know up in my face.

My hands clench the ball as I clear my throat. The entire room freezes, anticipating. "Thank you for coming."

There's nothing I can do about my deep voice, but I do my best to soften it.

I look at Devon, and he sticks his tongue out at me.

I huff out a laugh, because it helps.

I take a breath and walk to the podium.

You've got this, Jack. So what if you made mistakes early on in your career? You've given the best years of your life to this town. I wrestle with my nerves, stuffing them down inside a chest and wrapping a chain around them.

I speak. "What happened three days ago was an accident. I was leaving the stadium after a workout, actually backing up from my parking spot, and didn't see the young boy on his scooter behind me. I backed into him and broke his arm and sprained his ankle. His prognosis is good." I push the words out with force. "The truth is there's no salacious story here. Accidents happen every day, and thankfully no one was more seriously injured. I'm grateful for that and plan to follow up with Timmy and his family."

Some of them gape at me. Besides a five-second interview on the field when my adrenaline helps me power through a microphone in my face, this is the most I've said to the press since being drafted. Coach knows about my issue, and during press conferences after games, he lets me sit silent while he breaks down the game.

Another reporter jumps forward.

"Were you distracted when you hit him? Some witnesses say you were on your phone."

My lips tighten. Witnesses, my ass. No one was there.

"Are you aware Timmy's been offered money to sell his story? There are claims you yelled at him and refused to call the ambulance—"

"I can answer that," comes a small voice from the back, and the entire place swivels to see Timmy in his wheelchair as his mom pushes him forward. The reporters dash to the back.

Shit.

I step back from the table and stalk through the throng to where he is. A male reporter jabs a mic in my face. "Did you know he was coming today, Jack?"

"No," I mutter, edging around him.

Lawrence is calling for me to come back, but fuck that; I can't let these reporters hound this poor kid.

I finally get to him and toss him the ball. He catches it, and my hand goes to his thin shoulder. He's a skinny thing, hair buzzed short, wraparound black glasses. Wearing a number one bright-yellow Tigers jersey (mine), he looks up at me.

"Hey, little man. You don't have to answer anything. These reporters can be hard to handle."

He frowns at me. "I know you said I shouldn't come, but Mama said she'd bring me, and it's hard to tell me no when I nag."

I glance at Laura.

She shrugs and smiles. "He begged all night. I guess he's watched ESPN these past three days. He was worried about you and how they said you were probably drunk."

Why would I be drunk leaving the stadium? No one even cares. They just assume.

Reporters are crowding us, and I send a glare at them. "Back off, will you? He's just a kid."

But Timmy likes the attention, because he's already talking to John from ESPN, who's managed to weasel in on the other side of his wheelchair.

"Timmy, tell me what happened." He sticks a mic in his face.

Timmy gives John a look, his chin tilted up in a determined way. "Okay. Mr. Hawke did *not* yell at me, and whoever said that is a liar. He called the ambulance right away and even came with me because Mama didn't know where I was. I took a bus to Nashville and rented one of those scooters and snuck past security into the stadium parking lot."

"Are you a big Tigers fan?" John asks, darting a look at me. "A lot of people aren't these days."

I grit my teeth.

Timmy nods. "Jack sat with me while they reset my arm and put a cast on. He didn't leave until midnight. And I am not selling a story, because there's no story to tell." He sweeps the reporters with an evil eye, and I bite back a grin.

Yet part of me had wondered if perhaps his mom was going to make something more of this. I couldn't help but notice they don't have much. Clean but old clothes, their address a small apartment in Daisy . . .

Daisy?

I freeze, recognizing the connection, but I let it go when Timmy keeps talking.

"Mr. Hawke is my favorite Tigers player, and I was hanging around the stadium hoping I'd see him. I get bullied at school, and I was sick of it, so I skipped school that day to see him. I waited for him to come out." He grimaces. "Really, it's my fault."

"No, it's not. Don't say that," I say, scowling. "I should have double-checked it was clear."

"How serious are your injuries, Timmy?" a reporter asks, sending me a scathing glance.

I can't win here.

"I'm fine! I go back to school Monday." He grins. "I like the wheelchair, but I don't really need it. Mama says it keeps me still." Another grin. "I'm hard to manage."

"Why did you come today, Timmy?" John asks, eyeing me. "Are you being paid any money?"

My temper spikes. *Is he for real?* I think my face must say what I'm thinking because John pales.

"To support my favorite team and player. What y'all say about him is just not true. He paid for my hospital bills and he . . . and he . . ."

"What?" John asks.

Timmy bites his lip and gives me an "I'm sorry" look. "He's coming to Daisy to have breakfast with me tomorrow . . . and he—he's going to be hanging out with me a lot."

What the hell?

All eyes look at me. I throw a glance at Lawrence, who's moved next to me with Devon. Devon laughs, and I can see the wheels in Lawrence's head spinning.

They both know I haven't agreed to any of that . . .

"He's going to come to my school, too, and give a talk about what it's like to be a famous quarterback."

I sigh. Timmy is quite the manipulator.

Timmy stares up at me with big eyes. "And he said he wants to support our little town by participating in our play this year. My mom is the director!" His face brightens as he turns back to the reporter. "He's going to be my best friend!"

"Wow, Jack," Devon murmurs next to me. "Didn't know your schedule was so fluid. Wanna come help me do some shit too?"

"Go with this." Lawrence's green eyes gleam. "Spin it. Because this just fell in your lap . . ."

I stare down at Timmy while he talks to reporters, taking him in, recalling how small his little body was when I dashed to the back of my

SUV and saw him lying there, his arm broken, the scooter snapped in half. I recall the terror I felt. It's a wonder I didn't kill him.

"Is all this true?" The question comes from one of the female reporters, and she's got a glimmer of tears in her eyes after talking to Timmy, when he was describing how his dad had recently passed away. He might possibly be the perfect poster child for *Let's make Jack Hawke look good.*

I let out a deep sigh. I don't like using this situation at all, but . . .

"Yes. Timmy's a great kid. We're gonna be great friends."

Chapter 10

Elena

"Can I buy you a drink, pretty girl?"

The male voice comes from my right at the bar just as I'm sucking down a tall glass of ice water. Sweat dots my forehead, and my mascara is smudged—I can see it in the mirror across from the bar—so I know for a fact I am *not* pretty right now.

I don't even glance at him, although a cursory look in the mirror tells me he's tall with clipped hair at the sides and with spiky hair gelled and sticking up.

"Not interested." I signal the bartender for another glass of water. "Hit me again. Less ice this time, please," I tell him as I dab at my face with a napkin, then my chest.

Mohawk leans in a little closer, and I smell expensive aftershave, something with cool tones, like the sea. "Really?" he murmurs. "You trying to run me off? I'm kinda scary at first, but once you get to know me—"

"Try another *pretty* girl." I am not in the mood for men—especially after last night.

The bartender sets down the water, and I attack it.

Mohawk chuckles. "You're a thirsty one."

"Are you still here?" I say, pulling my phone out of my crossbody purse and pretending to scroll.

"Yeah. And I'm surprised you aren't asking for an autograph by now. You come here often? I haven't seen you, and I know everyone who comes in here. These are my stomping grounds."

Autograph?

Okay, curiosity makes me turn and give him a full-on look. He's tall, about six two, and lean, with purple-tipped hair and tattoos up his arms, disappearing into his clothing.

I arch my brow at the dress shirt he wears with red lightning bolts all over it. "I don't come here ever. Actually it's my friend's birthday." I point out Topher and Michael and some of his friends. The guys are dressed as T-Birds with pompadour hair, black leather jackets, white T-shirts, and combs in the back pockets of their jeans. A couple of girls—Michael's entourage—are wearing Pink Ladies jackets and poodle skirts. It's *Grease* everywhere. Topher strikes again. We had dinner early at a Thai place on Second Avenue and then popped in here to dance. Topher planned the entire event. It's one of the things I adore about him, how he loves to make other people feel special.

Mohawk watches them dance to "Who Let the Dogs Out" and then turns back to me, an amused smile on his face. He checks out my long teased hair, the red stilettos, the suffocating black leather pants, and the off-the-shoulder tight black shirt. "I guess you're Olivia Newton-John at the end of *Grease*? Hot Sandy?"

"Mmm. You're super smart."

He isn't deterred by my sarcasm. Although, on a better night, I might have been flattered or even asked him about that print on his shirt. It fits him perfectly, tight across the chest but not clingy, the sleeves perfect around his muscled biceps. Tailored. Expensive. Not a shirt for me, but the fabric is interesting. Romeo might like a new bedcover. I make a mental note to search for it online.

"The name's Devon Walsh, by the way." He looks at me expectantly, as if waiting for me to do something—so I do a slow golf clap.

"Nice. That's a girl's name."

He cocks his head. "Seriously, you don't know me? Even with this?" He brushes a hand through his spiky hair. "It's my calling card. Has been since high school."

"Some men peak in high school, Devon. I wouldn't brag about it."

He throws his head back and laughs, eyes gleaming. His face is handsome—a nice nose, although it looks as if it's been broken once, a slight imperfection. Two small black hoops are in his ears. A silver eyebrow stud winks at me under the strobe lights, accentuating the straight lines of his dark brows. Toss in the neon-blue leather jacket he's carrying over his arm, and he's . . . interesting.

"Tell me where you got that shirt."

His lips twitch. "You *are* amusing. And I haven't peaked. Still climbing." He rubs his shirt. "You like it, huh?"

I nod.

"Wanna touch it, babe?"

I roll my eyes. What is it about me these past two nights that I've caught the attention of two very different yet hot guys? Must be the leather pants tonight. They scream *Looking for a good time.*

But what was it about me with Jack? Because he saw me in my work clothes . . .

I turn back to the bar. "Don't *babe* me. Or *pretty girl* either."

"Then tell me your name."

"No."

He chuckles. "Just the first name. We can get to last names later."

And by later, he means . . . yeah, right. Not doing that again.

I nudge my head at a brunette across the bar from me. "Try her. She's more your speed; plus she's looking at you like you're a king-size Snickers."

He shrugs. "Nah. You caught my eye. Once I saw you, everyone else just disappeared. I mean, I'm not a photographer, but I can picture us together."

I laugh. "That is a terrible pickup line, but points for perseverance."

"I can't stop myself; they just roll off my tongue. And usually those lines work. Usually all I do is say my name, and girls fall at my feet. Sorry." He grins, not looking apologetic at all.

"Not interested. All I want to do is hang out here for a while, then head home to Romeo."

"Romeo? You got a guy?"

"Pet pig."

He laughs and plays with his beer bottle. "Would it help my case if I said you have the ultimate privilege of speaking to the best wide receiver in the countr—"

"What?" I start, my glass nearly slipping from my hands.

His lips turn up in a slow grin. "Ah, you like football. I play for the Tigers here in Nashville. You're welcome." He takes a bow.

I shake my head, the wheels spinning. "I don't know anything about football." I throw a quick glance around the dark club, scanning it for Jack, my heart leaping in my chest. Don't football players travel in packs like wolves? I don't know why I think that, but . . .

He orders another beer from the bartender and takes a long swig. "But you've heard of me, right?"

"No."

He gapes at me. "This is a travesty. A true crime."

"Mmm." Still no sign of Jack as I scan the club, but there are so many nooks and crannies and dark places I might be missing him.

"Are you here alone?" I ask.

He smirks. "Actually, no. It's also my birthday—how serendipitous is that—and a few of my friends and teammates took over the VIP room."

He said *serendipitous*. I soften. I do love big words.

"Really? A VIP room. Huh." I'd *love* to see Jack again. Maybe toss my water in his face. Maybe have a good old-fashioned southern hissy fit.

Devon nods. "I just popped out to hit the men's room and saw you over here slinging back drinks—"

"Water."

"Okay, water. And just thought you might want to join our party, but I can see that you're not interested . . ." He scans the barstools, disappointment on his face.

"Is it cooler in the VIP room? It's hot out here."

He looks back at me, eyebrow arching. "Yeah. Wouldn't it be nice to get out of this crush of people and have a conversation?" His gaze sweeps over me again, lingering on my cleavage.

I tug my shirt up. "And by conversation, you mean . . ."

He laughs. "Conversation can lead to whatever you like. There are a few private rooms in the VIP section where we can go—"

I lean over and thump him on the forehead. "Stop that."

"Ouch!" he says, rubbing the place I hit. "Why'd you do that?"

"Because you're too smooth and flirty. How on earth will you ever meet a nice girl if all you do is throw off these 'Let's get naked' vibes?" I pause. "But because I happen to love your shirt, I'll cut you some slack. I wouldn't mind getting away from the loud music. Is there food?"

Is there a Jack Hawke?

His eyes light up. "Hell yeah. And birthday cake. You aren't going to thump me again, are you?"

"Maybe, maybe not. Lead the way to the VIP room. Let's do this." I slam my empty water glass down on the bar. I don't know where my nerve comes from right now, but if Jack is in the VIP room, it might be a chance for me to . . .

I don't know.

But I want to see him.

"Follow me, babe. You'll love everyone."

"Uh-huh."

He guides me to an area roped off with red velvet cords to the left of the club, near the back. I didn't even notice it when I walked in before—or the bouncer who's guarding the entrance.

I look over my shoulder and give Topher and Michael a thumbs-up sign. I elbow Devon. "My bestie knows I'm with you, so no funny stuff."

"Ah, I wouldn't hurt you for the world."

My nerves are stretched thin as we breeze past the bouncer, walk down a hallway and inside a dimly lit room with a smaller bar and a raised dais for a dance floor. Nicely dressed servers roam the room with platters of champagne. A longer table of food lines the back wall, filled with cold shrimp, fruit and cheese, and little quiches. I eye those.

There's a window that faces the dance floor, and I see Topher, although I'm certain the regular people out in the club can't see inside the bar. I hadn't even noticed the window.

"There's quite a crowd in here," I murmur as I pull my pale-pink cat-eye glasses out of my purse and slide them on. They're bigger than my white ones and have little jewels on the sides. My dress-up pair.

Devon leads me around the room, randomly calling out to people. Men slap him on the back, wishing him happy birthday. He glances down at me a few times, as if to introduce me, and I grin because he doesn't even know my name. Several women rush up to him, pressing kisses to his cheek, edging me out of the way, and I let them and step away, drifting back to the food. I grab a plate and load it up. After snatching a glass of champagne, I stand in the shadows and survey the area. I've never seen so many big muscular guys in one place, and I feel small even in my heels. Beautiful women, and I mean freaking supermodel types, dot the room, hanging on muscular arms and cooing at the men. Not my kind of place, and all at once, my bravado about finding Jack sinks like the *Titanic*. I came in here on an impulse without thinking too hard about it, but it's clear I don't fit in here. Even with these stupid pants!

I'm stuffing a quiche in my mouth just as Devon reappears. "You snuck off."

I chew and nod. "Food."

"I can see."

"Do not judge. I believe food should be appreciated."

"I admire any woman who doesn't eat salads constantly."

I smile around a shrimp. Devon's not too terrible—even if he is a bit of a player. "Unless it's a pasta salad, maybe with some tortellini and a pound of bacon, am I right?"

"Totally. I could go for a bacon sandwich right now." He slides in next to me and watches the crowd.

I wave my hands at a group of pretty girls dancing on a raised dais, the music in here piped in through speakers from the ceiling. "It's your birthday. Why aren't you out there getting some action?"

"Meh. I think I've screwed every girl here at least once."

I cough and almost spit out part of my shrimp, and he pats me on the back. "Babe, you okay?"

I swallow down my bite. "Devon, look, I'm not a hookup. I don't want to give you the wrong idea."

"I think the thump on my forehead was a clue."

"Good. I'm just here to see if J—"

The crowd parts, and there he is. Every hot-AF inch of him—dark hair swept off his face; chiseled jawline cut like glass; sinful, sensuous lips full and pillowy. He could be a movie star. I squint. Wait. Clarity slaps me in the face. Isn't he the . . . Adidas guy? My mouth parts. He is! I definitely recall seeing his face on a billboard in Times Square when I lived in New York. That was several years ago, but damn, I had sex with . . . *that*.

Whatever.

He's standing near the back, and three women are all over him—a redhead, a brunette, and a blonde. Color me not surprised. He's got a harem of every flavor.

My chest rises, and I set down my plate of food and narrow my eyes at him.

"J-a-c-k. There you are."

Devon follows my eyes. "You a Jack Hawke fan? Want to meet him?"

Fan? *Fan?*

And meet him? I fucked him!

I straighten my shirt to make sure my chest is adequately covered and tug up my pants, ready for battle. I don't know why, when it comes to Jack, I don't dwell on my usual politeness or inherent shyness. Something about him brings out the warrior in me. Maybe it's because Preston screwed me over, and I'm angry in general, or perhaps it's because I was really into *Greg*—

"You could say I know him. Excuse me, Devon, someone owes me an apology."

His eyes flare. "You *know* Jack? *He* owes you an apology?"

"Winner, winner, chicken dinner." I set my plate down on a passing platter and point my stilettos in his direction.

I'm going to kill that quarterback.

It seems to take forever to cross the room to get to where he is, and I feel people looking at me. No doubt they're wondering who I am and why I'm so much shorter than the supermodels. F them. I may not be the usual for this crowd, but I will get my say.

I have to actually push through several people to get to him, using my shoulders to jam my way into his little circle. This isn't me at all, but I'm running on adrenaline. I come to a halt about three feet away while he gazes down at a redhead in a tiny cutout black dress that's at least two sizes too small. She's got ruby lips and the biggest set of breasts I've seen on a girl so skinny. Good for her. An elegant hand curls around his biceps as she smiles up at him and chats. I cock my head, noticing how he looks past her, nodding his head, but he isn't actually talking, just taking it in, a slightly bored expression on his face. Oh, he's responding with nonverbal cues in all the right places, yet his mind seems far away.

I know because I stand there for at least three minutes, tapping my feet, getting my nerve up. Kinda hoping he sees me first. But he doesn't. I'm too short.

On the other side, the blonde has her arm on his other shoulder; she's leaning in, her silky hair brushing against his fancy button-up shirt, another expensive piece of tailored art. She's speaking, too, agreeing with whatever Miss Red is saying. Then I'm distracted; his sleeves are rolled up, and my eyes get tangled up on those forearms again, how taut and muscular they are, how tightly he held me the night before, his hands on my hips as he thrust inside me—

Stop this nonsense right now.

"Jack Hawke," I snap, and it comes out sharper than I thought it would.

Everyone around him stops talking.

He lifts his head slowly, and it seems to take a million years, only I'm sure it's just a few seconds until those honey-colored eyes meet mine. His lush mouth parts as he sweeps me over from head to foot, recognition dawning on his face. A slow flush crawls up his neck to his face.

Then he frowns at me, as if I've done something wrong—when he's the one who's a liar.

That's right, buddy.

I bet you thought you'd never see me *again.*

Yes, he wrote me a note with a cell number, but was it even real?

The girls check me out, and you know how that goes. They give me a once-over, rather dismissive and amused, taking in my glasses, teased hair, sweaty face, and pants. God, who can forget these horrible, tight, sticky pants? How the heck will I ever get them off me? Scissors.

"Elena."

The way he says it, drawing out the syllables, the texture of his deep voice making me shiver.

I close my eyes briefly, feeling the force of his focus and presence like a huge hurricane that's blowing straight in my face. He's primal. He's the god of fucking.

And I climbed him like a tree and enjoyed every moment.

And he did too.

I had him begging for it. Begging me to—

A tingle zips down my spine.

Screw that tingle.

I inhale a deep breath, my fists curling at my sides. "*Weatherman*, where are my panties?"

Chapter 11

Elena

Jack does a slow blink just as Devon appears next to me, and although I'm not looking at him, I feel his eyes darting from me to Jack.

Jack shakes off the girls and moves toward us, his focus squarely on me, a scowl burrowing into his forehead as he leans down, keeping his voice low. "What are you doing here? Why haven't you called me?"

Oh. Okay, maybe the cell number was real. I was too mad to try and also worried some weirdo might pick up, and then I'd have to ask, *Are you Jack Hawke, famous football player I had sex with who kept my panties?* I would have gotten around to calling the number eventually because my curiosity would have driven me nuts, but today I just needed . . . a day to process.

I feign composure, tilting my chin up. I ignore his last question. "I happen to love this club. I party here all the time."

He studies me. "No, you don't. Did you know I'd be here tonight?"

I scoff, frowning. What is wrong with him? "No."

"Are you a reporter?" he snaps.

I gape. *Jesus.* He may be the most beautiful man I've ever seen, but please.

"I'm a librarian," I hiss. "I shelve books for a living, for God's sake. I don't have time to stalk you. I just want my undies! I spent hours sketching that design. It took weeks. Do you have any clue how hard it is to make those so that when you touch them, the image changes? They're priceless panties!"

I'm close to a come-apart in public, and I don't do those—I don't. Mama taught me to hold it all in. *Smile. Say please and thank you. Don't cause drama. Don't be the object of gossip. If you're angry, say "Bless your heart," and move on.*

But *bless your heart* just won't cut it here.

"Stop saying *panties*," he hisses back, tossing a look around the room. He takes my arm and tugs me over to the side. His hands are gentle but a brand on my skin, a current that runs from him to me.

He lets me go, his gaze lingering where he touched me, as if he was just as aware of that electricity as I was. "How did you get in the VIP room?"

Devon, who's been following us, approaches. There's an odd look on his face. Maybe it's surprise. "Dude. She's with me."

Jack rears his head back, as if he's been slapped, and I guess he didn't notice Devon following us. He puts laser-sharp eyes on him. "Is that right? And where did you meet her? Because seeing her again, here, is weird. I think she's scouting hot spots to pick up NFL players. Everyone knows you own this club and I own Milano's—"

I push my finger into his broad chest. "How dare you? I didn't even know who you were. Trust me; if I'd known you weren't the *weatherman* I was supposed to meet, we never would have . . ." I inhale. I can't even finish that sentence.

Devon looks at me, then back at Jack. "Wait. You and her?"

Jack lets out a deep breath and gives Devon a sharp nod.

Devon's mouth opens. "She's the one you told me about?"

Anger stirs hotter, my face flaming. "You've talked about me to your teammates?" I cross my arms. "You two are the worst. Just full-of-yourselves athletes going around and picking up women willy-nilly—"

"You picked *me* up," Jack mutters, easing in closer until we're almost chest to chest. "You sat down with me, and now that I think about it, how do I know if that whole 'Oh, you have a blue shirt on, so you must be my date' was legit? You didn't even sign your real name on the NDA."

What? His words give me pause, and I frown, trying to process. He did say how private he was, and I get that, but to be this paranoid . . .

Devon rubs his chin as he takes us in. "I just met her at the bar, and I picked her up—"

I snap my fingers at Devon. "You did *not* pick me up. I only came to find Jack."

"Ouch," Devon replies with a smirk.

"And you just happened to be here tonight?" Jack asks.

"Yes," I say.

"I see."

Some of that tightness leaves his face, and we stare at each other, both of us breathing harder than is necessary. He's just so . . . full of himself!

"I am not."

I must have said it aloud.

I shake my head. "I don't watch TV. I don't know football. Even if I did, I'd avoid you both like the plague. I like my dates to be sweet. Also not liars."

Jack winces. "Elena . . ." But he doesn't finish it, and Devon takes over.

"I'm sweet," Devon says with a pout.

But I'm barely listening.

I study the planes of Jack's face, trying to understand him. He's not . . . he's not the same man from last night. That person was into me, his kisses deep, like red wine, dark and rich and intoxicating—

Forget that.

"I just came back here to get my *underwear*."

Jack scrubs his face, his tone softening. "Elena, please, this isn't the place. People listen to every conversation I have. Can we just talk somewhere more private?"

Like his penthouse? Ha.

I shake my head. I get that he's famous. He was on a billboard in New York, but . . .

"Was nothing real with you?" I ask.

Devon looks away from us, fidgeting, and I guess I'm saying too much, and it draws me up. Ugh. This isn't me. I don't walk into VIP rooms and approach superstar athletes. I lick my wounds and move on.

My anger deflates, and a long exhalation leaves me. Fine, fine.

I've had my say. I should go. I eye the exit.

"Elena, wait . . ." He shoves a hand through his hair, the golden highlights glinting. "Look, it's just . . . this is such a coincidence, and a VIP party is the last place I'd thought you'd appear." He pauses. "This isn't how I wanted to see you again."

Yeah, because he had three girls with him.

"Hey. I don't think we've met," comes a male voice who's joined our little circle. "Aiden Woods, quarterback. Saw you walk in. Love the pants."

Damn these pants. I take my eyes off Jack to see the guy who has slid up next to us. He's young, a classic boy-next-door type, his chin square, dimples in his cheeks. He takes my hand and shakes it.

"Alabama, chill. She's with Jack and me," Devon says in exasperation.

Aiden—or Alabama—gives me a wide smile. "You open for a foursome too?"

"She doesn't do that," Jack growls. "She's not a jersey chaser."

I don't even know what a jersey chaser is.

"Huh. I haven't seen you around. You got a name?" Alabama asks me, ignoring them. He hits me with light-blue eyes and an award-winning smile.

Jack bumps his shoulder with his. "No, she doesn't have a name for you. She's with me. She's a lady."

Well.

Well.

First *I* picked him up, and now I'm a lady? Does he have emotional whiplash?

Jack's got his focus on Alabama, who seems cool as a cucumber, even after the shoulder bump. I sense backstory.

"I like ladies," Alabama murmurs, giving me a cocky grin. "I take it you're friends with Jack. How did you two meet?"

I lick my lips, choosing my words carefully. I may be angry with Jack, but I don't want to cause any problems for him. "We just met," I tell him.

"Really?" he replies. "Because he's barely taken his eyes off you since you walked up. Did you call him 'weatherman'? Is that a cute nickname you two have?"

Alabama is pushy—but charming with that southern accent.

"No," I reply. Short. Succinct.

Jack's nose flares as he watches us. He leans down and whispers something in Devon's ear, too low for me to hear. Devon watches my face, listening to Jack and nodding.

"I bet they're plotting to get you away from me," Alabama murmurs as he leans his head down to me. "Jack's a bit territorial. You sure you guys aren't dating?"

"Nope." We just had sex.

"Which means you're available?"

Good Lord. I stare at him. "Do all football players just assume every woman in the place wants them?"

He lifts his hands. "Yeah."

Jack and Devon finish their conversation, and Devon sends me a big smile. "Um, you ready to get out of here?"

Jack's eyes cling to mine, searching before looking away. "I'm sure she is," he says tightly.

He's getting rid of me.

"So ready," I mutter.

Alabama gives me a disappointed look, but I don't think it's so much about him finding me attractive but more along the lines of who I am to Jack. "Hey, it was nice to meet you. Maybe I'll see you again."

I nod.

Devon hooks my hand through his bent arm, and we leave the VIP room. He is oddly quiet, his brow pulled down as we go back to the bar.

I plop down on the barstool and send a glance up at the huge glass window where the VIP room is.

Is he watching us right now?

Or is he already squished between three models?

Who cares?

Devon lets out a long sigh, his gaze following mine. "Trust me; he's watching now that he knows you're here. Jack never misses anything."

I signal for another water, taking a long sip on the straw. Topher and company are still dancing, the song "Greased Lightning," and I'm betting Topher talked the DJ into it. Topher sees Devon next to me, his grinning face telling me he knows who Devon is. I grimace and hold my hands up. *What are the odds?* my face says. He blows me a kiss.

"Your bestie?" Devon asks.

I nod.

"Jack's my best friend, has been since college days; plus we live together. We're brothers in a sense, I guess. I'd do anything for him."

"Escorting women out of the VIP?"

He grimaces. "It wasn't like that. He was protecting you. If reporters knew he was seeing you, trust me, they might not leave you alone."

"Were reporters in there?"

"No, but people in there might talk. He doesn't trust easy, especially Aiden."

I order another water and sigh, feeling let down about Jack—about how *different* he was tonight.

He settles in next to me, concentration on his face, as if he's choosing his words carefully. "Also, he did *not* give me details about last night. He just wanted to know *who* you really were. In fact, I've never seen him—"

"I'm no one." I shrug.

Devon nods. "Tell me—did Jack leave you his cell number?"

"Yes." I guess he did.

"He never does that. I bet five people have that number." He waggles his brows.

"Well, I'm not calling him."

"Uh-huh."

"I won't."

"Sure, sure."

"I'll thump you again."

He grins and checks his watch.

"You late for somewhere?"

"No. Just waiting."

"For Jack?"

He gives me a hesitant nod. "Yeah, he wants to talk to you. He told me to get you out of there. He doesn't like Aiden talking to you. Thin ice there."

"Oh."

He nods. "Think about it. Football players at the top get there because number one, we're talented as hell; number two, we're highly competitive; and number three, we all want that glory and the money. It's a team sport, but you're always looking out for yourself. Alabama wants to bring Jack down hard and take his spot." He clinks his beer with my water glass and leans down. "Dance with me. I love this song."

"Really? Who sings it?" It's Sam Smith's "I'm Not the Only One."

He rolls his eyes and takes my hand. "Who cares? Let's just dance."

He tugs on my hand until I agree—he's like a sweet puppy—and leads me out to the dance floor.

Devon takes me in his arms, his hands on my waist, mine on his shoulders, and we sway to the slow song. He keeps a respectable distance and stares down at me, a look of bemusement on his face.

"What?" I ask.

He just smiles, his teeth a flash of white on his tanned face, and like Jack, I guess he's outdoors a lot. "I see why he likes you. You're really an open book, you know. Your face says exactly what you're thinking. No guile. No subterfuge. When you were, um, asking for your panties, it was refreshing . . . to see him flummoxed. Women flock to him, and all they say is 'Yes, Jack, whatever you want, Jack.'" He chuckles. "After you've been around as many women as we have, you figure out the real ones."

His large hands drift to my lower back, close to my ass. I give him side-eye. "Watch it there, Mohawk."

He laughs. "Also, I give him sixty seconds before he's down here."

I blow at a piece of my hair. "You're convinced that he cares that I'm dancing with you? Please. Let's make a bet. A buck he doesn't show."

"Damn, I like you. Okay, you're on."

I count to sixty in my head, and the song changes to another slow one. "He isn't here. Not that I wanted him to be. You owe me."

Devon thinks, his gaze going back to that window. "Right. Okay, let's play it a little meaner. Double or nothing?"

I nod. Why not? For one thing, I do want to see Jack—because hello, panties. I need them back.

Devon arches a brow. "I'm going to play dirty; you feel me?"

Play dirty?

And before I can respond to that, Devon stops our dance, putting my back to the window. Wrapping an arm tight around my waist, he steps in closer. His hand moves my hair, and he kisses my cheek, much like Topher would, yet his lips skate over to my ear. He nips my lobe, and I giggle because it tickles but mostly because the entire time he's murmuring, counting the seconds. To anyone else, I imagine it appears as if we're in an embrace and he's sucking my neck area. "One, two, three, four, five, six, seven, eight, nine, ten—"

"Devon!" Jack says from next to us, a good two inches taller than Devon. He scowls as he puts his hand on Devon's shoulder. "What the hell? I said keep her company, not make out." His voice is all growly.

Devon lets me go, holding his hands up in a placating manner. "Sorry, man. You said to get her out of there, and a good song came on. Couldn't stop myself." He winks at me, sticks his hands in his jeans, and waltzes off the floor. I hear him whistling.

"You can pay me later, Elena," he calls from the edge of the dance floor as he gives me a jaunty wave. He strolls up to the brunette at the bar and leans his head in. No doubt calling her *pretty girl.*

Jack looks back at me, his gaze indecipherable as it drifts over me. "Pay you for what?" He shakes his head. "Never mind. Come with me. Let's find a private room."

He holds out his hand for me to take, and I stare at it. His tone screams alpha, and every atom inside me vibrates from being near him.

Couples move around us, the beat of the song playing getting faster, matching the pounding of my heart.

"Elena. Come with me. *Please*," he adds softly when the tempo of the music grows. "We can't talk out here. It's too loud."

At least I got a *please.*

"No." I brush past him and head for the exit of the club. En route, I pull my phone out of my crossbody and type out a text to Topher that I'm heading home. No one expected me to stay as long as they'd planned, so I drove myself. They'll close this bar and hit a few others.

"Elena, wait," Jack calls behind me as I weave through the crowd and reach the exit. I feel him behind me, the heat of his skin, the smell of him, spicy with hints of pine and male.

I don't turn around, but I do see a few girls whipping out their phones ahead of me, snapping pics and probably videoing. I dip my head and stare at the ground. If he's as hot with the media as everyone says, I don't want to be part of that, especially when it's obvious I don't fit in with his crowd. I recall those "Yes, whatever you want, Jack" willowy creatures in the VIP room.

Yeah, Jack and I don't go together. That is crystal clear.

Chapter 12

Jack

Fuck.

Why can't I take my eyes off her heart-shaped ass in those pants as she weaves through the crowd to get away from me?

Away from me.

How long has it been since a woman didn't want anything to do with me? I can't remember. I guess middle school, when I was a skinny runt. It wasn't until I played football that women flocked to me.

She breezes past the crowd and exits, slamming the door behind her, but I'm right behind her. Relief settles over me as I take in the night. Finally, I'm out of that club. I rarely go there anymore, but with Devon's birthday, I knew it was important I do the mix-and-mingle thing. It's hard, pushing myself to be "on," especially with all this other shit going on.

She turns a corner, and I jog. I can't let her get away from me this time. But I knew I had to get her out of that VIP room, because rumors can start from the smallest thing.

There's a cold drizzle when I catch up with her on the sidewalk. She doesn't care, not even whipping out an umbrella as she stalks. She strikes me as the type who doesn't care that she's getting wet. I wish I had one for her as I try to keep pace with her, sticking my hands in my pockets.

What do I say?

Shit.

I don't even know how to talk to a girl these days.

"Where you going?" I start with.

"My car. Home. Away."

My lips twitch, and I see her throw me a glance.

"What's so funny? And why are you following me? I have pepper spray, you know."

I nod. "Good. You shouldn't be walking to your car alone. I'll make sure you get there."

She presses those full lips together. They're a hot pink tonight, and my eyes invariably go to the upper part, a deep V there, noticing how it gives her a just-kissed look.

"Stop staring at me. I'm a stalker, remember? I followed you to Milano's and the club."

I grab her hand, and she stops and looks down at it. I let her go, but at least she's not walking away from me anymore. "Elena. I'm sorry I said that."

"Then why did you say those things?"

"Because I'm stupid." I exhale. "You showed up in the VIP room, and you had that on." I wave my hand at her hot outfit. "It surprised me. It's a well-known fact that Devon owns that place, and women hang out there just to look for us. Plus, I had you in my head as someone else. All prim and proper . . ."

My eyes go low, taking in the way her shirt keeps slipping down her shoulder, revealing the black lace of her bra. Her height hits me around my upper chest, and I dig her small frame, all my protective instincts flaring up—especially when I saw her wrapped up with Devon on the dance floor. Sonofabitch. He was playing me. He isn't into her. Right?

What if he is?

I roll my neck.

She's pushed her glasses up to hold back her auburn hair, and her face is mostly devoid of makeup, skin like porcelain, her lashes dark and thick, fluttery fans as they blink up at me. I recall last night and that pencil skirt and demure Peter Pan collar.

"I like you all buttoned up," I admit grudgingly.

"Why?"

I shrug, feeling bemused. "I don't know. Maybe it's just you."

"Oh."

We stand there in the soft rain, staring at each other, and I clear my throat. "I'm sorry for lying to you. I wanted to tell you my real name half a dozen times. I didn't, because it felt good to know you wanted me for me and not because of who I am."

She looks away from me, watching a group of people laughing as they walk past us. They don't seem to look at us, but I'm jonesing to get off this street and away from everyone.

"Are you into Devon?" I blurt, surprising myself.

She levels ocean eyes at me. "If I were?"

"Then I'll back off." Motherfucker. I will not back off.

"Back off from what? We aren't a *thing*, Jack."

"Is that so? Even after last night?" I watch her closely, trusting body language way more than words.

Her chest rises, and a slow flush colors her cheeks. She swallows and chews on those lips, and my body responds, hardening.

"You're not into him, or you wouldn't have flushed." Gaining more confidence, I take a step closer to her. I reach out and touch a strand of hair, letting it trail through my fingers, recalling how I tugged hard on it the night before, increasing that pressure more and more, waiting for her to tell me to stop, but she didn't. She groaned and came, her pussy tightening and spasming around my cock. Need washes over me. Just to have her one more time.

"We aren't done, Elena. Come to the penthouse with me."

Her little hands clasp together, and she opens her mouth, but nothing comes out. Instead, she takes off walking again, and I blink, following after her. "What did I say?"

She's reached a green car and hits her clicker. "You really know how to woo a lady, Jack. I guess you think all you have to do is snap your fingers, and I'm going to join you in that penthouse for some frolicking."

Frolicking? I grin. "I'm not looking for a relationship, and you've just broken up with someone. Did I read you wrong?"

The rain kicks up, falling harder, drenching us both—yet neither of us seems to care.

"First of all, I don't do one-night stands or two-night ones. You don't know me at all."

"Okay, then let me get to know you." I nudge my head at a coffee shop down the road. "Let me buy you a coffee. Get to know me."

Shit.

Shit.

I hate public places where the owners don't know me.

But . . .

A cold wind blows, and I frown when she shivers. She wipes at the rain in her eyes.

"Here," I say and unbutton my shirt and whip it off and hold it over her head. It doesn't help much, but at least she's not getting any wetter.

"You should have worn a coat," I mutter, staring down at her. "It's forty degrees and raining."

She glances at my now-soaked white T-shirt, then meets my eyes again. "You a weatherman now?"

I grin. "Rain. It's wet."

She gives me a wan smile, and a long sigh leaves her chest—and I see a distant expression growing on her face. "Here's a tip for the next time you have sex with a girl: don't lie about who you are, and don't leave before she wakes up. Bad form."

That fucking nightmare that woke me up.

Part of me hesitates as I consider trying to explain it, but . . .

I don't know her. My gut senses she's genuine, but . . .

You can't really trust anyone, a voice tells me. Whatever I share with her might eventually be passed on, even if it's just to a friend, and then that friend decides to tell someone else. Pretty soon it will get leaked to the media, and they'll concoct a story out of it. After all, it wasn't just Sophia who betrayed me. Harvey's sister profited off the story of my life after I was drafted, an article in *Sports Illustrated* that detailed my early years with my mom. It reeked of lies, painting Harvey as misunderstood and blinded by love.

"You're right. I should have stayed. I should have pulled you in my arms and woken you up." I grimace. "I'm not good with stuff like that."

She studies me for several seconds.

"Elena, I don't know how to do this."

"This?"

I hesitate before answering. "Look, can we just start all over?"

Without waiting for a reply, I stick my hand out and take hers. "Hello. I'm Jack Eugene Hawke, quarterback. I collect cheesy coffee mugs and magnets from every city I've been to. I can do a push-up with you on my back—yeah, I thought about it today. I read a lot, mostly thrillers. I grew up in a small town in Ohio. My mom is dead. Don't know where my dad is. I love to sketch but am too embarrassed to show anyone. I won a national championship my senior year, the Heisman when I was a junior. I'm actually . . . shy. Dwight Schrute from *The Office* makes me laugh until I cry. And recently, I've discovered I have an insatiable penchant for hot librarians."

She looks down at the concrete, then back up at me, and for some crazy reason, I feel winded as her blue-green gaze holds mine, my breath held, waiting for her reply. I've never said a few of those things to a girl. *Never wanted to.*

"That wasn't bad. Thank you."

I'm still holding her hand, and my thumb brushes against her wrist. "Why do I hear a *but* there, Elena?"

A long sigh comes from her as she eases her hand out of mine.

Nerves fly all over me. "Elena . . ."

She's taking a step back from me, and shit, I don't want her to. It feels like she's just going to disappear at any minute . . .

"I need to get going. Nice to meet you, Jack. Take care."

She pivots and ducks her head out of the protection of my shirt and moves to her car.

"Elena!"

She turns and looks at me. "Yeah?"

I lick my lips, my shirt clenched in my hands, rain falling harder now, the drops hitting me on the face. "You're the first girl I've been with in a year."

I don't know how long we stand there; maybe it's only a few moments, but I'm cataloging everything she does, committing it to memory. The way her eyes flare, the rise and fall of her chest. Disbelief crosses her delicate face, her gaze searching mine.

Then she turns back around, opens her car door, and gets in.

I close my eyes, and a long sigh comes from me. *You suck so bad, Jack.*

She backs up and drives away, and I watch her taillights get smaller and smaller.

I look up at the dark sky, processing, planning.

I whip my cell out of my pocket and press Lawrence's number.

"Yo!" he answers. "Where did you go? I can't find you in here. Quinn can't either. This place is packed. Devon said you took off. We should talk—"

"Did you find out her last name?"

He pauses, and I can hear the music from the club bleeding in through the phone. "This girl is not your type, Jack."

"Who is she?" My hand grips the phone.

"You should be focusing on your career right now. Let's have a meeting with your agent this week. Maybe we can get that Adidas endorsement back—"

"It's dead. Aiden told me tonight he's already got a meeting with them. Let it go."

He lets out a string of curses. "Sonofabitch. That young buck is riding your coattails so hard—"

"Don't care about the money, Lawrence. Tell me about the girl."

He sighs. "Elena Michelle Riley from Daisy, age twenty-six, librarian. Father dead, mother alive. One sibling. Never been married or arrested or dated a professional athlete. Moved here from New York and moved in her grandmother's house." He pauses. "I'm never doing this shit for you again. I'm supposed to be fixing your image, not checking out your hookups."

I detect hesitation in his voice.

"Yeah? What else?" I want to know fucking everything about her.

"She lives with a man."

Jealousy spikes.

"His name?"

"Topher Wainscott. Your girl is taken. Let it go."

Topher . . . hmm.

"Address?"

He blows out a long breath. "Seriously, Jack? You can't show up at her house. She never signed that NDA."

"I'm not an idiot, Lawrence. Give it to me."

He rattles off an address, and I imprint it to my memory.

"Thanks. Later." I hang up on him while he's still lecturing me about not getting involved.

I'm walking to my Porsche, and just before I open the door, I pause, backpedaling in my head. Shit. I accused her of being a stalker, and here I am . . .

Fuck it.

I know how she looked at me tonight in the VIP room, even when we were "arguing." I know she came three times, and she never has with a man. I know she giggles when I kiss the inside of her knee; I know how she moans when I suck that spot on her neck—

Yeah. Oh, yeah.

There's something there, and whatever it is, it's something I want again.

Chapter 13

Elena

Around eleven, I pull up at my house and dash inside from the rain.

After pouring a small splash of Pappy from Nana's well-stocked cupboard, I pace around, thinking about Jack. I picture him in the rain telling me *who* he was, and I can see there's more to him than just a bad-boy football player, and it's a little dangerous and a whole lot of sexy.

A shaky breath comes from me.

Forget him.

Even if it was the first time for him in a year. Right?

But why has he waited so long?

Was it the pain of his breakup with his ex and then the book she wrote? Maybe.

And he's . . . shy?

I can't imagine it, because he knew exactly how to charm me at the penthouse.

Then again, for a man like him, maybe he wasn't referring to sex, per se, but to himself in general. Maybe sex is a whole new category for him, a way he lets himself go—

And now I'm horny.

Ugh.

Inevitably I end up in my sewing room with its high ceilings and heavy antique chandelier. This used to be Nana's room, where she'd make me and Giselle matching dresses. Her sewing machine still sits in the corner, an ancient black Singer made of heavy cast iron. My space is directly in front of the bay window, a drafting table where I sketch my designs, a professional serger, and two sewing machines. Mannequins and dress forms dot the room, each one covered with one of my lingerie. Silk, lace, sequins, thread, ribbons, and scraps of fabric are arranged in neat order on shelves that Topher helped me put together.

A piece of paper, an email I printed out on Friday, sits on my drafting table, and I pick it up and read it again.

> Dear Elena,
>
> Thank you for your interest in our company and the sample sketches.
>
> We currently have an intern position available in the design department. This position is for a year with the possibility for full-time employment with benefits. I realize this isn't quite what you had in mind, but we'd love to talk to you about applying. Please give me a call and we'll set up a meeting. I'd love to see your designs in person.
>
> Marcus Brown
>
> CEO of Little Rose Lingerie

Disappointment hits me as I take a sip of the whiskey, the burn smooth and gratifying. I emailed Marcus a few sketches a few weeks ago along with the link to my blog. I don't know what I expected . . . maybe that they'd embrace me and offer me a real position.

Things don't work that way, Elena.

I *don't* have any experience in fashion—just an eye. My degree is in English.

I rub the letter. This could be a big step, but spending most of my time running errands and getting lattes for the real staff isn't what I had in mind.

Then there's Mama. She'd have a heart attack if I quit my job, the one she called a few influential friends in Daisy to get for me. Plus, she'd be mortified if she knew I was drawn to lingerie. The gossip would kill her.

I toss the letter aside and plop down in the dark-green velvet Queen Anne chaise longue in the corner and glare up at the chandelier.

I laugh out loud at the ludicrousness of me quitting my job.

Nana would have told me to go for it. She always encouraged my ideas, pushing me to get out of Daisy and see the world. When Mama pouted because I wasn't moving back to Daisy after graduation from NYU, Nana threw a big party for me in this very house to celebrate my first job at a publishing house. Nana loved it when I took a trip to Europe alone. She always looked at me like she *got* the wild spirit inside me.

I push those memories away and set my glass down on the side table and pull out the scrawled note Jack left me in the penthouse, tracing my finger over the sloping stroke of his handwriting.

I left him there in the rain.

A little smile curves my lips. I walked away from the hottest man I've ever seen.

I wonder what he'll do about it.

Because if men like Jack want something, according to their highly competitive nature, they'll make it their goal to get it. That came straight from Devon.

We'll see . . .

◆ ◆ ◆

My phone wakes me up, and I curse.

Romeo, who's been snuggling with me, digs his face further into my arm, making an unhappy sound as I reach over and grab my cell off the nightstand.

"Wakey, wakey!"

I groan at her chipper tone. "Mama. It's eight in the morning."

"And it's Sunday. You promised me two weeks ago you'd come to church today!"

"Stop yelling," I say and straighten up in the bed. "Did I really tell you that?" I scrunch up my nose, vaguely recalling her badgering when I was getting my ends trimmed last week at the Cut 'N' Curl.

"Young lady, do you have a hangover? Drinking isn't good for the soul."

Then why did Nana leave me a cupboard of expensive whiskey?

"Jesus drank wine, Mama, but I just got in late. What's the big deal about church today?"

"Don't you worry about that, darlin'. But you did promise."

"Mama, I need to work around the house." I want to sketch and clean up some. It's been a busy weekend, and I've barely had time to think.

"God does not listen to excuses."

He also doesn't dance for hours, then face off with a quarterback either.

I sigh.

"Wear something pretty—one of your little blazers with a skirt."

My tone lowers. "Mama, what did you do?"

"Nothing at all. Aunt Clara and I will meet you outside at nine, and we'll walk in together."

"The Daisy Lady Gang?"

"I don't even know what that means. You and Clara made that name up. Wear your contacts. Wouldn't hurt if you put on some makeup . . ."

I smell fix-up. I should go full-on hooker to church.

"Also, you never told me how the weatherman worked out—"

"It didn't."

There's a small silence, and I can picture her in her stately brick house on the other side of town, just a few blocks away. Those wheels in her head are turning, wondering why I'm not offering more info. She's probably tapping her heels, drinking her coffee, already dressed and ready for church. Heck, she's probably cleaned her whole house already since waking up.

"Well, I never liked him. He always says we're gonna get snow, and we never do. You can do better."

"Right."

"Did you hear that the high school got a new basketball coach this semester? Brett Sinclair. Nice boy. You went to school with him. He married some city girl from Los Angeles—a singer—and you know how wild they are. No one is surprised. No kids either. If the preacher doesn't work out—"

I fumble out of bed, kicking the covers off me as I stand up. "Preacher! Mama, no. Hell no."

"Elena Michelle, I am still your mother. And you promised you'd come. It's his first Sunday, and you know all I'm doing is trying to fill the pews and make him feel welcome. It's what I do. I support the church."

She *is* involved. Runs a Wednesday-evening ladies' Bible class. Takes food daily to the elderly or sick who can't get out. Checks in with the women's shelter in town.

But that's not all she's doing.

Dammit.

"What did you say?" she asks.

I must have cursed aloud. "Nothing. Just stubbed my toe."

She exhales. "Look, I know Topher already told you about Preston and Giselle. They won't be there. They went to Mississippi to tell Preston's family. I'm sorry, love. You'll find someone—"

"Jeez, I don't need a man to be happy!"

"Uh-huh. I'll see you at nine. Get dressed. Bye."

"Mama—"

And she hangs up on me.

Shit.

One hour.

I look down at Romeo, and he kinda grins back at me. "Traitor," I murmur and scratch his nose. He loves Mama.

My leather pants on the floor catch my eyes, and I snort. I didn't have to cut them off, but I came close last night after spending an hour googling Jack Hawke, then downloading that horrible book about him. I only got through the first chapter before I tossed it across the room. According to Sophia Blaine, she met him at a postgame party and immediately fell head over heels in love—only she didn't realize he was a drunk and abusive. I'm sure those specific details are outlined in the coming chapters, but I don't think I have the heart to read them. I hate that my place of former employment actually published her book.

I pick the pants up and look over at Romeo. "Mama's lucky these are absolutely shitty, or I'd put them right back on."

Romeo sticks his head under the covers.

Exactly.

I walk down the sidewalk toward the arched wooden double doors of the First Cumberland Church, a nondenominational congregation that sits right next to the library on West Street. It's the biggest church in Daisy, boasting over 300 members—350 on Easter and Christmas. It's an old structure, built from bricks that used to be red but were recently painted a startling white. Lots of opinions about that at the beauty shop.

Taking a deep breath, I straighten my outfit, a white shirt with tiny pink butterfly buttons I sewed on myself. On my hips is a vintage black velvet pencil skirt, something I found in the attic. Nana's. Lucky for me, she and I share the same curves. Still, the skirt is snug. Might need to go easy on the carbs for a while.

Serves Mama right that I left the blazer behind. She better watch out. I'm feeling rebellious.

"She's lucky I even came," I mutter to no one.

Mama is getting out of her Lincoln and calls my name, waving me over. Tall and thin, she's stately with her coiffed blonde hair, elegant blue suit-dress, and midheel black pumps. Classy. She and Giselle are replicas—beautiful, cool, and reserved.

Her sharp blue eyes run over my outfit, lips tightening at my shoes. She sighs. "Pink shoes? Really? That's not like you."

But they are; she just doesn't see it.

Good thing Topher and I are both a size eight. He was snoring loudly when I tiptoed in his closet and picked out the brightest, sluttiest pair I could find.

"Cynthia, leave the poor girl alone."

I smile when Aunt Clara bounds up next to me, wearing a bohemian-style dress with purple flowers and lace. I grin. She looks a little mussed, her little feathered matching hat not quite on straight. She and Mama are ten years apart in age and are as opposite as night and day. Most days, Aunt Clara feels like my older sister.

"I love your shoes. You should wear them every day. I bet Mr. Rhodes is going to flip," Aunt Clara says, crooking her arm through mine. "He's going to be up there preaching, get a peek at those, and lose his place in the scripture. *Saint Peter, save me from this woman!*" She does a Hail Mary.

Mama slaps her on the arm. "Stop that. We aren't even Catholic."

"Mr. Rhodes is the preacher, I assume," I say as we walk.

"Yes!" Aunt Clara says. "You've missed all the good gossip at the Cut 'N' Curl this week. Goodness, did you hear about that Tigers football player and little Timmy Caine—"

"Never mind that," Mama says as she slides in on the other side of me and pats my hand. "Let's make a game plan for the preacher."

Aunt Clara does a fist pump in the air. "The Daisy Lady Gang strikes again. We own this town. Nobody compares to our casseroles—or your mama's matchmaking."

"The plan is . . . there is no plan," I say curtly.

Mama continues, as if I didn't speak. "His wife died three years ago, bless her heart, and you know he's lonely."

I picture an old man with gray hair and a Bible.

Lord.

Help me.

I let out a sigh. "You both need to be committed to the nuthouse. If I'd known this was your plan, I never would have promised."

Mama shrugs. "I just think you need to start dating; that way it will be easier when Preston and Giselle, you know . . ." She sends me a careful look.

"When they get married," I say flatly.

Aunt Clara makes a gagging motion.

Mama scowls at her. "Stop it, Clara. This is serious. Elena is the oldest, and she should be the one getting married. She's going to be an old maid—"

I send a beseeching look up at the sky. *Lord, I'm serious. I know I haven't been the best girl, especially this weekend, but please help me deal with my pushy mother.*

"Stop wavering, and come on, Elena," Mama says, tugging on my arm.

I glare at her. She's done worse. My senior year in high school, when my boyfriend suddenly dumped me a week before the prom, she called a girlfriend in Nashville and convinced her to send her college son down to take me. He did. He showed up in a limo with a rented tux to match my dress, plus a beautiful corsage. We went to prom and barely spoke to each other. My friends were so infatuated with him they spent most of the time talking to him and not me.

Mama is a well-oiled machine with secret ways. Scary.

"Mama. This is the twenty-first century. I don't ever have to get married. I can live with Topher until the day I die," I say, lowering my voice as several parishioners walk past us, murmuring "Good morning" as they take us in.

Mama eyeballs them, too, her spine straightening. "Let's not discuss Topher."

I know she has an issue with him, although it's not that he's gay—which is surprising. But he is a *man*, and he does live with me, and that causes talk in town. When she first questioned me about Topher living with me, I got ruffled and put my foot down hard. Nana left me that house, and it is *mine*. I may let her push me around some, but when it comes to the people I love . . . nope.

The steeple bell rings, and I drag my feet, debating running back to my car.

Mama knows. "Look, you're already here; just shake his hand at the door, and that's all I ask. You *do* work at the library—right next door. You're going to meet him eventually. Plus, you never know when you'll need a preacher. They can be handy. He's quite forward thinking, too, painting the church white and asking for new hymnals. He's like you. Modern."

He is nothing like me.

Aunt Clara gives me a grin. "What she's not telling you is she invited him to Sunday lunch. She's made a chicken casserole and homemade yeast rolls. Heard there might be okra and cheddar mashed potatoes."

"Ohh, big guns," I say.

"And we're using the good china." Mama beams.

"Monogrammed napkins?" I ask.

She nods.

"And I bet you got fresh flowers for the table," I add.

She grins.

I curse under my breath.

Aunt Clara holds her hands up. "FYI, I got nothing to do with the preacher. It's that weatherman I want to hear about. I heard he's quite a *player*." She giggles, and I narrow my eyes. Topher. Those two are thick as thieves.

"Topher told you?" I hiss at her. When did he have time? I bet he texted her. Ugh.

She just grins.

We open the door and walk inside. Mama immediately bypasses several members at the entrance who call out her name, giving them her practiced smile as she drags me toward a man near the front of the auditorium.

Mama nudges me in front of her like a prize goat.

"Patrick, dear, this is my daughter Elena." She's got her hand on his arm like a vise as he turns around.

I arch my brow at her. Oh, a first-name basis. I'm not surprised.

Okay. Well. Patrick Rhodes is a nice-looking man, scholarly almost, with thick sandy-colored hair and intelligent eyes behind black-rimmed modern-style frames. He's not too handsome—like *someone*

I know—and even resembles my ex from college. Mama. I sigh. She knows my type.

"Hi." His voice is nice and deep, and he's tall with a lean build that fills out his blue suit very well. He's younger than I expected, maybe midthirties.

What happened to his wife? I'm sure Mama knows.

Her hand is tight on my arm, as if I might bolt for the door at any moment. She's holding us *both* hostage. Maniacal woman.

"Elena is the town librarian. She does the most adorable story hour on Tuesdays and Thursdays with the preschoolers. She loves kids so much. It's why she became a librarian."

I groan inwardly. Lie! She's making me out to be some ready-to-settle-down-and-have-kids woman. I want to someday when I meet the right person. I love my job because there are books, but story hour with the three- and four-year-olds is like herding angry cats. Topher does a better job than I do.

She's still talking. "You should stop by sometime. They have a new biography section." Mama flashes a smile at him. "You did mention you love biographies."

"I did indeed." His voice is a tad dry, and he raises an eyebrow at Mama.

I bite back a grin. He's no dummy, and I bet he's seen plenty of matchmaking mamas since his wife passed. He knows dang well he's being maneuvered into a wedding about a year from now.

Aunt Clara whispers in my ear as Mama keeps talking to Patrick. "I'd do him. I may have to start coming more regular."

"Yeah, what would Scotty say about that?" I whisper back. "I'm betting he walked to your house last night and left before dawn. Hussy. When are you going to make a decent man of him?"

She gives me a little pinch on my arm—subtly, so no one notices—and I cough to cover up my laugh.

I dart a look at her face, and she's glowing. Probably thinking about Scotty putting his mail in her slot . . .

She blushes at my scrutiny. "I like it on the down low—isn't that what you kids call it? More exciting."

She elbows me, and I see that Mama is glaring at us, and I figure we've missed something.

Oh yeah. The preacher.

Mr. Rhodes meets my eyes; then his gaze drifts down and lands squarely on my shoes. Four-inch heels and delicate. I pranced around in them for several minutes trying to get the feel of them.

His gaze comes back to my face, a slow grin there. "Nice to meet you."

I nod as he takes my hand and shakes it. "Welcome to Daisy, Mr. Rhodes. I'm glad you're here." And I am. The former preacher was seventy and had needed to retire years before.

"Call me Patrick, please. Cynthia talks about you constantly. She says you're doing the play again this year, *Romeo and Juliet*? I'm going to check it out myself."

Talks about me constantly to him? I wince.

She really *is* worried about me. Underneath all her blustering about how I need to settle down, she must sense I'm at a crossroads; something inside me is stirring to break out. She's probably terrified I may move back to New York.

"Of course. You should." I paste on a smile.

There's a tiny glint of interest there in his gaze.

Well, heck, if the shoes don't deter him . . .

Nope. Nope. Nope.

I could never be a preacher's girlfriend or wife.

I like whiskey and vibrators and sexy lingerie—

"Thank you, yes, glad to be here," says the deep, unmistakable voice behind me, and every muscle inside me stiffens in disbelief (and relief?) as I turn to see Jack. He's just come in the door and is chatting with the couple designated to be greeters. Mama totally dashed past them, but he hasn't.

A dark scruff shadows his jawline, as if he didn't have time to shave, and his hair is slightly damp, as if he's recently showered.

"What the heck?" I say.

Mama elbows me. "Who is that?"

"J-a-c-k."

Aunt Clara giggles. "And now she's spelling words. Somebody get the smelling salts."

What? No. I shake my head.

"Why, I believe that's the Tigers quarterback," Patrick murmurs. "Wow. You really did fill up the pews, Cynthia."

Mama just shrugs.

Jack slowly turns and looks at me.

He gives me a smile, a flash of white teeth on his tanned face, his eyes crinkling in the corners. He rakes a hand through his dark waves, his gaze sweeping over me before coming back to my face. He gets a hesitant look on his face, seeming to waver, but then takes the steps to reach us.

"Elena."

He says my name slowly, the tone warm with a hint of bemusement.

I feel a slow blush starting at my toes and growing all the way up to my face.

I can't even. My ability to *even* is severely warped.

What . . . is . . . he . . . doing . . . here?

Several seconds pass as we stare at each other, and in my head I'm seeing him last night in the rain . . .

Clara has popped out her lace fan, and she's swishing it around furiously.

Mama turns beady eyes on me. Waiting for an introduction. I refuse.

My mouth opens and closes more than once, and Jack sees it all.

How flustered I am.

He can probably see my nipples tightening inside my bra.

He's wearing low-slung jeans, tight and fitted through the legs, leather loafers, and another button-down, this time a navy-and-yellow windowpane design. Those sleeves are rolled up to his elbows, the hair on his muscled forearms sun kissed.

"I'm going to get my seat," Mama says to no one in particular, but she doesn't move a hair.

"We should. We don't want those Palmers getting the back row. Don't they know that once you claim a row, it's yours forever?" comes from Aunt Clara.

No one budges.

"I hate it when they do that," Mama murmurs. "I've been here longer than they have. That is my seat. We should make a rule about that."

Aunt Clara nods. "And your husband, God rest his soul, was the mayor of this town for fifteen years. You're a pillar of the community. Practically royalty."

Patrick clears his throat. "Uh, the front row is typically always clear. At least that's how it was at my last congregation."

"No one likes the front row. Put some whiskey up there, and they might come," Aunt Clara says in my ear, but I'm barely noticing, looking at Jack.

He's still standing there, eyes on me. He hasn't stopped looking!

"Let's go save our row, Cynthia," Aunt Clara finally says loudly and shoos Mama into the auditorium.

They scurry away, tossing looks back at us.

Now it's just me, the preacher, and the football player.

Definitely the beginning of a bad joke.

Jack breaks our gaze to shake Patrick's hand.

"Jack Hawke. Glad to meet you. Nice place."

They share a much firmer handshake than he and I had.

"Welcome," Patrick says with a big smile. "I'm a huge fan, actually. Used to play in high school. Wide receiver. What brings you to Daisy? You know Elena?" Patrick arches an eyebrow.

"I do. And a couple of others here in Daisy—" Jack says, then stops when the choir starts in with "Amazing Grace."

"Oh, sorry, that's my cue. Have to go." Patrick nudges his head toward the auditorium. "First day and all. Great to meet you." He gives me a smile. "You too, Elena. I'll see you at auditions hopefully?"

"Sure."

And then he walks away, his rather nice frame disappearing through the doors that lead to where the choir sings. There'll be a chair up front for him to sit in while the song leader leads the choir.

I frown, turning back to Jack, finding my voice. "What on earth are you doing here?"

He winces, and what I think is a guilty expression crosses his face. "I swear, I didn't know you'd be *here*, but this day just got a whole lot more interesting."

I replay his words in my head. "So you just happened to come to Daisy today—for church?"

"Not exactly."

"Ms. Riley!" The voice comes from the door as Timmy Caine bounds into the foyer. I smile, glad of the distraction, when he rushes me and wraps his good arm around me, the other one in a cast. The white plaster has names written in bright colors. I see Jack's and a drawing of a Tiger that looks a whole lot like Jack's tattoo on his back . . .

With thick wraparound glasses, a tiny frame, and clothes that I think have been worn by someone before him, Timmy is small for his age and one of my favorite students who pop in the library. He's had a rough time, his dad passing away last year in a drunk-driving accident. He was coming home from the Piggly Wiggly when a car ran a red light and plowed into his driver's side. He died at the scene. Mama was terribly upset, taking food and visiting with Laura for several days.

This little town is gossipy, but when one of our own needs us, people stick together.

Jack ruffles Timmy's hair. "Hey, little man. I beat you here. Told you I would. My car is fast."

"Thank you for meeting us for breakfast! And for the new bike," Timmy says. "Those banana pancakes at the diner were so good. Mama says we'll have to do it again."

He took the Caine family to breakfast?

Jack smiles. "Next time, we'll try the waffles. Sound good?"

"Yeah!" Timmy dashes away and peeks into the sanctuary. "The place is packed. We'll have to sit on the front row. Mama, remember that time Mrs. Claymont was singing in the choir, and her teeth came flying out?"

I laugh, recalling that story from Mama, then suck in a breath, connecting the dots from the googling I did on Jack Hawke last night. I watched snippets of his press conference online, getting the highlights, but the kid he ran over was never named since he was a minor. I eye the cast on Timmy's arm and look back at Jack.

Jack has been watching me, and when I look up at him, he reddens. "Elena, I know what you're thinking. I didn't mean to hurt him."

"You don't know what I'm thinking," I say softly as Timmy darts around the foyer, grabbing crayons and a program for the service. He keeps looking over at Jack and grinning.

Laura has reached us and stands next to Jack. "You did *not* have to come to church with us. Breakfast was plenty." She gazes up at him and smiles, and dang, I forgot how pretty she is with her bobbed golden-brown hair and peaches-and-cream complexion. She's a few years older than me but was one of those popular pretty girls in high school.

My hackles rise until I stomp them right back down.

I have no right to be jealous of Laura.

Timmy tugs at her hand. "Come on. I don't want to miss when they introduce the preacher. I heard he's tall. I want to be tall." He grins at Jack. "Are you staying?"

Jack looks at me, his face unsure. "Ah, I'm not sure." He glances down at his jeans. "I'm not really dressed for church."

Then why did he walk in here?

Timmy glances from me to Jack. "Do you know each other?"

"Yes," Jack says.

"No," I say at the same time.

Timmy frowns. "Adults are weird."

"We are," Jack agrees, then turns his attention to Laura, who has her hand on his shoulder.

She gives Jack a hug, and I . . . I . . . frown.

She smiles at us and opens the door to the sanctuary. "Seriously, Jack. Don't feel like you have to stay. We'll see you later."

Later?

They wave goodbye and disappear through the door, and Jack turns back to me. There's a long silence in the foyer as we eye each other.

Why *did* he walk in the church?

Is he interested in Laura? She's not one of his jersey chasers, but she's absolutely pretty. And they've obviously spent some time together.

The foyer is empty, and he's just watching me, hands in his pockets, and I can't seem to find my words.

He gives me a grin, looking much more relaxed than last night. "You should have seen your face when you saw me. Priceless. I should have taken a pic. I mean, your mouth was open. Flies could have gotten in." He pauses. "Are you mad I'm here?"

I give myself a mental shake. Am I? I don't know. "It's church. Everyone is welcome."

He smirks, a rather boyish expression on his face. "It feels as if we can't stop running into each other. Is that fate?"

"It's something."

"Hmm. I have your panties, Elena." He pulls a piece of the fabric out from his front pocket, just a few inches, but the sequins are *right there*.

My mouth gapes as I dart my eyes around the foyer. Still empty.

"Because you knew I'd be here?" How is that possible?

"No, I didn't know you'd be here, but I hoped to see you today."

Oh.

His finger rubs at the fabric, never taking his gaze off me. "Do you want them?"

I lick my lips, my finger twitching with the urge to snatch them away from him.

"Come get them."

I shiver at the authority in his tone, at the tug I feel when he talks, that husky, dark voice . . .

I curl my hands into little fists.

How dare he bring those panties to church? With Mama right here.

I'm *really* going to kill the football player this time.

Chapter 14

Jack

"Where are you going?" I call after her as she pivots and sashays down a hallway and to the left, straight for a room with a closed door. I tag along, feeling unsure and nervous as a kid about to ask a girl out on a date for the first time.

Without answering, she opens the door and indicates for me to follow. I try to get a read on her face as I stalk past her. Her little hands are clenched, and there's a vulnerable bent to her shoulders that I don't like, and I hope I'm not the reason for it. I don't want to be. I want to be . . . shit, I don't know, except that I haven't been able to get her out of my head. Does she have any idea how much *trust* it even took for me to have a conversation with her last night outside the club?

The room is slightly darkened, the only light coming in from a small window that overlooks the manicured back lawn of the church.

There's a huge window that overlooks the sanctuary, and I check it out. I find the women she came in with on the back row—one blonde, the other with auburn hair like Elena's.

The window is one way, judging by the glass, much like the VIP room. A speaker is in the top corner of the room, and I hear the soft drone of the choir as they sing.

"They can't see us?" I ask. "Church has its own VIP room. Cool." I sound like an idiot.

"Yes. It's for nursing mothers." She's turned to face me, her chest rising.

Oh. Okay. I never went to church growing up, and I haven't stepped in one since one of the players got married a few years ago. I didn't grow up with religion, not from my mom and not in foster care with Lucy.

"Ah. Nice."

We stare at each other.

Why can't I think of anything else to say?

Because you've never had to work for it, asshole.

She leans against the door, as if needing a quick escape. "Want to explain why you're here?" Her tone trembles around the edges, and it only ramps me up, knowing I can affect her.

"I happened to have breakfast with Timmy and Laura this morning. We planned it yesterday after the press conference. They also invited me to church, and I followed them here, not really sure if I'd come in or not. What are the odds you'd be at the same church?"

"There are only two in town, so fifty-fifty."

"I saw your car in the parking lot. I don't know what I expected. If I hadn't seen you in the foyer, I might have sat down and tried to catch you after it was over."

"I see." She chews on those lips.

"You drove away from me last night, Elena. After I told you some stuff I don't tell anyone." I ease in closer to her, hot awareness zipping down my spine. And I know exactly what that prickle means. I want *her*. Bad.

She clasps her hands in front of her. "Jack, look, you seem like a nice guy—"

"I'm not."

She frowns. "You are."

I start. No one ever says that. "Then you need to read some of those articles about me."

"I did. Forget that. Those opinions don't matter. I saw how you looked at Timmy and see how the press is portraying it. I don't believe everything I read, Jack. Also, Quinn thinks you hung the moon. Plus, you apologized very well last night."

"I was sure I screwed it up, because you left."

She bites her lip. "You did take your shirt off for me in the rain."

Why is she standing so far away from me? I take another step closer, eyeing her curves in that skirt.

She holds a hand up. "And we had a . . . nice . . . Valentine's Day." Her lashes flutter for a moment. "And I forgive you for lying and leaving. But it can't happen again."

And by *it*, she means sex.

She sounds as if she's reciting a speech, her spine straight, eyes stern enough to give me doubts about what the hell I'm doing. I waver for half a second before roaring back. I saw how she looked at me when I walked in. Like I was a lollipop she wanted to suck.

"I've seen you naked, Elena. It very much did happen. And quite spectacularly." I stare at her face, taking in the soft curve of her cheek, the way she fidgets from one foot to the next.

A small laugh comes from me. "I don't think I've chased after a girl this hard since high school. I did bring you back your . . . item. Doesn't that make you happy?" I enjoy the blush that colors her face as I pull that scrap of fabric completely out and dangle it in front of her.

She takes a step closer. "So were you just going to show up at my house and hand them over? Because that's fascinating. You obviously know where I live."

I hesitate. "Yes."

"How?"

"I had someone look into it. You have to come closer if you want these *panties*."

"Fine." She's now two inches from me; I can feel the heat of her skin, the shirt she's wearing close to brushing up against my chest. I inhale her scent, fresh with a bit of—

"Did you drink whiskey before you came?" My words are incredulous. "Do you have no respect at all?" I chuckle.

She tilts her head up and gives me a glare. "It was a leftover sip from last night! If you had to live in this town and deal with my family—who, by the way, are doing their best to set me up with Patrick—"

Jealousy crawls all over me. "The preacher? No way. He's not for you. You're too wild."

"No, I'm not!"

I grin. "Want me to tell you the ways you're wild?"

She ignores me and makes a grab for the panties, and I jerk them behind my back. She reaches behind me, grappling for them, her tits against my body, firm and hard and so freaking perfect.

"Give me those," she hisses.

"Take them."

"You're too big!" She makes another move for them and comes close to getting them. I dance off from her, and she follows me, teetering a little in her heels, making little grabs, but I switch hands and put them farther from her reach.

"Jack Hawke, give me my panties." She looks up at me, little puffs of air coming from her chest.

"Give me a kiss first."

Her arms fall at her sides, pretty eyes wide. "Why?"

"Because I can't stop thinking about your lips."

"You want them around your cock?"

I groan when that dirty word leaves her lips, then laugh at the surprised look on her face, as if she never expected herself to say that. "Maybe. We didn't do that. But I'd also like a long, breathy, make-out kiss, the kind you give me when you haven't had several gin and tonics."

"Oh." She looks confused, and I suck in a sharp breath at what I've said.

Make-out kiss?

Too soon, too fast.

My mouth still won't stop.

"I want you, Elena," I say softly.

She sways a little, as if she's dancing, and I move in closer until I can see the white flecks in those big eyes, the way her lashes are thick and curled, the way her skin is so perfect, creamy and—

She yanks the panties from my hands. "Aha! Mine, thank you very much." She laughs up at me, red lips curving up, and my heart skips a beat.

"You tricked me." I wrap my hand around her nape, tugging her hair down from her updo until it spills down her back. I arrange it until it falls over her shoulders, the strands silky and soft, the red and gold colors blending together.

"What are you doing?" she says, frozen, her voice hushed, laughter gone. "We're in *church*."

"You said *cock* in church, so this is nothing."

"I could have been referring to a rooster."

"You weren't."

She blushes.

"I'm going to kiss you, Elena. Right here in the nursing mothers' room."

"I don't think you should."

"Right now in this instance, I am. I don't think I paid nearly enough attention to your lips on Friday night." My lips hover over hers, and I tilt her head up. "If you want to run, now's your chance."

Her breath comes out in little pants. "You better not kiss me."

"Then move away from me."

"I shouldn't have to."

"You really should, or it's going to happen."

"No, it isn't!"

Her breath hitches. But she doesn't move a muscle.

"Last chance," I say softly, tugging on a piece of her hair.

"Stop that."

I laugh. "You're like an angry kitten. But you aren't moving. I'm not holding you, Elena."

"I can't move!"

"Same."

She takes a breath. "But it's church, and we shouldn't."

"People kiss when they get married here."

"You're infuriating." Her eyes are on my mouth as her tongue comes out and dabs at her lips.

"I want to show you so many things, Elena."

"You mean like sex things? Because I may be a little inexperienced, but I assure you I can keep up quite well—"

"I know." I laugh and press my lips against hers.

Chapter 15

Elena

I forgot how beautifully he kisses, his lips soft at first as they meet mine, parting my mouth, widening it slowly with little nips, his tongue delving deep, sliding against mine. His hand lands on my hip before sliding around to cup my ass. "Elena," he murmurs against my cheek and takes my mouth again, sure and fast, his tongue tangling with mine. He tastes divine, sweet and dark mixed together, and we go from zero to a thousand in five seconds, starved and ravenous, our hands all over each other. Mine slide up his chest, stroking the expensive fabric, the rustle of my touch against him more erotic than it should be. My nipples bead inside my bra, erect and aching, and I grab his hair, sinking into him and letting go of all the misgivings I have. Why not? Kissing him is like holding an exploding star, hot and vibrant and lethal—and I want it. Just one little peck, I tell myself. Besides, it's the kind of kiss you write in your diary; it's the one you'll remember when you're old and gray.

He groans and presses me closer against him, letting me feel the hard length inside his jeans. I sigh into his mouth, my hands digging into his shoulders. He doesn't do anything shyly or slow when it comes to this; no, he gets right to the heart of what he wants.

Somehow in the craziness of kissing, I'm pressed against the wall, and he's raised my hands above my head, his mouth moving down my neck, sucking hard, then pressing small kisses there. He says my name. God, I really like when he says my name like he wants to eat me up. My skirt has hitched up, and he's ever so slightly grinding his hips against—

A man's voice, Patrick's, booms through the speaker, and we break apart as Patrick begins his sermon.

We are going to hell.

Jack's chest rises. "Elena, this is so good between us—"

Before he can finish, he grimaces and stumbles back and sits on the couch next to a group of rocking chairs. "Dammit," he mutters and rotates his left shoulder, his fingers digging into his skin. He's gone white, his face drawn and tight.

Breathing hard, I bend down next to him. "What happened?"

He shakes his head, his throat bobbing as he winces. "Old injury. It flares up at the worst times." He leans his head back, taking in big gulps of air as he presses his hand against his shoulder.

"What can I do?"

He stares up at the ceiling, still too pale for my taste. "Nothing. I need some heating pads, meds, and a deep massage." He closes his eyes. "Just give me a minute."

I try to help him get comfortable on the smallish couch, but it's no use with his huge frame; he's actually bigger than the couch.

"Can you take Aleve?" I'm digging around in my purse and pull a bottle out.

"Yeah." He takes three pills from my hand and throws them in his mouth and swallows.

"Let me get you some water from the kitchen." I stand, and he takes my hand and pulls me down until I'm back with my knees on the floor.

"No, don't go."

He grips my hand as another spasm hits him.

"Jack, please, you're worrying me. Should I phone the town doctor? He's no fancy athletic doctor, but he does house calls, and I'm sure he'll come here. Mama knows his family—"

"No, thank you; that's kind." He slowly eases himself to sitting, his breath labored.

"Is this a football injury?"

His eyes find mine. "Not originally."

Odd answer. "Then what is it?"

He doesn't answer but heaves himself up more, straightening his back and slowly moving to stand. I move with him, supporting him. I'm small, and I'm sure I'm not much help, but I try.

He flicks hazy eyes at me. "I need to get back to Nashville. I have a whole routine I go through when this hits, and I can't do it here. Would you . . . could you . . . drive me?" He flushes.

"Whatever you need."

"I hate to ask you."

"I can tell."

He nods. "I'll get a town car to bring you back."

"Of course."

I'd agree to anything right now to get that grimace off his face.

Moving slowly, he walks to the door, me beside him. My panties are lying on the floor where I dropped them, and I bend down and stuff them in my purse.

He huffs out a laugh. "You're either going to be pissed or amused when I tell you something."

"Yeah?"

"I had those in my pocket last night."

"You are a sicko, Jack Hawke. You had those the entire time and never offered them to me? I may never forgive you." I smile.

"Carried them around all night, like a little secret I had all to myself. Then you walked up to me, and I thought I was going to pass out in shock." He leans against the wall next to the door, pausing for a moment to rub his shoulder.

I shake my head. "Why didn't you just give them back?"

He sighs. "Thought about it. Probably should have. Wanted to see you again."

"Jack." I shake my head, bemused by his interest. "What am I going to do with you?"

"First thing is get me out of this church without anyone seeing I'm in pain. Think you can do that?" He gives me a searching look. "If just a hint of an injury gets out . . ."

Right. His career. He's overly paranoid about everything. "You're speaking to the unofficial and unwanted leader of the Daisy Lady Gang, so yeah, I'm slick. I know this church like the back of my hand. Hand me your keys, and I'll pull around to the back. All you have to do is leave this room, go right all the way down the hallway, and there's a side exit before you reach the kitchen. Got that?"

He nods. "Smart. My keys are in my pocket. Do you . . . can you get them for me?"

I nod and pat his right pocket, sticking my hand inside as he leans his head back against the wall.

"Elena . . . ," he moans when I grab the metal keys, brushing my fingers around something hard.

"How on earth are you excited and in pain?" I'm whispering, and I don't even know why except that I'm close to him, and he's so beautiful and . . .

He huffs out a laugh. "It's been a while for me. And it's you, I guess."

Well.

I let out a shaky breath and hold his keys up. "What are you driving?"

"Black Porsche. When you come out, it's to the left, next to a big Lincoln." He sends me a look. "Can you drive a stick? This car is kind of my baby, and the thought of you grinding gears—"

"My nana taught me to drive a tractor when I was ten. I can handle your fancy little car. The issue might be getting you in it."

"I'll take care of that. Meet you outside in three minutes?"

I give him a nod and open the door.

He grabs my hand before I can exit. "Elena . . ."

I look up at him. "Yeah?"

He licks his lips, a look on his face I can't decipher. "Thank you."

I smile. "For what? I'm helping you get out of here and back home. I'd do that for anyone."

He flashes a half grin, half grimace. "Yeah, I think you would. What I meant is thank you for . . ."

"What?" I'm whispering. Again.

"For being you. For forgiving me for lying. You have more capacity for kindness than most."

I shake my head at him. "You just haven't met the right people, Jack."

"Maybe." He closes his eyes as another flicker of pain crosses his face.

"Okay, I'm going to get your car."

He nods.

"Jack?"

"Yeah?"

I glance down at our intertwined hands. "You have to let me go."

He flushes and drops my hand. "Sorry. See you in three."

I exit and shut the door behind me, scanning the area. Usually there are people dashing to the restrooms or latecomers still coming in, but since it's the preacher's first day, it's quiet as a . . . church. I snort and dash out the front door and head to the sleek black Porsche.

I slide inside and adjust the leather seat, my nose filling with the scent of him inside the interior, all male and *him*. I rub my hands over the steering wheel, caressing it, thinking about Jack driving it . . .

Forget daydreaming. Right. I have a mission.

I crank it, and the engine rumbles, powerful and ready to eat up the road. I whip it in reverse and drive over to the side entrance. He's already waiting for me outside, his shoulders straight, his face stony.

I jump out and open his door, and he walks to the car, pauses for half a second as he takes in the low passenger seat. He lets out a string of curses, and I grimace as he manages to bend over and arrange himself. He attempts to reach for the seat belt, but I beat him to it, pulling it across him and snapping it together.

"There," I say.

I'm rising up when he tugs on my arm, pulling me back to him.

"Things were just getting good in there, and . . . I may not ever get another kiss." He cocks an eyebrow. "Am I right?"

Instead of answering him, I just smile and shut the door and get back in and speed away from the church.

Chapter 16

Elena

Where are you?

Your car is still at church. Everyone can see it.

Did you leave with that football player?

Elena Michelle, you missed Sunday lunch.

Okay, okay, I'm sorry about the preacher. But I think he liked you!

FYI, I saw on the internet that Jack Hawke has a drinking problem. He is NOT marriage material.

I sigh as I read the series of texts Mama has sent me. Nothing about Jack screams drinking problem. He's viscerally alert and focused, too competitive to allow alcohol to rule him. I'm not sure how I know this, but I do. Yes, he had the scotch on Friday, but there's nothing wrong with a good whiskey. Plus, he didn't even have a drink in his hand at the VIP party.

And then there's Aunt Clara's texts:

You should have seen Cynthia at lunch. She chewed so hard I thought her teeth might break. You're with Mr. Hottie Footballer, aren't you? Sneaky devil. Take some pics for me. Bare-chested? Dick pic? LOL.

I put my phone down as the young male trainer approaches. Gideon something. We're inside Jack's penthouse, and he's just wrapped up a session of working on Jack's back and shoulders. "He needs rest. I've worked out most of the kinks, but if he has any more pain, just give him the Aleve again. He won't take anything harder because of drug screens." His next words make my eyes flare. "He really does need rest. No *workouts* today; know what I mean?"

"I'm not *with* him." *Get a grip, water boy.*

"Uh-huh." He eyes my neck for some weird reason.

I open the door. "Jack and I are *friends*."

He blushes all the way to the roots of his gelled hair at teacher voice. "Sorry, I just assumed. Jack, ah, women, everything I hear—"

I open the door wider. "Please don't assume. I'm sure you have other things to do on a Sunday afternoon. Goodbye." I smile politely in a way that says, *I may appear sweet, but don't mess with me, bucko.*

He walks through it, and I shut it firmly.

We arrived here about two hours ago. After I called Quinn, who lives in an apartment close by, together we got him up to the penthouse through a side entrance and a private service elevator.

Gideon arrived in fifteen minutes, whipped out a massage table and oils. Jack changed into athletic shorts, crawled on top of the table, and the trainer went to work. My eyes kept going to that black-and-yellow tiger tattoo on his back, that snarl, the sharp teeth bared and ready to bite. I barely recall it from our night together, just catching glimpses, but mostly I didn't pay much attention to his *back*. I really should have. It's menacing looking but beautiful. I'd like to trace my fingers over it . . .

When I turn, Jack is rolling his shoulders in the den, an eased expression on his face. I try to focus my eyes off his broad chest, but it's hard. The muscular pecs, the ripples of his tight six-pack, the slight V where his hips meet his black shorts. Even his thighs are powerful, thick and taut as he does a few stretches.

I look up at the ceiling. *Lord. Have some mercy.*

Also, my buzzed memory does not do him justice.

Quinn pops in from the kitchen area. "You hungry, sir? I can whip something up."

"I swear, Quinn, if you don't stop calling me that, I'm going to fire you," Jack murmurs as he scrubs his face and walks over to click on the TV. ESPN pops up, the volume low. "I'm kidding, but come on; we're almost family."

I cock my head, detecting a wistful tone in Jack's voice.

Quinn straightens. "Right."

Jack grabs a bottle of Gatorade Quinn set down on the coffee table earlier and kills it, his long tanned throat sucking it down.

I look away.

Just as my stomach rumbles.

Jack pauses. "You hungry, Elena? I guess that massage went right through lunch."

"No, I'm fine." I skipped breakfast this morning, though.

Another growl.

"Liar," Jack says as he walks over to me. He's not quite back to his usual athletic grace and prowess, a slight hitch in his broad chest as he focuses on keeping his left arm down and loose at his side.

"I can order pizza?" Quinn offers.

Pizza? After I missed Sunday chicken? Regardless of the setup with the preacher, that is my favorite meal. I imagine Mama's got leftovers in some Tupperware right now.

Jack reaches me where I'm still idling near the front door. I should get out of here. Casserole is calling.

"What do you want? We can call anywhere and get it delivered? Milano's?"

I look at a point over his shoulder.

"Not your favorite?"

"Just . . . can you put a shirt on?"

Quinn chuckles, and I think I see a pleased expression on his face as he watches us.

Jack grins. "Nah, I like walking around like this. It makes you flustered, and I don't think that happens often."

Who is he kidding? Everything about him makes me wired.

Without looking at Quinn, he says, "Call up Milano's. Salads, pasta with bolognese, and extra bread? Unless you want something different?"

"Extra?"

"You ate a lot of bread on Friday. I want to be prepared."

"Hmm, I did." I twirl a piece of my hair, then stop, frowning. When did I become a hair twirler?

"It's the least I can do after you driving me here."

But it wasn't a hardship at all, especially with all that hotness right next to me. He actually fell asleep—I don't know how—and I spent most of that time darting looks at him, wondering why he'd gone to the trouble of trying to see *me* again.

For sex, Elena. The man wants to bone you.

I nod. "Food is good."

"Milano's is the best. Good call on buying that place, sir, but count me out," Quinn says. "It's my day off, and if you're good, I'm heading out."

He glances at Quinn. "Hot date?"

Quinn looks from me to Jack. "Ah, yeah."

I squint at him. Quinn's lying. There's no date. I feel the untruthfulness like I do when Aunt Clara tells me Scotty isn't slipping in her back door at night.

"Who? I didn't know you were seeing anyone. Lucy never mentioned it," Jack asks, interest on his face.

Quinn has a deer-in-the-headlights look on his face, much like the morning I forced him to eat my omelet while I tried to pry personal info about Jack out of him.

"Uh . . . well, I . . . yeah." Quinn stares at the floor. "Let me call in that order to Milano's."

"No need. I can do it. Didn't mean to pry about your date. Your business and all," Jack murmurs, a look of disappointment flashing over his face before he locks it down.

I frown. It's almost as if Jack *wants* Quinn to confide in him. Lucy?

"Are you two cousins?" I ask. They look nothing alike.

"No," Quinn says when it becomes apparent Jack isn't going to. He throws a look at Jack, as if looking for help, his face unsure. "She . . . um . . ."

"She was our foster mom," Jack adds quietly. "I lived with her after my mom died. Quinn came to her after I was already in college."

Foster care. I file that away, wondering what happened to put him there.

"I see. She must be a special lady."

Jack nods.

Quinn clears his throat. "She's amazing. Jack even moved her here from Ohio after he was drafted. He bought her a huge-ass house out in Brentwood, and when I got in trouble with the law, Jack gave me this job—"

"I'm sure Elena doesn't want to hear all that."

Oh, but I do! I'm fascinated, trying to work out the dynamics here.

But the truth is I don't think Jack wants me to know too much about him.

"Elena's cool—" Quinn says before Jack cuts him off.

"Quinn, don't you have a date?"

"Yeah, right. I'll go." Quinn grabs his phone and heads to the foyer, brushing past me. He leans in, keeping his voice low. "Keep him company for a while, Elena?"

His face is earnest.

"Why?" He's Jack freaking Hawke. Why does he need me?

He throws a look back at Jack, who's walked back to the den. "Look, he's a stand-up guy. Misunderstood a little. Plus, I overheard how you showed Gideon the door. Ballbuster." He pauses, his expression hardening. "You won't . . . hurt him, right?"

Hurt him? What on earth? "Of course not."

"I knew it." He grins, his face lighting up. "He likes you, you know. Asked me twenty questions after you left the penthouse. Wanted to know everything you said. He saw your note in the bathroom. He laughed for a good five minutes. Said you were a firecracker."

And then he's out the door.

When I head back to the den, Jack's already on the phone ordering our food, giving instructions for the driver. I roam over the den, my shoes already kicked off, taking in the modern furnishings, black leather sofas, sleek armchairs, heavy glass sculptures that adorn end tables—things I barely noticed the night I was here. No photos or thriller books on the bookshelf. Not one single cheesy mug or magnet in the kitchen, either, or I would have remembered it because I cataloged everything when I cooked. All I found were the basics of a nice kitchen: stainless steel pots and pans, expensive white china.

Nothing meaningful.

Cold and sterile.

I stand at the huge floor-to-ceiling glass windows that overlook downtown Nashville. Beautiful view. And close to the stadium—only a block away. Convenient.

From the reflection in the glass, I watch as Jack approaches me, still bare chested.

"Food will be here soon." His voice is quiet, as if he senses my unease now that we're alone.

"Why did we come to the penthouse instead of where you live?" I turn around to face him, and his face is unsmiling, a little frown there.

"Why would I?"

"Because you'd be more comfortable there? This isn't a home. There are no pictures of you or trophies. And don't you live with Devon? I'm sure he would have helped you get situated instead of calling Quinn."

"Right."

"You don't trust me?" I cock my head, not angry but just curious. I understand now his need for privacy based on what I've read, but to think of living like this, being so defensive with every single person you meet—it must be exhausting.

He eases down on the couch and pats the seat next to him. "Come on; sit down."

I sit, keeping about three feet between us, keeping my hands clasped in my lap. "Tell me about that scar on your shoulder."

He frowns.

Yeah, I saw that bundle of raised skin, about the size of a nickel, when he stripped for the trainer. Somehow I'd missed it before.

"It looks like a bullet wound." I smirk at his surprised glance. "Besides being the mayor of Daisy, my daddy was a doctor. He loved to entertain me with medical photos. I've seen it all. Knife wounds, gunshots, broken legs, even a shattered wrist once—that was weird." I grimace. "He expected me to go to med school, but I didn't."

"You're smart enough."

"Maybe."

"Hmm." He gives me a bemused look. "Maybe you should get a closer look at my scar, Dr. Riley." He scoots over closer, his leg pressed against mine. The heat from his skin emanates like a furnace.

I touch his shoulder, tracing my finger lightly over the raised skin. “It’s not your throwing shoulder, because you’re right handed, which is good.”

“Yes.” He’s watching me carefully, eyes searching my face. “But how do you know it’s a bullet wound?”

“Well, first off, I’m southern, duh, and everyone in Daisy deer hunts or owns a firearm. I personally don’t like guns, but I’ve been around them all my life. Even had a date once in a deer stand. Worst time ever. It was early and cold and high up in a tree, and all I wanted to do was go home. I’m guessing a handgun at close range. It looks like it might have hit your brachial plexus, that bundle of nerves that controls arm function. Have you had surgery on it? While people think gunshots to the shoulder aren’t life threatening, they can damage blood vessels and cause severe pain—especially if there are fragments still floating around in your muscles; am I right?”

“Hmm.”

“And I bet you were younger when it happened, based on how it’s faded.”

“Elena . . .” He frowns.

He’s retreating. Not telling me everything.

I drop my hand from his warm skin, swallowing. I shouldn’t be touching him, even to check out his injury . . . but . . .

“I get it. You’re *private*.”

He lets out a deep exhale. “It’s not that pretty of a story.”

“Scars usually aren’t.”

“I don’t like to talk about it.”

“Because you think I’m going to run to the *National Enquirer* and tell them?”

He just shakes his head and grabs the remote, clicking on a show with Asian characters, and settles back deep into the couch, propping his feet up on the glass coffee table. “Okay, fine, it *was* a bullet. I got shot when I was a kid.”

"Oh."

A flush darkens his face, and I see the vulnerability that cloaks him, even as he tries to shutter his face.

And normally, I'd let it go, but I can't. I want to know more about Jack, more than just the legendary quarterback.

"Were you in some kind of gang? Did you defend some girl's honor in high school?"

He stares blankly at the TV. "Why is it so important?"

"Because it tells me *who* you are."

His sharp gaze turns to me. "You first. Who's Topher?"

"Devon didn't tell you?"

He shakes his head.

"He's my gay roommate."

"The one who fixed you up with Greg Zimmerman, famous weatherman. He's tall and dark haired, by the way. I'm much better looking."

I arch a brow.

"I looked Greg up. I just wanted to know who my competition was. Are you going to go out with him? A redo?"

"Are you jealous?"

"I figure that's your type."

I stare down at my clasped hands.

There are several moments of silence between us, and I feel him watching me intently, dissecting me, making a decision as a long sigh comes from him. "Elena . . . the man my mom lived with shot me."

My heart drops as my gaze clings to his. "Jack, that's terrible."

He nods, his eyes seeming to drift back to a memory. "He was a piece of shit. He hit her. Slapped me around. Even came close to drowning me once in the lake behind our house. Claimed he was teaching me to swim, but the asshole held me underwater. It's why I still can't even swim."

Horror washes over me. "Jack—"

"No, let me finish. She loved me, but she loved him more, you know? Even though he drank and had a vile temper. She couldn't quit him. One day I came home from school, and she had a busted nose, and I snapped. He had me against the wall, and I thought it was over. My mom pulled a gun on him . . . he took it away from her."

Dread fills me.

He takes an uneven breath. "He killed her, then shot me."

My hand takes his, threading our fingers together.

He looks down in surprise, then back at me. "You didn't know any of this?"

I shake my head, my heart heavy. "No."

He sighs. "It's in Sophia's book, although she embellished quite a bit."

"I did download it, but I haven't gotten far. It's crap."

His thumb caresses the upper part of my hand. "I—I got the gun away from him and killed him. I was fourteen. The police had been to our house enough to know that it was self-defense, but that's how I got my scar. And according to Sophia, that's why I'm a drunk and an abuser—just like him. I used to party hard . . ." His voice trails off. "I was just full of fire then and had all this money. I don't even know who that kid was. Like Aiden, maybe. Rash and invincible and arrogant as hell."

I smile. "You're still arrogant."

He laughs, and the tension from his story eases from the air.

"Thank you for telling me."

He gives me a long look. "Hmm, you're easy to talk to."

I glance at the TV, nerves flying. "Didn't know you liked K-dramas."

"Yeah, I've been waiting for this stupid guy to kiss this chick for about ten episodes, and if something doesn't happen soon, I'm writing an email to the producers."

"It's subtitled, *and* it's a romance? Wow."

He takes in my open mouth. "I won't judge you for eating a pound of bread when we met, and you don't judge me for my K-dramas."

"Not judging. Who is who, and what is going on?"

He points at the TV. "It's called *Once I Saw You*. That guy is Lee, and he's a badass who loves to fight and argue with everyone. He's totally misunderstood. She's Dan-i. They met when he spilled a soda down her dress; then she slapped him in the face, and now he can't stop chasing her around campus."

"It's a college romance?" I can't keep the incredulity out of my voice.

"It's good! The feelings are intense. I'm invested."

"So he's in love with her, and she's not into him?" I watch as Lee and Dan-i argue about her going on a date with someone else. "Is he used to getting what he wants all the time?"

Jack's eyes are locked on the TV. "He's, like, all in with her, but I can't tell how she feels. I mean, he saved her from a blizzard once, but she kind of had a crush on one of his friends at the time. He's doing his best to show her he's a good guy, but he's got emotional issues, and it comes out wonky when he talks to her. He's never been in love and doesn't know how to talk to her."

"Complicated . . ." I bite back a grin.

"I know you're over there laughing at me, but I can't look at you, because I have to read the subtitles."

"You are so weird."

"You have no idea." He laughs. "But the dynamic of their relationship sucks you right in."

"Oh my God. You're a closet romantic!"

"Am not." He's grinning at me now, a gleam in his eye. "I'm a big tough football player."

"So? You're watching a budding romance between two college kids like it's crack!"

"It is crack! They haven't even kissed yet, and it's killing me! What's wrong with them? Why doesn't he just grab her and lay one on her?"

"Because then there wouldn't be a show!"

"True that." He throws back his head and laughs, then straightens, his gaze on my lips. "Elena. Speaking of kisses . . ." His hand tugs on me until I'm closer to his face, his skin like fire when I place my palm on his chest. To stop him or—

"Jack. We shouldn't get frisky."

"Frisky, you say?" He laughs. "And I disagree," he murmurs. "FYI, you have a hickey on your neck from church."

My eyes flare, and I press my skin where he kissed me. "Jack Hawke, you jerk. That's why Gideon kept looking at me. Now I'll have to cover it up." I sigh, no heat in my voice. I enjoyed it just as much as he did.

"Maybe you need another one on the other side. A matching set." His hand slides around my nape, massaging the skin there, drifting down to my shirt. He toys with the buttons. "I want to undo these real slow."

"Too bad you're injured," I murmur.

"Hmm." He tilts my head up to his. My heart jumps at the desire in his irises, the dilated pupils. "I'm dying to kiss you again. You gonna let me?"

I love that he asks me first. Waiting for me to accept. Underneath that tough exterior is a man who doesn't hurt women.

"Elena?"

From the moment I saw him in church, no matter my declarations that he's dangerous to my heart, my gut knew I wanted to be in his arms again.

"Kiss me."

He does, almost hesitantly, as if giving me a chance to move. But I can't. I sigh in his mouth, nipping at his lips with my teeth.

He increases the pressure, his lips slanting over mine harder, insistent. Time stands still as we kiss. His chest is silky under my fingers, soft from the oils. Moving up, I touch his face, scraping my nails against that scruff on his jaw, and he opens his mouth wider, devouring me, arching closer. He smells delicious, all male and primal. His tongue battles with mine, sucking, then letting it go, exploring me, flicking against mine. They go on for a while, these deep kisses, rocking me, making my skin flame as I brush against his chest.

I feel weightless and heavy at the same time, my legs scissoring, wanting . . .

His chest rises as he pulls back and presses his forehead against mine. "I can't move much . . . my shoulder . . . will you . . ."

I've gone and lost my mind, because he doesn't have to tell me what he wants. I move and straddle him as he pushes my skirt to my upper thighs, caressing my bare thighs.

"What is this?" He's looking at my soft beige thong, the brown fringe at the top.

I press a kiss to his neck. "Barbarian Princess set made with chamois, a soft leather imported from Spain."

"You made them?"

I nod, feeling shy as I plant my face deeper in his neck, my hands toying with the hair there, twining my fingers through it.

"They're pretty, but . . . can you take them off? I don't think I can."

"I'm not taking my panties off again."

"Then how will I fuck you?"

My entire body clenches at the image his words paint. "Who says we're gonna f-u-c-k?"

His hand tangles in my hair, tugging until my scalp tingles, sending a bolt of lightning straight to my core. He kisses me hard then, his mouth demanding and rough, before skating across my cheek to my ear. "I do," he whispers in my ear. "But if you don't want to . . . I can still make you come, Elena."

"Hmm," I breathe as my hips swivel against the tent in his shorts, sliding against him, feeling the hard ridge of him against my skin through the thin crotch of my thong.

"Is that a yes?" He groans, dark lashes fluttering against his cheeks.

"Yes," I say, moving against his shorts.

He bites his lip. "Don't stop doing that. Please."

I gasp when his finger eases under my panties and meets my slick flesh. His thumb circles, rotating on my favorite pressure point.

"Jack . . ." My voice is uncertain, wavering, as I second-guess. This desire is so fast with us, and I'm not used to it, not used to feeling this out of control with a man. I dated Preston for three months before we got to the good stuff, but with Jack, that's all I can think about. I've never been too adventuresome with sex—part shyness, the other part never having the right partner who took the lead and *showed* me what I wanted.

"Do you want me to stop?"

"I'll die if you do."

"Can't have that," he rumbles against my neck.

His fingers are skilled, slick with my wetness as he parts my folds and delves inside, dipping in with a fast stroke before circling my bud, his thigh muscles tightening under me as he strains for better access. "Undo your blouse." His tone is gruff, and I can't get the buttons free fast enough, my hands shaking as I slide the buttons through the slits and tug the end of the shirt free from the waistband of my skirt. He never stops that maddening touch, fingering me one heart-stopping second, then back to circling. Sharp prickles of pleasure build at the base of my spine, pushing me higher until I'm gasping for breath. Orgasms are rare and precious to me, requiring work and effort that my past lovers never took the time for.

"You're beautiful," he murmurs, staring up at me.

I laugh, bemused that he'd think so. I whip my shirt off, and his mouth parts. He stares at my barely there leather bra. "How the hell am I supposed to *not* fuck you?"

His need for me arouses me more, makes me brazen as I undo the front clasp on the delicate demicup bra, my breasts tingling at his gaze.

"I've only got one good hand, and it's on your pussy. Come closer." He bites his bottom lip.

"Like this?" I ease up until I'm on my knees, hovering over him.

"Closer."

I scoot in, not wanting his hand off me, but he knows what I want and never stops. His head arches up, and his mouth takes a nipple, his tongue flicking against my areola, the sharp edges of his teeth scraping against my sensitized skin. The scruff on his jaw brushes against me, prickling. My hands clasp his hair, hanging on to him.

I hadn't planned on this. I really didn't mean for this to go so far . . .

"Don't let your head roam; stay with me," he says, moving to the other nipple and sucking hard, taking as much skin in his mouth as will fit.

It pricks in a delicious way that surprises me and feels so good, the way he wants *me*, desire flushing his cheeks.

He's got two fingers deep inside me, soft and easy, and I arch back, giving him more access. They flutter inside me, caressing against one place, and I jerk and tense at the new rocket of heat that spikes over me.

"G-spot. Ride my hand." Sweat beads on his temples, his face tight with concentration.

"Am I hurting you?" I gasp out. I think back to Gideon's words.

"No, no, no, don't stop. Shoulder be damned, I'm going to fuck you; I'm going to bend you over this couch after you come."

I picture it in my head, his big body behind me, hands digging into my hips. "Keep talking."

He huffs out a surprised laugh. "Elena, where have you been all my life?"

"New York, then Daisy," I murmur. "Tell me more, Jack."

His tawny eyes gleam at me. Wolf. "More what?"

"Don't play the dumb jock. Dirty talk, Jack, now."

He groans and moves his left hand then, the injured one, where it was resting by his side. He runs it down my chest, his fingers closing around my nipples and plucking them.

"Jack . . ."

He wraps his hand around my waist and grips me tight. "I'm going to fuck you against the wall, too, Elena. With your ass in my hands and your feet digging into my back. We didn't do that yet. On the ride here, I couldn't stop thinking about it."

Oh, oh . . .

My heart shudders in my chest. How can I ever handle a man like this? He's raw and hot and primitive. I tremble and catch a reflection of us in the glass of the floor-to-ceiling windows. I'm on top of him, my hair trailing down my back, my hands in his hair. I look . . . decadent and almost beautiful.

"Jack . . ."

"Baby, please come. I *need* to fuck you," he rumbles.

Be mine, I think he says, but I'm not sure, and that can't be right, because I know what this is. It's just sex. It's just two people who want the same thing, and damn, why haven't we been doing this nonstop since the moment we met?

Because he is who he is, and you are who you are—

"Elena, stay with me. Me and you, right now."

He's shoving his gym shorts down, his thick length popping out, long and hard and veiny, the mushroom head flushed and tight, a bead of wetness there. He grips my hips and slides me against him, a long guttural growl coming from him as our flesh meets. I grind against him.

"Come." His fingers play with me, circling, the silky feel of his velvety skin skimming my folds. He's almost inside me, if I move just a little, and I'm past all reason, my mind full of him, and his touch has my body climbing and searching, yearning, until I'm right there so fast that it takes me by surprise. The pleasure barrels into me like a train, and I tremble as it takes over and washes over me, covering me with vibrating sensation. The universe moves, and I'm powerless in its wake and ripples. I swivel on him, shuddering, making him slick, riding it out.

Jack pulls my face to his and kisses me hard. "Elena, Elena, Elena . . . you're so—"

The doorbell rings.

Chapter 17

Jack

Elena climbs out of my lap, jerking her skirt down. Her panicky fingers work on the buttons of her shirt she picked up from the floor.

"It's our food," I say, enjoying watching her. Goddess. She's the sexiest woman I've ever met, and she doesn't even know it.

"You missed one," I murmur. "Middle button. Also can you throw me a blanket?"

"You're cold?"

"Steel pipe in my pants."

She blushes and dashes over to the armchair and grabs one of the fur blankets and tosses it back at me.

She darts over to the mirror above the desk and pats down her hair, trying to straighten out the mess.

"Oh my God. I look insane."

"Yep."

She throws a glare at me.

"What? You do." I grin.

Ding-dong! Ding-dong!

"Our pasta's going to be cold if you don't get that," I say, laughing because she's now trying to put her hair back in some kind of bun, but it's clear she doesn't have the tools. "Man, that bread is going to be good, and all you want to do is fix yourself."

I move to stand, and she points a finger at me.

"You. This is your fault. Don't move. I'll get this."

Blowing out a breath, she gives up on her hair and marches to the door. I don't have the heart to tell her that her skirt is on backward, the slit that was in the back now obviously in the front. And her shirt is crooked, one side tucked in, the other hanging out.

Damn, I love getting her ruffled. Contentedness washes over me. Something about her grabbed me from the moment she sat down with me at Milano's, and it's so new and refreshing, and she doesn't care *who* I am . . .

Unease trickles in.

But what the hell am *I* doing? I was ready to fuck her right here on the couch without even thinking about protection.

I don't have a view of who's at the door, but the voice is instantly recognizable. Lawrence. I wince. He's been sending me texts all day wanting to know how the breakfast with Timmy and Laura went and if I took any pics he could post on social media. I hadn't. It never crossed my mind. I know I need to be spinning this and making the story into *Football player spends time with young fan*, but . . .

They're murmuring, but I can't hear them. I frown. Lawrence can be a bulldog when it comes to protecting me—that's what I pay him for—but he isn't the smoothest when it comes to women.

I've eased myself up to standing as they walk back into the den. Wearing a suit and his slicked-back Wall Street hairstyle, he walks ahead of Elena, whose face is blank, when normally she's so expressive. It's one of the little things I dig about her, the way I can read her. Milano's: nervous as a poodle. VIP party: pissed. Church: shocked. Our kiss: hot as hell.

Then I see the papers she's carrying in her hand.

Fuck. My eyes shut briefly. I was getting around to approaching the NDA topic, but Lawrence beat me to the punch with probably the finesse of a bull in a china shop.

"You aren't answering your phone, asshole. And you know that makes me nervous," is what he says as he walks in. He takes in my lack of shirt and pops an eyebrow. "I called Quinn when I couldn't get you, and he said you had a spasm today—and that you had company. I brought new papers for her. You okay?"

"Good." It still twinges. I've had worse injuries than this one on the field, yet this is the one that nags me whenever it wants to pop up. But it's never hurt quite this bad. I don't tell him that.

"Nice. You have training camp soon. You want to be on top."

"I will be."

"Right."

"Anything else?" I ask, getting more tense as I watch Elena slap the papers down on my desk, then walk down the hallway to one of the bathrooms.

Lawrence watches her leave. "Good. Privacy." He takes a few steps closer, keeping his voice low. "Talked to the principal at Timmy's school. He's down with you meeting some young fans, signing some footballs. I told him low key, no school-assembly-type thing. Good?"

"Make it casual. No media."

"What the fuck is the point if no one takes a photo, Jack?"

I inhale, knowing he's right. "You can take one photo for Instagram or whatever. I don't want this to become a circus. I don't want reporters outside Timmy's school or his apartment. Laura wouldn't like that." She said as much at breakfast, and I want to make sure their lives aren't upturned.

"Fine." He breathes out a heavy sigh. "Timmy wants you to do this play thing. How are you going to manage that?"

I heave out a groan. I do *not* want to be on a stage. I picture me up there, weaving on my feet, my face bloodred, trying to get the words out. Hell no. My heart races at the mere thought.

He reads me. "Do you have any clue how hard it is to manage you when you aren't helping? Just go, and see what happens. Maybe you can be an assistant to the director or some shit."

I nod, not liking the anxiousness in the pit of my stomach. "Yeah."

He looks over his shoulder. "She still hasn't signed the NDA. Told me so at the door. What the fuck? And she's here now? One word to the press about an injury and—"

"She knows about the shoulder. She was there when it happened."

Lawrence lets out a string of curses.

"She won't tell, Lawrence."

"Uh-huh. You've known this girl for three fucking days." He shakes his head. "Be glad Sophia never knew that injury keeps popping up."

True. Sophia knew about the scar because everyone in my hometown knew the details of that story, and it has circulated around me for years. Plus, Harvey's sister wrote her article. I never got around to telling Sophia about my occasional pain, mostly because it happened rarely. I hesitated when it came to her, which should have been a clue that she was wrong for me.

Yet I told Elena. I could have brushed it off as a minor football thing, but I didn't. I told her the story from start to finish, and I can't recall doing that since Devon.

Lawrence is giving me details about Timmy's school in Daisy, quieting when Elena walks back in the room. She doesn't meet my gaze. Her clothes have been straightened, and her hair is smooth, the long strands gleaming, as if she's brushed it. Fresh red lipstick is on her lips. She snatches the papers from the table and sits down at the desk a few feet away from us, her head bent as she thumbs through them, pointedly ignoring us.

Great. I run my hands through my hair.

"Is that all, Lawrence? We're waiting for lunch to arrive." I give him a pointed look. *Get the fuck out.*

He nods and pivots. "Don't see me out. I know you're hurting. I'll let you know what day and time for the school thing plus the other we discussed." He gives a nod at Elena. "Nice to meet you, Elena."

She never looks up. "Of course."

I grimace. Her voice is quiet, polite, exceedingly so. But she didn't say *Nice to meet you too.*

Lawrence is oblivious and glances at me and gives me a thumbs-up and leaves.

I walk over to her, taking in the stiffness of her shoulders. "Elena . . ."

She holds a hand up. "Nope. Let me finish reading this fascinating document—which is backdated to Valentine's Day, by the way."

I cringe, knowing exactly what else is in those papers: a firm statement about consent and age; explicit description of sexual acts she'd do, from foreplay to anal, things she puts a check next to or doesn't; an agreement of complete confidentiality for the entirety of her life, right down to the details of personal information including my cell number, the Wi-Fi password at the penthouse, the location of my apartment, even Lucy's address in Brentwood. Lawrence and my lawyer came up with the language.

"What did Lawrence say to you?" Part of me is anxious at her expression—the other side of me, well, I want her to sign it.

"He's a jerk."

"He's my jerk. Elena."

She ignores me, her fingers trembling as she turns the page. "What strikes me as the most ludicrous is that you'd actually sue me for *five million dollars* if I speak to *anyone* about our private life. Hate to tell you, but Topher and Aunt Clara know we had sex. Already told him, and he told her. No telling who she might tell. She's a stylist at a beauty shop in a gossipy small town. You should hear the things they talk about in there."

She's trying to get a rise out of me.

"Good luck," she adds. "I don't have any money. All I have is my house, and it's not worth that. We might be in court for years."

"Elena, please—"

"No, you don't have the right to say my name like that." She dips her head, her hair swinging to cover her face. "This is so . . . ridiculous and grotesque. I must have been trashed. What was I thinking?"

I lean against the wall at the disdain in her voice. Shit.

"I wish . . . I wish I had read it, because I never would have had sex with you, Jack."

A long sigh comes from me. "It would make me feel better about us, Elena. Think about it. You sign, and we can start all over again—"

She stands, little fists curled, a defiant tilt to her chin. "How many girls have signed this? How many women have you kept at this fuck palace?"

My lips compress. "No one has been *here* since she was. I didn't need an NDA until she did what she did. You're the first girl I've even wanted to be with. No one else has been *offered* an NDA."

"I'm *so* flattered." She throws her eyes around the room. "You never even took Sophia to where you really live?"

"No."

"How long were you with her?"

"A year, give or take."

She shakes her head, eyes flaring. "You really don't trust anyone."

"Can you blame me?" My voice is low. "I have a career to protect. And my privacy. I don't want any more stories about me, Elena."

She licks her lips. "For a weird reason, I really thought you walked in church to see me, but really it was all about these papers."

"Not true."

"Oh, I think it is. Deep down, this NDA has been on your mind."

I pause. "Yes."

"I'm surprised you haven't brought it up earlier."

I dreaded it . . . maybe because I sensed she'd be offended.

My skin crawls with unease, but all I can see is Sophia on *Good Morning America*, talking about our sex life, how I beat her up when she got out of line. Even though she never had one police report or photo or a hospital record to back her up, that shit still got published. It was my word against hers, and when I don't give interviews . . .

Sure, I put out a comment through Lawrence saying it was untrue and even tried to sue her, but it was pointless, a waste of money—and people ate it up. Even Coach grilled me when it came out. Shit. That was a tense few weeks, but he knows the man I am. Adidas was incensed at the book, especially when I refused to publicly comment about it.

"I want to trust you, but . . ."

"Right. Walls." She picks up the papers and wads them into a ball. "This is what I think of your NDA."

I close my eyes, a hard anvil landing on my chest, and it's not so much about the fact that she isn't signing it but that I've disappointed her.

"You're right," I mutter. "You are better than me. You deserve a nice guy and not a banged-up bad-boy superstar football player. I hear you. Do you think I like this? Being alone? It sucks, okay; it fucking sucks. Next up, she's writing an article for *Cosmo* about how I forced her to have an abortion."

She bites that lip and looks away from me, her eyes glistening, and I pause; shit, is she going to cry—

"That isn't true, Elena. She was never pregnant. I'm not like that. I may have grown up with a man who slapped me around, but I respect women."

"I believe you." Her words are quiet.

Thank God.

Her ocean-blue eyes are clear when they land back on me. "I will never tell a soul about our night. I will go back to Topher and Aunt Clara and swear them to secrecy. If I stumble across you at a restaurant or a VIP room—which is highly unlikely—I promise to not even give you a second glance. Besides, you have plenty of other options, don't you, Jack? Why not ask one of those supermodels at the VIP room to be your penthouse girl?"

Been there. That road is bleak and empty.

And those girls aren't Elena, with her pouty lips and little skirts and glasses.

She scoffs. "Tell me, what do I get out of signing the NDA? Jewels, evening gowns, galas, an allowance, a new car—"

"Stop. It's not like that. It's not a transaction."

"Well, it sure seems like it. What happened to good old-fashioned hanging out and seeing where it goes? Maybe a date. Maybe more conversations about who you are and who I am? Because I refuse to be some girl you bang when you're horny and need a warm body who's signed some stupid papers. I'm a person. And full disclosure . . . ha ha . . . I don't *want* to be your hookup, okay? I don't! I'm team boyfriend all the way, Jack."

Her chin is tilted up, eyes blazing at me, and I wonder how I *ever* thought she was shy.

My throat tightens. Here's the part where I should say something right and good and fix this mess, maybe tell her that she makes me feel like no one ever has . . . but fuck, I don't know how to even be myself with a girl anymore. She's right. My walls are up. I'm living in a fortress.

She looks at me. "I'm waiting, Jack. I just said some real stuff. Say something."

Several moments pass as we stare at each other, and I'm racking my brain to figure out how to get us out of this conversation, to get her on my side—and back in my arms.

"Whatever," she mutters.

Dammit. I've waited too long, and she grabs her purse and shoes and stalks to the door.

I should beg her to stay. *I should.* Because it feels like that—like I'd be willing to walk across hot coals just to get her to be with me.

Shit.

That is just . . . crazy.

I barely know her!

I clamp my lips together as she opens the door.

She looks back at me, a flash of vulnerability on her face, as if waiting for me to stop her.

I just stare at her, getting a good look at her face, that long auburn hair, those big eyes. Fuck. I'm never going to see her again. She's done. I feel it.

She lets out a sigh and darts out, brushing past the concierge fellow who's in the hall holding our food.

Dammit.

Chapter 18

Elena

"Alert, alert! Douchebag and fiancée approaching the library!" Topher calls to me from the front desk as I shelve a new shipment of YA books. My hands tighten around one as I come out from behind the stacks and glance out the tinted windows.

Preston and Giselle. They're arriving in his Lexus in the parking lot. I watch as he walks around to her side and helps her out. She wraps a hand around his arm, and they march toward the door.

Someone stops them on the sidewalk, and Giselle holds up her ring. Glowing.

I let out a sigh. I've been avoiding them all week. Not in the mood to deal with something I clearly should. Preston started calling on Monday, leaving voice mails and texting again. I never responded. Giselle took up the cause on Tuesday evening, coming by the house, but I didn't answer her knock.

On Wednesday, Mama barged in and asked me to talk to them. She was businesslike about it, reminding me that Giselle is my sister and always will be, and I need to make things right.

My lips tighten. Why should *I* make things right? He dated me first!

On Thursday evening, Aunt Clara popped over, surprising me in the middle of a sewing session. I slammed the door to my secret room and joined her in the kitchen, where we shared some bourbon. We barely talked about the engagement, but I knew that was her mission, to convince me to sit down with them. Instead, I told her about Jack and the *stupid* NDA. We ended up outside on the screened-in porch, a little tipsy, talking about men and sneaking cigarettes she'd brought.

And now it's Friday, and Preston and Giselle are here to double-team me. Perfect.

Topher slides in next to me and pushes up the sleeves of his Nirvana shirt. "I'm gonna protect you, Elle."

"I know you would, but I don't think it's going to come to blows. Preston isn't a fighter—or much of a lover."

Topher's eyes never leave Preston's face as they continue to chat outside. It's a sunny day for the end of February. "He's an uptight prick. I bet he never got hugs as a baby."

"She did, though." Mama especially doted on her. *Pretty* is key to her, and she showered Giselle with attention, the good daughter who's now working on her doctorate in physics.

I watch as she gazes up at him, a soft expression on her face, the way her eyes glitter. *Love.* I want to spit.

I've been extra . . . not really angry . . . but disillusioned since I walked out of Jack's penthouse several days ago. I almost thought . . . he might try to stop me, but he didn't.

But he's been back to Daisy. I heard all about it at the Cut 'N' Curl yesterday when I popped in to get Sun Drops for me and Topher.

Why, he's just the sweetest man. Polite and gracious! He signed over three hundred footballs for all the kids at the elementary school! Little Timmy right next to him. Such a handsome fellow! That came from Birdie Walker, the school secretary. She was getting her roots touched up by Aunt Clara, who met my gaze in the mirror and grinned like a loon.

I just rolled my eyes and sat down in a chair, pretending to read a magazine, and listened.

Every student and teacher got to meet him one on one with Timmy and Laura! It took almost all day!

Oh, so Laura was there. Nice. Why don't they just get married?

I hear Ms. Clark even slipped him her phone number! I wonder if he'll call! She's so pretty. He looked interested!

That was it. I groaned and maybe glared a little at the mouthy secretary. Ms. Clark is barely twenty-two and gives everyone her number. She's also his type.

Whatever.

I flounced off from the Cut 'N' Curl, part of me . . . annoyed that he hasn't tried to find me.

Is that crazy?

But he was in Daisy and didn't even come by the library. It's right across from the church! If he was so gung ho about me, then why not try harder? Where's that competitive nature of his?

But . . .

It's over between the football player and me.

I wadded up that NDA and *almost* tossed it in his face.

I walked out.

And he didn't follow.

Right.

Aunt Clara appears like magic next to Preston and Giselle, her eyes darting to the library windows, but the windows are tinted for the sun, and anyone looking in can't see me and Topher.

Because if they could see our dagger eyes, they'd run.

"They'll be here in a minute." I head to the front desk and position myself behind it. Thankfully, it's noon, and the place is quiet, with only a few patrons here—some at tables, some at the computers for the free internet. I pat down my hair, tamed and up in a french twist. I fix my glasses and reapply my red lipstick quickly, squaring my shoulders.

The three of them walk in, gazing around at the space. It's an old building, but it's beautiful, completely renovated since I took over—pristine, shiny tile flooring and new crisp-white shelves. The walls are a cool gray, the artwork from talented students at the high school, drawings of historic buildings in Daisy. Even the church is on the wall. To the right is a carpeted kids' area, complete with toys, puzzles, and puppets for story time.

Giselle's eyes glance over everything, but I doubt she really sees it. Her brain doesn't work that way. She's all about facts and equations.

Preston meets my gaze, his brown eyes searching my face, and I . . . I feel absolutely nothing.

He takes in Topher's glare, pauses, and walks over to a shelf and pretends to look at the audiobooks. Pussy.

"Can we talk?" Giselle asks, an uneasy smile on her face as she reaches the desk. She's wearing cream slacks and a soft blue blouse. If I squint a little, she's almost Mama.

"Sure," I say brightly. "I've been waiting to see that ring! It's all everyone is talking about!"

I can do this!

Aunt Clara comes around the desk like she does it every day—she doesn't—and aligns herself next to me. Giselle grimaces, moving her eyes from me to Clara.

"Alone?" Giselle asks.

Aunt Clara frowns.

"It's fine," I tell Aunt Clara, still smiling. "Giselle and I have barely had a minute alone since she got back and started dating Preston! Why, I can't wait to hear how things are. Weddings are so exciting!"

I mean the words to be as real as possible, but when she winces, I know I struck a nerve. Maybe I need to tone down the peppiness.

Aunt Clara pats me on the arm. "I'll go check out the romance. Got any hot-vampire books? I want full-on sex scenes."

I nod. "Sure do. J. R. Ward. Read the whole collection. You'll love it."

She gives me a final look and heads to the shelves.

Giselle stands stiffly, looking uncomfortable. "Elena. I'm sorry."

Plain and simple.

It's what I expected.

She's a direct person.

"For what? Stealing my boyfriend or the engagement?"

Her face flushes. "I know we haven't really talked about everything, and thank you for never telling Mama that. I didn't tell her about seeing you with that football player. I keep secrets, too, Elena."

I recall the day when I caught them kissing in his office. It was mid-July and scorching hot when I walked from the library to his office on my lunch break. My head churned with how our relationship was floundering. Between Topher living with me and the lingerie—things weren't right between us.

I expected to find him behind his desk, working, excited to see me bringing his favorite club sandwich from the Piggly Wiggly deli, only she was in his arms. My first reaction was shock, and I gaped at them in disbelief. Then hurt slammed into me. Then anger roared to the surface, and I yelled at them and slammed down his food, splattering ham and cheese and tomato all over his desk, and stormed out. I marched right over to the Cut 'N' Curl, fists curled, ready to tell my family what they'd done, *especially* Mama. I fumed with glee, picturing Giselle falling off her pedestal.

I got all the way to the doors of the beauty shop and stopped.

I pictured Mama's crestfallen face, how angry she'd be with Giselle. Part of me relished the idea, but I paused, battling with emotions, thinking hard about how their betrayal might change our family forever. My daddy died way too soon in a car accident, and even Nana's husband died in his forties from a heart attack. For years the women in the Riley family have stuck together, carved out a life, the Daisy Lady

Gang. Although Giselle always rolled her eyes when Aunt Clara called us that, deep down, she was part of our group. Did I want to rip that apart? Did I want Mama upset? Mama might have gotten over it after a while, but Aunt Clara never would have. She's closer to me than anyone.

Family is all I have, really. It's been entrenched inside me since I was little. It's why after Nana died, I stayed in Daisy. Christmases at Nana's, Mama's meddling, Aunt Clara's love life. All those memories swirled in my head. I didn't want to break us up or cause a rip in the fabric of our lives—and that kiss was definitely a tear.

I didn't want it to ruin everything we'd had for years—over a stupid man.

So I composed myself and walked in and announced that I'd broken up with Preston, and it was over. I made sure all the old ladies heard. Then I texted Preston and Giselle and told them to do whatever the heck they wanted. I used a few curse words.

Now, Mama believes Giselle picked up right where I left off. She didn't like it at first, always sending me anxious looks at Sunday lunches, but I played it off as best I could.

"Let's see this ring," I say, leaning over the counter, shoving books out of the way.

Giselle moves stiffly, placing her long elegant fingers on the desk.

"Wow. Princess cut. A full carat?" I ask, inspecting it like it's a bug. Not my taste. I like emeralds or rubies. Color.

"Yes. I—I didn't know he was going to propose, or I would have told you first, Elena."

"Uh-huh. I've been busy this week. Sorry I haven't gotten back with either of you."

She swallows, her face tight. "I never wanted to hurt you . . ."

"Yet you kissed him anyway." I smile.

She closes her eyes briefly. "Yes. I didn't mean to. *I didn't.*" Her throat moves, her voice cracking just a little, and I cock my head, not used to emotion from her. I'm the emotional one. That's my thing.

She's the cold one. "You walked in on something I didn't plan to even happen."

A lone tear falls down her cheek, and I blink. This is *not* like her at all.

"Then why did you do it?" I ask curtly.

We should have had a heart-to-heart months ago, but she's been busy, living in Nashville since she got back, studying at Vandy, while I've just buried my head in the sand and sewn my heart out.

"I swear, that was the first time in his office. He asked me to stop by to talk about your birthday in August. I . . . I . . . don't know what happened. He just . . . kissed me . . . and . . ." She blows out a breath, hands wiping at her cheeks. I grab a box of tissues and hand one to her. She takes it and dabs at her eyes. "Do you have any idea how hard it was growing up in your shadow? How the whole world gravitated to you when you walked in the room? Funny, sweet Elena with all the creativity."

I sputter. "What on earth are you talking about? You're the pretty one. You're getting your PhD at twenty-three. I couldn't even do medical school."

She shakes her head at me. "You burn bright, Elena. Nana saw it. She loved you the most. I'd see it on her face when she showed you how to sew, when she taught you how to drive, when she gushed over your adventures in New York." She pauses. "She left *you* her house! You have all her things: the clothes, her little knickknacks, *the whiskey*, the beautiful staircase we used to play on, the sofa where we took naps, the swing outside on the tree . . ." She bites her lip. "Even Aunt Clara. You're so close to her."

Oh.

Nana left me her house. Mama and Aunt Clara got shared ownership of the Cut 'N' Curl as well as monetary gifts. Giselle was bequeathed farmland in Daisy.

"I am the oldest, Giselle. And that land is worth a lot of money. Close to Nashville, beautiful hills. It appraised at two hundred grand. I'm sure it will only increase."

"It's not about the money. You got the house because Nana wanted you to have it. She loved you more." I hear the jealousy in her tone, and I start. She never acted like she cared at the reading of the will.

She sniffs. "I didn't want to cause any rifts, so I never said anything."

Ah, and that's where we're alike. Peacemakers.

Only we've been avoiding a real conversation for months.

And maybe Nana did love me more. I don't know. She did gravitate toward me—and me to her. Two peas in a pod.

"You never wanted to learn to sew. Daddy taught you how to drive." I pause, feeling silly for trying to contradict her feelings. People feel how they feel. You can't change that. I sigh. "You're welcome to any of her things, Giselle. I never meant for you to not have a personal item." I glance over at Preston, who's out of earshot. "Are you saying you were interested in Preston because you were . . . jealous?" There's always been that little competition between us. While I came in second at the county spelling bee in middle school, she won her year three years later. While I got a partial scholarship to NYU, she got a full ride to the University of Memphis.

NYU is much more prestigious, a little voice whispers.

She frowns. "You say you didn't go to medical school, but you could have if you'd wanted to, but you chose what you love. You always stand up for what you believe in. You're . . . brave."

No, I'm not. I think about my lingerie.

"And I know about your lingerie."

My eyes fly up to hers. "Preston. Asshole. You better keep your trap shut."

She huffs out a laugh. "Of course I won't tell."

"Good. 'Cause I might have to pull all that pretty blonde hair out."

I might be serious.

She smirks. "There it is. Fire. And here's the thing; if you'd *really* cared about Preston, you would have told Mama the truth, and you would have confronted me months ago! Do you know how many times I waited for you to snap at Sunday lunch? But you *never* did. Because you didn't really love him."

"And you do?"

She nods. "From the moment we met, I knew there was something there. I tried to ignore it, but he kept texting me, and I didn't . . . know how to handle it."

Instant attraction—at my own house. It stings.

She must read my face. I can't hide anything. "It wasn't about taking what was yours, Elena. I hate that he and I happened like that. I do, so much. It's going to haunt me forever. If you hadn't sent that text to us, I never would have dated him, you know. I would have walked away."

Maybe. But he and I were already ruined after that kiss.

"I found a hot one, Elena!" It's Aunt Clara, who's been hovering near us, yet she's managed to grab a romance book.

I straighten up from the desk as she approaches, waving it in the air. "I'll take it. Just read a hot scene. Whew." She fans herself, eyes on mine. *You okay?* they ask.

I don't know. A sister's betrayal is hard. And it wasn't even needed. Preston should have broken up with me first. They did things in the wrong freaking order.

Life is messy, love especially. I hear Nana in my head, but I'm not sure my pride is ready to listen. It still *hurts* that I trusted both of them.

Preston approaches the desk, probably seeing that we're winding down our conversation. He gives me a once-over, lingering for half a second on my shirt, and I bristle. It does have little hearts all over it and is quite cute with the red velvet collar, but he better keep his eyes off my breasts.

He drops his gaze immediately and takes Giselle's hand, lacing it with his.

"Everything good?" he asks us.

I smirk, recalling his full set of pajamas, average build, and mediocre penis size. His inability to find my clit!

"Did you ask her about . . . you know . . . ," Preston says to Giselle, giving her a nudge.

"What?" I say.

Giselle inhales a deep breath, her eyes regretful as she flicks her gaze at Preston. "I really don't think that's a good idea."

"I do," he mutters. "It's perfect."

Aunt Clara slams her book down on the counter. "Y'all might as well spit it out. We ain't got all day. I have hair to cut."

Giselle closes her eyes.

I frown at Preston. "Ask me what?"

He frowns back. "Your mama suggested we might have the engagement party at your house. It's the biggest house in town, and the community center is booked, and the church has renovations, although we'd want alcohol there, so that's really not an option. I have a huge family in Oxford, and Giselle has her friends from Memphis, and well, *I* think your house would be perfect."

He is such a dick!

I glance at Giselle, and her face has reddened. She says, "You know how Mama is. Once she gets an idea—"

"Yeah, I know." I can't identify what emotion ripples through me, but I power through it. I put on a smile. "*My* house is perfect! Let's do it!"

Giselle blinks, and Preston tosses an arm around her. "See. It's fine. Told you. Elena is the best."

The best? Ha.

Giselle waffles; I can tell by the way she's wringing her hands, her gaze trying to hold mine.

I stare down at the books on the desk instead.

And they mumble a few more words, apologizing for something, but I'm barely listening, my head racing. A party. I'll need to get the shrubs trimmed, have the rugs and curtains cleaned . . .

Aunt Clara whisks them out the door, and Topher is next to me, arm around my shoulders.

"You heard?" I saw him darting by periodically.

He nods, face grim as he watches them get in the Lexus and drive away. He gives me a squeeze. "You know you don't have to host a party for them, Elena. Not really. They could do it in Nashville somewhere."

"No, I do. I really do. I have the prettiest house in town, and it's a sister's duty to help. She did spend time there. It has special memories. Daisy is her hometown."

"You are too kind. Also, he's an ass. He was totally checking you out."

I shrug. "It's the boobs. Guys can't help it."

"Elle, honey, it's *you*. I wish you could see you how everyone else does. Fucking Preston. I hope Giselle knows he's got a roving eye." He pauses. "I honestly think you intimidated him. He never liked me living with you."

I wince. "I never said that."

"I could tell. Dirty looks and all."

"He's going to be her husband, so let's focus on the positive. He's . . ." I stop, not able to think of one nice attribute.

"Well, we know he was a horrible lay."

I laugh.

"And he never liked Hog from Hell," he adds. "Didn't Romeo crap in his shoes once?"

Yep.

"He never put the toilet paper back on when he finished a roll!"

I nod.

"And his nose hairs need to be clipped."

I snort. "You should have seen his toenails. Gross."

Topher stares down at me. "Are you terribly upset? Usually I can tell, but not today."

I let out a long sigh and give him a nod. I expected the tears to come when I first saw them walking in, but they never did.

"You know, I talked to Greg."

"Yeah?" I ask.

He nods. "He really wants to meet you."

"Uh-huh. We know how my last blind date turned out."

"I'm serious. I showed him that picture of us at Halloween—you know the one, where you dressed up as the tart and I was the priest? He was super into it." He waggles his eyebrows. "Just sayin' . . . he likes your kind of sexy."

I pick up a book and run it through the scanner. "Nope. Between Preston and Jack, this girl is *done* with men."

Chapter 19

Elena

The following Monday evening after work, Topher and I walk into the community center after dinner. Just a block from my house—like most things in town—it's on Main Street. It used to be the old elementary school until the new one came along several years ago. The center holds bingo nights and chess clubs in the cafeteria, ballet and salsa dancing are taught in the classrooms, and plays are in the gymnasium.

There's a crowd of people, maybe thirty, when we stroll in, some sitting in chairs, some on the stage already working on the backdrop and blocking, while others are congregated in a huddle, reading the back wall. The list of who made the auditions.

"Well, my audition sucked," I say to Topher as we look around. They held them last Friday night—after my debacle with Giselle and Preston.

Laura, our director, clipboard in hand, stands front and center near the stage, congratulating the actors. The curtains that frame the stage are a tattered black velvet, draping softly in thick folds. **Daisy Elementary School** is scripted on top of the concrete wall, and two roaring lions stand sentinel on either side.

Timmy is next to Laura, beaming. He throws a wave and runs across the gym floor, shoes squeaking on the hardwood, legs pumping. I guess his ankle is better.

"Ms. Riley, Ms. Riley, you got Juliet!"

He wraps his good arm around my waist.

I laugh down at him. "Well, actually, I don't think anyone else tried out for that role."

He pushes up his black goggle glasses. "You're perfect for it, and guess what?"

"What?"

He jumps up and down, like he might pop. "I've kept it a secret for a week, but did you notice that no one auditioned for Romeo?"

"Oh, I hadn't noticed." It was a hectic evening with people coming and going. I read some lines and then left.

"Guess who it is!"

Unease trickles over me. Who's the one person Timmy would be this excited about? No, no . . .

"Jack Hawke!" Timmy exclaims with a happy squeal. "He's going to be Romeo! I've been dying to tell everyone, and now I finally can! What do you think about that? Isn't it awesome?"

"Awesome," I breathe.

I look over at Topher. "Did you know?"

"I may hang out at the Cut 'N' Curl, but I don't know *everything* in this town. That one slipped by me and the beauty shop. But it's great for our theater program. Maybe we can use the money to do some improvements. We need a new spotlight and microphones."

Timmy runs in circles around us. "It was a big secret! He—he kind of wanted to just help out Mom and be an assistant, but that is just silly. I told him how much it would mean if he had a real part. A hero's part. Jack needs to be a hero. I asked real nice and everything."

He begged. I'd bet my house on it.

Timmy stops and looks behind me. "And there he is!"

He dashes off without another word, and I pivot, heart flying in my chest, butterflies fluttering.

Jack stalks in the gym like he owns the place. Wearing jeans and a tight black-and-gold Daisy Lions long-sleeved shirt, he pauses, nearly stumbling, when he sees me.

Our eyes cling.

I drop my gaze.

Dammit.

He's still amazingly hot.

I sneak another glance from behind Topher's shoulder. Jack's face has that scruffy look, and maybe those are dark circles under his eyes, but it's dim in the gym. We need new overhead lights too. Half of them work, half don't.

"Finer than frog hair," Topher murmurs with awe in his voice.

"Traitor," I mutter.

"And those eyes. They glitter like topaz. No wonder you rode that stallion."

I elbow him hard.

He grunts. "Sorry. I hate him—for you. I'm team Elle all the way."

Unhappiness at those words washes over me. "No, don't hate him. Too many people do, and he . . . he doesn't deserve it." I think about that story he told me about his scar. How hard it must have been to have lost his mom and then take the life of another person. I can't imagine the violence of it, the anguish, the aftermath that came with it. I grew up with stability and so much love—he didn't.

Topher puts an arm around me, watching my face. "Regrets, Elle?"

Yeah. I wish I kissed him one more time—one of those breathy make-out kisses he does so well—so I could play it back in my head for the next few years.

"No. He stuck to his guns. And I did too."

"Hmm."

I shoot him a look. "I have principles. He reduced sex to a professional transaction. He wants a regular hookup without giving anything of himself. I can't do that. I'd be the one crying when he got tired of me."

"Nobody gets tired of you."

I lean on him, emotion clogging my throat. "Topher, the men I fall for always leave." I dart a look at him. "Not that I fell for him or anything."

"Mohawk has entered," Topher adds as we see Devon come in the door behind Jack. He's wearing a black shirt with a skull on it, a studded belt, and dark jeans.

Realization dawns, the enormity landing hard on my chest now that the shock has worn off. "I'm going to be seeing a lot of Jack for the next few weeks."

"Yeppers. Close proximity. Kissing bits. Lovemaking scenes. Death scenes. Crying. Lot of star-crossed-lovers romantic shit."

"This is going to be hell," I mutter as both men stalk toward us.

"Feels like fate to me," he murmurs. "I mean, have you actually thought about the odds of you meeting him at his restaurant, then the club, *plus* the Timmy connection? Destiny is pushing you together."

I sigh. "Destiny is a bitch. I want to slap her. You need to lay off the romance novels, Topher."

Devon jogs over to me, outpacing Jack, who is hanging back to talk to Timmy.

He runs a glance over my Chucks, high ponytail, leggings, and baggy NYU sweatshirt. "We meet again, pretty girl. I sure have missed you. When are you going to come back to my club? VIP is always open for you."

I adjust my white glasses and smile. He was sweet to me at the club, and he totally reminds me of Topher, only straight.

"Oh, shut up, and give me a hug," I say, and he grins and swings me around. "Guess I still owe you for that bet."

"You can make it up to me some other way soon." He winks.

"I'll thump you." I punch him on the shoulder, and he rubs it like it hurt, grinning.

After I introduce him to Topher, they shake hands briskly. "Nice to meet you," Devon says. "I play with Jack. Wide receiver. I'm *sure* you've heard of me."

I roll my eyes.

"Oh, I know who you are. This one doesn't watch TV"—Topher points at me—"but I catch a game now and then."

Jack approaches us, and I can't help but eat him up, the way he moves, the grace of his body.

He stops just outside our little circle, and for a moment, I see uncertainty on his face.

Devon turns to him. "Dude. Found your Juliet. Yeah, Timmy told us." He flashes me a smile. "Guess you know who Romeo is. My number one man is going to rock this play." He slaps Jack on the back, getting a grimace in return.

Jack looks at me, those golden eyes holding mine until I can't look away. I feel pinned by the intensity of them, caught and entranced.

I convinced myself we were done, and now here he is, making me feel things I shouldn't. Damn those butterflies. I squash them down.

"Elena. How are you?"

The rumble of that cool, husky tone slides over me. I take a deep breath.

He's being polite. A little standoffish.

Fine, that's how we'll play this.

"Super. You?"

He smiles faintly. "Super."

He takes in the room, unease on his features. "What do we do now?"

Topher points to the front of the stage. "You missed auditions, but this is where the magic happens. We're doing a modern version of

Romeo and Juliet. More Baz Luhrmann than old-school Shakespeare, gangsters with guns and black outfits. We won't get to wear tights, and I'm a little disappointed."

Devon laughs. "I'd love to see you in tights, Jack."

Jack doesn't smile. "Yeah. Cool. Love that movie. How many people come to this thing?"

"About two hundred. Not a big crowd, but interest is growing. With you here, I imagine it will be covered up with people. Thanks for volunteering." Topher grins. "Although if I know Timmy, he probably weaseled you into it."

Jack nods, frowning. Something about him is off.

What part of Topher's words bothered him?

It isn't Timmy, because I saw how Jack treats him, with kid gloves and a genuine, if rather bemused, smile on his face.

Is it the idea of a huge crowd of people from Daisy being here to watch him?

But that doesn't make sense. According to Birdie Wheeler, half the town is already in love with him.

Also, he plays football in front of thousands of people.

Millions watch on TV.

Oh . . . maybe it's—

"Do you like Shakespeare?" I blurt.

He swivels his head back to me, eyes cool. "English major. Got my degree, even though I could have gone to the draft early. My mom always wanted me to get a degree because she never did." He shrugs nonchalantly, but I sense deep emotion in that movement. "I did it for her."

English major. And he graduated for his mom.

"Well, how interesting," Topher says with a smirk. "Elena is also an English major. She got the library job without a library science degree."

"I did apply at the high school for a teaching position, but there wasn't one available. I love the library. It worked out for the best."

Jack raises an eyebrow. "What was your specialty? British lit for me."

I chew on my lips, and his eyes follow my movement. "Um, American is my favorite."

"Right, how could I forget? Mark Twain. 'Go to heaven for the climate, hell for the company.'"

My lit-loving heart pounds. "'They did not know it was impossible, so they did it.'"

"Nice. How about, 'If a man could be crossed with a cat, it would improve the man, but deteriorate the cat.'"

I smirk. "Speaking of, I still have a cat if you want him, but he's more of an outside tom now. He runs around the whole neighborhood." I rack my brain for another quote. "I got one: 'The two most important days in your life are the day you were born and the day you find out why.'"

He mulls, rubbing his jaw. "How about 'Don't wait. The time will never be just right.'"

"Or 'Any emotion, if sincere, is involuntary.' I love that one." I grin, then remember I'm mad at him.

He huffs out a laugh. "Is this some kind of face-off where we see who knows the most Mark Twain quotes?"

"I can go all night," I say.

"Hmm," he murmurs, his lip curling. "Mark Twain battle. I sense a contest."

"We should do it," I say.

"I dare you to try."

"Is that a challenge?" I tuck my hands inside my pockets. They tremble. It's *him*. I haven't been able to get him out of my mind since the penthouse, wondering how he is.

If he's as lonely as I am.

"Name the time and place, Elena."

I suck in a sharp breath at the way he's looking at me, those eyes warming.

And shit, he has no right to say my name like that, as if he's savoring it.

My eyes stare at his lips, the fullness, the softness mixed with strength—

I look around and realize Topher and Devon are looking at us strangely.

"What?" I say.

"Nothing," Devon murmurs.

"Just awed by y'all's memorization abilities," Topher says. He looks at Jack. "Are you familiar with *Romeo and Juliet*?"

Jack clears his throat. "Yeah, I've been refreshing myself all week."

I picture him laid up in his bed, sans shirt, turning the pages of the play. Maybe reading glasses on his face. My face feels hot.

This is *really* going to be a long month.

"Hey, guys," comes a familiar voice behind me, and I start and turn, my eyes widening at the sight of my sister.

"Giselle? Are *you* doing the play?"

She dips her head and nods. I haven't seen her since the library. Mama cooked lunch on Sunday, but she said she wasn't feeling well and didn't come.

Wearing a tweed jacket, dressy slacks, and heels, she walks over to us. I guess she came straight from her classes at Vandy. "Mama said Laura mentioned no one signed up to play the role of nurse, and well, I thought I might give it a go. You don't mind, do you?"

I want to frown but put a smile on. "Of course not."

But . . .

She's never shown one iota of interest in the fine arts.

I flick my gaze behind her. "Preston here?"

"No." She grimaces. "He hates this stuff."

Right. He never came to any of my plays.

"Well, welcome to the crazy." I do what any good sister would. I motion her to join our circle, introducing her to Devon and Jack.

She shakes hands with them and grows quiet, her finger twitching at the seams of her jacket.

Jack frowns, a pucker on his forehead as he takes her in, then turns back to me, a question in his eyes. I give him a nod and let him connect the dots. *Yeah, she's the one who's with my ex.*

Devon smiles at us, appreciation in his gaze. "You two look nothing alike."

"Elena's the fun one," Giselle murmurs.

"And you're the smart one," I add.

She pushes up her glasses. "Well, you're the one everyone adores."

I blow out a breath. What is up with her? I push it aside.

"She's recently engaged," I say. It's a non sequitur, but her ring is right there, glittering up at us.

Jack starts, looking at Giselle's hand, then giving me a lingering look that I avoid.

"Congratulations," Devon says with a smile. I don't think he ever stops smiling. "Shame. I was hoping Elena knew some single ladies."

"Elena knows everyone in town. I'm sure she can hook you up." There's a wistful tone in her voice, and I frown, about to disagree, but I realize she's right. I do know everyone. Even though I moved away, as soon as I came back, I fell right into getting reacquainted with everyone in Daisy, either through the library or the community center.

I look at Devon and Jack. "We're having the engagement party at my house for Giselle and her fiancé in a few weeks. You guys should come." I groan inwardly. Why did I say that?

Jack starts and glances at Giselle. "Is that so?"

She nods. "Yes. Please come. I'd enjoy getting to know Elena's friends."

I shouldn't have even invited them. It's not *my* party. I'm just hosting it.

"My schedule is tight," Jack says, shrugging.

That means no.

Devon laughs. "I'll be there. I'm digging this town. What should I bring? Wine? Whiskey? Beer? What's your favorite, Elena?"

I smile, my face burning at Jack's odd behavior. I need some distance from him, from his coolness, like now, but I hang tough. "Just you and a smile."

"Bells on, babe. So tell me about the single girls in Daisy."

I nod. "There's a teacher at the elementary school, Ms. Clark. Twenty-two. Long blonde hair. Drives a red convertible Mustang. Might be your style. She auditioned. I'm sure she's here somewhere. Everyone gets a part if they want it."

I dart my eyes around the gym until I find the teacher. She's talking to a group, but her eyes are focused on Jack like a laser beam. I picture her dashing up to Jack and fawning all over him like those girls at the VIP room.

Devon slides in closer. "Oh, tell me more. Does she have a ruler she can pop me with?"

"Ask Jack," I say, grimacing, even though I try *not* to. "He got her phone number when he visited the school. Heard from Birdie Walker he was very interested."

Devon sends Jack a hard glance. "Did you now?"

"She pressed it in my hands." Jack glares at me.

He should have ripped it into shreds!

Elena. Stop. He isn't yours.

Tell that to my body.

Annoyance rises, with him for being Romeo to my Juliet, with myself for daydreaming about him all week, and finally with Giselle for being part of something that's always been *mine*.

"You should totally call her," I snap.

Jack's nose flares, his eyes glittering. "I will. Thanks."

"She's right up your alley."

"Really. Glad you know what I like."

"VIP-room perfection," I say curtly.

A muscle pops in Jack's jaw. "Elena . . . ," he starts but stops, his face like granite.

We stare at each other, and the air around us feels tight.

Giselle frowns, looking from me to Jack. "Uh, is everything okay?"

"Fine," I scoff.

Topher clears his throat. "Nice evening out. Wonder if it will rain?"

I could throw out a weatherman comment, but I bite my tongue and force myself to keep my lips zipped.

How is he able to bring out this childish side of me?

I'm acting like a jealous girlfriend—and that is not what I am!

But ever since I heard about Ms. Clark at the beauty shop, it's been stewing.

And he just said he'd call her.

And obviously, he probably hasn't even thought about me again.

A long exhalation leaves Jack's chest, and he murmurs that he wants to go talk to Laura. He turns and leaves, his back stiff and tense.

"Well, that went great," I mutter.

Later, after Laura has given some brief instructions about rehearsal dates and times and introduced everyone, the cast settles in chairs at a long table. Read-through time.

Jack sits next to me, the heat of his leg close to mine. I scoot over to give him more space.

He shook every hand in the place before we sat down. A couple of people asked for autographs, and he signed their playbooks. I tried to not watch him, but it feels impossible. He's the kind of man people stare at. He's earnest and kind when he talks to them and not at all cocky. Once or twice, though, I caught a red flush on his cheeks when people got close to him, and it makes me wonder . . .

Patrick sits on the other side of me, playing Tybalt, Juliet's cousin. Topher sits directly across from me, playing the sparkling Mercutio. Giselle occupies a spot at the end of the table, head down, glasses perched on her nose as she thumbs through the playbook. Ms. Clark plays the prince, although in this case, since the play has a majority of male roles, it's princess. Suits her, I think, watching as she reapplies her lipstick as she sits directly across from Jack. She keeps reaching over the table and touching his arm, commenting how much she loves football and the Tigers.

Please.

Control yourself, Elena.

Devon is at the back of the gym, shooting hoops with Timmy.

"Let's start and see how far we get tonight with a read through," Laura announces with a smile. "Scene one starts with Sampson and Gregory from the house of Capulet. It's fun and snappy. Tybalt enters, and he's ready for a fight."

Patrick laughs. "I'll try to be angry. We could end the play early if I just tell them about loving your neighbor and all."

Laura raises her head and smiles, her eyes drifting over his face. "You'll be great, Patrick."

I arch my brow.

Well.

Laura continues, clearing her throat. "Then Romeo comes in, lamenting his love for Rosaline. Scene two brings Paris and Capulet discussing Juliet's marriage. Next, Romeo and company show up at the masquerade—and it's love at first sight! The last scene in act one is when Romeo kisses Juliet. We'll take a break after that and see if there are any questions."

Patrick nudges me and leans in and whispers, "Nice. You and Jack are going to be great."

"So awesome." My voice is flat.

He raises an eyebrow, voice low. "What? I could have sworn I felt sparks at church. He walked in, and well, you sort of melted."

Melted? I blink at the preacher. "Don't know what you mean."

He chuckles. "Cynthia will be devastated we didn't work out."

I wince. "Sorry if she tried to throw us together. Pretty sure she had the wedding all planned."

He shrugs. "Hard to date a preacher. You have to memorize the entire Bible before the first date."

I laugh. "You're going to be great for this town." I nudge my head toward Laura. "Sparks?"

Patrick blushes a deep red.

Jack leans in on the other side of me, his leg pressed against mine now. "Can you stop flirting with the preacher? I can't hear Laura."

I stiffen in my seat and hiss at him, "I was not flirting."

I expect him to move back to his bubble, but he doesn't, that taut muscled leg not moving one inch.

Fine. I'm not moving either.

We begin the read, and I forget about him, getting lost in the words and language.

Jack/Romeo reads his first line, and I come back to reality.

His voice is beautiful, deep, and husky yet lacks his usual confident tone.

I'm not sure if anyone else even notices, but I do. I've heard him talk, the cadence of his syllables, his mouth on my skin . . .

I dart my gaze over to him. Is he okay?

"A little louder," Laura says.

He nods and reads louder. It's perfect, the emotional inflection spot on for a man who is experiencing unrequited love. For a moment, dread filled me as I wondered if he was a bad actor, but he isn't at all.

But . . .

I glance down, and his hands are clenched under the table.

I frown, taking in his expression without being too obvious. The furrowed brow, the concentration on his face.

Realization hits. He . . . he doesn't like this. Even though he's *flawless* in his execution. Is he this unhappy about me being here? Oh. I deflate a little. Maybe he never wanted to see me again, and tonight was a shock.

Minutes pass, and we get to the last scene in act one, where Romeo and I meet and kiss.

I can't look at him as we pause for the kiss, which we don't do—obviously. This is just a read through.

Keeping my eyes down on my playbook, I say, "Then have my lips the sin that they have took."

Jack replies, "Sin from my lips? O trespass sweetly urg'd! Give me my sin again."

We pause to allow for the second kiss, our heads rising up to stare at each other. His face is a mask.

"You kiss by the book," I say to him, looking right into those amber eyes. I hate it when my voice trembles.

The nurse interrupts Romeo and Juliet, Giselle's voice saying her lines, and I clear my throat and look down at the table.

It's clear as day that this play is going to *kill me*.

Chapter 20

JACK

I heave out a long sigh as we wrap up our read through, rolling my shoulders and my neck as I stand. My entire body is tight and wired, yet exhaustion ripples over me, as if I've come off the field after being sacked. I shake it off. Literally. I do a few stretches with my arms and shoulders, mentally shoving down the stillness of the past three hours.

I'm acutely aware of Elena as she stands, gathering up her things. I watch as she puts her purse crossbody-style over her shoulder, the motion delicate and fine, graceful. She's barely showing any skin at all, just the creamy part of her wrists and hands. Swallowing, I stare at them—

Dammit.

I'm bad off, turned on by a *wrist*. My eyes rove over the soft curve of her neck, the auburn hair that's up and trailing over one shoulder—

"Hey, Jack. I just want to thank you again for visiting our school," comes the high, squeaky voice from the girl who's appeared next to me. Blonde. Young. Lots of jewelry and makeup. A short dress. Ms. Clark from the elementary school, whom I barely recalled until Elena reminded me. "I can't believe you're doing the play. The entire town appreciates you. It's so sweet."

Sweet?

It's hell. I almost stumbled when I sat down at that table to read. But I did it, hands tight, my body pumped with adrenaline. Admittedly, it wasn't as bad as a group of reporters shooting questions at me, but still, it makes me squirm knowing that I have to speak in front of people I don't know.

"You're welcome," I say politely, then move to walk around her, my gaze on Elena, who's already walking away. She chats with Topher briefly before striding toward the exit. He appears to be staying behind to help with props.

"There's a little tavern near here. Some of us are headed there. Would you like to join us?" Ms. Clark grabs my arm, and I stop and look down at her. She *is* pretty and willing, if that gleam in her eyes is anything to go by.

"No."

She bats long lashes. "Are you sure? It'll be fun. Dartboard, pool tables, great ambience."

"Positive."

She pouts, but I murmur goodbye and step around her, eyes on Elena.

I have to jog because she's already disappeared out the gym doors, her ass swaying.

"Elena!"

I catch up to her as she stomps down a dark hallway toward the exit. I don't know what I'm going to say, but . . .

She keeps on walking, face straight ahead. "Not going to have a drink with Ms. Clark?"

"Guess you heard. Sharp ears. Not interested in her." I tuck my hands in my jeans as we pass by silver lockers, some of them rusty and dented. "Did you go to school here?"

"Yes." Those pretty eyes find mine before looking away. "You said you'd call her."

I blow out a breath. Dammit. That was stupid, but she pushed me, and I pushed right back.

I take her hand, making her stop. An uncertain look crosses her face. "Jack. What do you want with me?"

I don't know.

And after she walked out of my penthouse, that should have been the end of us.

And I'm probably going to hurt her.

But . . .

I can't forget her—her face, those lips, the way she talks to me like I'm an average person, no judgments, no care about who I am.

I ask what's been on my mind since I heard the news. "Giselle and Preston are engaged. Are you okay?" My eyes study her face, looking for clues. "That must be hard for you."

Her shoulders dip. "She loves him. I'm not sure I ever did."

I rock back on my heels. "I see. Over him already?"

"Maybe Giselle did me a favor."

"Maybe your one-night stand erased him from your memory." I smirk at her, wanting to make her laugh—or something. I don't like this hardness from her, that expression of reserve she has on her face.

She pulls her hand out of mine and takes off walking again. I follow her.

A long breath comes from her. "Isn't Devon waiting on you?"

"We drove separate. He left earlier. He just came to snap some pics." I pause. "He knew I wanted to talk to you."

"You knew I'd be in the play?"

"Laura told me."

"You could have come by when you were in town last week," she says curtly.

I grow silent, feeling surprised. "Figured you might need a break from me. You left angry. Wasn't sure how you felt about seeing my face again."

"*Ms. Clark* was glad to see you."

I laugh. She wants me to react and be angry enough to walk away. "You're jealous of a teacher who gave me a number I didn't even ask for."

She sputters as she comes to a stop. "No!"

"Liar," I murmur. "You were sending death glares to poor Ms. Clark all night. If looks could kill . . ."

"I was not!"

Damn, I love getting her riled up. "You can't stand the idea of me calling her."

She puts her hands on her hips, which look damn good in her black leggings. She advances toward me, her fingers poking me in the chest, while I stare at her deep-red lips. "And you're jealous of Patrick."

"You wouldn't stop talking to him."

"About you!"

I chuckle, feeling elated. "Can't stop thinking about me, can you?"

I back up to a locker, and she follows me.

"You are so . . . cocky! It's a little maddening." She shakes her head, her expression changing.

"What's making you frown?"

Her teeth pull at her lower lip. "Jack, earlier . . . I couldn't help but notice that you seemed a little off when you came in and when we sat down to read. You did amazing. Your voice is beautiful—" She stops. "What was it? Are you that unhappy about being here? About being around me?"

Ah, she noticed. People rarely do. All they see is this face and talent and just assume I'm comfortable in my own skin. "I'm doing this for Timmy—and it looks good for my image. Lawrence insisted, and he isn't wrong. I need to push myself more. I didn't have to agree to play Romeo—especially when it's hard for me to be around people I don't know very well. But I did."

A dawning expression crosses her face. "You really are shy."

I grimace. "Told you I was. Most people just assume I'm rude."

"You are not rude! You were so nice to everyone here."

"I am a nice person."

"Right. But you play football in front of millions. You boss around football players and tell them what to do. Is that hard for you?"

I smile, seeing that she's inched in a little closer. Curious girl.

"But when I'm out on the field, I'm the warrior."

"But here, will you be able to do the play?"

I think back to the read through we did. "I was a little nervous, meeting new people, getting adjusted. Everyone here is down to earth, and no one is throwing a microphone in my face. Plus, you're here. It helps. Keeps my mind on other things." I don't even realize it's true until I say it.

Her head cocks. Another step closer. "So what you're saying is . . . you're kind of socially awkward."

"Yeah."

Her mouth opens. "But you're so . . ." Her voice trails off.

"What?"

"Stop fishing for compliments."

I laugh.

"Is this why you don't give interviews?"

I nod. "I've never been able to relax with them." I pause, feeling uneasy for a moment before brushing it off. "Not many people know that, Elena."

She takes my words in, her emotions easy to read on her face—mainly confusion.

"But you don't seem to have a hard time with women. Apparently, they flock to you."

"I've never had to work for it."

She glares at me. "Arrogant!"

I smirk. "It's the truth."

"But why on earth would you agree to be Romeo?"

"Well, as it happens, this town kind of loves me. Plus, you're here." I let those words settle around us, watching the flush that starts at her neck and works its way up to her face. Does she have any clue how I wrestled with the idea of doing this play? Yet as soon as Laura mentioned Elena would probably be Juliet . . .

Her tongue dabs at her lower lip.

I rest against the locker. "Hmm, I think you want me to kiss you right now."

Another step. Her chest rises.

"This feels like high school, and we're having a tiny tiff. I'm ready for the makeup part," I say, pulling her hair out of her ponytail, sighing when it falls around the curves of her face. "Take your glasses off, Elena."

She tucks them in her purse. Takes another step closer. "You're bossy. I don't know how any woman has ever put up with you."

"I don't either. I don't deserve a nice girl. Keep talking." Because with every word, she's almost in my arms.

She tilts her chin up, her scent sweet and soft and floral, and I suck in a breath at the full force of *her*, the way my heart twinges, shifting around in my chest.

"And I do not want to kiss you. It comes with a price. My dignity. I have a vibrator at home, all charged and ready to go—"

"Fuck that. You will *not* use a vibrator. Not when I'm right here," I growl. "Do you think about me when you use it?"

"No." Her color rises.

I chuckle. "How do you imagine it, Elena? You underneath me, pliant and willing, begging for more?"

"No!"

"Me behind you. That's it. You love that. That sound you make when I slide all the way inside. Been thinking about that a lot. Feels like a year ago when I had you."

"Stop talking dirty."

"I think it's you under my tongue, Elena. That's what I think about, the taste of you. You came like that in the kitchen with me on my knees. Did you like that? Me worshipping you?"

She breathes heavily. "Pfft. I barely remember it."

I count the white rays in her irises, the way they make her eyes shine.

"You're a terrible liar."

"You should stop."

"Make me," I grunt as she takes that final step, her sweatshirt pressed against me.

"I will, Jack. Don't test me."

"Elena, you can't get me out of your head."

"Someone needs to teach you a lesson in humility."

"Please do."

She touches my chest, and I groan. "Fuck, Elena. *Kiss me.* Because I'm dying here. I'm barely able to stand up—thank God for lockers—and all it took was your *fucking* wrist to get me hard—"

She stands on her tiptoes and takes my mouth, and I rumble out my victory, my hands landing on her ass like they were made for that spot, picking her up and switching us around until she's against the lockers. Her legs curl around my hips, her lips pressed against mine, her tongue battling mine without reserve, all fire and heat. Her hands knead my shoulders, digging and caressing, pulling, tugging, *wanting.*

"All it took was your stupid forearms in Milano's," she mutters in between kissing.

"Good goddamn thing you sat down," I mutter back, sucking on her neck.

"Good thing c-l-i-t-s are your specialty."

"Elena," I breathe. "So many tricks up my sleeve . . ." My lips trail along her cheek. "I want to show them all to you."

I kiss her again, deeply, paying attention to the fullness of her upper lip, nipping at it, loving that sweet spot near her ear that makes her shiver.

"What are we doing?" she breathes.

"Making out." I shove a hand in her hair, holding her head to the side, slanting my lips across her for a hard kiss, sucking on her tongue in a decadent, rhythmic way, like I'm fucking her.

"I'm not signing that stupid NDA," she says.

"I haven't brought it up." I kiss her again, my hips swiveling into her pelvis. She arches closer, her hands pulling on my shoulders.

"Are you wet for me, baby?" I murmur, my hand easing between us, brushing against her apex.

"Damn you."

I laugh, rubbing my thumb across her leggings, rotating against her mound.

She shudders, her hands in my hair now, tugging me closer for another kiss.

Voices and people walking out of the gym reach my ears, and I press my forehead against her. "We're out in the hall for anyone to see. Not a good idea."

She wiggles out of my arms, chest rising rapidly, and takes my hand. "Come on. I know every room in this place."

She takes off, dashing down the hall, and I jog after her. I don't know what I'm doing, because I swore to myself I'd leave her alone, that I'd stick to her decision, but . . .

She stops at the door on the right, letting out a gleeful sound when it's unlocked. She pulls me inside a darkened room, the only light the glow from the moon coming in from a window. I take in a big desk and a wall of mirrors with a long bar along the middle.

"Ballet room?" I ask as she turns to face me, hair everywhere where my hands were. Her mouth is swollen, red, and lush.

Fuck, fuck, fuck . . . what is she doing to me?

"Yep, but we aren't dancing. Welcome to my second-grade classroom. Take off your clothes, Jack. Let's make this quick."

Heat pierces me, sweet and excruciating at the need in her voice. With Sophia, sex was never like *this*. Consuming and fast, as in I-can't-wait-to-have-you kind of feeling. Football kept most of my attention; I never thought about Sophia unless she was right in front of me. Elena . . . I can't get her out of my mind . . .

"This will not be quick," I say.

She pulls her sweatshirt over her head, her red lace bra making me groan. She toes her shoes off and shoves them out of the way. Leggings disappear until I see the tiny red thong, the contrast of the color against her pale skin intoxicating.

I groan, my gaze all over her. "Are you sure?"

"I'm not thinking clearly, and I don't want to. And you being Romeo is driving me crazy! Maybe this is the only way to work you out of my system."

I frown, not liking that statement. But her wariness is my fault. Since the moment I walked in, we've been sparring, and I know it's my distrust that makes her scared.

She said she's team boyfriend.

And I am *not* a boyfriend. Not like she needs. I just . . . can't go there. My mother loved Harvey, and look what it got her. I thought I cared about Sophia and—

"Snap out of it, and stop staring at me. We have to hurry," she says, dashing to the door and checking the lock. She moves swiftly, uninhibited in her near nakedness, her curves lush and creamy.

I sweep paper, pencils, and books off the desk in one movement, my body in full-on let's-do-this mode. So what if I'm in public? So what if she hasn't signed the NDA? Take this and run with it—and right now. I don't care about anything but getting inside her.

And if she wants to work me out of her system, sign me up.

"You're still dressed, Jack. Fix it." She approaches me, her nipples beading under that lace.

I whip off my shirt, unzip my pants, and shove them off, fighting with my black sneakers. I kick them across the room.

"Commando," she breathes, looking at my hard cock.

I fist myself, giving my arousal a pump, watching her eyes widen, her hands twitching at her side.

"Me. You. Desk." I hold her hot gaze, afraid if we stop looking at each other, this tenuous bond might break.

Her chest rises as she takes me in, her breasts straining against the lace of her bra.

"Come to me, Elena." I'm panting at just the sight of her, already thinking of how I want to fuck her. And then again. And again.

She reaches the desk and drops to her knees.

"Elena," I groan. "I want you on that desk, bent over."

"And I want you in my mouth. We haven't done that."

Her hands wrap around my length and stroke. I hiss when she takes me in her mouth, her tongue sliding down, then back up, her lips puckering around my head.

"Am I doing it like you like it?" she murmurs.

"You are." I don't recognize my voice. Torn. Ragged. It's not that I was celibate for a year, but the fact that *her* lips are on *me*. I've been sucked off many times—in clubs, hotel rooms, locker rooms—but not one of them compares to her plump, sassy mouth on me.

I stumble back, my ass landing on the desk, my hands wrapped in her hair, guiding her down as far as she'll let me. I let out a string of curses when I feel the back of her throat, my head lowering, the muscles in my legs tightening as the urge to come zips over me.

"Elena! I'm going to . . ." I groan, reaching for control.

Her eyes find mine. "Don't ruin this for me. This is my first time. Say some of your lines."

I focus on Romeo, managing to sputter out a few. They make no sense. Some of them are her lines.

"That's terrible. Use more emotion, like you did when Romeo and Juliet kiss."

I close my eyes, remembering how she gazed at me during the read through. "Thinking about kissing you just makes it worse."

"Well, then think about football or whatever."

"Impossible," I gasp out, watching as she unclasps her bra and takes me again in her mouth, firm, perfect tits against my legs. I reach down to brush my thumb over her rosy nipple, her breasts cushioning me as she takes long drags.

"Elena, shit . . ."

Her big eyes stare up at me, her lips tight around me, and it's a submissive thing, that she's on her knees, but underneath I wonder if she knows that it isn't submissive at all. She's got all the fucking power with me, and I don't think she even knows how much I want her. I clench the edge of the desk. I needed this. *Her.* Especially after the anxiety from earlier. This, *her*, soothes everything inside me.

She slides me between her breasts, slick and warm, as I pump between her cleavage. Her head dips, and she takes me inside her warm mouth and hums against me, and I . . . I . . .

"In my mouth," she murmurs, like she's said this a thousand times, but my librarian has *never* said those words to a man, and it makes me shudder, my chest heaving, watching her suck me deep. *Mine.* Territorial alpha claws to the surface, and I come with a roar, eyes on her face, searching, imprinting this moment in my head.

Breathing heavily, she swallows all of me, her tongue laving my dick.

I look at her magnificence for as long as I can until I collapse back on the desk, panting, body shuddering.

"Pants. Condom. Get it."

I hear satisfaction in her voice as she stands. "You'll need a minute. I think I did very well. A-plus for me."

"I am not an old man yet. Get the condom, woman. My legs aren't working."

She laughs, shuffling sounds reaching me as she goes through my jeans.

I'm dizzy when I rise up. She tears at it with her teeth as she walks over to me.

She glances down at my arousal and laughs. "How can you be ready again?"

"It's you. And don't laugh. He's sensitive. He might get soft."

She laughs again, doubling over, and I chuckle, watching her, feeling comfortable and easy. Maybe this is what incredible sex is, when two people crave each other—and not just their bodies but their personalities.

"What's taking so long?" I ask, sitting up more. "You're wasting precious time."

She holds the condom package up to her face, squinting. "Crap!"

"Amateur. Give it to me."

She dashes over to her purse on the floor and slides on her glasses, her face horrified as she glares down at the wrapper. "Jack! I ripped it! There's a tiny hole in it. Do you have another one?"

"That one's been in my wallet forever." I stand, weaving a little, my legs still like jelly. "Do you have any at your house?"

She shakes her head. "No, tossed them a while back. Expired."

I rake my hands through my hair. "Is there a store here in town where I can buy them?" I'm going to die if I don't have her again.

Her eyes flare. "You can't just waltz in the Piggly Wiggly at nine at night and pick up a box of Trojan Magnums! Everyone knows your face. What if the cashier takes a pic?" She pauses. "How do you buy condoms?"

"Amazon. Fake name."

We study each other, eyes searching.

"I have plenty back at the penthouse."

"Of course you do."

I study the planes of her face, trying to read what she's thinking, but her hair hides her face.

She walks over to her bra and puts it back on. Next come her shirt and leggings.

Chucks are next.

Dammit! Why did I bring up the penthouse?

She picks up her purse and pushes up her glasses.

I grab my shirt and slide it on. I grab my pants and put them on. "Fine. I'm going to the Piggly Wiggly, and then we're going to your place. Don't they have those self-checkout things?"

She huffs out a laugh. "Have you ever used one?"

"No, but it can't be too hard."

"It can be a surprising pain in the ass. Self-check or not, everyone in town will know by tomorrow."

"I'll wear a hat. I have one in the car."

"Won't work. Your hotness is world known, apparently, by everyone but me."

We stand there for a few seconds, and it feels as if I should say something here.

Invite her to your real home, Jack.

But I can't.

I want to, I do, but how can I trust what I'm really feeling right now?

I don't even know what *this* is!

She watches my face, and I know what she sees—me retreating. Fortifying my castle walls. Digging a moat around it.

She inches closer to the door, her hands behind her back, probably on the doorknob.

With fumbling fingers, I button my pants. "Elena, don't go."

Why am *I* always saying that?

There's a long silence, the only sound our breathing in the quiet room.

"Elena, I didn't plan on this. I just wanted to . . . kiss you, and then I don't know. Let's go somewhere else."

A smile crosses her face, tinged with regret and wry acceptance. "I know exactly what this was. It was you walking in this gym, and me wanting you, and you wanting me. Just two people without commitments. Isn't that what you want, Jack?"

I close my eyes briefly. "Yes."

A long silence wraps around us as we stare at each other.

"That's what I thought." Her eyes drop to the floor, then rise up to meet mine. "See you at the next rehearsal." She scans the room, her gaze everywhere except on me. "Do you mind putting the desk back together?"

And then she's gone, opening the door and walking away from me.

I don't try to stop her.

Chapter 21

Jack

"The MRI isn't great. You need surgery, Jack. It's either that, or you're going to take a hit on that shoulder, and the damage to your tendons might be irreparable." Dr. Williams gives me a sympathetic glance, his hand holding my thick folder of records. He's the best orthopedic in the state, well known for treating superstar athletes, from tennis players to baseball greats.

I came in last week for some x-rays and the MRI. Since the episode at the church, I've had another spasm that hit me while I was working out at the stadium. I was lifting when it hit, nearly making me pass out with the pain. Thank God Aiden wasn't in the gym that day.

I exhale. "It isn't even a football injury."

He nods, taking a seat behind his desk and considering me. "Right. It's an old wound, but the way you use your body isn't like the average person. If you didn't play football, you might never have had any issues, but as it stands, your tendons are being pulled away from your bone. I can reattach them, no problem."

"Thank God."

"Don't get too excited. Have you had a particularly hard fall lately?"

I grimace, recalling the defender who yanked my face mask and slammed me down during the Super Bowl. The five interceptions that followed. "Super Bowl."

He nods. "I'm assuming you still want to keep playing?"

I feel dizzy and grip the edges of my chair. "Hell yes. I still have good years left, Doc. I'm twenty-eight!"

He taps a pen on his desk. "I'll be frank. I've done surgeries like this, and even when things go well, including rehab, some athletes never get back to full one hundred percent."

My heart drops. I know the stats on shoulder injuries for quarterbacks. Even for a college player, once news of a shoulder injury reaches the NFL teams, it affects their draft status, pushing them down in the ranks. Few teams want to take chances on a player with an injury. For a seasoned player like me, it could be less playtime, early retirement. Fuck that. "I'm not *most* athletes. I'm the best. I've been using massage, needling, cupping, everything for the past few years. I even pay out of my own pocket for treatment. And those guys you're talking about have the injury on their throwing arm. This is my left shoulder."

"True, true. I just want you to know what to expect. If you take a hard fall again, even after surgery, you might injure it again."

My stomach lurches. "Fine. Lay it out for me, then. What should I expect? Summer camp starts in June, and I want to be ready for it." I pause. "Shit. I'm doing this play for the next month."

"I saw that on ESPN. Nice touch."

"Yeah. The fans like it." Even though it makes me uncomfortable as hell, my image has improved slightly. I haven't gotten any glares when I take my table at Milano's lately. But fans are fickle. And if they knew I had a shoulder injury. Damn. They'd be ready for Coach to trade me in a heartbeat. They'd fall in love with Aiden. He's poised and ready . . .

He continues. "Let's pencil you in for early April. The first two weeks you'll be moving hand to mouth only; then we'll progress to driving around week six. After that, we'll see about summer camp."

"Damn."

"I know you like to work out, Jack, but take it easy. Stick to running. It's the off-season. Go on vacation like a normal person. Take it easy for a while."

Take it easy? Yeah. Not gonna happen—not if I want to keep my spot.

"I'll manage."

He arches a brow. "You got someone to take care of you while you recuperate?"

Lucy, although I hate to ask her. She'd jump at the chance, but she has a new husband, and they're planning a cruise around the world in April. There's Quinn. I could ask Devon, too, but shit, he's got his own life going on, and I hate for any of the players to see me weak, even him. Elena comes to mind, but I push that thought away. Not even going there.

"Yeah." I stand up, feeling . . . shit . . . a little lost. Just the thought of not being able to play the game, to do what I do best in life, makes me feel like I want to barf. And I can't even confide in anyone except Coach. I'm . . . alone.

The doctor rises up with me, and I guess he reads my face. "It's not the end of the world, Jack. You still have some games left in you."

"A Super Bowl?"

He laughs. "You come close every year . . ."

"Right. But never a trophy."

He smiles. "Sure would be nice to have one for Nashville."

I nod. "You do the surgery, and I'll get us one."

But as I leave his office and head to my car, I'm not nearly as confident as I sounded. Fucking Harvey. Even from the dead, he's haunting me. My head goes back to that day, the memories tearing through me, those shots that took my mother's life, the one he pointed at me. And he would have shot me again if I hadn't somehow reached up and wrestled the gun out of his hand. I was so small then, a runt of a kid, a lot like Timmy, my muscles and strength not yet honed by dedication to football. I closed my eyes and pulled the trigger, and when I opened them, he was dead, a bullet in his forehead. I swallow, fighting that anxiousness that rises up whenever I picture him and Mom on the carpet, blood seeping. I ran to her and screamed until the neighbors ran inside the house. Then I cried in the ambulance when they refused to tell me whether she was alive, and it wasn't for the pain in my shoulder but anguish for the only person who ever cared about me.

Only she hadn't cared enough to leave him.

I hate that I came last with her.

I hate that her *love* killed her.

Who needs that kind of emotion? Nobody. Especially me.

"Stop torturing yourself with that game. I have news." Lawrence sits across from me inside my apartment as I watch the video from the Super Bowl. He showed up after my doctor's appointment, wanting to get the lowdown.

"Yeah? It better be good." I'm tense, watching the screen, preparing myself for that last interception I threw. Shit. I wince as I fire the ball to Devon, overthrowing his outstretched arms, a Pittsburgh lineman catching it and running it all the way downfield for the touchdown that ended the game for us.

"Sophia reached out to me this morning."

Flinching, I turn to look at his smug expression. "What the hell did she want?"

He grins. "Seems she's broken it off with the hockey player."

I arch a brow. "Am I supposed to care?"

"She wants to see you."

I frown. "Why? We've skillfully avoided each other for a year."

He shrugs. "She says she wants to make amends. Make her apologies. There's a charity gala next week, and she'd like to be your date."

I bark out a laugh. "Amends? Hard to take back a book she published, Lawrence. That deed is done. We are done. I care nothing about seeing her again."

"Hmm, but she's still dangling that *Cosmo* article. She says you might be able to convince her not to write it. Weird, right?"

Very. I ponder it. I can't trust anything she says. "She's up to something. Tell her to find some other sucker." I flick off the TV and stand, heading into the kitchen to grab a Gatorade and chug it down.

He follows me. "All that is true. She's not worth your time, but if the media could see you together . . . being friendly . . . well, it might put some of those rumors of you beating her up to rest."

Elena pops in my head. She believed me when I told her that I didn't hurt women.

We've spent the week rehearsing together, and she's been polite, yet keeps her distance, her only emotion the feelings she puts into Juliet when we're on stage together. Last night Laura made us go over the balcony scene three times until we got it right. My hand clenches as I remember how I stood beneath her balcony window the prop guys had made, hearing her profess her love for Romeo. My heart pounded as I listened to her words, even though I knew they weren't for *me*. We were face to face, our eyes clinging to each other, saying those flowery lines, and shit, shit, I felt every one of them like a prick to my heart.

But as soon as those lines were done, she pointedly didn't look at me, talking to everyone but me. I like her ethics. I like that she knows what she wants and doesn't play into my hands.

But . . .

I can't stop thinking about if this were a different world, and I could let myself just . . . let go.

A long exhalation comes from me.

"Are you even listening to me?" Lawrence asks, eyeing me quizzically. "You're thinking about that play again, aren't you?"

"No."

"So what about just walking in with Sophia at the gala? I'm not saying you have to get cozy, but I'll sneak some pics, and we can spin it as 'Old lovers now turned friends.'"

"No."

"Dammit, Jack! It would help, and I'm sure you can turn on that charm of yours and convince her to not write that article. Would it kill you to *pretend* like you like her?"

I throw my Gatorade in the trash. "She ruined any trust I have. Never going there again."

He crosses his arms and is about to speak when a knock comes at the door.

I march over and open it, shaking my head at the person there. "Shit, Aiden, don't you have better things to do than annoy me? And how did you get my address?"

"Hello to you, old man." He barges past me and enters the den, taking in the spacious apartment, the modern leather furniture, the artwork of the city skyline on the wall, my Heisman Trophy on the bookcase along with several MVP plaques. He does a circle, looking at photos of me in high school and college. He faces me. "Nice digs. I need a decorator. Moved in across the hall this week, by the way—couldn't resist the proximity to the stadium. I was surprised when the real estate lady said she sold you yours a few years back. Guess we both have great taste. And before you go all ballistic on me, I didn't know you lived in the same building. There isn't a lot of upscale real estate close to the stadium. I got lucky. Devon around?"

I walk in after him. "You moved into the building? Good God. You stalk me in the gym and now here? You need a life, Alabama."

He snorts. "We both know all I want to do is work out. And I want you to help me."

I snort and cross my arms. "Why would I help you?"

Aiden loses some of that charm on his face, color rising on his cheeks. "Because you said I fucking hesitate! I can't stop thinking about it, and if you don't help me, then I'm going to be knocking on your door every damn day until you tell me what I'm doing wrong."

I smirk, plopping down on my leather armchair. "You have a quarterback coach for that, punk."

"He's on vacation! And no one's as good as you."

I smile. "I know."

He sits down on the couch. "Come on, Hawke, don't make me beg. Let's watch some tape."

"You just missed it. He was just watching the last game," Lawrence adds, eyeing us both. Probably figuring out how he can get Aiden for PR. "Did Adidas sign you?"

Aiden's teeth grind. "No. I'm not big enough for them, apparently. Word is they're going with the Pittsburgh quarterback."

"Damn," I mutter. "Assholes."

"I know, right!" Aiden sits up straighter. "Look, turn that TV back on, and put it on where I was on the field. I'm serious, Jack. I've watched the tape a thousand times, and to me, I look spot on, but shit, maybe I'm missing something."

He scrubs his face. I take in the sweat on his face, the workout gear. I grin because I got in his head, and he's worried. Damn. He reminds me of me at his age, eager and dumb . . .

"You partying all the time, Aiden?"

"No, sir!"

"Good."

He nods eagerly. "Right. Won't make your early mistakes."

"Watch it, Alabama."

He holds his hands up. "Right, right. You're cool now. Cold as ice. And I don't believe anything that girl said about you."

Hmm. I study his face.

I shrug, thinking back to how he throws. "Look, it's just instinct—that you get from experience. You have to learn to read the players, know where the lines are going to break apart, and react. Takes a hundred professional games to get there, Alabama. This isn't college anymore."

He gets up and paces around. "Right. I know you like being number one, and that's cool—I can accept it—but you know my time is coming. You'll be gone someday, and what if I still don't have it?"

"I am not going anywhere." My voice is hard and firm. Not until I get that trophy in my goddamn hands. I refuse to think about my surgery.

He levels me with a hard look, scrutinizing me from head to toe. "Missed you at the gym today, and that is weird. Busy working on those lines for the play? Been seeing that girl from the VIP room, the one you followed out of the club? Gotta tell ya, that isn't like you. She's giving you a run for your money, I bet. I like girls like that. Make you work for it."

I put a bored expression on my face, not rising to his bait. "I can do all those things and still never hesitate."

He blows out a breath. "Dude. I'm begging you! Come on—just a few pointers."

I ease back in my chair, enjoying the hell out of this. An idea looms. "You got a girlfriend, Alabama?"

"Who has time?"

I nod. "Right. But I need some help, you see, and you just might be able to help."

"Tell me."

"Sophia Blaine. Seems as if she's free and looking for a hot footballer on her arm at a gala."

"Jack, she wants you—" Lawrence starts.

I hold my hand up. "Not really. She wants a superstar—doesn't really matter who it is."

Aiden has paled. "That chick who wrote that stupid book about you?"

His street cred just went up a notch in my book. "Yep."

He runs both hands through his hair. "All I need to do is take her out?"

I nod. "And convince her not to write some stupid article. Get it in writing."

Lawrence snorts. "Dude, that will not work . . ."

"No, Lawrence. Look at him," I say. "He's young and handsome, and she doesn't know he didn't get the Adidas deal. Play that up, Alabama. Show her a good time, and get her to agree that you don't want anything written about your hero, Jack Hawke. Can you do that?"

"Hero? Ah, shit." He grimaces.

I laugh. "Your hero. You adore me. You love me so much."

"I feel sick," he mutters.

Lawrence brings up a photo of Sophia on Instagram, although I'm sure Aiden remembers her at parties with me. I lean over and check out a selfie of her at the beach, pouting at the camera with pink glossy lips as she lounges back on a chair wearing a bright-yellow bikini. I feel nothing when I see her—not even an inkling of missing her.

Aiden shoots me a look, clear interest in his eyes. "You gonna be pissed if I fuck her?"

"Your life, not mine."

He mulls it over. "She's gorgeous."

"Warning. She bites."

He lets out a long sigh. "Okay." He glances at Lawrence. "How do we do this?"

Lawrence shakes his head. "Son, I hope you know what you're signing up for. She's a snake."

Alabama grins. "I'll wear some big boots." He plops back on the couch. "Now turn on the TV, and tell me what the fuck I'm doing wrong."

Chapter 22

Elena

Around four in the afternoon, I drive over to the Cut 'N' Curl and dash inside.

Mama has her hands in Birdie Walker's hair, touching up her roots. She was here last week, and I swear these ladies just come in for the company. I say my hellos and dart to Aunt Clara's chair. "I need an updo. Something classy, maybe a pretty french twist. You got time?"

She cocks her hip and takes in my tailored dress suit, a soft lavender set that Nana used to wear, only I hemmed the skirt a tad shorter and adjusted the lapel of the blazer for a more modern look. No use letting Nana's beautiful style go to waste, and I swear I can feel her personality in the fabric, daring me to go after my dreams.

"Nice suit. Where you going all fancy?"

I glance over at Mama a few feet away. She doesn't fool me for a minute. She may be nodding her head at everything Birdie says, but I know her ears are tuned in. "Just a meeting in Nashville. Got off early from the library to make it."

Aunt Clara grins and pats her chair. "Get up in here."

I nod and take my hair out of the messy bun and take the chair.

She runs her fingers through it and meets my eyes in the mirror. "You're really meeting that football player, aren't you? You don't have to lie to me. I'm ready for it. Let's rope him in. You play your cards right, and there just might be a wedding at that church before Giselle's."

I huff out a laugh. "No date, I swear. Meeting."

She never stops brushing my hair, but I can see the wheels in her head spinning. "Huh. Job interview, then? That's a power suit if I ever saw one."

"What job?" Mama asks from across the room.

I groan. Bionic ears.

"Not a job interview! Just a meeting!" I call out, and she narrows beady eyes at me.

I drop my gaze. I swear she knows when I'm lying.

Aunt Clara's fingers go to work on my scalp, and I lean back and let out a sigh, letting the stupid anxiety of being near Jack at rehearsals this week drift away. Being his Juliet is . . . excruciating. And we haven't even kissed onstage yet, both of us just pausing and slightly hugging, pretending like it's happening. It's coming soon, when Laura is going to insist on us actually doing it. And dang, just being near him drives me batty. And of course, we can't forget that blow job the first night, when I couldn't resist him once he goaded me into kissing him. I could blame it on the jealousy of Ms. Clark, but deep down, I just wanted one more taste of him. Literally. I smirk at that, recalling how much he wanted me, that tiny bit of heady power I felt at his feet. The way he looked at me, as if he'd never get enough . . .

Who knew doing *that* would give me all the control—

"You're smiling. What kind of meeting?" Aunt Clara asks as she twists my hair up. She leans down to my ear. "It's that flimsy lingerie, isn't it? I saw that one with the little cats on it. Snazzy. A little too sparkly for me, but Scotty might get excited. Think you can make one in my size? I thought about squeezing my hips in that one but didn't want to damage it." She giggles.

I nearly jump out of the chair but grip the edge of the seat. *"Who told you?"*

She titters, her face settling into lines of mirth. "Shhh. Girl. Nobody. I just happened to drop off some of your mama's leftover casserole that Sunday you missed church and saw all of them fancy things on the dress forms. Quite creative, you are. I may have read an email you'd printed off."

"Aunt Clara! That was private! And that door was locked! I make sure every time I leave the house."

"I grew up in that house. All it takes is a bobby pin, Elena. And I didn't mean to pry—okay, I did—but you've been so secretive every time I come over about that room; I was worried you had a hot man locked up in there."

I let out an exaggerated breath. "You are too nosy. And to punish you, I will never tell you anything."

"I have access to all the Sun Drops in the whole town. You need me."

I glance around at the ladies waiting for their appointments, the other stylists who work here. I land on Mama. "If you tell her, I'll kill you."

Her hands grow still in my hair, and for once her gaze is serious as she meets mine. "Honey, I won't."

Mama finishes up with Birdie, and they chat as they head to the counter at the front. I think I'm safe until Birdie stops at my chair. In her late fifties, she's as gossipy now as she was when I was in school and she was the secretary. "Elena, you're looking well."

She's lying. Between rehearsals with Jack and being ramped up about my meeting with Marcus and the lingerie company, I have dark circles under my eyes, and my face is decidedly pale. I murmur a thank-you and return the favor. I can dish out the southern sweetness like everyone else.

"How's that play going? Ms. Clark can't stop talking about how fun it is, although I do think she wishes she'd auditioned for the role of Juliet. She is younger than you and would have been perfect." She grins. "I think she has quite the crush on that handsome quarterback. They'd make an adorable couple."

I meet her gaze in the mirror, and I don't know where the words come from except that Ms. Clark is a sore spot with me, even though Jack hasn't shown any interest. She'd probably sign that NDA in a heartbeat. And dammit, she is younger than me, but I'm Juliet!

"He has a girlfriend, I'm afraid. He talks about her constantly."

Birdie leans in. "Really? Who?"

I feel Aunt Clara's muffled laughter behind me.

"A girl he met on Valentine's Day. Maybe you saw the picture of them—pretty sure it was on one of those gossipy TV shows Topher watches. He's really smitten. Maybe you should tell her so she doesn't fawn all over him at practice."

"Huh. *Fawn*, you say? I'll have to tell her you said that." She sniffs, arms crossed.

Well.

Shit.

How could I forget that Ms. Clark is her freaking niece?

In for a penny . . .

"Do that. Pass it along. Hate for her to be let down or *embarrass* herself."

She huffs and marches off.

"You done and did it now. You let your temper out. She'll tell her exactly what you said, probably embellish it."

I blow at my hair. "Dammit."

"Stop your cursing, Elena Michelle." Mama appears next to me, giving me the once-over. "Nana's clothes look good on you. Now, where are you going?"

"Nashville."

"And?"

"Just a meeting for public librarians." I hate lying—I do so much—and I shouldn't even have come in, but I wanted my hair to be smart and savvy. Should have just done it myself.

She nods, seeming to accept that. "Saw Patrick having lunch with Laura at the diner yesterday. Looks like you've got some competition, dear. Maybe you should call him."

"He's not interested, Mama. I think it was the pink shoes at church." I smile.

She harrumphs. "I knew it. You scared him off on purpose. But he is in that play with you. Just flirt a little—but not too much. You know, compliment his shirt or quote some verses—"

"Mama! I don't even know any verses off the top of my head, and Laura is perfect for him. You should see them at rehearsals. They laugh and play with Timmy. They make a cute couple. Let it go."

"Is she all over him? I knew it. That girl has always been pretty, and I know her husband dying was just awful—bless his heart—but I really thought Patrick liked you."

"Mama, Laura is not a flirt. She's one of the sweetest people I know."

She sighs. "But Giselle is getting married, and now the engagement party is at your house—"

"Thanks to you."

"And I just want you to be happy."

"I am ecstatic."

"And I know when you're depressed. You get those bags under your eyes—"

"My eyes are fine—"

"And you get all secretive. Are you dating that football player? He's practically a Yankee."

"Ohio is the Midwest, Mama. He grew up in a small town. Definitely not a Yankee."

"That's worse. He's a hayseed."

"Mama! We live in Daisy. You can't get much more rural than this."

"And I read about all those women he dates."

I sigh. "Don't read stuff on the internet."

"You didn't answer me. Are you the girl he met on Valentine's Day, the one you told Birdie about? Wasn't that the date with the weatherman—or was it him?"

Dammit. She's so close to the truth. Has Giselle or Preston told her?

I smile. "Mama, all this talking has made me parched. Can you grab me a Sun Drop?"

She huffs and turns to grab one of the sodas out of the old fridge behind her. She hands it over, and I twist the top off and suck it down. "Those things aren't good for you. Too much sugar."

"Hmm." I figure as long as I'm drinking, I can't answer her.

I'm saved by the mailman. Scotty waltzes in, wearing his smart blue-and-white uniform, a wad of packages and letters in his hands as he strides to the front, eyes all over Aunt Clara.

I bite back my grin as everyone in the place stills. He is a good-looking man, single, and owns a small farm on the outskirts of town. With sandy hair, hazel eyes, and an engaging grin, he's muscular and fit too.

He's one of Daisy's most eligible bachelors, except he's in love with my aunt.

"Mail," he calls, and I'm glad Aunt Clara's done with my hair because she practically sprints over to him. I take in the way she laughs up at him, the way his eyes heat as he stares down at her. Sadness tugs at me, and I chew on my lips. I want *that*. I want a man to gaze at me as if I hung the moon, as if one moment away from me is too much, as if he doesn't ever want to walk away, as if he doesn't need a piece of paper before trusting me . . .

"Scotty! What do you have for us today?" Aunt Clara smiles brightly up at him.

He blushes. "Oh, just some hair stuff. Want me to put the boxes in the back?"

Mama whispers, "That man is smitten."

I start, wondering how much she really knows about the late-night visits and sexy times Aunt Clara tells me about. Not much, I bet. She wouldn't approve.

Mama frowns at them as Aunt Clara leads the way to the storage room where they keep the hair products. I notice she shuts the door just enough that we can't see them. Secret kissing, I bet.

I break the silence, hoping to divert Mama's attention. "Mama, stop worrying about me, okay? I'm fine."

She looks back at me, running her eyes over my hair, touching some of it. She smiles wistfully. "You can't tell a mother that, dear. We always worry. You go have your meeting, and I'll see you at Sunday lunch this week."

I stand and take in my hair. Pretty. Soft. Not too uptight. I straighten my suit and look at Mama. I pull out a couple of twenties and leave them on Aunt Clara's counter. She'll try to give them back, but I always pay. I head to the door, and Mama follows me. She takes my arm before I can leave. "Elena, I'm sorry about suggesting your house for the engagement party. It just slipped out before I thought about it. That house stands for us and our family, you know, and I guess that's just what I was thinking."

I give her a hug. "It's fine, Mama."

She nods, her eyes searching mine. "Good. I thought as much, but sometimes you're hard to read. You hide stuff from me."

Because she expects me to be the perfect little southern girl.

To follow along with what her idea of me should be.

I open the door and look back at her. "Don't you dare invite Patrick to lunch again. Or I swear I'll wear my tart costume from Halloween."

I grin and shut the door before she can reply.

I come out of the meeting with Marcus onto the busy sidewalk in downtown Nashville. It's nearly dark, and a soft rain has started, and of course, I have no umbrella.

My phone rings. Topher.

"How was it?" he asks.

"Good news: they loved my designs and would love for me to be part of their team. Bad news: still not a real job offer. They want an intern. A twenty-six-year-old gofer—without benefits. It's crazy." I hold the phone to my ear and walk briskly in the cold air, heading toward my car I parked about a block away.

"Well, the library is a drama zone. You just missed two toddlers scuffling over a dinosaur book. Slaps were exchanged. I thought two mamas were gonna come to blows over who started what. I just now got those two settled down, and a hundred more are begging for books. I just wanted to call and check in on you. I should have come with you."

"Somebody needs to run the library. I should hire a part-timer."

"Elle, you sound down." I hear little voices coming through the phone. I picture him at the library, toddlers pulling on his Red Hot Chili Peppers shirt. "Don't be. You're going to figure it out."

I sigh. "I wish I could go back in time and tell myself to get a degree in fashion."

"You were born with that talent, Elle. Somebody is going to sit up and notice. Plus, you have the blog and the Instagram account—"

I snort. "Romeo has more followers on IG than I have."

"Well, maybe put some lingerie on him. Jammies for Hammies."

I laugh. "I love you."

I come to a stop outside a small quaint bakery. My stomach howls as the scent of sugar and melted butter wafts from the door as someone exits.

"You got quiet on me," Topher says. "Did you go in one of those fancy boutiques, the ones with the custom cowboy boots and leather jackets? I love those." He lets out a wistful sigh.

"No, better."

"Must be food. You're at that Thai place we went for Michael's birthday."

"Warmer. Think sweet." I eye the placard outside the store, reading the pies of the day.

"You're at that little pie shop, aren't you? The one on Second Avenue." He pauses. "You're close to the Breton Hotel—you know that?"

I ignore that. "And the special today is key lime, my favorite." I can practically taste the tart mixed with buttery crust in my mouth. "It's practically dinnertime, and this is what I want. Sugar."

"Get off the phone with me, and go get you a slice. Bring home a whole pie. I'll cook tonight, and we'll split it after. Love you, Elle."

I get off the phone and head inside the bakery. A long sigh comes from me. *Sugar, make me happy.*

I take a spot at one of the booths, settling my purse and garment bags with my lingerie on the seat next to me. I eye the bags, recalling my interview. Marcus, the CEO of Little Rose, met with me personally. He was incredibly nice and complimentary of my work, his eyes lighting up especially at an off-white set featuring tiny quotes from *Romeo and Juliet*. I'd found the silky fabric online when I'd first heard about the play.

The waitress, a young girl dressed in a white dress with ruffles on the hem and a soft-pink apron, sets down my slice of pie. I groan as the first taste hits my tongue. With a hot cup of coffee, I polish it off in record time, and when she comes to take my plate, I put in the order for the whole pie.

It's not until I'm at the counter and she's ringing me up at the cash register that I have a tiny freak-out. I can't find my wallet. With customers waiting in line behind me, I scrounge around in my purse, digging and pushing everything to the side. It's not here. Crap.

I rack my brain, slumping when I realize that when I got my wallet out to pay for my hair, I must have dropped it on the floor or maybe left it on Aunt Clara's counter.

"Everything okay?" the checkout girl asks, eyeing me as if I might dash out the door without paying.

"No, fine. Just give me a minute. Let these other guys check out. I'll be back." I flash a smile and dash back to my booth, getting down on my knees and feeling around the edges of the seat just in case it dropped out when I sat down. Nothing. No wallet.

I get back up and take a seat. I could call Topher, but he'll be closing up the library, and I hate to ask him to drive all the way into Nashville. Giselle might still be around the city, but I brush that aside. It's Friday, and she probably has plans with Preston.

I pull out my phone and scroll until I find the contact I want. I've had his contact in my phone since I knew it was real, but I've never used it.

Here goes nothing. I send a text to *Weatherman Wannabe.*

Chapter 23

Elena

He sweeps in the bakery like a king, his tall frame taking up most of the space at the entrance and all my air. I sigh. He's wearing tight black running pants, a long-sleeved matching shirt, and a Tigers knit hat, which hides all that magnificent hair. Intense eyes rove over the patrons, landing on me. The predator has found his prey.

I wave.

He arches a brow.

Two women gape at him, one of them elbowing the other as they whisper. I'm not surprised when they dash over to him, faces tilted up, eyelashes batting. He pauses, looking at me and then them. I shrug, and my eyes say, *Your fans. Go ahead. I'm not going anywhere. I have no wallet.*

He holds incredibly still as they ease in, his face earnest as they ask him questions. They laugh up at him and push a pen and paper they've grabbed from their purses. He nods politely but absently, not really listening, much like his demeanor in the VIP room. I imagine he's focusing on not . . . being rude? I take in the rise of color on his cheeks, the way he fidgets as they lean in closer. One of them whips out her phone and takes a selfie of him and her together. Still, he maintains an expression that, if you glance, looks sincere and easy, but he *is* uncomfortable—and it amazes me all over again that this gorgeous man with enough charm to entrance millions (once you get to know him) plus a famous talent that has brought him so much success . . . is *awkward.*

It feels like a little secret between us, and I can't stop the small smile that pulls my lips up.

His gaze meets mine as two other women join the crowd. He mouths "Sorry" over their heads at me and turns back to do another autograph. He frowns, swallowing, as another girl insists on a selfie, some of his control slipping. They don't even notice, and I wonder how many people actually look at him and see a *real* person with boundaries. None.

I sit up straighter, watching everything, every nuance that crosses his face.

It must be difficult to live in the limelight constantly. He loves the game but doesn't enjoy the attention that comes with it, yet he pushes himself, all the while never trusting anyone, keeping his distance, not letting anyone too close.

Oh, Jack. If only . . .

He nods and slips by the girls, but one of them grabs his hand and reaches up and plants a kiss on his cheek, pink lipstick smeared everywhere as he tries to avoid it. Checkout girl. Doesn't she have work to do?

I heave out a breath and stand up, leaving my things in the booth.

I march over to them and shoulder my way into the midst of the women. "Excuse me," I say to the tallest one, a skinny brunette who's trying to edge me out. I don't think so. The pointy end of my heel hits her foot, and she starts and gives me a look and steps back. That's right. I might be short, but I have stilettos. Beware.

I apologize profusely in a deepened, dripping southern accent and step around her, remove checkout girl's hand from Jack's arm, and give them all a sweeping look. I let out an amused laugh, bordering on annoyance, one Mama uses when someone has made her mad, but she still wants to be polite. "Sorry, ladies, but could you please let go of my boyfriend?" I bat my lashes. "He's been very nice signing autographs and taking photos, and I haven't seen him *all day*. I'm sure you ladies understand." I temper the words with a fake but seemingly genuine smile. "Plus, he's obviously tired from all that exercise." I wave my hands at his running gear. "He needs some air."

They gape and murmur.

"Of course. We didn't know he was here with someone," one of them mumbles, checking me out as she moves away from him. I smile and attach myself to him like glue, pressing my blazer against his arm. Not moving one inch. Feeling not one ounce of jealousy. Just protective.

"Thank you for the autograph," the tall one says, pressing a card in his hand as she limps away.

I roll my eyes. Good grief. Can't the man even walk in a bakery without being slipped phone numbers?

Checkout girl pouts as I tug him away.

He grins at me and follows me to the booth. "Boyfriend?" he murmurs. "Nice."

If he only knew it's the second time today I've claimed him . . .

I throw a look over my shoulder and hiss, "I saved you. You hated that, and don't split hairs here. Plus, we need to hurry. Checkout girl might be close to calling the cops on me for loitering, especially now that she knows you're here for me. She might do it just to get me out of the way."

He grins and spreads his hands. "And here I am, ready to rescue you. Forgot your wallet, huh?"

"Don't look so happy about it." I shove the check at him, and he looks down at it, bemusement still on his face. "A slice of pie, coffee, and whole pie? What kind is it?"

I nudge my head at the pink box on the table. "Key lime."

"I like key lime."

"So does Topher."

He laughs and tugs his wallet out of one of the zippers on his pants. After pulling out a wad of bills, he tosses them on the table and looks over at me. "You headed home?"

"Thank you. I'll pay you back at practice on Monday."

"Hmm."

I glance over his shoulder and see that the women have left, all except for checkout girl, who's eyeing us. She also has her phone out. Great.

"Why are you downtown?"

"Meeting with a lingerie company." I pick up my garment bag and purse as he takes the boxed pie.

"Yeah? How did it go?"

I pause, feeling confused, not at the question per se, but just at the fact that being here with him is easier than I thought, seeing him outside play practice, with none of the tension that's been between us since the blow job.

Don't think about that right now.

"You okay?" He frowns, easing in closer. "You have a weird look on your face."

"Fine. It was fine. They want an intern. I'll have to pass."

"I see. Sticking with the library?"

I nod, trying to keep the disappointment off my face.

He tosses an arm around my shoulders, tugging me close as we walk past the counter to the door. I look up at him, arching my brow.

He shrugs. "What? Just playing it up till we get out of here. Maybe we should kiss since that one girl is still watching?"

"No. I think I handled it."

He grins. "Your loss."

We reach the door right as the light rain outside turns to a full-on downpour.

He sighs. "I guess you don't have an umbrella?"

"Nope."

"Great. You came to Nashville knowing it was going to rain all day and didn't bring a coat or an umbrella."

"I didn't know it was going to rain all day, weatherman!"

He laughs and takes off his knit hat, his hair falling like silk around his chiseled cheekbones.

He pauses. "And now you're frowning."

I huff. "Why do you always look so pretty!"

"Woman, I am a grown-ass man. I am not *pretty*."

"You are, and it's so annoying."

He rumbles out a laugh and sticks the hat on my head, tucking the loose strands into the knit so they're covered. "There. At least your uptight hair won't get wet."

"It's not uptight. It's chic."

"I like it down."

"Fine." I whip the hat off and pull at my hair, tugging at the pins until my tresses are falling around my shoulders. I tug the hat back on. "Happy?"

"Not yet." He lifts up the neck of his long-sleeved shirt, pulling it over his neck. I flare my eyes. "Jack! You can't go shirtless. Women will maul you."

He laughs, and I see he has on another one underneath, short sleeved. "I came prepared for a cold run. You did not." He reaches over and slides the shirt over my head. "This is supposed to stay dry even when it gets wet."

"Oh." I gaze down at the shirt. It fit tight across his chest but flows around me loosely.

I look up at him. "You're going to get cold. All I needed was the money for the pie. You didn't have to do all *this*."

"I don't want you to be cold, Elena."

My breath hitches as we stare at each other. A few moments tick by as we take the other in. He breaks our gaze. "Where did you park? It's dark, and I'll walk you."

I nod, feeling disappointed for some reason. "Right. About two blocks from here, right off Second Avenue near the Marks Building. Maybe you should just go, and I can wait for the rain to let up."

He nudges his head at the checkout girl, who is probably taking pics of Jack Hawke with a poorly dressed woman. "Leave you with her? Don't think so."

He takes my hand. "Ready to run?"

I nod, and he flings the door open to a curtain of rain. We take off down the street, flying past storefronts and people who were smart enough to bring umbrellas.

I never see it coming when it happens, although I shouldn't be surprised. Here I am, sprinting in stilettos in a too-snug skirt, alongside a man whose gait is three times the length of mine. So yeah, when my heel gets stuck in a grate and I topple down knees first on the concrete, it pretty much seems like the final straw in a very long day.

Chapter 24

Jack

"Elena!" I bend down to her body and pull her up. "Shit! I'm sorry. I didn't even see that grate. Are you okay?"

Rain pelts us as she huddles against me. "I think so. My knees hurt, but I can walk." She squints through the water as it falls on her face. "How far did we get?" She starts off again, and I pull her back and under an awning. Lightning strikes in the distance, making her flinch.

I glance down, eyes widening. "You've skinned them both. Blood is running down your legs. Dammit. I'm sorry I ran too fast."

"Don't apologize. It wasn't your fault. My skirt is too tight, and these heels . . ." She grimaces, bending down to get a look at her legs. "They're fine. Nothing a little soap and water won't fix when I get home."

Nope. She is not driving like that. I guess I muttered it, because she cocks her hip, then winces. "I can drive."

"No, you can't. Plus it's a monsoon out here." I look up at the sky as the wind picks up.

"Hang on," I say and bend over and sweep her up in my arms.

"Jack Hawke, you can't carry me all the way to my car!"

I duck out from under the awning and take off at a sprint. "I know. But my place is closer. Put your head down in my shoulder, and hang on to your stuff."

She opens her mouth to say something—knowing her, it's to protest—but another bolt of lightning flashes off in the distance.

"Besides, this is good for me. Cardio. How much do you weigh?" I grin, feeling exhilarated.

She snorts. "Like I'd tell you. Just stop talking, and get us there already."

I huff out a laugh, hitching her up higher and jogging for the Breton about a block away. I weave in and out of pedestrians on their way home from work, feet slapping against wet concrete, concentrating on not slipping.

She glares up at me, clutching her purse and garment bag. The pie box is on top, and I don't even recall giving it to her, but I must have. She has a death grip on it. I start laughing, and shit, I don't even know why except that she looks angry and wet.

"Why are you laughing?" she calls over the rain.

"I don't know! You always make me laugh."

A smile starts across her face, steadily getting bigger until she's giggling. "Oh my God, if you drop me and this pie, I will never ever forgive you."

"Don't worry. I'll save the pie."

"You will not get one piece!" She blows at a piece of wet hair in her face.

I gaze down at her, laughing more, then sobering as emotion claws at me, soft yet somehow terrifying as it tiptoes its way inside my chest. A knot forms in my stomach, and I can't seem to take a breath, and it has nothing to do with running.

It's the girl in my arms who's got me freaked out.

◆ ◆ ◆

"I'm dripping everywhere," Elena mutters as I ease her down to her feet inside the foyer of the penthouse. She plops her purse, garment bag, and squashed pie box on the table near the door.

"But you look super sexy," I tease as she whips off the knit hat and takes off her shoes.

"Wet is the new thing, I hear."

"Hmm." I tear my eyes off her face and take in her knees again, wincing at the scratches there.

"Whoa! Give me a warning next time," she says as I sweep her up again and carry her into the den, setting her on one of the chairs. "Jack, I'm soaked! I don't want to ruin your furniture."

"I'm more worried about your knees than my stupid chair." She looks up at me, hair wet and stuck to her face, her clothes dripping. Mine aren't any better. She shivers, rubbing her arms as she stands.

My body clenches as I take her in, how her skirt clings to those full curves. *Mind out of the gutter, Jack. She isn't here for that.*

"Do you mind if I use a towel?" She chews on her bottom lip. "Maybe borrow some old clothes? I can get them back to you at rehearsal."

I blink, realizing I've been staring at her longer than I should have. Right, right.

I nod. "Yeah."

She heads to the bathroom, and I dash to my bedroom, yanking open the drawers of my chest for something that might fit her. I find a pair of shorts with a drawstring and an old practice shirt from my college days. After I knock on the door, she reaches out and takes them, a fluffy white towel wrapped around her chest. I see creamy shoulders and avert my gaze. "Put these on, and when you're dressed, let me take a look at those knees."

"Jack, you don't have to do that. I can wash up in here."

"No. I want to see them. Meet you in the den."

"Thank you." Her lashes flutter against her cheeks as she nods, taking the clothes and shutting the door.

Five minutes later, after changing into a pair of joggers and a T-shirt, I come out to the den holding antiseptic and bandages. She's sitting back in the chair I put her in, hands clasped as she looks around the room. Her expression is reserved, her shoulders tense as she waits for me, and I sigh.

Fucking penthouse.

She doesn't want to be here, and I know it, but my real home is two blocks from here.

Would you have taken her there anyway? a voice says in my head.

I don't know!

Maybe.

Stop.

Just stop.

You need to stay away from any romantic involvement with her.

Plus, she's too good for you. She wants more than you can give. Remember.

Right.

But it's . . . her.

And I've never . . .

She smiles at the wad of bandages I have in my hand. "You look serious. Are my knees that bad?"

"Uh, yeah." Shit, I can't seem to think straight. I sit on the floor in front of her, my eyes running over her from head to foot. I clear my throat, and my voice is gruffer than I intended. "You look good in my clothes."

She blushes, and I watch as the color rises.

"What? Why are you staring at my face?"

I focus on her knees. "Never realized how much I enjoy a girl who still blushes."

"Oh."

We stare at each other. I exhale.

Have I ever stared at a girl this much in my entire life?

What the *fuck* is wrong with me?

Her gaze drops first. "Warning here. One reason I couldn't do med school is I'm a big scaredy-cat when it comes to blood. Crazy. I passed out once when a window broke at Nana's when I was trying to lift it. It was old and stuck, and I pushed too hard and cut my hand. It bled everywhere. And I hate pain. Like, I might cry."

"Right. Your knees," I murmur as I tear open an alcohol wipe and brush it across her lacerations. There are several on each knee, and I dab as gently as I can.

"Stings! Oh my God!" She inhales a sharp breath and clenches the side of the chair. "Jack, Jack, talk to me; tell me something good or funny or something, please!"

I huff out a laugh. "I love Justin Bieber's music. Listen to it when I run." I give her a fake hard look. "You are sworn to secrecy. If Devon knew, he'd never let me forget it."

She gives me a wide-eyed look. "No way."

"Yes way. 'Love Yourself' is my favorite."

"Sing it."

I hum the first few lines.

"Don't stop," she murmurs, eyes on my face.

"Kinda hard to concentrate and work on your knees."

"Pretty pleeeeaasse."

I scoff but start the song again, singing the words, getting all the way to the chorus. I feel my own blush rising. I can't sing worth shit.

I look up at her. "How you feeling?"

She's watching me intently. She licks her lips. Swallows. "You know any Taylor Swift? I mean, if you like the Biebs . . ."

I laugh. "Right. That's me, football player who digs pop music. Sorry, don't know all the words to hers."

She arches a brow. "How about Meghan Trainor's 'All about That Bass'? That's my theme song, and if you sing it, *maybe* I'll leave you the pie."

"Hmm. Your theme song should be something by Lizzo, maybe 'Good as Hell.' I see you like that—a hair toss, checking your nails, and walking your fine ass out the door."

"But if you know Meghan Trainor . . ." She winks. "I'll make it worth your while." Another blush. "Pie, I mean. *Food.*"

"Hmm. How about one of those make-out kisses?" I keep my head down, carefully tearing open one of the wide Band-Aids so she can't see my face. I want her. And it's not going away like I need it to.

"Okay, it's a deal—because I don't think you know it."

"Mmm, 'All about That Bass.' Let's see, I seem to recall that song . . ."

"You don't know it!"

"Oh, Elena, I so know it, every fucking word." My eyes find hers.

"Sing it." She bites her lip, anticipation evident by the gleam in her eyes.

I burst out laughing, putting the last Band-Aid on her knee. "Again, our secret."

"Right."

I don't know who I am when I stand up, grab the remote to use as a microphone, and belt out the song. I stumble over the words a little, making up words that fit, but the song is mostly the chorus, and I give it all I've got.

"Can you dance a little? Do one of those body rolls?"

I roll my chest. I'm not a terrible dancer, yet she's crying/laughing, tears rolling down her cheeks.

"Damn, girl. You make me do crazy shit."

"If football doesn't work out, I'm sure you can sing backup for some pop star."

I plop down on the couch. "I sing all that shit in my head on the field when I'm pissed off and need to calm down. When I'm nervous too. That first practice for *Romeo and Juliet*, I was humming 'Dark Horse' by Katy Perry under my breath."

"Shut up."

"True story." I spread my hands. "I'm basically a teenage girl."

She shakes her head at me, her eyes shining.

I pat the seat next to me. "Come on. Let's watch my K-drama. There's a new episode this week, and I haven't seen it."

"Thank you for fixing my injury," she murmurs as she stands.

I jump and take her hand and help her as she walks over to me, my baggy navy shorts swishing. She's rolled them under a few times, and they hit around her upper knees.

I click on the remote, my arm going around her shoulders and pulling her against me. She doesn't protest, sighing as she leans into me.

"So what's up with Lee and Dan-i? Have they kissed yet?"

"No. Dammit. I mean, what's wrong with them?"

"Guess they still have things to work through?"

I watch the characters on the show. Lee is running after Dan-i after he saw her on a date with another guy. "He has trouble talking about his feelings. He's holding back."

"Why?"

"He's never been this crazy about a girl, I guess. Doesn't know how to handle it."

Her head fits snugly on my shoulder. "Hmm. What about her?"

"She likes him, but she's scared. Past issues. Terrible boyfriend from before."

"Silly people. Why don't they just talk?"

"Right."

We get quiet, and I inhale, feeling like . . . like maybe we aren't discussing Lee and Dan-i anymore, but *us*.

"Elena?"

"Hmm."

I glance down at her. She wears a blank expression, fighting drowsiness. "You know that feeling of déjà vu? Where it seems as if something is familiar and has happened before?"

Her eyes close, flutter open, then shut again.

I smile. "Sleepy?"

"Tired. Hard week with Romeo. He drives me crazy at rehearsals. Always looking at me and . . ." Her voice trails off. "Yeah, I get déjà vu. We've watched this show before; maybe that's it?"

Her eyes close, her mouth parting softly.

I give her a few minutes to settle into sleep before I reply. "No, it's not that. It's as if I've *dreamed* about this before—you here with me, images of us together . . . just this feeling of . . ." *Completeness* comes to mind, but I disregard it. "Like if there was such a thing as a past life, which I'm not some woo-woo person and don't buy into souls that always end up together, but if I *did*, I'd say we had something before . . . like a whole life . . . shit, that is totally stupid. I'm only saying this because you're asleep, by the way."

She gives me a little snore, and I push hair out of her face.

Mine.

No, Jack.

Not yours.

You don't do those deep feelings . . .

I sigh and focus back on the show, watching as Lee tries to explain to Dan-i how he feels, but he gets quiet and stalks off. *True, man. I feel you.*

But damn—I'm legit losing my mind with Elena.

What the hell is wrong with me?

You know what's wrong with you, asshole.

Love ruined your mom. Sophia nearly ruined your career.

Right.

Caring for someone isn't what I need right now. I have to focus on my upcoming surgery and image problems. And if I want to win a

Super Bowl, I absolutely have to give everything, starting with training camp. Elena is just an interlude before football.

And once the play is over, I'll never see her again.

But why do I feel so . . . wrong?

Sure, we can fuck, but she wants more.

Everything I *can't* give her. Full trust, *commitment.*

A long exhalation leaves my chest as I lean my head back against the couch.

Chapter 25

Elena

I don't know what wakes me up. My eyes blink open in the darkness of a room that is vaguely familiar, and the pillow underneath my head is plush and soft. Jack's bed. The clock next to my bed shows it's ten o'clock at night, and I start. I must have fallen asleep, and he carried me in here. Clothes still on. I ease up to sitting, glad for the moonlight coming in from the window as I sweep my gaze over the room. Where's Jack? My body warms at how sweet he was to me earlier, and his singing? Terrible. I smile. Has anyone ever seen this side of him? That softness? The care he takes when he's worried?

I slip out of bed and pace the room, checking the master bathroom. Empty.

I pad out to the den and see him stretched out on the couch, one arm off the couch and on the floor. He put me to bed but didn't join me, when it clearly would have been more comfortable. Yeah. He needs his distance just like I do. With a glance I see that he's hung up my clothes on a hanger and draped them over the chair at his desk. My garment bag and purse sit on top of the surface. I don't see the pie anywhere, and I figure maybe he put it in the fridge. He can keep it. He deserves it after doctoring my knees. I chew on my lips and head to the kitchen, moving quietly, to look for a pen and paper to leave him a note before I go.

I get it written, thanking him for everything, and walk back into the den, setting the note on the coffee table. I glance down at him, my eyes tracing the planes of his face, the full lips that are slightly parted, the mahogany hair that falls across his face. Damn. Just damn. All that hotness—right here. I exhale.

His eyes pop open, finding mine. "Elena."

I grab my chest. "You're awake! I thought you were asleep."

"Hard to sleep when you're staring at me." He grins, easing up to a sitting position, rolling his shoulders.

"You couldn't have been comfortable out here."

"Nah, I was fine. You passed out during the show."

"Sorry. This week caught up with me."

He stretches as he stands, and I swallow at the fact that he's removed his shirt at some point, the muscles of his chest flexing as he rolls his neck and pulls at his arms, as if he's warming them up. His gaze flicks over me, lingering on my mouth before looking behind me. "You were just going to leave?"

I nod.

"You think I'd let you walk to your car this late? Hell no."

I cross my arms. "I'm a big girl. Plus this is a safe neighborhood."

"With pockets of bad. It is downtown."

"I'll be fine." I take a step away from him, decidedly not looking at his taut muscles.

"Hmm, aren't you forgetting something?" He gives me a heavy-lidded look.

I lick my lips. "No, all my stuff is on the desk. Thank you."

His body moves closer, his hand reaching out to brush against my mouth. "You owe me a kiss, Elena. For the song."

My chest rises.

"Give it to me."

Shivers wash over me at that tinge of authority in his voice. I like it so much, that heat in his tone.

You got this, Elena. Just kiss the man, and be done with it—maybe on the cheek just to irk him—and that's totally what I plan to do, but as soon as I ease closer to him and feel the heat of his chest under my hands, my body takes over. I slide my fingers up and wrap them around his nape, my eyes holding his. I have no self-control apparently when it comes to him, and no matter what my head says, that I shouldn't get lost in his lips, I already know I *want* to. I'm dying for his mouth on mine again.

Just one, just one, just one.

I tug his head down and lick at his lips, and he parts them, letting me in as I kiss him softly. He sighs against me, his arms wrapping around my waist to pull me tightly against him. He lets me lead, and I do, exploring him, tasting him, groaning at the smell of his skin, at the brush of his chest against his shirt I'm still wearing.

He takes over, his fingers digging into my ass, his lips slanting across mine, harder, more insistent.

"Elena . . . ," he murmurs. "I've never loved kissing this much." His mouth takes mine again, and I melt into him, my leg hitching against his hips. My fingers tug on his hair as he runs his hand down my thigh, stroking and kneading. "Can't resist this," he rumbles against my neck. "I put you in bed and wanted to get in there with you so goddamn bad."

Desire fires off inside every part of my body, and I tremble. It's so fucking hot with us, an electric wire from me to him.

And I know, *I know* what this is. Sex. Just sex, but when will I ever feel like *this* again? This connection. This feeling as if I might die if I don't have him. I should stop, I should.

Because he's going to hurt me.

He's going to—

He's the one to break us apart, holding me, staring down at me, his throat working. His chest moves rapidly. "One kiss . . . shit . . . Elena. If you don't go . . ."

"I don't want to go." I close my eyes. What am I doing? This is his fuck palace! "You once said you wanted me bent over this couch. I haven't stopped wondering what I missed."

He inhales a sharp breath. "Elena . . ."

"You actually said, 'I'm going to fuck you from behind.' I think. Maybe I'm missing the exact wording, but it was hot, that image you painted in my head."

I remove his shirt I'm wearing, feeling nervous.

But I'm brave. And I hang on to that with tenacity.

This is what I want.

"Elena . . ." He bites his lip and meets my gaze. "Please don't stop whatever you're doing. Please."

My fingers push down my shorts. I unsnap my bra, and my breasts sway as I tuck my thumbs in the waistband of my thong, teasing it down a little, then pulling it back up, enjoying that flare in his gaze. His chest heaves, and his eyes glitter.

Gah, I'm a madwoman. Crazy. I don't know who I am right now—maybe my real self—it seems so easy with him. The freedom. This *want*.

"You gonna make good on that promise, Jack?"

He groans, watching me. "Yes, *fuck* yes. Leave the panties on. I want to take them off."

My lower body clenches at his words. "Take your shorts off, Jack."

He palms his cock. "You do it." He pauses. "But no sucking me off. This is about *you*."

"Hmm," I say, stepping into him, sighing when my nipples press against his skin. I shove down his shorts, using my toes to push the fabric down. His arousal is hard and long, thick with veins that throb as I brush my fingers over his mushroom-shaped head.

He shudders and wraps his hands around me, our skin finally pressed together. "God. Elena . . ."

"No one's ever said my name like you do."

He pauses and cups my face. "Good."

I smile at how breathless he is, the stillness of him, that hint of anxiousness on his face, as if he's afraid I might disappear.

He stares down at me, an unsure look on his face.

"I'm not disappearing."

His eyes close briefly. "I'd die if you leave."

He kisses me, his fingers brushing at my nipples, then his mouth following, his tongue flicking across my breasts, sucking. Pushing them together, he massages me, his tongue and teeth wreaking havoc.

"Are you wet for me, Elena?" he says in my ear.

"Since the moment you walked in the bakery. What are you going to do about it? Maybe you should tell me *all* about it."

He huffs out a laugh and slides his hand inside my panties, his thumb rotating against my nub. I sway on my feet, arching into his fingers as one slips inside me before coming back out.

Another deep kiss. More groans from him as he maps out my body.

"You're being mean, and you're not talking dirty," I gasp after a few moments.

"Saving up for something good." Another finger goes inside me, rotating and tantalizing my sweet spot.

I grasp his length, dancing over the wetness from his tip, stroking it down and back up.

He hisses and shoves my underwear down. "Do you have any clue how many times I've pictured you here with me?"

"How many?" I suck on his neck hard, wanting to leave my imprint on him so that when this is over, he'll see my mark and want me all over again.

"A hundred at least. You spread out, me behind you . . . shit . . . you in my lap . . . you on the floor . . . you against the wall. You won't get out of my head."

He turns me to the back of the couch, placing my hands on the edge of the high back, and my body knows what to do, bending over, ready for him.

I gasp when his hands run down the curves of my back, his lips brushing over my shoulder blades, skimming down my spine, his mouth biting my ass.

I look over at the window at our reflection, and he's on his knees behind me, hands palming me as he spreads me apart and licks down my body. His fingers seesaw inside me, stroking me, teasing me as I wiggle to get him back to that bundle of nerves.

"Jack," I cry out as he flicks his tongue against my core, still not where I want him, his fingers and mouth dancing over me, spreading me and drifting over every inch, even those secret places no man has ever tread. My legs scissor, arching into him, moving closer, desire making me dizzy as I clutch the back of the couch.

"I like you like this," he murmurs. "Weak. I don't want you to come until I'm inside you."

"Jack," I grind out, pushing my body back against him. "I need . . ."

"Shhh, just a minute." He stands and grips my hip with one hand, the other on his hard length as he slides his swollen cock along my cleft, teasing me, not quite entering me. Over and over, he grinds against me. "Baby, I want to fuck you without a condom so bad. Never done that in my life. Not once." He reaches around and barely touches my clit, just a soft flick. Heat flashes over me, that spiral of need tightening. "Can I, Elena? Please . . ." His cock teases my entrance, then disappears, making me shudder.

He's begging me, and I can't breathe. And it's him, all him, driving me insane. He's never done this without protection. I don't have time to ponder it, but it feels like an important moment. My words are ragged. "On pill. Recent gyn. Clean—"

He doesn't wait for me to finish and slides inside me all the way to the hilt and holds still for two seconds before letting out a primal growl, pulling all the way out and then back, his thrusts slow and deep, swiveling his hips when he reaches the end, grinding against my ass. "Fuck," he says. "Your pussy is so tight. So wet, baby, so wet."

I mumble nonsense, lost in this feeling, his silky hard length thrusting inside me. I lay my head on the couch, keeping my eyes on the reflection of us in the glass, the need on his face, the concentration as he looks down at us joined together.

I lose myself in watching us, my body pliant and soft against his hard one. It's beautiful, the way he wants me. And the beauty of it is that it's not just about the sex between us; it's about *him*, his awkwardness, how he gets me, how he carried me in the rain. Emotion tugs at my heart; it's more than sex for me, and maybe I knew it from that first time with him on his knees in the kitchen, which is crazy and insane, but there it is. This, this, *this* is worth any anguish later. It is. What if I never meet anyone like him again? What if I never feel this *feeling* again in my lifetime? I'll take it. I'll take it a million times to have him. A zillion.

His fingers circle my clit, in tune to his thrusts, his breathing ragged. "Elena, harder?" There's a plea in his voice.

"Harder."

He leans over me, his mouth on my neck, sucking hard, sharp prickles erupting, delicious ones that make me inhale. "More," I beg. I want him to lose control with me, to think back on this and wish he had me forever.

He grunts, pulling on my hair, making my throat arch up, those fingers never stopping their dance, precise and intoxicating. He stops to hold my hips with wild hands, his grip slipping over the sweat on my body. He twists inside me, his fingers leaving bruises when they land, and I gasp out my encouragement. "More, more, more," I moan.

"Fuck . . ."

"I haven't come yet," I remind him breathlessly.

He growls. "I'm gonna fuck you all night, I swear. You'll get there."

"Now." My hand goes to my clit, and he brushes it back.

"Mine." He thrusts faster, leaning over me again, his finger swirling, faster and faster, his mouth on my neck, sucking, and my body stiffens, tingles building at my spine, skating up my body, seeping into my soul. Us, him. The sound of his breathing, the sweat that drips down his face, the slap of our bodies. My mouth opens for a cry that never comes, reaching higher, higher . . .

"Mine, mine, mine. This little pussy belongs to me, Elena. I make you come—you got that? None of that vibrator shit."

A muffled laugh comes from me at the ownership in his voice.

"Are you disagreeing?" He pulls out of me.

I throw a look back at him, tossing my hair. "Why are you stopping? Are you crazy? Do you know how hard it is for me to orgasm?"

He teases my entrance. "Not with me."

"Jack Hawke, I was almost there." I swallow thickly. "If you don't—"

He laughs and drives all the way in, and I groan, wiggling against him.

"Faster."

He complies, moving wilder, the slide of him perfection as our eyes cling. It makes my neck ache to look back at him, but he's beautiful, the way he moves, that desire low and heavy in his eyes. His mouth parts as he tugs at the hair on my mound, grinding down as he brushes maddening circles over me. He shifts our angle, going deeper, thrusting, a harsh male sound escaping his throat. The universe that's us explodes, sparks raining down around us.

My lashes flutter as my release hits me like a waterfall, falling and falling into a ride of sensuous pleasure. I ride it out, my hands grasping the edge of the couch, tearing at it as my body clenches around him, spasming against him.

"Elena, yes, yes, like that, so sweet, so perfect . . ." He groans and pulls out of me, turning me around, lifting my face up. He stares down at me for a long time and then kisses me hard. It feels like ownership.

He picks me up, and my legs go around his waist.

"You didn't get off," I say, resting my head against his neck, inhaling the scent of him.

"Not done yet. Don't go to sleep on me."

"Pfft. As if."

A lamp falls over from an end table as he walks me to the wall. Neither of us glance at it. "At least it didn't break. Are you going to break me?" I tease.

"Only in the best way, baby."

I shudder and grind my pelvis against him, my wetness sliding over his cock. "Promise?"

His eyes flutter. "Hmm."

His hands cup my ass as he puts me against the wall. "Lock your legs."

I do, and he adjusts my body, thrusting inside me, moving me as if it's effortless, and I sigh at how strong he is.

I must have said it aloud, because he huffs out a laugh. "Fucking you is like breathing. *So easy, so good.*"

My back digs into the wall as he pins me there, his eyes on my face.

He slides inside me, and I groan. "Elena . . . ," he pants. "You . . . you . . . make me . . ."

"I know." And I do. I get what he means. This kind of sex, it . . . it can't be normal. *Can it?* This consuming need and desire, this fire that licks at us, that makes his eyes burn for me, that puts that expression of emotion on his face . . .

Does he always look at me like that? As if he'll never let me go? As if I'm . . . vital to him?

I don't know. Maybe it's just his face with every girl—

No.

I let that go and focus on him and this moment. My walls tighten around him, and my kisses deepen. I murmur naughty things in his ear, my heels pressing into his ass. He roars his release, his body shuddering, his face buried in my neck with my hands in his hair.

With careful hands he carries me back to the bed, and we crash down on it together. Our chests rise rapidly, almost in sync, as we stare up at the ceiling. The only sounds in the room are us, soaking it in, our breaths loud. The silence isn't uncomfortable, but I wish he'd say something. I look over at him on the other pillow, and he turns his head at the same time.

I swallow.

He watches me.

I open my mouth to speak but chew on my lip instead.

He arches a brow. "Best you ever had, right?"

I pop him on the arm. "You're supposed to tell me it was the best *you* ever had. That I am the queen of everything. That you can't wait to do it again."

He grins wider. "Better than that first night—which was hard to beat."

True. I was a little drunk on Valentine's and thought it was incredible, but this—this was me at full awareness.

I shrug nonchalantly. "Maybe. My silver bullet isn't nearly as arrogant as you are—"

He moves faster than I thought he could, rolling me on top of him. "Are you asking for another lesson in *who* owns your orgasms?"

I laugh down at him, tracing my finger over his eyebrows. "Maybe."

"Give me five minutes."

"Slacker. My bullet has a battery."

He growls. "You best toss that thing out. I'm here now."

My lips land on his scar on his left shoulder. "How's your shoulder doing?" I ask, rising up to take him in. "Hey, why are you frowning?"

He looks away from me, then back, his hands idly playing with my hair. "I've got to have surgery on it."

There's a pause as we study each other. I take in the seriousness of his face, that glint of worry in his eyes. "I'm sorry. That can't be good for football, right? Can you still play?"

He sighs. "Maybe. Probably. We'll see." A furrow builds between his brows, and I rub it away.

"I'm still wrapping my head around it. If the surgery goes haywire or I don't heal up right, it could mean the end of my career. And if people think I'm injured or not at the top of my game . . ." His voice drifts off. "Since the moment I knew I was talented, football has meant everything. It's been the one stable thing in my life since I was fifteen. I can't lose it."

I nod, seeing and feeling his worry. "You need it."

"I do."

"What was it like for you . . . without your mom?"

"Like someone tore a limb from me. She was the kindest person, but she took shit from Harvey. She kept thinking he was going to change, I think. He didn't." He gets a faraway look on his face. "Sometimes I think I'm . . . uncertain around people . . . because of him. He scared me. I fucking walked on eggshells around him. Any little thing would set him off. Cold dinner, messy house, my face."

I picture him as a little boy, frightened of the man his mom refused to leave. I don't like it.

"And Lucy, your foster mom, she was good to you?" I'm hanging on his every word, aching to figure him out.

He nods. "I moved in with her when I was fourteen . . . after everything happened. She was widowed, a retired schoolteacher who had all these rules about behavior and exercise. She stuck by me, pushed me to try new things, or I might never have put a football in my hands, but when I did, it was like . . . *home*."

He *has* known goodness. I want him to have had everything.

"What about you? You lost your dad young, right?"

"They think he fell asleep and ran into a tree. It's just been me and Mama, Giselle, and Aunt Clara. My nana passed two years ago. It's why I moved back home. For some reason, I haven't left." I pause. "And how did you know my dad was gone?"

He winces. "Lawrence looked you up after I asked him to. That's how I knew your address, remember?" He exhales. "I was determined to see you again."

"NDA." My eyes narrow.

"Let's not discuss the NDA. It wasn't just that. It was *you*."

"You wanted to teach me all your wicked ways."

He laughs. "My wicked ways? You blew my mind. Glittery panties with unicorns. Please. How am I supposed to just let that slip away?" His hand strokes my leg, turning me so that we're facing each other. He glances down at me. "How are your knees?"

"Hmm, my doctor was excellent. Very good bedside manner."

His eyes hold mine. "How good?"

I ease on top of him. "Best I ever had."

"Knew it."

"Stop smiling like that."

"Like what?" He shifts until his hard length is at my apex.

My breath stills. "All cocky."

"You want this *cock*?" He picks my hips up and maneuvers so he glides inside me, slick and hard as he pushes deep. I moan as he slides back out and then in again.

"Hmm, I think you do . . ."

"The dirty talking is all I'm here for," I murmur. "Maybe another orgasm. Maybe pie."

"No pie until you come again." He moves fast, flipping me over, hovering over me as he settles between my legs, hitching one over his arm.

"Promises, promises," I pant as he holds my hands above my head and thrusts inside me. We move like it's a perfectly choreographed dance, his strokes soft and unhurried, his mouth on mine, kissing me slow, savoring me.

"You're all mine."

His thumb arrives and drives me insane, circling as he takes his time. I lose myself again in the feel of him, the way he looks at me, the emotion that carries me away when I come apart and call his name.

He goes over with me, eyes honed in on mine, something . . . *something* there in the way he looks at me as we ride it out together.

I close my eyes, holding him. Does he feel *this* too? How good we are?

You're mine, he said.

But . . .

For how long?

Chapter 26

Elena

I take down the last drape from the front windows in the dining room and fold them carefully. Velvet and a deep brown, they've been up for nearly twenty years, but they're classic and hang beautifully—although they're a bit dusty. After a good cleaning and pressing, they'll be perfect for everyone by the time the engagement party arrives in a few weeks. We've picked a date after the play, and I am going to do it right. Lots of food, a bar for drinks, snapshots of Giselle and Preston around the house . . .

"Elena! Your phone keeps beeping with texts, and now it's ringing," Giselle calls from the kitchen, where I left her earlier, polishing silver. "It's Weatherman Wannabe? Is that the football player? Want me to bring it to you?"

"Crap!" I stop folding and dash to the kitchen, skidding in my fuzzy cat socks. I need to put shoes on.

"She's practically falling down to talk to him," Aunt Clara says slyly as I grab my phone and answer it, ignoring her grin as I clear my voice.

"Hey."

"You left before I woke up." His voice is low and husky, and I picture him still in that big bed when I left around five o'clock this morning. It's nine now. Did he sleep this long?

"I did," I say, heading out to the screened-in back porch, mentally taking notes of the leaves I'll need to clean up that have swept in from Romeo going in and out.

"I had to get back before anyone noticed my car wasn't home. Plus, I planned a cleanup day for Giselle and Preston's party."

"You left your purple underwear."

"Lavender. And it's a present. I know what a weirdo you are about panties."

"Just yours. They're in my pocket now."

I guess he's not in bed.

Background noise of him rustling around hits my ears. "What are you doing?"

"Just left the gym, where I ran. Getting in my car. Did you really think you were just going to run away?"

"No, I mean, I didn't know if you'd want to, you know . . ." I stop, biting my lip as anxiousness hits, part of me excited that he's called, the other side of me disappointed that I really should get back to work.

"Want to do a late lunch? You can come over, and we can call Milano's?" he asks.

Back to his penthouse.

"We're cleaning. It's one of the only days I'll have to get everything done. Between the play and work, I need to trim the shrubs, get the carpets cleaned, polish the hardwood, power wash the sidewalk. Everyone's here now. Maybe Preston later. There's a lot to do."

His car starts, and there's a long pause. "This party . . . isn't it going to bother you?"

Giselle waltzes out to the porch and grabs one of the extra brooms. I glance down at her ring, waiting for the wince that usually comes when I see it, but it doesn't hit my heart like it did in the library. She gives me a wave, and she mimics throwing a football and waggles her eyebrows. She arrived bright and early at eight o'clock, an unsure look on her face as she came in and took in the house. I can't remember her actually being here since the Fourth of July, when she met Preston. She must feel really guilty.

I wait until she goes back in the house before answering. "In the grand scheme of things, she's family. We may not have it all together, but we're in it together. Nana used to say that."

"And Preston? On Valentine's Day, you were definitely upset about him," he adds. "Do you always fall in and out of caring for someone so quickly?"

I sputter. "What kind of question is that?"

"A good one."

I huff, thinking back to what Giselle said in the library, how if I had really loved him, then why hadn't I told Mama or at least confronted her? "Everyone in Daisy knew he picked right up with her after me, and she's my *sister*. How do you think I felt?"

"So it's just your pride that's hurt. Not your heart?"

Why is he asking such hard questions?

I exhale. "If my heart was broken, I wouldn't have agreed to the party."

"Hmm. You might. You're a kind person. I don't like him," he growls. "And I'm annoyed that he gets to see you today."

"Jealous of my ex and the preacher. Tsk, tsk."

"I can hear you smiling through the phone."

I laugh.

He sighs. "Okay, so you don't want to see me."

"It's not that."

"So you *do* want to see me. There's always dinner . . . or whatever." His voice deepens.

Play it cool, Elena. Protect your heart as much as you can.

Mama comes out with Romeo in her arms. She's dressed him in a blue sweater I knit last year. She sees me on the phone, and I wave at her that I'll be off in a minute.

She leans in, ignoring me, and whispers, "Elena, the sewing room is locked. Don't you want to use it for the party? We could put some chairs in there. Giselle thinks we'll have at least a hundred people here."

I groan.

"What's wrong?" Jack asks.

"Nothing. I have to go," I say.

I click the end button without even saying goodbye and blow out a breath as I stand and head back into the house while Mama follows me.

"Didn't mean to interrupt your call," she says as we walk in the kitchen.

"No, it's fine." I glance at the sewing room door. "I really don't want to use my workroom. All my stuff is everywhere. Material is a mess. Machines are hard to move. Let's leave it be." I keep my voice firm, eyes on hers.

"Okay. Your house, your call."

I breathe out a sigh of relief, feeling winded, as she wanders into the den.

Two hours later, I'm polishing the cherry staircase when I hear car doors shutting out in the driveway. Preston? Did he bring someone? He still hasn't arrived, and Giselle keeps texting him to see when he's coming.

"Topher, can you see who that is?" I call from the top of the staircase.

"Got it, Elle!" He jogs into the foyer from the kitchen and opens the front door.

"Holy shit!" I hear him call from the front porch.

Holy shit means something big, especially since Mama clearly heard him as she stomps in from the kitchen, cleaning cloth in one hand, glass of ice tea in the other.

I mutter and tug down my old Daisy Lions gray sweatshirt, which was clearly too many layers for this kind of work, and head down the stairs. I wish I'd talked to Jack more on the phone. I wish . . .

Aunt Clara meets me at the bottom and follows me. "Who is it?"

I fling open the door and step outside on the porch.

Jack, Quinn, Devon, and Aiden talk as they walk around the front of the house, looking at my flower beds.

What the heck?

I freeze, inwardly cursing my lack of lipstick, crazy topknot, and old Chucks. And I'm sure I have dust on my face.

Mama heads down the sidewalk toward them. Topher watches with bemusement from the porch.

"You're that football player" is her greeting, her eyes raking him over from head to toe, taking in his black designer skinny jeans—which cling to his thigh muscles—and turtleneck with a blue flannel shirt. Dang it. I sigh. How does he manage to look hot in *everything*?

"Yes, ma'am. You must be Elena's mom. Good to meet you." He sticks his hand out, and she pauses before taking it.

I look up at the sky. *Lord, if you're up there, please let her be nice . . .*

"Well, it's about time we had a formal introduction. You ran off from church and took Elena with you. She missed lunch. She never misses one of my meals. I cooked that one especially for her. And the preacher was there. He was disappointed."

No, he wasn't! He likes Laura!

"Uh, yeah. Sorry about that. Elena offered to drive me home. Emergency of sorts." He flushes and looks at me. Mama follows his gaze, her face blank.

Blank is not good. It means her wheels are turning. It means—

Oh, who cares!

I look like hell!

I scrub at my face, pushing strands of my hair that have fallen out and are sticking to it.

Mama focuses back on Jack, arms crossed. "Is all that stuff true about you on the internet?"

No, no! Why does she always have to get right to it?

Jack sticks his hands in his jeans. "Well, which part do you mean? There's a whole lot." He pauses. "I've done some things I'm not proud of, but that was a long time ago."

Oh, smart. Blanket statement that covers the DUI and the partying . . .

"That book some girl wrote about you. I read part of it. It was terrible!"

I close my eyes.

"No, ma'am. Not true. She just wanted money, and people love to talk about me. I tend to not say anything back, and it drives them crazy."

"Because you're famous." Mama puts her hands on her hips. Wearing old jogging pants and a T-shirt with the pink Cut 'N' Curl logo on the front, she's not dressed in her usual slacks and blazer, but you'd never know it by her regal stance.

"I just play football."

Oh, Jack. Please. You're famous.

"Well, I never heard of you," Mama retorts. "We never even had a football team here in Daisy. School is too small."

Devon laughs. "Even me, Mrs. Riley? You've heard of me, right?"

She swivels her head to him, probably eyeballing the hair, tattoos that peek out from his sleeves, and those black earrings. "No, but you're memorable. What color is that in your hair? You need to come see me. I'll fix it."

He laughs. "Devon Walsh, wide receiver. Pleasure to meet Elena and Giselle's mom. Nice girls you have." He takes her hand and kisses it.

She blinks.

Young James Bond steps forward, all brawn and blond. Even today, he's dressed in a black turtleneck and dark jeans. "I'm Quinn, ma'am. I do security for Jack. Beautiful property here. Love the town. Jack drove us around for a few and showed us the sights."

The sights?

Mama starts. "Security? Bless. Do you carry a gun?"

Quinn laughs, looking at Jack. "No. I usually just stock his fridge and arrange his schedule, stuff like that."

"Well, that must be boring."

Mama!

"Keeps me busy and out of trouble, ma'am. Jack and I are sort of foster brothers."

"I see." She lasers in on Aiden. "And you?"

"Aiden Woods. Best quarterback on the team." He shakes her hand.

"Watch it, Alabama," Jack murmurs. "You're only here to be of use. I can send you home at any time."

Aiden smiles sheepishly, nudging his head at Jack. "He's better than me. For now."

Mama takes it all in, her foot tapping, before turning back to Jack. I can't see her face, but I know she's sizing him up, deciding if he's to her taste. She's playing back all that stuff she read online, the book, probably recalling how he went to Timmy's school.

I hold my breath, waiting for her reply.

If she calls him a hayseed . . .

He fidgets as he shifts from one foot to the next, color rising on his cheeks as she stares at him. His eyes land on me again, and I shake my head at him. *Mama has you in her sights,* my eyes say. *Beware!*

She lets out a long exhale. "Well, about those things I read . . . gossip is a terrible thing. Ruins lives. People need better things to do with their time. I appreciate everything you've done for Timmy and Laura. I heard you bought back their house she lost when her husband died. I'm sure you didn't have to do that."

My eyes flare. He did that? How does she know?

She knows everything . . .

"Stop stalling. Cynthia is scary." Aunt Clara pokes me in the back. "You better get down there before she runs them off."

She wouldn't!

She might . . .

Topher laughs from the front swing, where he's sat down. Wearing old jeans and a faded Queen shirt, he's taking it all in. "Ms. Clark and Birdie Walker have driven by the house twice since they pulled in. Lunchtime in Daisy is causing a traffic jam. Guess it's hard to miss an Escalade, Range Rover, and the red Maserati. Wonder who that belongs to? I'm betting Mohawk."

"Cars and people driving by are not the issue! There are four football players in my yard, and I don't know why," I exclaim.

"I know. It's awesome." He grins. "We haven't had this much excitement here since, well, never. I should go get my diary and jot this down. Good material. Maybe take some pics." He sighs. "Although you did leave that pie at his place. I should hate him for that."

"You aren't moving a muscle. I might need you." I go down the steps toward Mama but hang back a few paces, wavering as I pretend to bend down to tie my shoe. I'm totally waiting to see how Jack handles Mama, and vice versa.

Why is he here?

Why am I so nervous?

Mama sweeps her eyes over the four men. "Well, why are y'all here?"

It's as if she reads my mind. Dammit, is it true that you eventually turn into your mother the older you get? No, absolutely not. Please no.

Jack flashes a smile. "To work. Elena mentioned you had a party to get ready for, and she had a lot to do. Said she couldn't have dinner with me."

I stand; color blooms on my face. How dare he tell her that? Doesn't he know that once she knows we are . . . *whatever we are* . . . then she's never going to leave him be?

"Well, if there's no time for dinner, there is always time for lunch on Sunday," she declares.

Fell right into that one! I glare at Jack.

Giselle and Aunt Clara appear next to me. Like me, they're in sweats, no makeup, and bad hair. At least I'm not alone as we slowly inch closer.

"We can't hear well from the porch. What on earth is going on?" Giselle hisses.

"The gods answered our prayers and blessed us with eye candy. Big muscles and handsome faces," Aunt Clara murmurs, fluffing her hair.

Giselle winces. "Preston isn't coming. He said he's working late."

On a Saturday—when we need all the help we can get? I frown.

"Does he work on the weekends a lot?" I whisper, keeping my eyes on the group in front of me as they talk.

Giselle nods, her expression hesitant. "He is the new guy at the firm."

"Did you really tell Jack you wouldn't have dinner with him? You have to eat, Elena." Aunt Clara giggles. "I went to bed late last night, so don't think I didn't see that your car was *not* in your driveway."

No privacy. Ever.

I elbow her. "Did I tell you I called Scotty to come clean the oriental rugs? He has one of those cleaning machines. Maybe he can slip over to your house later and clean *yours*."

Her eyes widen. "You hussy! You did not!"

I check the time on my phone. "He'll be here soon. He was thrilled, even offered to do it for free, especially when I told him you'd be here helping us."

"I'm going to put rat poison in your tea," she whispers.

I laugh.

Giselle sighs. "Everyone knows y'all are a thing. I don't know why you won't just make it official, Aunt Clara."

She huffs. "I'm ten years older than him! It's ridiculous. Everyone will think I'm robbing the cradle." She looks down at her shirt. "Dang it. Now I need to go change clothes before he gets here."

I grab her arm before she can head off to her house down the road. "You will not. We all look like something Romeo dragged in, and you are not going to show us up."

She sighs. "True. I don't want to miss one minute. I'm curious to see if your mama will tell the boys what to do or if Jack will try to take over. He likes to be in charge; I can tell."

We gaze back at the group, and they've moved to Jack's black Escalade, Mama right behind them.

"Jack's got a power washer," Giselle murmurs as he pulls it from the back of the vehicle.

"And a hedge trimmer that looks brand new from the Home Depot," Aunt Clara adds with a sigh. "Elena, do you think he went and bought it just for us?"

"I have a perfectly good one," I mutter. "It's in the shed."

"Who's the blond dude? He's not a football player?" Topher says from the other side of me. I guess the curiosity got to him, and he decided to join us.

"Quinn. Jack's foster brother."

"Nice," he says, walking up to the men and introducing himself to Aiden and Quinn.

Mama looks back at us. "Elena? Aren't you going to say hello to your company?"

Where are your manners? is written on her face. Right, right.

Giselle hooks her arm in mine, Aunt Clara on the other side, and the three of us approach the group. Daisy Lady Gang.

Jack's gaze is on me, lips twitching. "Elena. Good to see you."

Good to see me? Please! He had me all kinds of ways last night! My body remembers clearly.

"Nice of you to come help," I say weakly.

"Thought you'd need some extra hands, and these guys don't have anything better to do."

"We could be watching game tape," Aiden mutters, and Jack smacks him on the arm.

"Patience is a virtue, Alabama. Pick up that trimmer, and start on the flower beds. Might bulk you up," he tells Aiden. "You try to keep up with me in the gym, but you're puny. Need help carrying that box?"

"No." Aiden picks up the trimmer and stalks off, calling over his shoulder, "You owe me—and not just for this."

"What else should we do, Jack?" Devon asks, and Jack sweeps his eyes over the house, looking at ease as he tells everyone what to do.

"Wash off the sidewalk and front porch." He points at the others. "Quinn, you and Topher work on the leaves in the yard. I'm sure Elena has rakes. Maybe wash the outside windows."

"Rakes are in the shed. Topher knows where," I say. Might as well join in.

"Check the backyard too. Collect the leaves in trash bags," Jack adds.

As the guys amble off, I ease in closer, brushing at my hair. Again. It's no use. "Um, thanks for coming. You didn't have to do all this."

His lips tilt up. "Hmm."

We just stand there. I swallow. I'm not looking at Mama, but I feel her staring at us.

She nudges me. "Elena, get some drinks out here. There's ice tea or water or Sun Drops from the Cut 'N' Curl. I closed it today, but here's my key." She presses it in my hand. "Take Jack with you to carry them."

"Sure." He nods, eyes on me. I don't think he's *stopped* looking at me. "Never had a Sun Drop," he murmurs.

"Citrusy soda. Addictive. Bottled in Middle Tennessee," I say.

Mama squints at him. "That's because you're a Yankee. In the South, we drink them all the time. You heard what I said about lunch tomorrow. You coming?"

Jack pauses, his face flushing. "I appreciate the invitation, but . . ." He looks at me, and I shrug.

All your fault, buddy.

"I, um, already have plans."

I frown. Really? It's the off-season.

But I know what it is.

He wants a little, but not a lot.

I get it, and I'm fine.

Totally fine.

"Next time, then." She shoos us away. "Go on; stop gawking at each other. I'll finish the staircase. Y'all can work on the screened-in porch when you get back."

It's like I'm a teenager all over again, and she's ordering me around. Jeez, this is *my* house. Fine.

I take off for the beauty shop across the street, and Jack follows me, keeping pace.

Ugh! Why didn't I at least put on lipstick this morning?

"Are you mad at me?" he asks quietly after a few steps of silence.

I dart a look at him, then back at the road in front of us. "For coming?"

He nods.

"No. I just figured I'd see you Monday at rehearsal."

He frowns at that. "I didn't see Preston."

I scoff. "Is that why you came? To stake your claim?"

"Partly. Plus, I wanted to see where you lived."

"I'm right off Main. Everyone knows my house."

"It's a beautiful place."

"Thank you. There's still a lot I want to do: modernize the kitchen, redo the hardwood, add a garage—that's next for sure."

"Nice."

Our conversation is so . . . mundane! What is wrong with me?

Plus, I'm irked he turned down Mama for lunch.

Let that go, Elena.

I head to the door of the shop, unlocking it and heading inside. After clicking the lights on, I walk over to the white fridge and grab one of the cardboard boxes on the top to put the drinks in.

Jack is behind me. "I wish you'd look at me, Elena. Should I not have come? I just wanted to see you, and you sounded like you needed help."

I shut my eyes. He's not only great at orgasms, but he's *kind* . . .

But . . . part of me is terrified.

He's going to crawl inside my heart.

He's going to break it into a million pieces.

"Yes. I'm glad you came." I whip around, and he's eased in closer, backing me up against the fridge.

He wipes at my cheek. "Smudge on your face."

"Dusting."

His elbows land on either side of my head against the fridge, eyes holding mine. "I can't believe you left me—then hung up on me. No one treats me this bad."

I cock my hip, feigning confidence I don't have. "Figured I owed you one for the morning you left me."

His head dips as his nose runs up my throat. "Also, you left a hell of a hickey on my neck; hence this awful turtleneck. Didn't want your mama to see it."

My breath hitches. "Jack . . ."

He kisses my ear, his teeth nipping at my lobe. "Yeah, say it like that again, all breathy, and I'll forgive you for leaving me . . ." His chest presses against me. "I like your mama. She's feisty. No wonder you turned out so wild. Little hellion."

"I am *not* wild! I'm a librarian."

"You keep saying that, but you've got a streak in you, and I like it." His hand skates down to hold my hip. "This is what I wanted when I woke up. You. In my arms. Me inside you. I might have even pulled out the handcuffs. You missed out."

"I have my own handcuffs. Pink and fuzzy . . ."

"Wild woman."

"You best get rid of that tent in your jeans before we walk back," I whisper.

He kisses my throat. "We're going to get your place nice and pretty, Elena. And when everyone is gone, I'm going to do bad things to you in your bed. Is it one of those big old-fashioned ones, high off the floor?"

"No, it's a new king-size one," I say, sighing as he tugs at my hair, pulling it down.

He stares down at me. "I love your hair, the color, how long it is."

"I'll just have to put it back up. And we can't do this in the beauty shop."

"I just want to kiss you."

"Uh-huh. Never knew a man who loved to kiss so much." I slide my hands up his shoulders, tangling in his hair. "Now stop talking. Mama's probably timing us. If we're here too long, she'll barge in."

He laughs and takes my mouth, groaning as our lips cling.

And I'm lost all over again.

How will I ever let him go when it's over?

Chapter 27

Jack

I tuck a Tigers hat on my head and exit the SUV and open the door of Leo's Pizzeria, the place in Daisy Elena swore was the best place in town for takeout. I ease in the door and check out the interior. Busy as hell for nine o'clock at night on Saturday in a small town, but she's starving after all the work we did today. I grin for no apparent reason other than I have to feed her, and if she wants pizza . . .

A few patrons I recognize from the school give me wide-eyed looks, then send me a wave. Friendly but not jumping up to mob me. I like that and wave back. Don't feel like small talk. Just want to get back to her place.

"Do you have garlic knots?" I ask, recalling how she loves bread.

The cashier is a girl with braces, wearing a red Leo's hat and an apron. She glances at me, then does a double take. "Uh, yeah. There's six in an order." She blinks rapidly.

"Right. Two of those, then. A large cheese, a large supreme, and a large pepperoni." Damn. I'm probably ordering too much for just us, but I don't know exactly what she likes. I left her at the house, laid out on the couch with that little pig in her lap, her lids shutting. She swore she just wanted a nap. I smile. She best get one, because I've got plans . . .

"Anything else?" the girl asks, staring hard at me.

I look down to take out my wallet, used to the avid attention, yet it always feels strange at first. Takes me a minute. "You got anything for dessert?"

"We have homemade chocolate pies. The owner's wife makes them every Friday. They're usually gone by tonight, but we have three."

I nod. "Throw those in."

She tells me the total, and I swipe my card.

She hands it back to me. "Uh, are you Jack Hawke?"

There it is. I put on a smile and look back up. "Yeah."

"I saw you on TV today."

I inwardly groan. "Well, I hope it was good." Because it probably wasn't.

She pushes up her glasses, and I automatically think about Elena. This could have been her a long time ago, a teenager working at a store, waiting for college. I wonder what she was like in high school. Total nerd, I bet. Shy. But not. Wild. But never showing it. I bet she ran the yearbook club or the library society with an iron fist. I wish I knew her then. Ah, hell, who am I kidding? She wouldn't have looked at me twice. Football player. Jock. Never talked unless I had to.

"It was on *The Today Show* this morning, the weekend edition," the cashier says, bringing me back.

I frown. "What was it?"

"It was a video of you running with a girl in your arms. It was pouring rain, and y'all ducked inside a hotel. There was a photo too—looked like you and Ms. Riley in some bakery."

Dammit. Should have seen that coming.

"Can I get your autograph?"

"Uh, yeah." My head is a million miles away as I sign a napkin she pushes at me.

I take a deep breath. I'll need to warn Elena. I wince, hating to put her in the spotlight like that. If reporters start showing up here . . . fuck, I'm surprised they haven't already with the play, but since that first pic with me and Timmy at the play, they've seemed to fade away. Not much long-term interest in a feel-good story for those jerks. Whatever. I may have started this with the intention of cleaning up my image, but I like Timmy and Laura. Genuine, honest people.

Pizza and the rest of my order in hand a few minutes later, I get back in my car just as my phone rings.

"What happened?" I ask Aiden. He left Elena's around two o'clock so he could get ready for his date with Sophia. He must have left the gala early if he's already calling . . .

"Is that any way to say hello?"

"Just tell me what she said. Everything." My hands clench the steering wheel, and I realize that her dangling that *Cosmo* article in front of me has been on my mind more than I thought.

A long sigh comes from him. "Sophia is hot, man. Smoking."

"Uh-huh."

"She was real into me too."

"Just get to the point, Alabama," I growl, anger ratcheting up, and it isn't because I even fucking care that he was with her, but I'm so goddamn annoyed that she's manipulating me.

"Look, I showed her a great time. We had dinner, danced, but she said she wants to see you, and she'll sign whatever you want."

I lean back on the headrest. "You failed, Alabama."

"I did not! I did everything you wanted, man—I did, but it's you she wants to see."

I curse. It was a half-assed idea anyway. My gut knew she wouldn't be satisfied until she laid her eyes on me and said whatever she wanted to get out.

"Does this mean you're not going to help me? Dude, come on. I put all my charm out, and I got that in spades—women fucking adore me. I did my best—"

I hang up on him and call Lawrence, my teeth gritted.

"Yo! What up? Tried to call you earlier. Have you seen that video of you and Elena? It's not bad. Very chivalrous. I'm still waiting for her NDA—"

"Fuck that. Get with the lawyers and send the tightest nondisclosure you can come up with to Sophia. She'll never say one fucking word about me again as long as she fucking lives. Do it now, Lawrence; I want this mess over and done with. Tell her once she signs it, I'll meet her. She can say her piece. And then it's done. Got it?"

I hear him rustling around, probably writing it down. "Got it." He sighs. "I know you hate this. I'm sorry, man. You sure you can deal with her?"

My jaw pops. I don't know what it will be like to actually *see* her again.

But I want her out of my hair. Forever.

Plus, it makes my gut clench to picture Elena and her whole family reading about whatever shit she decides to come up with next. And now that reporters know Elena's face, they'll get a name soon, and what if they hound her, dig into her past, figure out the lingerie?

Later, I pull into Elena's driveway. Topher's car is gone still. He left to hang out with Devon and Quinn at the Razor. Pretty sure he just wanted to give us some time alone.

Taylor Swift music is blaring from a speaker as I walk in the door, and Romeo pops out of a little tent in the den and glares at me. I'm not sure how I feel about the little pig. He follows Elena everywhere, throwing snippy glances at me.

"Hey, dude," I say. "Where's your mama?" I walk into the spacious kitchen, setting the food down on her island. Romeo sits at the doorway, watching me.

"Want some garlic bread, little piggy?" I pull out one of the garlic knots and dangle it in my fingers.

His snout twitches.

"No?" I take a big bite. "So good, mmm."

He shuffles, dipping his head as he gets up off his haunches and walks slowly to me, eyes on the bread.

"You can have this, right?" I say, bending down to scratch his head.

Give me, give me, his brown eyes say.

I hold it close to his mouth, a little unsure about those teeth. He snatches it faster than I thought he would, and I jerk and fall back on my butt. He gives me a condescending stare—*Amateur*—and runs back to the den.

Laughter comes, and I look over at Elena, who's come in, hair wet, wearing long pajama pants with unicorns on them and a tank top. "Are you scared of Romeo?"

"No! He just startled me. His teeth nipped me."

"You trying to bribe him with bread?"

I stand up, scoffing. "No."

She wanders over to the pizza, takes out a slice from the supreme, and takes a big bite and chews. "God, this is so good." She sways over to the cabinet and pulls out plates, grabs napkins and sodas from the fridge. I watch her, the way she moves, hips swishing, completely at ease as she arranges our food. She takes a seat on a stool and pats the one next to her. "Come on; let's eat." Her eyes drop. "Thank you for today, by the way. You guys did everything so fast. Saved me so much time."

Nerves ramp up as I take her in, not wanting to end our camaraderie. I need to tell her about Sophia.

Shit. I don't want to.

I take a slice and eat instead, my head weird, messed up.

How will Elena feel about me seeing Sophia? Is she going to freak out?

What *are* we?

Do I really need to tell her?

Somebody will tell her . . .

Damn, it's been such a good day.

Do I have to go and ruin it?

She laughs, her eyes gleaming over at me.

"What?" I say.

She takes a drink from a Sun Drop. "Are you even aware that you're humming to Taylor Swift? I love this song."

I grin, relaxing. For a minute there, I thought she might see how torn I am.

I cock my head. "'You Belong with Me'?"

"Damn. You even know the name of it." She giggles. "Hmm, high school song about the girl who wants the guy who's dating the cheerleader."

"I was just thinking about what you were like in high school."

"Badass nerd."

"Knew it. You wouldn't have looked at me twice."

"Oh, I would have looked all right." She sends me a little grin. "Sing it for me."

I roll my eyes. "Can't a man eat in peace? And why do you want me to? My voice is terrible."

"Sing it! Sing it!" She pounds her fists on the counter.

"Dammit, woman. No. Your knees were a special case. How are they?"

"Fine. Please, Jack, pretty please. I promise to do whatever you want later . . ." Her eyes glint, a wicked gleam there—and I'm lost.

I set my pizza down and pick up the chorus, singing along with Taylor as she goes to the verse about the guy in his faded jeans and how the girl wants him even though he's with the wrong girl, when she's the one who understands him. She knows his favorite songs and his dreams and wants him to see *her*.

Elena watches me avidly, her chest still, as I wrap up the song. I should feel like a total idiot. But I don't.

It's her, and shit . . .

She gets me.

I can hum Taylor Swift all day long, and she might be the only person who knows it.

There are a few moments of silence when I finish, the stereo bleeding into another song.

She's staring at me . . . like . . . like . . .

I don't want to hurt her.

"Elena, I have to tell you something."

She pauses, frowning at my short tone as she picks up another piece of pizza. "Sounds serious."

"I'm going to meet with Sophia soon."

Her eyes flicker, her face carefully blank. "You're still talking to her?"

"No. I never want to see her again, but she wants to meet. She says that she'll sign a document that she'll never talk about me again. That's the only reason I'm going. She wanted me to go to this gala thing, but I sent Aiden, and he was supposed to—forget that. It's me she wants."

"Ah. Is that why you turned down lunch tomorrow?" She pats her mouth with a napkin and stands.

I pause, grimacing. No, that was just . . . I don't know . . . shit . . . too much, too soon.

I can't answer that, so I say, "I don't want to see her—you know that, right?"

The kitchen grows tense, and I swallow, seeing hesitation on her face, that tiny bit of distance that's—

"Elena, if I don't, then who knows what she comes up with next? She's dangling this abortion issue, and I just don't want you to get the wrong idea when you see it or hear about it or—"

"Did you ever love her, Jack?"

I lick my lips, thinking for a second. "No."

"You hesitated."

"I dated her. She came to games and parties. I *cared* about her."

"Have you ever been with a girl you couldn't live without? College?"

"Never had the time it took. Never wanted to get too involved. Football always came first."

Her face shutters more, her eyes down as she stares at the pizza. "I see."

"Are you angry?"

She taps her fingers on the island, mulling, then looking up at me. "I'm not angry about you seeing her. She betrayed you."

Thank you, Jesus!

"I'm over her."

A wry, wan smile comes from her. "I know. You let girls go and never look back."

I frown, not liking that tone at all. "Elena, can we just forget her and move on?"

"Sure." Her hands tremble as she closes the pizza boxes and picks up our plates and puts them in the trash. She darts her eyes at me. "What's going to happen when the play is over . . . with us?"

I frown. I . . . I don't know.

Will she still want to see me?

Will she, I don't know, get tired of the distance I keep . . .

"We can talk about that later. We just . . . need time." It's a total cop-out, but my gut has knotted up. I'm scared, okay, fucking scared.

She plucks at a napkin.

"Are you sure you're okay?" I'm hanging by a thread, searching her blank face, wondering what else I could have said. The room feels tense, and I'm scared she's going to tell me to take a hike—

Fuck it.

I walk over to her and lace our hands together. I stare down at her. "I'll be thinking about you when I see her. Just you. Even when she's sitting across from me. You . . . I *trust* you, Elena."

"Do you?"

I do—it's tenuous and fragile, but it's there. Otherwise I never would have had sex with her without a condom or even shown up today. If I didn't trust her, I would have been firm about that NDA from the get-go, but I've let it go.

"I don't want her."

"I'm not worried about *her*, Jack."

Then why does she look so . . . wrong?

She needs reassuring, Jack. She needs you to . . .

But . . .

No, I can't get into *feelings* yet.

It's too soon!

It's ridiculous and insane to think I might be—

Stop. Just stop. Take it slow. Slow.

So I ignore my thoughts and do what works. I tilt her head up and kiss her long and slow. She pulls back, her hands resting on my chest, big sea-green eyes clinging to mine.

I press my forehead against hers. "Baby, don't let her get in your head. Kiss me back, *please*."

"She isn't in my head. You are . . ." She parts her mouth to say something else but doesn't, a long exhalation coming from her.

We stand there, and she's thinking, and I'm anxious, not wanting this to fuck us up . . .

She seems to come to a decision and smiles softly, tangling her hands in my hair as she reaches up on her tiptoes and presses her mouth to mine.

I groan, deepening the kiss, hoping she can see how I feel about her like this, with her in my arms. I sweep her off her feet and, never taking my mouth off hers, push past the kitchen and to her bedroom.

Chapter 28

Jack

Three days later, I walk into Milano's at three o'clock in the afternoon. The place is dead—the lunch crowd gone, the early birds not here yet. All as planned.

Bernie, the maître d', points to my usual table in the back. "Your guest is already here."

I grimace. Of course she is.

I walk to the back and see Lawrence and my lawyer, both lingering near the bar area. I give them a nod. I need witnesses in case this thing goes haywire. Lawrence got the papers from Sophia yesterday, all signed and perfect. Is it really possible that all her bullshit is behind me?

We had a phone call where Lawrence suggested that since I have the contract, I could stand her up, but that isn't me. I'm a man of my word, and maybe a small part of me wants to see her, to get her confirmation for myself.

She stands as she sees me, elegant and tall in a short red dress with a deep-plunging neckline. Her white-blonde hair is long and wavy, her face perfectly made up, lips curved in a slight knowing smile. A silver-chain necklace is around her neck, bolo-tie style, two perfect diamonds dangling on the ends. Classy but not ostentatious. Expensive. I should know. I bought it for her on her birthday. We broke up four months later. Bitterness pulls at me, and I inhale a deep breath.

"Jack! It's been too long," she says with a wide smile and attempts to give me a hug, pressing her breasts against my suit jacket. There's a brittle gleam in her eyes, part defiance, part . . . something else.

I untangle her from me. "Please, have a seat."

She pouts red lips as she sits. "So cold, Jack. I expected it but thought you might be at least a little happy to see me."

My teeth grind. I must have smiled, though, because she returns it.

"I knew you'd come. Aiden was very sweet, but you . . ." She laughs, the sound tinkling. "Well, we both know this was long overdue."

I arch a brow. Did we? I would have been happy to never see her again in my life.

She takes a sip of her white wine, thoughtful, intelligent eyes watching me. I stare back, my face carefully blank. She's the only daughter of wealthy, doting parents; status and power rule her world. I should have seen past the pretty face to the shallow girl underneath, but she seemed genuine when I first met her. Vivacious with an outgoing personality, she filled up the empty spots when I didn't feel like talking. People gravitated toward her, her engaging laugh, the way she smiled, and I mistook it for sincerity.

"Indeed. You got me right where you want me."

"I signed your papers," she breathes. "I'll never say another word about you."

"You did."

"Don't you want to know why?"

I smile grimly. "I gave up trying to figure you out when you published that book, Sophia."

"Money, of course. Half a million for that." She pauses, her fingers drawing circles around the wineglass. "I was angry with you, Jack. I wanted you to commit to me." Deep-brown eyes stare up at me.

"Yeah."

"And then I met Rodney."

"Heard that went south."

She shrugs. "He isn't nearly the superstar you are, but he kept me occupied. He wants me back, you know."

"Good to have options."

She flicks a strand of hair over her shoulder. "He's not you, but I think he loves me."

"Great. Lock him down. Isn't that what you want? Marriage to a pro athlete? Money? The lifestyle?"

Her lips purse, her eyes remorseful. "I wanted that with you, but you never let me in, Jack."

True. She never went to my apartment. I never took her to Lucy's house. I never shared anything too deep. And I spent a year with her. There's something not right about that, but I push it away.

"You've got serious commitment issues, Jack." She sighs, brushing her gaze over my shoulders. "I imagine it's hard and rather sad to never have the guts to fully commit to anyone."

Her words sting because I hear the ring of truth in them.

A long sigh raises and lowers her slender shoulders. "Anyway, I wish . . . I wish we could have worked out."

"Then why all the lies?" I snap. "Why do you want to talk to me, Sophia? You've gotten your revenge with the book. I didn't think we had anything else left to discuss."

She takes a long drink. With a shimmer of tears gleaming in her eyes, she raises them up to mine. "Jack, how can you be so immune to what we had? I *loved* you." Her throat bobs, and a tear traces down her face. Seemingly embarrassed, she flutters her hands and dips her head as she reaches for tissues in her purse.

I inhale at those words. She threw them at me several times, especially those last few months, her face always begging me to return the sentiment, but I never did. I was good to her, I gave her my time and devotion, and I never looked at anyone else. I admit I might have come to love her, maybe, someday, *if* she'd been the person I thought she was.

Still.

Hearing her say *I loved you* makes me uneasy. She said I have commitment issues, and hell, she's right about that, and part of me knows it goes deeper than just people betraying me and using my success for their own gain. All of my feelings of insecurity can be traced right back to Mama and Harvey. Love means making yourself vulnerable; it means giving power to someone to hurt you. Who needs *that*?

Was my inability to truly commit and love Sophia *why* she hurt me? No.

She did that herself; she made the choice. She's shallow, and when something doesn't go her way, she figures out a way to make it work.

I clear my throat. "Lies aren't love, Sophia. You wanted to manipulate me when you left. You thought leaving me for Rodney would spur me to action. But it didn't. And when that wasn't enough, you hurt me. You knew how private I was."

I think about Elena. She's not a liar. She'd never do this kind of thing.

Sophia shakes her head, her throat bobbing. "I regret it. My family hates all the attention it garnered. Rodney hates it."

Surprise ripples over me.

I sit back, frowning, trying to get a read on her.

She reaches out to touch my arm, and I pull back.

"What do you want?" I ask, my voice gruff. "Closure?"

She sniffs, dabbing at her eyes. "I don't know. Maybe. It's just we were together for a year, and you'd never had a girlfriend that long. I gave up on you too soon, Jack. I should have been more patient. I had to see you to see if . . . if . . ."

"What?" I say.

She winces. "If there was any feeling left for me? If maybe we could get past this and move on, maybe see each other sometimes."

My mouth parts. "You're joking?"

She bites her lip. Swallows. "No. I know you haven't been seen with anyone since me—well, except for that video of you with some girl. I . . . I just wanted to . . ." She takes a deep breath and looks at me, longing in her eyes. "Jack, I still want to be with you."

What? Confusion takes over. Does she actually believe that it would be that easy? She *shredded* my trust. I take a deep breath. "If we got back together, what would you do when everyone asked why you're back with the man who *hit* you?"

"I've thought about that. I'm willing to say it wasn't true."

I feel off kilter. "And you think that's all it would take for people to just forget about it?"

She nods, leaning in, her scent wafting around me, heavy and floral with a hint of jasmine. Perfume I bought her. "I do. I can say I was upset at our breakup. I can own it, Jack. For you."

"Might mean the end of your modeling career once people know you're a liar."

She leans closer, her finger tracing my hand. I pull away, and she grimaces. "I'm twenty-eight, and modeling isn't forever. And who knows—any news is good news for me. I can spin it however I want. Plus, it would be great for you—and that's worth it to me. Those fans would eat up a story about us reconciling. I love you, Jackie. I'm willing to be with you on your terms."

I cringe at the nickname. "I'm seeing someone."

She freezes, a look on her face as if I slapped her. A few moments of silence tick by as we stare at each other. "You aren't in love with her, or you wouldn't have come. You wanted to see me."

"I came because I said I would."

She looks down at the table, then back up at me, her eyes pleading. "Jack, we had something good. If you'd just give me a chance, you can forgive me. I know you have a big heart. We can start all over a little at a time, and you'll see that I mean it. I want this. I want to be a better person. I won't ask for marriage. I won't ask for anything but the chance to just be with you."

Her willingness to put herself out there like that makes me do a double take. I came here thinking maybe she wanted to hold something over me one more time, but now I see that she . . .

A long exhalation leaves my chest as I realize something I hadn't before.

I did hurt her, more than I ever realized, even though I tried not to. With my distance. With my walls. With my refusal to say words of love.

I can see the proof of it on her anxious face.

She does love me, as much as a person like her can.

I pause. How different would our relationship have been if I'd given more of myself? Would we still be together?

A thought niggles at me, sneaking in: *Aren't you just going to hurt Elena the same way you hurt Sophia?*

No.

But . . . I don't know.

Shit.

What is wrong with me? Why can't I just . . .

I clear my throat, coming back to the girl across from me. "Sophia, we are finished."

She closes her eyes, opens them, visibly shaken. "Everything I said was true. You broke my heart, Jack; you used me up and tossed me away—"

"I cared for you, Sophia. But you ruined what we had. Not me." My gaze hardens.

"You hate me." She pales, regret on her face as her gaze clings to mine, another tear tracing down her cheek. I hand her a napkin, and she takes it from me, her fingers grasping mine, trying to lace them together.

Untangling our hands, I let out a deep exhale. "Sophia, I don't hate you. Be happy. Go back to Rodney or just find yourself. Live your life."

Her voice, when it comes, is wobbly. "Are you happy?"

She's fishing.

"I have to go, Sophia." I stand up from the table but frown down at her, puzzling over what's on my mind until I realize that I want to tell her . . . "The girl I'm seeing . . . she's kind and good."

An incredulous look crosses her face. Her eyes narrow. Maybe it was something in my tone. Maybe it's because I've insinuated she isn't a good person.

I give her a nod, and I'm turning to go, when her voice stops me.

"I have one more thing for you." There's a sly look on her face, and I cringe, once again disappointed in myself for being blind when I dated her.

"What?"

She stands gracefully, hips never missing a seductive sway as she glides over to me, her wineglass in her hands. She drains the liquid and sets it back on the table. Gone are the traces of her tears, yet there's a hint of desperation on her face. "That girl in the video? Elena Riley. The *librarian*."

I stiffen. She's done her homework. "What about her?"

She laughs, and unease creeps over me.

"Stay away from her, Sophia."

Her features harden. "I couldn't care less about that ordinary girl. I just can't believe you're with her. Especially considering *who* she is." She gives me a knowing smile, a glint of *something* in her gaze I can't read.

"What about her?" I snap. "What game are you playing?"

A brittle laugh comes from her. "Oh, it's so good, what I know about her, but I'm not going to tell you. You'll figure it out on your own soon enough, I bet."

"Tell me what?" I grind out.

Swiftly, she grabs her purse, an effortless motion. Her face is smug.

My heart beats harder than it should.

"Sophia, tell me what you mean."

She brushes past me, her hands dragging across my shoulders. Another laugh. "Don't trust her, Jack. She isn't who she says she is. Think about that. That's my gift to you today."

My body tightens as she sashays away, a clever smile on her lips. She breezes out the door and out of my life forever, and I swallow thickly. Relief and victory are mine. So why do I feel like something just went horribly wrong? A heaviness settles on my chest, like a boulder that I can't push off.

What did she mean about Elena? What kind of betrayal was she insinuating? Did she mean the lingerie or something more sinister?

Don't trust her, I say in my head, and it plays over and over.

I freeze, shaking myself.

Wait. Who am I thinking about not trusting—Sophia or Elena?

I *can* trust Elena.

Right?

After talking briefly to Lawrence and my attorney, I get in my car, my mind churning, trying to figure out what Sophia was getting at.

She isn't who she says she is.

A text comes in. Elena. I let out a sigh of relief, needing a distraction from the emotional roller coaster that is Sophia.

You all done?

Yeah. All over. So glad.

Great.

I stare at her words.

Things haven't been easy between us these past few days, and part of it was Sophia, and the other part was . . . me.

Maybe I need to take a breath and reassess.

Don't trust her, she said.

But . . .

Fuck.

I want . . .

Elena.

You'll never commit to her either, a small voice murmurs in my head, *and once she figures it out, she's going to kick you to the curb so hard, and you might not get up.*

Stop.

I lock those thoughts down.

My throat feels dry as I twist the top off a bottle of water in the Porsche and chug it down. I need to see her.

Meet me at the penthouse.

Can't. I'm at work plus play practice is at seven. Are you coming?

I've been so caught up in worry over this meeting that rehearsal was an afterthought.

Right. I'll head to your house. Meet you there before practice.

Are you okay?

Am I?

I will be when I see you.

I set the phone down and start the car.

After an errand at the hardware store, I'm on the road toward Daisy and playing back Sophia's words.

Is there something in Elena's past she hasn't told me?

No. I toss that idea out.

Still . . .

My teeth grit. A seed of doubt is building and growing inside me, snaking around my . . . heart.

Feeling anxious and harried, I park my car in her driveway and jog up to her door, knocking briefly and going inside. I've spent the last two nights here. We've spent long hours in her bed, talking and making love. I've never been this . . . desperate for a girl. I've given her more than I have anyone. No NDA. No holding back about who I really am. She knows about my shoulder. Fear snakes over me, and I shove it down.

I stalk in, feeling off, sweeping the room.

"In the bedroom," she calls, and I walk down the hall and open her cracked door.

She's standing at the foot of the bed. Hot as hell. Black lace thong is on her ass, a lace bra hugging her breasts. I shut the door firmly, wondering where Topher is. Probably upstairs.

Focus, man.

She looks at me. "You look weird."

"Do I?"

She nods and walks over to me.

I want things to be okay.

I want this thing we have.

But on my terms . . .

And I wonder how long that's going to last?

Shit.

What am I doing with Elena? I'm going to hurt her *just* like I did Sophia.

Never hurt her!

I inhale sharply—shit—trying to regroup and focusing on her as she takes my jacket off, sniffs it, and gags. "Gross. I do not like this perfume."

Sophia picked it out, and it wasn't my favorite, either, but I keep my mouth shut, knowing better than to bring her up right now.

Elena tilts her head up at me, a fierce look on her face. "We are not going to discuss her. It's done. Now take that suit off. I'm wiping your memory like a Jedi mind trick. Elena is the only girl you want to see at Milano's," she says, waving her hands in front of my face.

A laugh comes from me, rough and unsure. "Have you been standing in that pose waiting for me to come in?"

"You bet. All planned."

"Vixen."

"I was giving you five more minutes, and I was going to pull out the vibrator."

"Liar."

She cranks up Taylor Swift as I quickly unbutton my shirt, tugging it out of my pants and tossing it aside. My pants are next. Socks gone. She hates socks on me.

She turns and jumps in my arms, her legs locked around my hips. "Let's do this. Nice and fast before we're star-crossed lovers."

Finally. She is in my arms, and I didn't even realize how much I needed it. I put my head in her neck, inhaling, all of my territorial instincts roaring to the surface. She's mine . . .

I groan and carry her over to the end of her bed, splaying her down as I hover over her.

Ask her.

"Elena?"

"Hmm?" She smiles up at me.

"Is there anything you need to tell me?"

She stills, holding my gaze. "Like what?"

It feels so wrong to even question her. It's . . . Elena. She's sweet and good and kind.

"Sophia . . . shit . . . Elena, can I *trust* you?"

Her eyes search mine for a long time, deeply. She knows what I mean, talking about me, selling a story if we don't work out—

"Yes," she says softly, and I close my eyes and kiss her.

Chapter 29

Elena

"O happy dagger, this is thy sheath. There rust, and let me die!" I stab myself with the fake dagger and collapse to the ground across Jack, draping myself over his chest, my face away from the audience. My hair is down in long waves and falls down my back. Wearing a thin ankle-length white dress with bell sleeves and a lace-up bodice, I'm in full costume tonight, opening night just three days away.

"Nice death, Juliet. Wish we could have just stayed alive," Jack murmurs.

I flick my eyes down at him. He's so carefree like this, none of that Sophia stuff in his head. His hair is swept back off his face as he lies on the stone like a slab one of the prop guys made. Wearing a tight black shirt, skinny jeans, and motorcycle boots, he sports a fake gold gun tucked in a holster. He looks fucking amazing. I've barely kept my hands off him all night.

He looks up at me.

I grin. "You just drank poison because you couldn't stand to live without me. Why are your eyes open?"

He cocks an eyebrow. "You smell good. Your fault. That dress is hot. Trying to figure out how to get my hand under it without anyone seeing."

I giggle, trying to keep it muffled. It's been two weeks of this, us at practice together, the intense feelings I feel every time he looks at me and says his lines, especially the ones where he talks about loving *me*.

No, Elena. Don't rush . . .

But I can't help it.

I'm flying high when I'm with him, when he's inside me, murmuring my name like a litany, his hands on my body.

But when I'm alone . . .

Taking chances, I remind myself in my head.

Isn't it worth it?

We might fall apart at any minute.

"What's wrong?" he asks softly, keeping his voice low. "Did I flub my line? Too much tongue with that last kiss? Shit. Too much tongue."

My lower body clenches at the way he kisses me onstage. The first time it happened was a few nights ago, when it wasn't required, but there he went anyway, laying one on me during the balcony scene. The whole crew watched us, and I didn't even care. "I don't think she meant *make out* . . ." I try not to laugh. "Your lines were great."

"I still worry I'm going to forget a line."

I shift slowly, managing to squeeze his hand. "I'll be here. Just picture them all as meerkats out there, wearing top hats and being ridiculous. Good trick I learned early on."

He pauses, still whispering. We've learned to turn our mics off so no one can hear us. "Hey, I scratched my car last night driving it in your shed. Saw it when I left this morning."

"Poor Porsche. You're lucky I made room for it."

"Aunt Clara waved at me this morning when I pulled out of your driveway. You want to come to the penthouse tonight? It's Friday, and you don't have to work tomorrow. I need to work out early, but we can hang out later. Watch some TV. I miss my K-drama."

I stare at his shirt, lost in thought. I haven't been back to the penthouse since we had sex there after the bakery; I've been brushing him off when he suggests it. And I probably *should* talk to him, but my pride keeps getting in the way.

I refuse to ask him to ask me to go to his real home.

I . . . I shouldn't have to.

"Elena? You're frowning."

I gaze up at him, tracing my eyes over the chiseled planes of his face.

"What is it?"

I swallow as his forehead furrows.

"Elle?"

I sigh softly at the nickname he's picked up from Topher. Amber eyes study mine, his thick lashes fluttering against his cheeks as he blinks. Everyone on stage fades away as clarity arrives, slamming into my heart like a great tidal wave.

I should have known.

And maybe I *did* know since the night he carried me in the rain. Who says love can't happen so soon? Because this feeling in my chest is so big it hurts.

I'm deeply, irrevocably in love with my Romeo. His awkwardness when he meets strangers, the way he holds me at night against him, the silly pop songs he hums, the way he *looks* at me.

I want to spend *every* night with him.

But not at his penthouse.

My throat tightens.

"Are you sick?" Jack says, his hand that's away from the audience rubbing my arm.

"No." I lick my lips. "Jack. I don't want to go to the penthouse. Ever. We should talk about it."

He has to know this. He has to *get* it.

He frowns. There's a long pause as we look at each other, and I watch his face, looking for any clues to see if he knows what's on my mind, and I think he does, because he grows still. "Elena—"

The sound of Ms. Clark's voice breaks him off. I'm not facing the front, but I know exactly where she is, stage right, saying her lines, wearing a long purple dress with a fur-lined cloak. The princess. She stamps her foot. "How am I supposed to say my lines when those two won't shut up?" she calls out.

My eyes flare, and I ease up and turn around, grimacing when I see Laura, who's got her head cocked as she watches us from the floor.

"They've been talking during my entire speech!" She tosses her golden-blonde hair over her shoulder and crosses her arms.

"Uh, sorry," I say, biting my lip as I ease off Jack and move to standing.

She gives me a death glare. "It's been happening every time you two are supposed to be dead. Would it kill you to let the rest of us say our lines? Also, all the kissing is ridiculous. There will be kids at this show. Can you tone it down a notch?"

Jack stands. "Right. Yes. We were just . . . discussing how to do the scene better."

"Uh-huh," she says. "Everyone here knows you two are dating, so just chill with the excuses. We've all seen the video of you two in the rain, running into that *hotel*. It was all over the TV. I honestly think your *relationship* is interfering with the entire play."

I smirk. Someone is bitter she never got a call from Jack.

I dart a look at Jack as he exhales and lifts his shoulders, his expression saying, *What do I say?*

Patrick comes out onstage, dressed in his red shirt and pants, playing Tybalt, who's already dead by Romeo's hand. He glances at Ms. Clark. "Oh, it was fine. It's not like it's opening night. We barely heard them backstage."

Crap, they heard us?

Ms. Clark looks at her manicured nails. "Still, it would be nice to have a practice where they aren't all over each other."

"You're right," I say, just wanting to keep the peace, even though I think she's clearly going on way too long about it. I flutter my lashes at her. "Would you like for us to start the scene from the beginning, or would you like to just say your lines?" *There's so few of them,* my sharp look tells her.

Her lips tighten. "Whatever Laura thinks" is her reply.

"They should do that death scene again!" Timmy calls from a folding chair on the floor. He grins up at Jack. "Jack looks awesome when he drinks that poison and falls down."

I smile.

Jack does a little bow. "My biggest fan."

Laura laughs. "Okay, let's pick up when Romeo comes in the tomb and sees Juliet? Ready?"

We all nod and get into our places.

And this time, when I stab myself and fall across Jack, he keeps his eyes tightly shut, never once opening them to look at me, like I want him to . . . so much.

"Two more days till the play!" Timmy tells us as we grab our things after practice the next day.

Jack ruffles his hair. "Can't wait, little man. Want to go throw some footballs for a minute?"

Timmy holds up his ball. "I'm ready!"

They laugh and head off across the gym.

I hide my smile. Does Jack have any clue how good he is with Timmy?

"Y'all look great onstage, Elle," Topher murmurs.

I sigh. "Yeah."

Laura nods. "Best couple ever. I'm so happy you guys are dating."

"Yeah." I nod, that trickle of uneasiness hitting me when someone uses that word.

He still hasn't come to Sunday lunch. He still hasn't told me *how* he feels . . .

Neither have you, a voice says.

But we haven't spent one night apart—at my house. I've gotten used to him getting up before the sun is up and making me coffee, then chatting with me on the back porch before I go to work and he heads off to Nashville. Then he comes back in the afternoon, and we eat and laugh and read, then make love. I'm living in a bubble of us. I feel . . . disoriented and at sea . . . waiting for the tide to push me back onshore, to reality.

Our play will be over soon, and then, yes, then, I'll make a decision for us to really talk.

But for now . . .

I just want him.

Giselle walks up, wearing a guarded look. She wasn't right tonight during practice. I take in the dark shadows under her eyes.

"You okay?"

She dips her head. "Yeah."

I watch her walk away, frowning. I don't like that slump in her shoulders at all. Are she and Preston okay? They seemed fine at lunch this past Sunday, but then my head was on Jack. I haven't really been noticing everyone else around me.

My phone rings, and I glance at the caller—my old boss from New York. He gives me a call every three or four months to check in and offer me a job.

I wave at Laura and Topher as I walk to the empty stage and sit down on the floor.

"Marvin! How are you?" I laugh. "Kind of late for you to call."

"Ah, you know me," his deep voice says. "Always working. How's library life and lingerie?"

I grin. When I worked for him, he'd catch me on my break sketching. An older man with a head of white hair and a big smile, he hired me fresh out of NYU as one of their copy editors. I climbed the ladder fast in two years, scoring a senior editor position, hungry for the work, missing my family more than I'd thought I would. I focused on romance, a small imprint of Blue Stone.

"You want a job?"

I laugh. "Again?"

I hear a crunch as a chuckle rumbles out of him, and even though it's nine o'clock at night, his time, I know he's still at his desk, munching on Doritos and drinking Diet Coke.

"Can't help it. My managing editor of our historical line just resigned, and I thought of you. You were one of my best editors, authors adore you, and I figured you might want to move back to where the fashion world really is."

I grin. "Dangling fashion as a carrot."

"Worth a shot. Fashion industry has to be ridiculous in Tennessee."

"You have no idea." I've given up for the time being, just taking one day at a time.

"You could have say over all manuscripts, hiring and firing, deadlines, schedules, and a nice fat salary. What do you make these days?"

"It would make you weep."

He laughs. "See. Come back to New York. My wife will help you find an apartment. She loves you."

Oh, he's a smooth one, bringing up Cora, his adorable wife, who fed me more than once at their apartment on the Upper East Side.

"You talk sweet, but . . ."

"Damn. You actually love that place, don't you?"

I giggle. "It's crazy. Mama is still driving me up the wall, and God, wait until I tell you about—"

I stop. I *almost* brought up Jack. My chest twists. I should be able to talk about us.

"What?"

"Nothing. Just excited about a new play."

"You love those. Right. Listen, let me send you the job description, and you take a look at it and get back to me. Maybe fly up here, take a look at the department, see what you think?"

My eyes land on Jack as he throws the ball to Timmy.

"Daisy is home now, Marvin."

Even if Jack and I don't work out, I love this place.

A long exhale comes from him. He munches on a chip. "Okay, there's something else, and I swear it has nothing to do with the job offer."

"Okay."

"You remember that book we published a while back, Sophia Blaine's story, *The Real Jack Hawke*?"

"Piece of trash."

"Ah, well, yeah, you were here when she came to New York and met with our team."

"I didn't meet with her. That wasn't my department." Uneasiness fills my gut. Two weeks ago after Jack saw Sophia, he came back strange, asking me if there was anything I should tell him, and while my former job did cross my mind, I stayed quiet. I'd told him I used to edit romance. Surely, it wouldn't matter.

"Right, right, but you are seeing him, Elena. Hell, I barely keep up with football, but my son does, and he told me he saw you in that video and a photo on a morning show."

I frown. "What does that have to do with anything? My personal life is private."

"I know, but Carla Marsden—you remember her—she handled that book, and she saw the video too. She came in and asked if I'd give you a call—"

"Marvin! I'm not telling her anything about Jack! I'm not Sophia Blaine." My voice has risen, and Jack darts his eyes at me, a questioning look on his face. I smile and turn to the side, putting my face away from him. "It's not cool for you to even ask me about him."

"Agreed. I don't like it, but she asked because she knows you and I are close. And she doesn't want you to write some nutty book about Jack. She wants *his* story. She was never thrilled with Sophia, even though that book sold like hotcakes—"

"His story is his. Why are you asking me?" My tone is aggravated.

"Because nobody can get close to him. His agent doesn't take publishers' calls for him. His PR guy doesn't respond to anything from Carla. No one even has an address for Jack to mail an offer. She can't get through."

"For a reason!"

He sighs. "But if he *did* want to tell his story, she wants it. And she's using me to get to you, and shit, I'm sorry. I've totally fucked up this convo when I really would love to have you back at Blue Stone."

My hands tighten around the phone. "Tell her I barely know him, Marvin."

And that stings, even though I know that isn't true. I *do* know him. But I don't know *what* we are.

"You're pissed at me."

I sigh. "You offer me a job, then throw that at me?"

"But I offer you a job all the time, Elena. I meant that. I only brought him up because her department is bigger, and she's foaming at the mouth to talk to him."

And underneath his big smile, he's a publisher. A good one.

"Would you get a cut if Jack signed with Blue Stone through me, Marvin?"

"Don't know. Maybe. Yeah."

I swallow, feeling shaken, just now realizing the ramifications of that video, how terrible for Jack to never have even an ounce of privacy. And Marvin is my *friend*—yet here he is, using me to get to Jack.

"I'm angry with you," I say tightly, lowering my voice to a whisper.

He sighs heavily. "Yeah. Cora said you'd be. But I had to try."

I circle back to Carla Marsden, whispering, "Tell her what I said tonight, and don't call me for a while. Goodbye, Marvin."

I end the call.

"Who the fuck is Marvin?"

I twist around on the stage. Jack stands on the floor about five feet away, his face stony, his eyes dark and hard.

"A friend from New York." How much did he hear? I lick my lips, dreading explaining about Marvin. Jack's trust is like lace, filled with sharp edges and holes. Barely there. Delicate.

"How good of a friend?" he grinds out, his chest rising as he crosses his arms.

I flinch. There's a sharpness to his tone that makes my skin crawl. Not that he would hurt me, but it's as if he's already judged me. I study his granite face, the careful way he's holding himself, so still and frozen. He's . . . angry.

I glance around. Everyone from the play has gone. Laura and Timmy must have left while I finished up my call.

"Jack . . ." I stand, my dress swishing around my legs. "Let's go back to my house—"

"No," he says coldly. "Let's do this here. Explain that conversation to me." He widens his stance. "Especially the part where you said, 'Would you get a cut if Jack signed with Blue Stone through me?' You were talking about me, and I know exactly who Blue Stone is."

I could have handled the anger he's feeling from hearing a one-sided conversation, but it's the icy look in his eyes that tells me he's not going to listen.

My heart dips. "Not here." I want to be home, around my things. I need to sit down with him and explain about how I used to work at Blue Stone.

His chest rises. "I am *not* going back to your house after hearing what I just heard. Who *is* Marvin? Lay it out for me," he barks.

I inhale a breath, my stomach in knots. I study his face, not recognizing him. "You're reading into part of a one-sided conversation, one you didn't hear all of. And don't use that tone with me."

"God damn it, Elena," he says, stepping back from me as I jump down to the floor. "Don't you dare do this to me. I *trusted* you."

"You never trusted me." I stop in front of him, adrenaline rushing, anger and fear of his insecurities riding me hard.

How can he judge me so fast?

Based on one comment?

And why did he sneak up behind me?

He shakes his head. "I did."

"No, you didn't! You've been waiting for a shoe to drop since you came back from seeing Sophia!"

"With good reason if you're talking to Blue Stone." His breathing increases as he seems to break and let go of himself. He scrubs at his face and pales, the enormity of *something* hitting him hard. "Shit, you . . . you played me so good. Sophia told me there was something, but I never dreamed—"

"You let her talk about *me*?" I suck in a breath. "That's why you came back so strange. All it takes is a real conversation, Jack, something we don't really have, and maybe we could have solved this. And as soon as this play is over, do you think we'll ever see each other again? Have you even thought about it? We don't talk about the future. We don't make plans. Besides, since you had me *investigated* by Lawrence, surely you knew that I used to work at Blue Stone. I told you the night we met that I edited romance books!" I'm yelling, and I hate it.

He rakes a hand through his hair, his voice low, calm, and steely. "Stop stalling. Just tell me who he is, Elena."

Dread fills me. I suspect it's not going to matter what I say. "My old boss. He calls me all the time and offers me a job."

His face flattens more. "And a book deal to sweeten it? How much money will you get?"

I close my eyes, emotion clawing at my throat.

He's putting me in a category in his head, right up there with Sophia. Liar. User. Manipulator.

It slices right through me. He'll never trust *anyone*. Ever.

He'll never—

My hands tighten around my purse as I drape it over my dress.

"I want the whole truth. What do you plan to do with what you know about me? You know it all, don't you? Stories about Harvey I never told anyone. How . . . unsure I get. My shoulder. Are you even on the pill?"

That slices into me deep like a knife, and I bite my lip, tears threatening, and I didn't think he could hurt me any more, but he's crushing me. Anger battles back, fighting as my throat tightens.

"I don't owe you an answer to those questions," I whisper. He already has my heart. And my pride holds me in her tight grasp, because why should I respond to such things when he should know how I am with him, he should *know* I . . .

He falls back on a chair, his head bent, shoulders hunched.

Tears come roaring back, and I can't stop them this time when they fall down my face.

"Don't cry, Elena, please. I can't handle . . ." His voice is ragged, tired. Done.

I hang on to my purse, needing an anchor to hold me upright and away from him, because everything inside is battling to take him in my arms and beg him to *see me*.

"I love you," I say, the words broken. "I knew you'd sweep me away—and in the end, you'd *crush* me. I stayed right with you all the way because I couldn't bear to not be part of your world!"

He doesn't move a muscle. "Sophia said she loved me too."

I let out a harsh laugh. "Right. Silly me. All girls say that. But I'm not just any girl, Jack. I'm *the* girl. The *one*. The one we joked about at Milano's that night we met. Deep down, I think you know—"

"I don't know anything anymore." He stands, a vulnerable, scared look on his face. His hands shake, and he sticks them in his jeans. He gulps in air. "I need . . . to get my stuff at your house."

His laptop. His clothes he changed out of before we came. A funny mug he brought to drink coffee from with me in the mornings. A thriller he put on my coffee table.

He turns, then pauses and says, almost as an afterthought, "Do you need a ride?"

Is he serious? I can barely breathe and he's . . .

I force control into my voice, but the edges tremble. "I'll walk the two blocks. It's a nice night. Please go ahead. The door is unlocked."

His jaw pops as he throws a look at me. The scared look is gone, replaced by a blank face except for a muscle ticking in his jaw. "I brought you. I can take you home."

I gaze at a point over his shoulder. "I don't want to be there when you walk out, Jack."

He hesitates for a second, then pivots and stalks away, shoulders swaying as he moves out of the gym exit and into the hallway. I bite my tongue to keep from calling him back to beg him to just believe in me.

I hear a door shut from the stage and turn to see Giselle there, horror on her face. "Elena, I'm so sorry I heard . . . I was grabbing some of the props, and then you two started talking . . . and . . ."

"It's okay," I push out, but I'm not okay.

I'm not. I'm not.

She drops her purse and runs to me and wraps her arms around me as I burst out crying anew. Her hand brushes at my hair. "You're shaking all over, Elle. Let it out, sweetheart; no one is here but me."

All I see in my head is his back. Walking away.

I love him. *I love him.*

And he's throwing it all away.

He's dismissing us without even *trying.*

He's letting go of us.

Emotion pummels me, and I weep on her shoulder for a long time, the finality of his words playing over and over in my mind.

She stares down at me. "What can I do?"

I close my eyes. "Nothing."

"I can kick him in the nuts."

I laugh hoarsely, not meaning to, but the image of Giselle attacking Jack . . .

She takes my hand, lacing our fingers together like we used to when we whispered secrets to each other when we were little. She wipes my face. "Come on, Elle. Let's get you home."

Home.

I nod, and we leave the gym, the stillness of the dark hall a reflection of my heart. We get in her car and sit there for a few moments, both of us staring straight ahead, absorbing. I feel numb. Tired. I picture him walking through my house, gathering his small amount of belongings, and leaving.

God. I took too many chances. I accepted each day as it came, hoping that I'd get a little more.

Love is messy, and it takes two people to work at it, two *willing* people.

Jack will never let his heart go. Emptiness gnaws at me as I think about tomorrow. And the next day. Emotion builds again, and I clench my hands, keeping it at bay.

Giselle holds my hand.

"I think he'd be gone by now," I say after a long exhale.

She cranks the car, and we drive to the house and head inside. His car is gone, of course. Topher meets us in the kitchen, eyes on me, worried. "What's going on? Jack came in, then left. He looked . . . messed up."

Giselle explains in a halting voice, from the conversation with Marvin to the one with Jack, and I head to the cupboard and get out the Pappy, pouring us all a drink.

I hand Giselle her glass, my hands shaky. I inhale a deep breath and look at Giselle . . . "Where's your ring?" I ask, shoving Jack down deep and focusing on my sister.

She starts and blinks. "Elena, let's talk about you and how you're going to get through this play—"

"What happened?" I say, frowning.

She swallows a sip. "I ended the engagement with Preston today."

"What did he do?"

"Um, sexting with his secretary at the law office. Found them on his phone yesterday. Very descriptive. Boob pics. The usual sordid *shit*." She swallows her drink.

Giselle never curses.

"That sonofabitch," I mutter.

"Asshole." Topher shakes his head.

Her blue eyes find mine. "I suspected something for a while. Those Saturdays at work. Late evenings."

"What is wrong with men?" I pour myself another shot. "Except for Topher. We love you."

"Good to know," he says, his gaze still watching me carefully.

She grimaces, staring into her glass. "Will you ever forgive me, Elena? I'm sick over it still. Dating him was stupid. Thank God I never slept with him. I think he put a ring on it just so I'd do it."

I cough as my drink goes down. "What the hell? You're *still* a virgin? At twenty-three? I just figured at some point . . ." I gape at her. She barely dated in high school. She never brought guys home from college.

She snorts. "You should see your face."

I shake my head at her. "You're an innocent! You have no experience with jerks like him. No wonder you fell under his spell! Oh my God. I will kill him."

She sighs, that anxiousness still on her face, and I know what she wants. She needs to hear it from me because she never has.

I sigh too. "I forgive you, Giselle. I did a long time ago. He is a mere speck, and you are my blood, and I love you fiercely, and nothing comes between family. It's all I have, and it means everything to me. This house, this small town, our memories. Do you know how lucky we are? Some families can't even stand to be in the same room with each other—they give up, but I won't. I won't. You are my *sister* forever." I feel tears itching to get out again. "Plus, you loved him. And I didn't, because I know what love really is. I love Jack." Those last words are whispered.

She bites her lip and hugs me. Pulling away, she says, "I'm sorry. And Jack is just scared. That day they came to clean up, he never stopped looking at you. You walked in the kitchen, and he followed. You went outside—he did. He watched you like you were the sun to his moon. The way you two say your lines . . ."

"That's pretend," I say. "For the play. Which is really going to suck." I inhale a deep breath. How will I get through it?

"No, it wasn't, Elena. He loves you."

My lashes flutter. "Yeah, then where is he now?"

Chapter 30

Jack

I don't recognize myself. What is this god-awful despair pricking at my chest? This sick feeling in my gut? Nausea rises and bubbles in my stomach, and I jerk the wheel of the Porsche off the interstate and onto the shoulder. Deep breaths rise from my chest.

I open the car door and run for the grass on the other side of the road, bend over, and vomit. *Elena. Elena. How could you? How could you rip apart that tiny faith I hadn't realized I needed so badly, that fragile conviction and hope that you were different from all the rest?* My head spins, and I clench my hands and lean against the car. She said he was a friend. She asked him what his cut would be.

It's my phone ringing in the car that brings me back.

Inhaling deep, I manage to get back in the car and pick it up.

"What the hell was that voice mail, Jack?"

Lawrence. I called him as soon as I got in the car. I don't even know what I said, still reeling from walking out of Elena's house.

"Elena used to work for Blue Stone. She was there when Sophia was there. Why didn't you know?" My voice is like gravel, dragged through rocks, slapped against boulders. "You didn't do your job."

"That never popped up." There's a silence on the phone. "I told you to get her to sign that NDA."

Remorse settles on my shoulders.

He continues. "You should have listened to me, and we wouldn't be here."

My head falls back against the headrest. Exhaustion hits. Hearing her say those words to Marvin, her refusal to explain herself, her declaration of love, so soon after Sophia's . . .

"I don't need you telling me *I told you so*, Lawrence."

He pauses. "Okay, let me talk to her and see exactly where she is with this."

My teeth grind. "She won't tell you anything."

"Then you talk to her."

"I can't. I just fucking can't. She makes me want to . . ." I close my eyes.

Because if she cries . . . if she looks at me with those big eyes . . . I just might—

"Fine. I can cut to the chase and find out what her plans are."

"She knows everything," I mutter. "How we handled Sophia, Aiden helping . . ." Shit, I hadn't even thought of that.

"The shoulder surgery?"

"Yes."

"Jack, fuck, why?"

Because I . . .

Because I . . .

I slam my fist against the steering wheel. "Just handle it. I can't talk to her."

Because I might lose it.

Can't even fathom the emotion clawing at my chest.

Even when Sophia announced her book, there was never this feeling of . . . despair.

"I need the space."

"Space? You can't quit that play."

"Never said I was." My voice shakes, wrestling for control.

How the hell am I going to face her again?

It's nearly eleven by the time I finally get home to the apartment. That knot in my gut still hasn't receded. I can't focus, barely getting my key in the door.

Devon meets me at the door, obviously ready for bed, his feet bare, a pair of pajama pants on.

"Lawrence called me. You look like shit."

I brush past him and head to the kitchen. "Where's the vodka? The good stuff."

"Freezer." He's followed me, frowning. "Are you okay?"

"No. But I will be." I pull out the Grey Goose, pour half a glass, and take a long drink. I fill it up. "Real soon."

"Tell me exactly what happened." He takes a seat at the counter.

"It's the usual. Girl meets boy. Knows who he is from the get-go, maybe. Spends time with him. Knows his secrets. Betrays him."

"Really? Did she actually say that? Because I know you. You shut down when shit happens. You don't talk and you—"

"She didn't explain it."

Devon heaves out a breath, hard eyes on my face. "But it's Elena. Think—"

"No thinking," I grind out, then take another gulp. I slam the glass back down on the counter. "Are you going to drink with me or not?"

He searches my face, and I know what he sees. Haggard face. Stooped shoulders. Fucking deceived. Again.

He gives me a sharp nod. "Pour it. Tomorrow we talk."

The next morning, Devon walks in my bedroom and yanks on the blinds. Sunlight blares in the window.

"Get up, asshole. You missed your workout at the stadium, and Aiden's been calling wanting to know why."

Grunting, I sit up in bed. "Tell him to fuck off."

Devon stares at me, sweeping his gaze over the empty bottle of vodka on the nightstand. "Been years since you got trashed, Jack. Not you."

I ignore him and scrub my face, weaving as I stand up. I move toward the shower. "What time is it?"

"Noon."

I start, my past dancing in front of me, the booze I consumed in my early twenties. It was nearly three o'clock in the morning before I passed out in the bed, replaying Elena's conversation in my head a thousand times. "Don't tell Aiden shit. I'll call him tomorrow or something." That's the last thing I need, my backup knowing about Elena.

"Okay. Lawrence came by earlier. He drove to Daisy this morning and was there when she opened the library."

Unease lands, snaking inside me.

"And?"

"He asked her to sign the NDA."

Anxiousness builds, my heart pounding. "What did she say?"

"More like what she did. She ripped it up and threw it in his face. Topher tossed him out of the library."

My head throbs, and I squint. "Did she now?" I picture her in her little skirt, hair up, face red with anger like last night, eyes blazing. "Figures."

"Hmm. She isn't an NDA girl, Jack. She's the one you keep." He lingers at the door. "I called her."

"Why?" I snap.

"Because I don't think she's—"

"What did she say?" And I hate the words, because they sound weak, and my chest hurts. I rub at it.

"She's as tight lipped as you are. The girl is a vault, Jack. I don't buy for a minute that she's talking to anyone about you. She isn't like that, and if you'd just stop—"

I feel dizzy. "I let *go* with her, Devon. I . . . I . . ."

"You fell in love."

My entire body shudders. Love? *Love.*

I don't even know what that is. I know that it's dangerous.

"At least talk to her."

I shake my head. "Whatever I say now, she might use it."

"You been with her every day for weeks. You've slept in her bed every night without coming home. You never do that! You were livid that night I danced with her. You wrangled us up to go work at her house! Every time you talk about her, you're different, Jack. When you look at her, hell—"

"Get out."

He frowns. "You're fucking up."

"I know. I trusted her."

"Maybe in your head you think you did."

I lick my lips, feeling unsure, waves of grief hammering inside me, a tsunami of emotions I don't want to dwell on.

Devon walks out, and I stumble into the bathroom, groaning when I see the dark circles under my eyes, the desolation . . .

Fuck that.

I can't be in love with her, because that will . . .

It will kill me even more.

Everything from last night piles up again in my head, and I lean over the counter, that nausea rising back up as images of her devastated face slam into me—when I confronted her, her anger, her quiet *dignity* when I pressed her.

But . . .

She gave me no real explanation.

I love you, she said. Those three little words linger, tugging . . .

Then . . .

Why didn't she tell me about Blue Stone?

Chapter 31

Elena

"Here, let me do that," Aunt Clara says as she comes in my bathroom and takes the curling iron from my hand and proceeds to take over doing my hair. She showed up after work to help me get ready. I'm moving on autopilot since two nights ago. And then Lawrence showed up at the library yesterday, dressed in an expensive suit, bulldogging his way through the door and barreling his way to me at the checkout desk. With a grim face, he slapped down another NDA, and I barely managed to hold myself steady when he asked me how much money it would take for me to sign it. I told him there wasn't enough money in the whole world. With anger flaring, I pulled out the scissors and cut it into small strips and threw them at his feet. The man sputtered and looked at me as if I had two heads. Topher took care of the rest, escorting him to the exit.

Last night at our last rehearsal, Jack arrived late, his face stoic. He spoke to everyone but me, except for when we ran through our lines. When it came to the kissing scenes, he told Laura he had a cold. I kept myself together, my hands clenched, my heart torn and angry and just . . . broken. Laura frowned at us, but whatever she read on our faces, she let it go and didn't press us.

After practice, he stalked out without a word to anyone, shoulders tight and drawn.

"Thanks for helping." I blink at my reflection, my throat dry.

"Want me to do your makeup too?" Aunt Clara asks.

I don't answer her. My face is pale. My head a million miles away, circling back to his cold demeanor. How could he just walk away . . . then send his jerk of a PR guy to clean up? My face feels tight, stretched over the bones, and I suck in a breath.

Don't think about him. Forget he ever existed—

"You okay, Elle?"

I nod, pushing a smile up. "Of course. It's only a play." I wave her off. "Just do whatever you want with the makeup. The more the better." I don't want to talk about him. Not now. I'm done. All I have to do is walk in there, say my lines, and leave. Finished. He'll go back to Nashville, and I'll go on in Daisy. As if it never happened.

She nods and gets to work.

Twenty minutes later, I'm dressed in leggings and a loose denim shirt that buttons for easy wardrobe changes that won't mess with my hair and makeup. I grab my costume for Juliet's first scene at the masquerade ball, a flimsy short white dress with lace. I frown, darting around my bedroom. Where are the little fluffy wings for the party scene? I worked on those for several days, adding little jewels and small roses.

"I can't find the wings," I wail as I run to the kitchen, where Aunt Clara and Mama are talking.

Mama studies my face. "Where did you have them last?"

I shake my head, feeling off. Disoriented. I chew on my lips. "I thought I had them hanging on the hook in my bedroom—"

She stands. "You're scattered, dear. Go check again. I'll look in the den."

I nod and go back to my bedroom, swinging open my closet again, riffling through clothes, checking the hook on the bathroom door. Tears form. Dammit. I'm not thinking straight. I just saw them yesterday! What is wrong with me?

I dart out of the bedroom. "Mama, did you find them?"

She doesn't answer, and I walk down the hallway.

"Elena." Her voice is low, off. "What is this?"

No. No. No.

I turn the corner, see the door to my sewing room open, Mama standing in the middle of it, her gaze on my dress forms. She spins in a circle, her face white as she takes in the samples. Barbarian Princess with the fringe seems to get most of her attention. "Did you make these?"

Aunt Clara comes in from the kitchen, bumping into me. She gives me a wide-eyed look. "You left it unlocked."

Mama turns to look at both of us, her eyes darting from me to her sister. "You knew?"

Aunt Clara nods and turns right around and walks away. I glare at her back. *Thanks for the support.*

"Mama, I can explain." I walk in the room, wincing as I see that she's moved to the glittery unicorn set.

"I'd like to hear it." She fingers the bra, examining the fabric, rubbing her hands over the sequins, her brow furrowing as she sees how it changes colors. She makes a noise in her throat when the unicorns flash. "Is this why this door is always locked?"

"I didn't want you to find them."

"Why?"

I close my eyes. It's now or never, and the truth is I'm sick and tired of hiding it. "I love making them. That meeting in Nashville was about this . . . a lingerie company."

She sits down at my drafting desk, flipping through my sketches. "You want to quit your job?"

I ease in. Wings are here. I pick them up, clutching them tightly. I take a deep breath. "I have to go, Mama. Let's talk later."

Topher comes down the stairs and enters the room. "Elena, you ready—"

He comes to a halt, eyes flaring. "Shit." He looks at Mama, then me, and walks right back out.

"Get right back in here, young man," she calls.

He pokes his head in. "Yes, ma'am?"

"Did you know?"

Topher gives her a resigned nod. "Elena's been dreaming about this for years—"

She cuts him off, her face tightening. "And Giselle, does she know?"

I nod, closing my eyes briefly. "Preston too. He hated it."

"Bastard," I hear Clara mutter from the doorway, and I guess she's gotten the guts to slink back.

Mama sits there, her head dipping. "I'm the only person you kept it a secret from." She swallows, emotions flitting across her face.

I shift on my feet and move to the chaise near the window. My legs are rubbery as I sit down. "I . . . I didn't want you to think bad about me."

She bites her lip, and I wince. I've only seen my mama cry three times. The day Daddy died; then his funeral, when she wept so hard none of us were able to console her; and when Nana passed. She's a rock, a solid piece of granite.

Moving closer, I grab tissues and push them at her. "Mama, please . . . I'm sorry I enjoy sewing these. I'm a disappointment to you."

"Stop that," she says, her face crumpling. "Please. Don't say that. You've never been a disappointment."

"I didn't go to medical school. I didn't get married and have babies right away. I barely come to church—"

"You would have been a terrible doctor. You hate blood, and your heart is too tender. Although it would do you good to listen to a sermon every now and then." Her shoulders cave in, tears rolling down her face, and it breaks me, to see this strong woman weep. "It kills me to think that you were keeping this from me when it was important enough for you to . . ." Her voice trails off, and she sniffs.

"Mama, don't cry, because if you cry, then I'm going to cry, and my makeup is already done, and it looks good, and Clara will have to do it all over again."

"Well, it's too late for that, because you're already crying."

"I know!" I sit down on the floor at her knees, emotions riding me hard, from Jack and now this. "Don't be mad at me for wanting to be different, please."

Her eyes find mine, shiny and wet. "Elena, how could you ever think I'd be mad? I'm surprised. Shocked at these . . . provocative . . . things." She shakes her head. "I just never dreamed you wanted anything more than the library."

"But it's never going to satisfy me. I want to make things that make me feel pretty, that are different from anything else."

"Oh, Elena . . . how could you think I'd judge you for doing what you love? Since the moment my mama taught you to sew, you took to it like a fish to water. How could you not tell me? Am I that terrible of a person? Do you think so little of me? Haven't I always supported you, even when I didn't agree? I let you run off to New York for college; I tried to keep my mouth shut when you stayed—I tried so hard when you went on that trip to Europe by yourself!"

It's the anguish in her voice that sends me over, and I wrap my arms around her waist. "No, never . . . Mama . . . this town means everything to you. Your church. Your friends. I didn't want you to worry about me embarrassing you."

Another tear skates down her face. "Well, I don't know why not. I love you, Elena. You are my precious baby girl, and I want to support you, even if . . . even if I don't always approve of you; you're mine, part of this family, and I thought you knew." She sucks in a breath. "A mother's love is unconditional, Elena. And I know I'm just a small-town woman who doesn't know much about the world, but you're different, and I know that; I accept it. You're not me. Maybe you won't ever get married and give me grandkids. That's okay. I just want you to be happy, Elena. I don't want to be the person who's the last to know." Her voice breaks, and I wrap my arms around her. She rests her head on mine. "I'm hard sometimes, I know, but in the end, I just want you to be happy. If making these things is a dream for you, I don't care what people think. I just want you to have everything. I want you to be the person you want to be." A long breath comes from her. "Don't you see that?"

She grimaces and wipes at my cheek. "You're the little girl who always did exactly what she wanted anyway. You have so many gifts, Elena, so much talent and creativity and drive. I'm so proud of you and the person you are. And I never want you to do or be someone you aren't. I want you to love yourself first and take your own path, even if it isn't mine but one next to me where you go further than I ever dreamed, where you're happy. My love for you is strong, baby girl. It holds no laws; it is limitless. I want you to be you." Her voice strengthens. "And I will trample down anyone who dares to mutter one spiteful thing about you in this town."

"I'm so sorry I never told you." I weep more, realizing that she loves me no matter if she doesn't agree with me.

She tilts my chin up, and I feel like I'm five years old again. "I will *never* ever leave your side. I am here."

Clara and Topher sit on the floor next to me, and I guess I hadn't even realized they'd come in.

"Nothing should ever keep us apart," Clara says, tears rolling down her cheeks.

"Why can't I be part of the Daisy Lady Gang? I'm not a lady, per se, but I like to dress in women's clothes," Topher whispers and wraps his arms around us.

"Might as well. Honorary member," Mama says softly, wiping her face. "We need to have some kind of induction ceremony like those sorority girls do. Cloaks and candles and a swearing in."

"And whiskey," Clara says, nodding. "We'll need whiskey."

Mama scoffs, but says, "Wouldn't hurt." She gives me a long, lingering look. "Hate to tell you, but you're gonna have to redo that makeup."

I give her a hug, holding her tight. "I won't keep you in the dark, Mama. I won't do it again."

She smiles. "Good. And when you become a superstar pantie person, if Birdie Walker says one damn word, I'm going to dye her hair bright purple like Devon's and call it a win."

I laugh.

"Come on," Clara says, pulling me to my feet. "We have a play to get to."

Chapter 32

Jack

The gym is packed when I arrive, chairs in two groups along the floor with an aisle, the bleachers bursting with people.

"Dude. Everyone is here to see you." Devon gives me a questioning look. "You got this?"

"Yeah."

"Liar. You gonna puke again?"

He had to pull over once on the interstate. Same thing happened last night when I drove down for the last rehearsal. My stomach is screwed up. I can't eat. I can't think. Thoughts of Elena mixing with nervousness over speaking in front of all these people.

"They're not reporters," he reminds me. "Just good people who want to see you. There's Timmy." He nudges his head as the tornado that's Timmy sees me and barrels over to us. He's got jeans and a slightly wrinkled dress shirt on.

I swing him up and give him a big hug. "You look nice, little man," I say to him, forcing warmth in my voice—when I feel so damn cold.

"You're late! Mama is asking everyone where you were!"

I grimace. "Sorry. Here now. Go tell her I'm coming."

He nods and dashes back down the gym floor.

"This is a one-night-only show. The last time you'll see Elena," Devon murmurs, sticking his hands in his jeans. "Think about that tonight."

"Yeah."

"Fine. Break a leg, then. Go on. I'm going up front. Elena mentioned they had seats for us and Quinn."

"Me too," Lucy says, coming in the door with Quinn and hearing us. She's a surprise guest. I mentioned the play to her a week ago, telling her about the people of the town. About Elena.

I didn't think she'd be able to make it since she's had a recent bout with the flu. Quinn picked her up since she doesn't drive much anymore, while I rode with Devon.

"I want a good look at this Juliet you've been talking about on the phone," she says, arching her brow. In her late seventies with bobbed brown hair, she's wearing black dress pants, a white silk blouse, and a strand of pearls I bought her for Christmas last year. They make me think of Elena . . .

"Yeah," I say tonelessly.

Her eyes are hazel and faded—but sharp. I haven't told her anything about what happened because I don't want her to worry, but Quinn . . .

I nod. "Should be three seats up front. I told Laura, and she reserved them."

She shoos me off. "Go on, then. Don't worry about us."

They wish me luck, and I wander off toward the front, but I pause, my chest knotted. I hang back, feeling eyes on me from every direction. My hands tremble as I hoist my duffel bag up on my shoulder.

Part of me wants to just . . . run away.

The other side of me . . . wants to see Elena. Last time.

Anxiousness rides me as people watch me jog to the stage, a wave of relief hitting me as I shut the door and climb the steps to the stage. Curtains are drawn, and everyone mills around with final prepping. Cast members huddle in groups, going over lines. Shit, I hate being late. I head into one of the dressing rooms for the men, thankful it's empty as I change out of my clothes and into Romeo's shirt, jeans, and black boots.

By the time I'm out, miked up, and waiting with the rest of the cast, I still haven't seen Elena.

Is she late?

Did she dread coming as much as I did?

"Jack."

I whip around at the sound of her voice, nearly stumbling.

She looks . . . beautiful. Her short dress falls above her knees, her wings in her hands. It was hell being around her last night at rehearsal, fucking awful.

"Have you been crying?" I say gruffly. Her face is perfect, but those eyes are road maps.

A slight smile. She thrusts a Tigers mug at me, the first one I bought when I got drafted to Nashville. "You forgot this. Guess you were in a hurry."

"Oh." I take it with stiff fingers, fighting . . . shit . . . battling with myself to not brush them against hers.

"Be glad I saved it. Clara wanted to throw it against the wall." She turns to leave.

"Elena?"

"What?"

A long exhalation comes from deep inside as she faces me again, and I say something I said I wouldn't, but I can't stop it, because the whole drive here, all I could think about was her, that torn, angry, yet resigned expression on her face when I left the gym.

I love you. I knew you'd sweep me away—and in the end, you'd crush me. I stayed right with you all the way because I couldn't bear to not be part of your world.

I recall the pride I read in her eyes that held her strong. Kept her from talking to me.

"What was your phone call about? I'd like to know so I can be prepared."

She gives me a professional nod, a wan smile. "Yes, of course. You stalked out without getting the whole story." Her expression is blank—God, I miss her emotions—and never changes. "In a nutshell, Marvin wanted me to see if you wanted to sell your story. He asked on behalf of a coworker, the agent who handled Sophia, who saw the video of us. They thought I'd be able to convince you or give them your contact info for a conversation."

Ms. Clark waltzes past us in her purple dress. She smirks at us. "Lover's tiff already, Romeo and Juliet? Can't say I'm surprised. You two don't go together."

Elena never looks at her, voice still toneless. "Fuck off, Sheila."

She harrumphs and flounces off, shooting eye daggers at us.

I focus back on Elena. "You never told me you worked there."

"Thought you trusted me. Assumed you knew. I was wrong. I would have eventually, Jack. It didn't seem pressing, but now I see that I should have said it right away." Her words are clipped, tinged with anger, and I find that I like that better, because at least it tells me that she feels something.

We're still staring at each other, and I can't stop looking at her face, the curve of her cheekbones, the way her hair falls around her jawline. "What do you want from me?"

She breaks a little then, wistfulness crossing her features before she shuts it down.

My control dips, that rabbit hole of emotion tugging at me. My arms ache to hold her.

But . . . shit . . .

She grimaces, looking pained as she plucks at the waist of her dress. "Absolutely nothing, Jack. I keep my promises. No one will ever know anything you told me."

I've never seen her so . . . hard to read.

Empty. Void of that usual light in her aquamarine eyes.

You put that there.

You blew up and walked out on her.

You ignored her words.

She frowns. "Are you good to go out there?"

I give her a jerky nod. "I'll be fine." I stare down at my boots. "Helps when you're out there with me. I don't even think about the audience."

"Well, at least I'm good for that. Meerkats work too."

I close my eyes. And I don't even know what I'm going to say, only that I don't want her to leave. I want her to tell me she loves me again. I want her to . . . "Elena—"

"Five minutes until the curtain comes up!" Laura yells, sweeping her eyes over us. She lands on me. "You ready?"

Elena walks away from me, as if she was waiting for the right chance, heading to the other side of the stage, where she'll enter.

I nod at Laura, my head spinning. I feel dizzy, and it has nothing to do with being nervous about speaking.

I'll never see her again.

I breathe heavily, as if I'm about to throw a pass to win the game, and the coverage is insane, covered up, and I can't find . . .

Dread, thick and dark, curls around me, wrapping around my chest.

Clarity settles around me, and maybe, maybe I knew from the moment she snapped back at me the other night without fully explaining, as if I should already know she didn't need to defend her phone call, but I shoved it down, locked my feelings away in a box, wrapped a chain around them, and tossed them where I put everything that makes me feel too much. She . . . she'd protect me until the end. I recall how she dealt with those women at the bakery, her fierceness, and then I'm lost, remembering sweeping her up in my arms and running for the penthouse.

Where she never wanted to go.

Where she never felt at ease, yet she . . . went.

I've fucked up with Elena. I've . . . I've judged her by Sophia's actions, when Elena *isn't* that girl.

She's never used me.

She's never pushed me to tell her anything, except out of genuine concern. I'm the one who willingly opened up more than I ever have with anyone else, and hell, even then I'm always holding part of me back.

I let *her* go.

Pushed her far away, scared. Afraid of my life repeating old mistakes . . .

But Elena isn't a mistake.

Even with my shoulder surgery looming, that gnawing worry about my future in the NFL, this month has been the happiest I've—

God.

She's the girl a man dreams of finding someday . . . everything I always wanted.

And I threw it back in her face.

I reacted without listening. I . . . fuck.

You lobbed another interception, Jack.

You lost the fucking game.

Chapter 33

Elena

Dressed in a knight's costume, Jack enters the masquerade party as Romeo and gazes at me with what Laura calls Romeo's "Dang, she's all I want, and I want my lips on hers" look. It's pretend.

I'm stage right, makeup repaired, wings on, acting my ass off.

He moves toward me, a dark flush on his cheeks, his lines not quite as sure as they have been. He's been floundering since the play started. I saw it right away, as soon as he said his first line. I watch him, encouragement in my gaze. Jack, Jack, Jack. *You are so beautiful. Don't let the people get to you* is what I hope he sees on my face.

He presses his hand to mine. We kiss. Barely. Pull apart. Gaze at each other as the party continues stage center.

"Then have my lips the sin that they have took," I say.

"Give me my sin again," he murmurs.

I swallow. He's jumped ahead a few lines, but I nod and kiss him again.

He slants his mouth across mine and sighs, his hand still on my face, our bodies closer than they should be.

"Elena." It's not loud, but it's audible and clear. The cast keeps on, never looking at us. His eyes search mine as he opens his mouth, as if to say something, but it's my line.

"You kiss by th' book," I say ardently—like the line calls for.

"Then I'll take another."

That is *not* the line. Nurse appears for her line, and Jack ignores her and kisses me again, his hands sliding into my hair. "Elena," he whispers in my ear, and I pull back, eyes big.

The mic is hot, catching it, and the audience murmurs. If they missed it the last time, they definitely heard it this time.

Giselle says her line, and Jack is supposed to leave the scene—only he doesn't. His eyes refuse to drop mine.

Giselle clears her throat, says her line again, and I come back.

One of the stage crew shrugs when I dart my eyes at him. He's waiting for Romeo to leave, only Jack is *still* next to me.

There's an awkward pause, until I flare my eyes backstage. *Close the curtains!*

The scene ends, the curtains falling at the end of act one.

I blow out a breath and dash stage right for a costume change. Jack follows me, and I whip around. The stage crew stares at us, but I barely notice.

"You can't do that onstage," I tell him. "They can hear you." I refuse to think about how it made me feel, his mouth against mine, wanting me to really kiss him back.

Giselle gets between us and points her finger at him. "You best get back over there where you're supposed to be, Romeo! You have the first line of act two."

He swallows, his throat bobbing, then turns and stalks away.

Giselle looks back at me. "You okay?"

I nod. Yeah. But we still have a lot of play left. What else is he going to do?

◆ ◆ ◆

By the time we get to the balcony scene, I'm sure he's lost his mind.

Halfway through a long line, he climbs up the ladder to my window—when he isn't supposed to—and says the rest of it. We're face to face, and I'm overwhelmed by the maleness of him, by the intensity in his eyes.

It's a play, Elena. Acting. This is the scene where Romeo wants to crawl in your bed and get busy . . .

But he's doing whatever he wants onstage, trying to get close to me when he's near me.

Focus.

I suck in a breath and say my line. "What satisfaction canst thou have tonight?"

"The exchange of thy love's faithful vow for mine," he says softly.

My lashes flutter. "I gave thee mine before you asked. I would give it again."

I screwed it up. That was all wrong. I left out so much. *Lord. Help.*

He stares at me. "Would you give it again?"

Oh my God. That is not his line!

I clear my throat. "My bounty is as boundless as the sea—"

He cuts me off, saying *my* line. "My love as deep, the more I give to thee. The more I have, for both are infinite. Forever."

He takes my hand and laces our fingers together. "Will you tell me again? No one's ever said it and meant it, Elena."

I shake my head at him, heart pounding. Hammering.

"I know it's not a line, but I have to know."

I dart a look at the audience, who are sitting on the edges of their seats. I see Mama and Aunt Clara. Birdie Walker gawking. Quinn and Devon, an older lady between them.

Nurse comes in, pulling Juliet away, but the play requires me to rush back out to the balcony to Jack. I have no clue what to expect.

I stumble through my part, exiting like Juliet, then running back to see him one more time. Young and reckless and silly girl. Her love will only end in heartbreak, and her Romeo will be banished after he kills Tybalt, and everything will crumble.

Maybe it's the unease on my face that pushes Jack, because he never misses a beat this time, his timing perfect, his lines not off script.

I'm a total disaster by the time we dash through the hasty wedding with the friar, and by the time the wedding night rolls around, well, all logical thought is gone. The man I love is in Juliet's bed, lying next to me, his leg pressed against mine as we pretend to awake to the sunrise. I'm wearing a long white nightgown—and he's in a long white pirate-style shirt and dark pants.

His hands hold mine as he leaves from my balcony window. I can't think straight. I'm dropping lines like crazy, ad-libbing to make it work. I can't stop thinking about the next kiss, the next time he holds me.

He steals my line again, changing it. "Do you think we shall ever meet again?"

Wait, what's my next line?

"I doubt it not," he picks up with a small smile. "You love me; do you not?"

I gape at him. That is not Romeo's line. Or mine.

"Do you love me?"

My hands clench. "Did I not say it was so?"

"Will my love forgive me for leaving when he first heard of it? It was only fear and insecurities that drove him thus."

I glare at him in exasperation. Laura, goodness, I can feel her staring at us in shock.

I shake myself, butchering the next part but getting it out. "Methinks I see you now, as one dead in the bottom of a tomb. Either my eyesight fails, or thou lookest pale."

He looks out at the sky, seeing the sunrise, and when Romeo is supposed to be sad to be banished from Verona, Jack isn't. He looks determined, a glint in his eyes as he looks back at me.

"One more kiss, and I'll descend."

Nope, we've already done that. Not doing it again.

He stalks toward me, gathers me in his arms, and puts his lips on mine, parting them slowly, carefully, almost as if he's afraid I might run. His left hand holds my hip, away from the stage, a brand on my skin as he deepens the kiss. His hand curls around my waist, and I melt against him, letting him in more, savoring the smell of him, the scent of leather and male, the feel of his hard chest against my breasts.

I push him, my chest heaving.

His eyes glitter down at me as his thumb brushes against my lips. "I love you."

He walks away from me, and I fight for control, gathering myself as I watch him exit off the stage. It's the last time Juliet sees Romeo alive. It's the last time . . .

"Juliet?"

I start as he climbs back up the trellis.

"Romeo, you're back. What a surprise."

Someone giggles in the audience. I think it's Timmy.

"Someone once said that the two most important days of your life are the day you were born and the day you figure out why. I know why."

Mark Twain? Wrong century! Wrong author!

"To meet you. To fall in love with you. Fate's a funny thing; she hits you with terrible things sometimes, making you grow up before you're ready. I never believed in destiny, but what if we'd never met? What if I hadn't been there at that exact moment when we were supposed to meet at . . . at . . . the masquerade party, where you were supposed to be dancing with someone else. But I was *there*. And there you were. And I had on the right shirt, er, costume, and you sat down with me, and my heart began to beat. Isn't that fate? Isn't that life giving us a chance? Isn't it? Please, tell me it is, because I can't walk away from you again without knowing you haven't given up on me."

I can't think of one thing to say. And I should, because by now even a two-year-old could figure out that we are doing a Jack-and-Elena thing here and not Romeo and Juliet.

He continues. "That same author also said that love is not a product of reasonings and statistics, but it just comes—none knows whence—and cannot explain itself." He pauses. "I didn't expect it, never dreamed it, never aspired to it. But here it is. Yours."

Juliet's mother enters the stage, a startled look on her face. No one knows what to do.

"Go," I whisper. "Please."

"Adieu, my love." After a long look, he climbs back down the trellis and walks away.

My soul cries for him to come back, to tell me those words again so I can soak them in, but he can't; we can't do this . . . whatever it is . . . in front of all these people.

I watch his shoulders, not able to tear my eyes away.

Chapter 34

Jack

The curtain goes down as the princess ends her last line, and a thunderous applause reaches our ears. Thank God! I'm so ready for this to be over so I can talk to Elena . . . instead of muddling and butchering poor Romeo's lines.

"Great job!" Patrick exclaims, clapping. "Big success."

Is he kidding?

Elena rises up from me, and I pull her back down. I scan her face, reading her, but since the messed-up honeymoon scene, we haven't spoken a word; instead I've been lying here with a hard-on with her draped across me.

"Elena . . ."

"Not right now, Jack. I can't." She stands and runs to stage right.

Fuck. I still can't get a read on her.

I head to my spot, an entire stage between us.

Laura calls out our names one by one, and we take our bows, the crowd on their feet, clapping.

Juliet's name is called, and Elena runs to the stage and takes her bow; then I take mine. I clasp her hand in mine as we take our bows together. Whistles and cheers erupt, and I grin sheepishly. This part hasn't been hard at all. The only thing on my mind was Elena. I didn't give a shit about anyone else.

The audience claps for three minutes. "Jack, Jack, Jack" starts up in the bleachers from some Tigers fans, and I give them a wave. Devon smirks at me from the front row and gives me a thumbs-up. Quinn moves his gaze to Elena, popping an eyebrow.

Yeah. I don't know yet.

Does she still want me?

Or has she had a good hard look at some of that darkness inside of me . . . and . . . shit—

Maybe I'm not worth the trouble?

Chaos ensues as some of the crowd pushes forward and jumps on the stage with us, Laura and Timmy and some of his friends he's got tagging along to talk to me. They all have pens and playbills out. I wince but try to cover it up. *Part of it, Jack.*

"Cast party at the Tavern in an hour, guys!" Laura calls out, a wide smile on her face. "Free beer and pizza courtesy of Jack."

Cheers go up.

She gives me a big hug. "Jack, thank you so much for doing this."

"I hijacked your play for my own personal use—"

"Shut up. It's you and Elena. The audience ate it up. A few reporters from the *Tennessean* were here. They inquired if they could interview you, and I said no."

I hug her again. "Thank you. They always print what they want anyway."

She smiles. "Well, there was nothing bad to say about you today. You and Elena . . . your chemistry . . . be still, my heart."

I throw a look around the crowded stage just as Timmy and company arrive.

I don't see Elena.

Two hours later, most everyone has left except for me and a few straggler fans still waiting in line to see me. I feel exhausted yet exhilarated after I finish the last autograph and selfie. Devon left with Quinn and Lucy already after saying their congratulations and goodbyes.

There's not a hint of Elena anywhere.

Chapter 35

Elena

I pop in the cast party super early, hug everyone, and eat pizza. No one mentions Jack, but you can tell by their questioning looks that they want to ask me what the heck was going on. Maybe it's my face that keeps them from inquiring.

As soon as he walks in the door an hour later, I head out the back exit and drive back home. I need time to think, to process, and I can't do it with him in front of me, wanting answers. I need space. I need *home*.

I fly in the house, whipping my costume off as I head to the bedroom, grabbing pajama pants and an NYU sweatshirt. One pour of whiskey later, I'm out on the back porch, heating lamps on.

Sitting on the steps, I blow out into the chilly March night and gaze up at the full moon. April is almost here. And spring.

The play is finally over. I close my eyes. God, I'm going to miss him.

"Figured I'd find you home." Jack's husky voice comes from the back door of the kitchen.

He sits next to me, easing his body down and gazing out at the faint outline of the rolling hills.

I don't look at him, but I feel him glancing over at me, making me self-conscious. I dip my head so he can't see my face.

The wind picks up, and I rub my arms. He gets up and heads back in the house before coming back with one of the jackets I keep on the peg by the kitchen door. He drapes it over my shoulders, his hands brushing at my hair before he takes the seat next to me, keeping a few inches between us.

A long exhalation comes from him. "I'm sorry, Elena. I freaked out over Marvin and assumed you were guilty. I was wrong."

Out of the corner of my eye, I see him scrubbing a hand through his hair.

"I lost my head. Does that mean I've lost you too?"

I meet his gaze, seeing worry mingled with fear in his tawny eyes. "You pushed me away from you like it was nothing."

His throat bobs. "It was pure unadulterated fear. Deep inside me, in a part I hadn't acknowledged yet, I'd already given my heart away to you, only to hear that conversation and think everything was blowing up in my face. All my protective instincts flared up. To be made a fool of again? To believe that a woman loved me? It felt ridiculous. Women who love me usually end up hurting me in some way."

"I'd never hurt you intentionally."

"I know. And now I screwed us all up."

I don't want us to be screwed up. I want us to be . . .

He flashes a brief sad smile, sighing as he looks away. "I gave you my heart tonight in front of everyone. It felt fucking amazing."

My stomach flutters.

"I'm also sorry that Lawrence came to see you and pissed you off." Regret lingers in the tones of his voice. "I did so much wrong, and it's my own damn fault for being . . . broken since the moment we met."

I sigh. "He's banned from the Daisy Public Library. Might put his face on a wanted poster."

"In his defense, he really does put me first."

I nod, circling back to something he said before. "You're not broken, Jack. Everyone has baggage they bring to a relationship, but you have to take a leap of faith."

He reaches in his front pants pocket and pulls out something and places something small and cold in my hand.

"What is this?" I hold it up in the light of the moon, taking in the metal object.

"My leap of faith. Key to my apartment. I had it made for you after I left Sophia, after she said I couldn't trust you. I was just waiting for the right time to give it to you, to get my nerve up . . ." His voice softens. "I meant it as a symbol that I wanted more with you, but then I'd get nervous and not bring it up. I felt so unsure. I've never loved anyone. I'm stupid." He sighs.

There's a long silence as we stare at each other.

"What are you thinking?" he asks.

I lick my lips. "I think I'm having a revelation."

"Yeah?" I see hope on his face.

He does love me. Oh, he told me onstage in front of everyone, but it wasn't until this moment that I let the *feeling* sink in. Let myself believe it. A man like him, who doesn't trust, was on the cusp of giving me a key, which to some may seem rather meaningless, but to him, it's the equivalent of a declaration.

He sighs, reaching out to trace the curve of my face. "Will you forgive me, Elena?"

I gaze at him, at the intensity of him, at the man who's been hurt so many times by people. And he's never loved a girl.

"Forgive me for pushing you away. Forgive me for not going to Sunday lunches. Forgive me for being broken."

Tears prick my eyes. "My nana used to say that broken people love the hardest because they appreciate the things that make their heart beat. Do I make your heart beat?"

He nods, his lashes fluttering as he comes closer, then pauses, looking uncertain. "God, Elena. I'm afraid you're going to push me away. I know I'm not perfect, that I need to work on this, but I can't let go of you. I spent two wretched nights without you. I never want to be this . . . sick again. I love you, Elena. So much. I don't even know how to describe it."

My breath hitches.

He says, "I want to wake up next to you every day and see what life throws at us. Will you try?"

Will I try? I'd walk over hot coals for him.

The elation that's been growing in my chest widens. My heart soars. "I love you, Jack. You're worth everything."

A smile grows, a bemused and awed expression on his face. "Thank God." He leans in and kisses me softly, his tongue sweeping against mine. "I'm not perfect," he breathes into my neck a few minutes later. "I can't win a Super Bowl to save my life, I get flustered around new people, I watch too many K-dramas, and your pig hates me. I don't have much to offer."

I laugh, feeling giddy. "Romeo does not hate you. Dislike, maybe. And I kind of like your Porsche."

He presses a soft kiss to my neck. "It's yours."

"I was joking!" I laugh as he stares deep into my eyes.

He holds my face steady with his fingertips. "I've never had *this*, Elena. I've never been with someone I couldn't live without. I talked about fate before, and the more I dwell on it, it just makes sense that maybe there is a reason for everything."

"What do you mean?"

"That sometimes, fate gives you a bad game, but in the end destiny straightens it out. And you win. You and I are going to win." He gazes down at me, and I suck in a sharp breath, seeing a man who loves me with all he is.

He brushes his thumb over my bottom lip. "Even if that fate is nonsense, I would have found you. Somehow. Maybe at a bookstore. Maybe when I had a flat tire in Daisy in front of your house when I came to visit Timmy—I don't know. We were always meant to be. There are too many things that brought us together. If destiny brought us together, that means she'll fight to keep us together."

He leans in and kisses me, hard and swift, and we get lost, me in the feel of him under my hands, him with his hand tangled in my hair.

He stands, sweeping me up into his arms, shouldering his way back up the steps.

I smile up at him. "Where are we going?"

He pauses at the back door. "I was just going to take you to bed, but now that I think about it, we could just go get married right now. I'm sure Patrick will do it. Laura mentioned being a notary once. We can get some witnesses."

I nearly jump out of his arms. I wiggle down. "Are you joking?"

He nods, a vulnerable look on his face. "Kind of. I don't know. It does seem fast. And insane. Definitely insane. But I've never felt like this. Okay, it's too fast. Right. I'm losing it . . . but what if you leave? What if you wake up tomorrow and decide I'm too much work?"

There he is. My beautiful man who just had a jolt full of love and trust and faith shot at him like a cannonball, and he's not quite sure . . .

"I think you're just caught up in the moment, Jack." I smile. "I kind of like it."

I manage to open the back door, and he follows me, a focused look on his face.

"You can wear your Juliet dress, and I can wear this." His tone is serious, all kidding gone, and I shake my head at him, my mouth opening, but nothing comes out.

We stare at each other.

I find my voice. "Mama will murder us; plus you have to apply for a license."

"So that's a no?" His face is extraordinarily intent, wolflike.

"It's a 'Can we have some great sex first and get on this later?' Mama will want to plan everything."

He grows still, amber eyes lit with a strange light. I think it's love. He blinks. "I just asked you to marry me, and you said yes—is that right?"

I gawk up at him. A laugh comes from me. "Y-e-s. Sometime soon."

He looks like a two-by-four just hit him. A little scared. But happy. A slow nod comes from him. "Deal. We'll figure it out later. Bedroom now. I want to be inside you." He leads us to my room.

I feel wired, taut, and tense, needing this, needing him. "Socks off," I murmur.

He whips them off and tosses them behind his shoulder.

I bite my lip as he unzips his black jeans and shoves them down. His shirt is next.

"You gonna leave me here naked?" Hot eyes drift over me.

He helps me take off my sweatshirt, groaning as he palms my breasts. Sighing, I push at my leggings until they're gone, and I'm standing in front of him in white lace panties.

"So pretty. So damn pretty." His hand skates from my clavicle down the cleft of my breasts to the apex between my legs. There's this look on his face. Awe. Reverence. Love.

He slides the lace down and drops it on the floor. "I love that you are always so open with me; did you know that? I love your eyes and your hair and the way you make me laugh. I fucking can't stop looking at you. Body made for me. And I'm going to take it real slow."

I'm already panting at the heavy-lidded look he wears. "Not too slow."

"Fast and hard?"

"Yeah, then the slow part."

"I'm thinking slow first."

I moan as he falls to his knees and nudges my legs apart, his lips dancing lightly over the smooth skin of my stomach. He licks the center of me, groaning.

Writhing, I wiggle closer to him, and he laughs against me, those eyes looking up at me. "Won't ever get tired of this. Never in a million years."

A lone finger glides inside me, slow and easy, his tongue on my clit, circling.

My hands land in his hair.

"Just like that first night, Elena. When I took one look at you and knew I had to see you again . . ." Another finger joins the first, rubbing against my wetness until I'm gasping, my hands clenching his hair.

I topple over the edge fast and viciously, making me cry out his name as the shock waves ripple over me, my body clenching around his fingers.

He presses a kiss to my inner thigh and hovers over me.

"Mine," he murmurs in my ear as he lays me down and slides inside me. He holds my hands above my head, lacing his fingers through mine. "Always." His eyes gleam down at me with passion, with love.

And love . . . love is all we know.

Epilogue

Jack

A few years later

It's March, and the windows in our house are up, letting a spring breeze blow softly into the newly remodeled kitchen. It's also clearing the smoke out.

"A little brown on top," Cynthia murmurs, staring down at the chicken casserole I pulled out of the oven. She pokes at it with a fork, her face expressionless, but I feel the disdain radiating from her. She just can't help it. It makes my lips twitch.

"Did you cook it on three-fifty for forty-five minutes like Cynthia said?" Clara asks me, sliding in next to us as she sniffs.

"I'll be honest, those Ritz Crackers are burnt," Giselle says, throwing in her two cents.

"Just scrape off the top. All the good stuff is underneath anyway," Topher says, working on putting ice in the glasses for the tea.

Cynthia pats me on the back. "I'm sure it's good, dear. It is her favorite, but she can eat my macaroni and cheese."

"All that pressure of hosting Sunday lunch. It got to him." Clara smirks. "He was too busy singing Katy Perry and forgot about the main entrée. Amateur. He might be a Super Bowl champion, but when it comes to cooking for his wife . . ."

"Katy Perry's 'Firework' is stellar," I murmur. "Did I tell you Scotty is coming? Yep. Any minute he'll be knocking at the door."

Her face flames. "You hussy!"

"Hmm, he jumped at the invitation when he brought the mail on Friday. I personally invited him." My eyes gleam.

"You just wait. The next time you come in for a haircut, I'm gonna cut it all off." She glowers at me.

Cynthia lasers her attention on her sister. "Just marry the man. Look at Jack; he made Elena official years ago. You're gonna get old soon, and then what will you do? Be a forty-something virgin?"

"I'm going to set the table!" She marches off, and we all laugh.

"She's really going to fix her lipstick." Giselle chuckles.

We gaze down at the terrible, awful chicken casserole. "I really wanted to do it right."

Cynthia gives me a hug. "Oh, honey, she'll eat anything—especially if you make it. Plus, between keeping up with you and that job with the lingerie company, she's too tired to care."

"What the heck is all the smoke?" Devon says, waving his hands as he walks in the kitchen with Quinn and Aiden.

"Do I need to get the fire extinguisher?" Quinn adds.

"Nah. Jack just ruined Elena's favorite meal," Giselle says.

"Slipping, old man. Did you hesitate? Need me to run out and grab some KFC?" Aiden gives me a grin.

"I got distracted," I exclaim. This is a big day . . .

"By his dancing and singing," Giselle says as she pops a piece of fried okra in her mouth. "Did you always want to be a pop star, Jack? Stick with football, 'kay?"

"He tried; bless his heart," Cynthia says. "Good thing I brought a backup." She nudges Giselle. "Go get the one I brought in the car. It's in a container in the back seat."

I'm not surprised at all that she brought another chicken casserole, but I act indignant. "You didn't think I could do it, even after you went over the recipe with me three times last week?"

Romeo runs in the room, his little nose sniffing the air. His gaze follows me as I head to the new custom stainless steel fridge and pull out a small cucumber and lean down to let him snatch it and dash off.

"There you go, bribing that pig. He still loves me most of all." Cynthia smirks.

"He naps on me every day," I counter. Not exactly true, but he has come around since I officially moved in two years ago.

She laughs. "Go check on Elena. Let me handle the rest."

She wants to take over, and I want to see my wife, my hands already jonesing to hold her.

I walk in the dining room, my breath hitching when my eyes find her. Wearing jeans and a soft-blue sweater, she's standing in the dining room, the sunlight catching her long auburn hair as she sets the table.

There's something about her that calls to every part of me.

She's *mine*.

We were married in August, as soon as my shoulder surgery allowed me to wear a suit. Six months from the first time we met, we stood side by side in her hometown church and said our vows, with Patrick officiating. She wore a long white dress Cynthia and her nana had both worn, an heirloom that Elena had altered with painstaking care, adding pearls and lace. I clearly recall her walking down the aisle to me, her hips swaying, that gorgeous hair down, with pink and purple flowers in her hands.

She took my breath then.

To know that she loved me.

That I was her *one*. And she was my *one*.

I whispered my vows, and it wasn't because I was unsure—no, there was not a hesitant bone in my body when it came to her and how she made me feel. I was blown away by her, the depth of my love, the wave of emotions that tugged at me every time she walked in a room.

After all this time I still sometimes gaze at her and just . . . stare.

How is this even my life?

How did I ever find her, this crazy love that destiny brought me?

The Tigers won the Super Bowl this past season, my shoulder repaired, me at the top of my game. But even that particular victory doesn't compare to her next to me in our bed, my arm curled around her waist when we sleep.

She resigned from her job as the librarian and took the intern job with Little Rose Lingerie, quickly working her way up the ladder to a paid position in their research and development division. She still makes her own things just for me.

My image repaired itself in an organic and real way, especially after the *Tennessean* wrote a kick-ass article about the play and how I professed my undying love for a certain small-town librarian. I still don't give interviews. And no one seems to care.

"Dada!" comes from little Eleanor Michelle Hawke, barely eleven months old, as she sits on Lucy's lap, laughing up at me, her little hands reaching out for me. I swing her up. She's got a headful of dark hair, big aquamarine-colored eyes, and two little teeth.

Elena laughs, her gaze on me, then Eleanor, the same love and amazement in her eyes too. I have everything. A real home filled with laughter. Trust. Love. Family. Things I never dreamed of having.

I give Lucy a swift kiss on the cheek. Her husband, Roger, sits next to her. They come to all the Sunday lunches they can in between traveling.

Elena appears next to me and wipes at the remnants of Cheerios on Eleanor's face. "Sweet girl. She loves her daddy."

"And he loves her and her mama."

She gives me a soft kiss as Eleanor coos on my hip.

"Can't keep their hands off each other. Always with the kissing. It's a wonder y'all ever get a thing done," Cynthia murmurs as she walks in with a casserole that is obviously not mine.

"It's sickening," Devon agrees, following her in the room.

"When can I babysit?" Topher asks. He's living a few streets over in a rental house. Elena and I have made her house our main home, although we spend time at my apartment in Nashville, too, mostly during football season—but it's this house that keeps us centered. This small town that I've grown to love as much as Elena does.

Quinn jumps in, standing shoulder to shoulder with Topher. "I'll help you, man. Pretty sure she hasn't seen *Grease* yet."

Hmm, those two . . .

"When can I teach her how to throw a football?" Aiden huffs. "'Cause her daddy ain't got what it takes."

"Watch it, Alabama. You're still the backup," I growl, then grin down at Eleanor, who's giggling as she tugs on my hair.

Scotty walks in. Guess he knocked, and we missed it. He holds up a string of several white balloons. "Will this work, Elena?"

She glows at him. "Perfect!"

"What's going on?" Cynthia says, her head cocked.

Elena smiles sheepishly as I wrap my arms around her.

"We have a surprise for you," I murmur.

"Well, don't drag it out," Clara calls. "What are the balloons for?"

I lace my hands with Elena's and stare into her eyes. "We're pregnant," I say, but I can't stop looking at her. Always her.

"Oh my God, again?" comes from Giselle, who'd frozen as she tried to steal another fried okra someone put on the table.

"We planned it," Elena says quietly, eyes on me. "All the babies. All the things we want."

"Hmm," I murmur and manage to kiss her again.

"The balloon is one of those gender-reveal things. Jack put me in charge so no one in the family would know until today," Scotty says.

"You never said a word!" comes from Clara, who is glowering at him.

Cynthia's eyes shine. "Well, I hope you aren't going to torture us by waiting until after lunch! Pop that thing."

I laugh, taking the balloon from Scotty. We thought about telling them as soon as Elena and I knew she was pregnant, but she wanted to do it like this, sharing the gender and the pregnancy all at once at Sunday lunch. We don't even know, having given the sealed envelope from the doctor to Scotty a week ago.

"Thanks, man." I glance at Elena, who gives me a shrug. *Go ahead,* her eyes suggest as she takes Eleanor from me.

"Nah, we'll eat first," I say.

"Stop that right now, Jack Hawke!" Cynthia exclaims.

Devon laughs. "Poor man. He's probably terrified. Two freaking babies."

"Chicken," Aiden adds.

Laughing, I pop it with a fork, and pink confetti flies up in the air and floats gently down to the floor.

A lump builds in my throat, and my chest tightens. Overwhelmed. I want my whole life to be like this: me and her and what's ours, sitting on our back porch, thanking the stars above for bringing her to Milano's and straight to my arms.

She smiles up at me. Wipes my face with gentle hands. Shit. "Oh, Jack . . ."

"Happy, baby, just happy."

Clara does a fist pump. "Girl! Daisy Lady Gang! DLG! The legacy grows!"

I just laugh, pull Elena closer, and kiss her.

ABOUT THE AUTHOR

Wall Street Journal, *New York Times*, and *USA Today* bestselling author Ilsa Madden-Mills writes new adult and contemporary romances with humor and heart.

She loves unicorns, frothy coffee beverages, and any book featuring sword-wielding females.

Please join her Facebook readers group, Unicorn Girls, to get the latest scoop and talk about books, wine, and Netflix: www.facebook.com/groups/ilsasunicorngirls/.

You can also learn more about Madden-Mills by visiting her website, www.ilsamaddenmills.com; signing up for her newsletter at www.ilsamaddenmills.com/contact; and visiting her page on Book + Main: www.bookandmainbites.com/ilsamaddenmills.